... 13 ...

Narrator's Note

Dear Reader

99.87% of books should be treated as sacred objects, not to be defiled by pen, pencil, crayon, highlighter or one of those special long rollers used to paint behind radiators.

This story is not one of those.

It has been designed with extra-special and expandable whitespace specificazilly designed for your personal use.

Make notes, create comments, doodle, draw, sketch, dance, go crazy.

Make a shopping list if you like. Make several.

Press wild flowers.

Practise photomontage, it's the new Leonardo.

And after you're finished, swap it with a friend and repeat the process.

And then another.

It would probably be best, however, if you have the permission of the owner, if there is one. If not, tag, you're it.

Singed: Victor, On E

P.S.

And don't forget to pronounce it properly. Don't diss de dots: it's "... 13 ...", not "13", not "thirteen". Those dots don't grow on trees, you know ...

Well, not healthy trees, anyway.

Preface

What follows is based on true events. Real true-life events that happened. Absolutely everything. Everything, down to the last comma and full stop. Backed up by the detailed notes I made at the time, and a photogenic memory. Unfortunately my cassette recorder failed when I momentarily placed it on top of an industrial shredder. Gulp, crunch, burp, splat, and that was that gone.

I think it was personal. It waited a couple of seconds before making a nee-ha-plink-plink sound.

Then it spat out the Off switch.

I couldn't believe it.

After that I religiously wrote down everything that occurred as soon as I had a spare moment, every single word, gesture, deed, tittle, tattle, you get the gist. I knew that it was going to be a story that had to be told. I wasn't aware at the time that I would be the one telling it. Hell, longest thing I normally write is "Job done" on a large invoice with no details attached. (Sometimes I vary it: "Done job". Sometimes just "Done". I'm crazy that way.) But that, as they say, is the way 7the cookie crumples. Which is why I sit here now in my lounge, typing up these notes, keeping those clear visual memories at the front of my mind rather than being distracted by the sight of the curvy young woman across the road washing her front windows, wearing a pair of very tight and tiny denim-coloured shorts and getting her tight white t-shirt wet, blissfully ignorant of the facts that I am about to reveal.

Daisy Dukes. I'm pretty sure they're called Daisy Dukes or something.

Woman's clothing isn't normally my thing.

Not normally.

Special occasions if absolutely necessary, if you know what I mean.

Real true life events.

Unfortunately ...

You know, one thing I've learnt in life is that it's largely composed of plans and what really happens in the end. Or what I call the gloop moments. As in you've planned a lazy evening watching telly, pretending you're just a normal suburbanite, maybe watch a good action movie or something, but unfortunately Boring Barra from next door pops in to return the hedge trimmer he borrowed two summers ago and drive you crazy wasting your evening discussing carrot diseases. Or you take a day off work to hold up a bank because of orders, you've got every detail down to a T, only it turns out to be a bank holiday, that sort of thing. And it comes to the point where you turn around to hit your head against a brick wall. But for some reason there's always an aquarium there, and there's this one fish staring at you. Just one fish. And she's been staring at you the whole time. And she stares at you for a few more seconds as if you're the stupid one. Then she blows a bubble. And it goes 'gloop'. And then she just carries on staring at you as if you're still the stupid one.

And I'm afraid we're facing one of those brick wall gloop things right now.

You see, it would be an accurate and precise portrayal of what happened if I was allowed to relate the exact events one by one, step by step, blow by blow. There's only one teensy-weensy problem. That little problem is, I can't tell you about them. Not the way I would if I could. And that's all due to a number of reasons, but primarily ...

Well I can't tell you that. Either.

However, let's use a little imagination here.

Think out of the tree a little bit.

Let's say ...

Let me think ...

Yes, I think I got it ...

Let's say that there was this judge, see, and, and a trial, and that sort of thing, you know what a trial is. We've all been on trial, haven't we? And this judge made a ruling in this trial.

An early ruling.

This is just a metaphor, of course. Not the actual thing that happened. Trust me. Think of it as an allergy.

And because of the judge's early ruling, and a combination of other events no-one can tell you about it.

Including me.

That hurts. That really hurts.

It really, really hurts.

And I've sworn not to use the X-word in this.

So all I can say is: it really, really, really hurts.

And I'm not going to use the X-word.

No, sir.

And breathe.

My only consolation is the image that always pops up in my mind when I think of all the newspaper editors out there. For five days they had been sharpening their pencils, slavering at the mouth (can you slaver anywhere else? No, let's not go there), preparing for an outpouring of the most juicy and lurid titbits –

Do you know, in the States they spell that tidbits?

– largely invented in the case of some of those publications who regard truth as an amusing concept which need not trouble itself to get in the way of a good story, but, hey, that's the modern world for you.

Though, to be honest, I think the world's always been that way. Julius Caesar probably had the same problem.

There's just a lot more of it and us around these days.

Actually, from what I've read good old Julius was rather partaken to inventing things himself, especially about the Gauls.

Or was that the Gools?

What is a Gool?

Anyway. I digress.

Note to self: stop digressing.

If I was going to wash windows, with water sloshing around everywhere, I'd wear an old pair of overalls or something. Much more comfortable for a start.

Daisy earls? Princes? Lords? Ducks? Daisy somethings.

Daisy ducks? Rhymes with?

No.

The, what did I say it was? Judge's ruling. That's the one.

That reminds me: vinegar. For cleaning windows. Must make up a shopping list, I'm short of pretty much everything apart from cheap brandy and toilet paper.

Why, I don't know. It's something to do with my shopping routine. Last month I had a cupboard full of tins of peaches. I don't even like tinned peaches. Where did they come from? You asking me? Who knows?

The judge's ruling.

Do tinned peaches grow on trees?

Can you buy tinned trees?

Life's full of questions.

Isn't it just.

Legs move on.

The judge's ruling stymied those editors, poor little darlings. The judge, a right hanging judge if ever I saw one, decided early on that the case was sub judice, sorry, *sub judice*, this spell checker doesn't like that if it's not in italics, and that no details about the defendant or plaintiff may be made public – "anything which might reveal their identities". What, exactly, might constitute "anything which might reveal their identities"? Would mentioning that one of the members of the jury was a statuesque blonde whose sexual allure was blunted by a taste for bright pink jackets and an overindulgence in glowing magenta eye shadow fall under the ruling? Describing the court room? Mentioning the dates? The season? The judge's predilection for ... Well, maybe that.

Yup, definitely that.

Oh, yes, definitely that.

My lawyer has just warned me that, if there was such a judge, and if there was such a trial, and if there was such a jury member as described, I may not mention it, for it will identify the said trial to those who were there. I pointed out that I would expect that those who attended the meta-follicle trial are probably aware of the fact, after all, it's hardly something they're likely to forget, and my mentioning a member of the jury with more sex appeal than fashionable taste is hardly likely to change that fact. He claims that the courts might see it rather differently if they – who "they" are, he never quite manages to explain – decide that I have transgressed the judge's original ruling, and decide to prosecute, which could lead to a sentence of not more than decapitation, or something very, very uncomfortable, like being sung to by Maggie Thatcher when she was alive.

You might be getting the impression by now that my lawyer's a bit of a doofus.

(Can't remember where I picked up that word, but I like it. Doofus. It's got a nice nasty sound to it.)

(Doofus ... Yeah. Ah Doo-Doo-Doo-dudoo-Doofus.)

He is. My lawyer that is. A doofus. I kind of inherited him from somewhere, worse luck. You know what they say about gift horses and not looking them in the mouth? Well, they're wrong because it might turn out to be my lawyer. He's scared of his own shadow, so terrified of making some legal misstep that would get him struck off that he speaks in legalese the whole time. I've never heard someone use "alleged" every third word. And as for "the aforementioned item" – well, you can have a fifteen minute conversation without being able to fathom whether he was talking about a blood-stained knife or the cup of coffee you offered him – or even the cup of coffee you've just poured over his head to drive a point home. He also hovers around behind me when he's here, nervously reading what I'm typing, just in case I commit some slander or libel for which he might be held to account. Or, to be more precise, he needs to know what I've written so that he will know what he has to deny should it come to that. Yes, Alfred Beazeley, you do, I know you do. You do do do. You might be quiet, but I can see your reflection in this screen.

(His name's not Alfred Beazeley, but I had to give him one you wouldn't recognise, and I think it suits him. If you're on a train and the person opposite looks like an educated, badly dressed dork with hair standing up all over, wearing an old suit that's having a fight with itself, that's probably Beazeley. Pat him on the head and feed him a goldfish sandwich, he'll be fine. Mostly. Till the sandwich runs out. After that, well ... maybe you should review your travel arrangements. Before he finishes chomping.)

Wash your hand afterwards, mind.

Count the fingers too.

So, back to our firm-busted pink jury person. Did she exist? Am I allowed to tell you? And if she did, and I am, to what extent did her actions – I'll lead up to those slowly, because, taken out of context, they might appear somewhat bizarre – influence the final verdict?

Well, that's not really for me to say, considering the venerable judge's decision, the old pillock. There may have been such a person, maybe there wasn't. Maybe there wasn't even a trial. I'm not saying there was or there wasn't. (Satisfied, Beazeley?)

Times like these I wish my mother had been Jewish so I could say Oi Veh with attitude.

But, what I will say is, if there was a trial, and all those poor slavering-at-the-mouth-only editors had been allowed to report on it, the following is what might – might, I repeat – have happened. I've got the notes. I've even got the computer. I had it specially made. It's got a 72 inch screen and a 40 inch keyboard with a unique little key that bleeps if you hit it quickly fast enough. It's got an extra P key top right cause I can never find the other one. Yes, somewhere between me and this snazzy, brand new laptop that story is going to come out. It's got the rams, the drive, the mouse, the memory, the megahertz, the mega-other-stuff, all the bits in the world, I've got the story and it's going to come out. Oh, yes it is. Even if I have to drop-kick this little beauty from here to Antarctica.

That. Story. Is. Going. To. Come. Out.

Now, where's that dot key gone to again?

Ah, there it is.

...

I like dots.

...

Can we make this thing do, like, a smiling face? One of those effigy thingies?

Thought not.

I'll pencil in a huge grinning skull later.

Cause I like it.

...

Yeah, dots and dots and lots of dotsy dots ...

Contents

Chapter I. The Court

Okay, so first I'll have to explain, sorry, invent, what the court case was about, and introduce the characters, the plaintiff, defendant, judge, jury and the rest.

Now what if I told you that the defendant was a small, mousy-haired chap with a wispy moustache and a limp? Maybe your next-door neighbour is a small, mousy-haired chap with a wispy moustache and a limp in his right leg. So then you get to thinking, "Oh, my god, it's him, I'm living next door to the small, mousy-haired chap with a wispy moustache and a limp in his right leg, I must move immediately before he gets a chance to slit our throats as we sleep!". Or perhaps you're the more get-up-and-go person whose first reaction is to burn the neighbour's house down with him in it, forgetting that you live in a Victorian terrace. One minute you're peeking out of the net curtains chuckling and trying to look sideways, the next you suddenly think, "Wait a minute, it's getting hot in here …"

That sort of thing does happen, you know.

In my world, quite a lot.

On the other hand, supposing you think, to take an example out of the air, "Well, my neighbour is a delightful young woman who has cute bobbed hair, a very pleasant smile and very nice legs with no limp in either, wears very short, tight denim-coloured shorts while washing her windows, has a delightful derrière with absolutely no resemblance to a small, mousy-haired chap with a wispy moustache and a limp in his right leg, so I'm okay". Suppose I'm deliberately hiding the identity of the defendant behind a small, mousy-haired chap with a wispy moustache and a limp in his right leg, when in fact the defendant was actually a delightful young woman with cute bobbed hair, a very pleasant smile, a delightful derriere and very nice legs with no limp who just happens to be your across-the-street neighbour and also psychotic and owns some very big sharp knives with pointy ends? What do you do now? Burn *her* house down? Nail up a sign outside her front door saying "It's Her! It's Her! It's the cute-bobbed-hair-limpless-young-woman-with-a-delightful-derriere!"? Look for a contract killer who isn't a police officer pretending to be a contract killer? Emigrate to the remotest part of the Australian Outback and disguise yourself as a sheep?

Of course the more perceptive will be saying, "Now wait a minute, we don't even know what the charges are. Or even whether this is disguised as a civil or criminal case. It could even be the Family Court." Well, you know what? Because of that silly stupid ruling I can't silly stupid tell you straight, now can I silly stupid?

But I swear I'll do my best, mind.

Without using the X-word.

How, I don't know.

But there has to be a way.

There has to be a way.

Let's try it this way – It was a dark and stormy night ...

No, can't see that working. Anyway, it wasn't a dark and stormy night, the weather was brilliant sunshine every single day apart from that one particularly specially weird day, and that was a particularly specially weird day. No, let's go for something a bit more traditional. Something – I know: Once upon a time. That's traditional, isn't it? Once upon a time there was – there was this person who wrote a book. Yup, it's coming through now, a book ...

A book ...

A Book ...

A book based on another person's life ...

Oh, yes, come to me baby. Booksy me, baby ...

Let's say that the second person accused the first person of character assassination. Yeah, character ... assassination. Got that? Assassination. Take a leak, Beazeley, I'm busy.

Not in here, Beazeley. Leave that potplant alone.

Anyway, I meant hike. Take a hike. Doesn't anyone around here speak Merican?

Sheezus.

With or without the potplant.

Beazeley's whining that he wasn't going to piss in any pot, he was moving it because of Fink Shway.

Well you just tell old Fink that if I catch him he'll be in deep you know what.

And, just to muddy the waters a little, in case that should ring a bell, person A and person B – the plaintiff and the defendant – were going out together, but not married. That's important to some people. They were not married. Repeat. Not Married.

Oh, look, Beazeley, a squirrel!

(Actually, in this story they were divorced, but don't let Beazeley know I told you that. Quick, scroll down before he sees that.)

So, anyway, it all ended up in court – I'll mention MI5 later, because the conspiracy theorists (or are they, hint, hint – that's the problem, start with an allergy, you end up with a bunch of red herrings) wouldn't forgive me if I didn't. It's – let's say it was – an English court (that's England, Great Britain, United Kingdom for anyone who might be confused), so we'll put it in somewhere with an old-fashioned Olde-Englande name; let's call it – oh, give it "Bury" somewhere in the name. As in Shrovesbury, Canterbury, Banbury Fair, Bury St Edmunds (what did Edmunds do that they wanted to bury him? Those southern softies pretend to be as cute as mince pies, but they can be right nasty nematoids when they choose). And, well –

that's it, we'll call it – yes, "Well" – Well-bury. Wells, you know, where the water comes from.

Wellbury. Wellbury High Crown Court. With added Assizes. Built in the time of Henry IX. The whole town – the old town, that is – was built in the time of Henry IX, including the railway and the strange hotel where everyone was staying.

And, boy, was that hotel strange.

You think the Hotel California was odd.

Oy Vey.

Oh, and let's put it in that Doomsday book thing, give it some breeding. Some ancestry.

Funny name for a book.

Probably means something different in Viking.

Right, so we've got a town name. Next, let me describe the physical layout of the court – a possible court. Let's make it a cross between Cubanism and that bloke who does stairs which go the wrong way up, Porter or Usher or whatever his name is.

(Anyone not interested in architecture or DIY might want to skip this bit, it could be a bit boring.)

(Though, having said that, anyone interested in architecture might want to skip it as well, I don't want any letters telling me that my description is physically impossible, that I don't know a gable from a gantry, or that the self-cleaving thruppenny widget with a failover twange was only invented fifty years later so it doesn't make historical sense.)

(Just thought I'd make that clear.)

Okay, let's go through this bit at a canter. Let's say that this court had been built in the days when they built things to last. Looking at it from the back, as it were, as I was, might have been, you would see the judge's bench, a raised, oak-panelled affair, about eleven feet above the well of the court.

(Do you think I should use footnotes rather than these brackets?) (Beazeley prefers footnotes, so brackets it will be.)

The jury box – oak-panelled, let's make everything in our court oak-panelled, that's what you'd expect in an ancient Olde Englande court house when they could afford it and didn't need to buy the flat pack soft pine look – the jury box to the right was raised to precisely one inch below that of the judge's bench. (Approximately 2.5cm in new money.) It was built on what looked like stilts or struts, angled in to the wall, like an Elizabethan balcony on a stage. Over time the stilts had sunk, and it sloped both ways. I imagine any jury in such a situation would be continually leaning to their left to stay upright. I mean the jury were (was?) continually leaning to their left to stay upright. Could have been.

Oh, and it tended to wobble if they moved too much.

Somehow I just knew that jury box was going to collapse sooner or later.

Probably.

It's my jury box, I made it, and I'm going to make to go Pop.

Crinkle.

And

Splat.

Sometime.

Sooner or later.

Okay. Witness boxes. Raised about five feet above the judge's bench. Why? Don't ask.

Equidistant between the two witness sentinel towers and the sloping, wobbly jury box are the lawyers' docks, defence and plaintiff standing side by side. The sides had been raised to five feet high. Which meant that, sitting down, a lawyer would only see an oak panel in front of him, unless he looked directly up, in which case he could admire the skylight which was the single source of natural light to enter the court, or possibly try to see patterns in the wet stain in the ceiling which were the last reminder of a dog which had once expired on the floor above it, lying there for three weeks during a hot summer before someone realised that the smell wasn't coming from the prisoners or the judge.

(That's one smell that can take me right back to that court, the slight whiff of dead dog mixed up with the heavy aroma of wood polish permeated by the sinus-jarring perfume some of the lady jury members had sprayed on. The dead dog had passed on some twenty years at that stage, but its pong lived on long after.)

Come to think of it, some of the perfume had the same staying power.

Beazeley's doing something funny with his fingers while looking confused. Actually he does everything while looking confused. I think he's trying to visualise the court by holding various fingers in different positions. He'll pull a muscle if he's not careful.

Thinking about it, it probably is a lot of detail take in so soon. But, remember, I have to camouflage this lot. Just use your imagination. Build your own court. Build your own jury. It's free. Legal. And non-taxable. At the moment. Anyway, I'll keep repeating the descriptions every so often so that I can get used to them. I mean, you can get used to them.

Did I say goldfish sandwich? I meant fish finger sandwich. No wonder they gave me strange looks at the delicatessen. I mean, asking for mayonnaise on your goldfish sandwich.

Cheese.

What sort of doofus does that?

Where was I?

Benches and docks and things.

Below and between the judge's bench, the sloping, wobbly jury box, the lawyer's cages and the elevated sentinels is the original well of the court. For some reason – perhaps the budget ran out – this was not raised, so the administrative staff of the court – recorder, usher, etc. – conduct their lives about ten feet below everyone else.

Finally let's have the public gallery, which overlooks everything else, rather in the manner of a long theatre box. The gallery was occupied by journalists and members, strangely enough, of the public. Shall we say that there were very few journalists and no members of the public present, or would someone smell a fishy?

Let's go with the lie for the moment, keep the numbers down, otherwise we'll end up with a cast of thousands which even dear old Mr de Mille would flinch at, they'll be packed in like sardines. Let's just say it was me – I'd popped in to get out of the rain – and another bloke, thin moustache, wearing a trench coat, collar turned up, dark glasses and a fedora. Let's say that he had MI5 written all over him.

The rest of the town: a quick invented description. I've got a few of those coffee-table type books in front of me we can use, Tudor Towns of Britain, Ye UK Olde-Fashioned Hamlets and Cities, that sort of thing, so if we mix them up a bit we can get a good picture of somewhere that might exist: a medieval castle going to wrack and ruin; an old cathedral; a hotel, covered with rose creepers and wisteria, window boxes holding peonies, petunias and hollyhocks. The hotel was small – not too small, but struggling to cope with the influx of – of the judge, jury, plaintiff, defendant, recorder, myself and the bloke in the fedora. And some others I'll get to in a minute or so. Oh, and we need Jasmine. Thatched cottage walls covered with Jasmine and Honeysuckle, I think we should definitely have some of those somewhere, I rather enjoy the delicate fragrance of Jasmine and Honeysuckle on a warm English summer's day. And we have to have at least one traditional pub. A low-beamed, quaint old pub called the Baby's Arms. Chuck in a small university on a hill. A casino on the edge of town. Rolling farmland and fields outside town. Narrow little alleyways of small shops all over the place. That sort of thing. Your average Olde-English picture-postcard, chocolate-box little large town.

There's also an old knocking shop still knocking around somewhere, but I never got to visit that, only Beazeley did.

Beaezeley says that's not fair, he never went near no knocking shop.

Don't worry, Beaze, your secret is safe with me.

Oh, look, Beazeley, a sorrel!

He he.

Right, that should do it for the setting. Next we'll start on the characters. I reckon they're going to be great fun in making. Each one is likely to give Beazeley a minor heart attack. Poor chap. So young, so nervous.

First, time for a quick cup of tea and a little thought.

Thinking about the characters, I can change names and locations and looks and that sort of thing, but I can't really change the final score. Those who loved and won – none – those who loved and lost – many – those who will never make it to the end of the story. Bit of a bummer, that. Especially those who loved and lost. It would be so nice to have a happy ending for everyone.

Actually, it would be nice to have a happy ending for anyone. This is not going to end well.

Hey ho.

Hello, the postman's just knocked on the young woman's door, the one across the street. I hadn't noticed her going backside.

He's carrying a large box. Must be something to do with furnishing. She only moved in last week.

Doesn't look too heavy.

Two knocks, eh. That looks well dodgy. I thought the pedestrian only knocked once.

Hello, hello, she's opened the door, he's going inside, the door's closing ...

Let's hope her husband doesn't turn up suddenly.

Hey, maybe she's single.

If I get a second free I'll try find out.

Right, cup of tea and then on with the characters.

Rich tea biscuits.

Chapter II. The Characters

Have you ever noticed how hard it is to tell what someone is like by their appearance? Their characters, that is. Take my neighbour, Boring Barra. (Incidentally that's a pseudonym, last thing I want is Boring Barra nipping over to ask why everyone thinks he's boring, it would be like trying to explain the idea of "wet" to all the oceans in the world at the same time, with the Atlantic nipping out for a fag and then coming back and asking you to repeat what you've just been through, while the Pacific decides it needs the loo, now.)

If you saw a photograph of Barra you might think, well, middle-aged, middle-class, bit overweight, thinning hair, face a little pudgy, probably married, kids grown up, looks like your average easy-going neighbour. The same mistake I made when I first met him and said hello as any good neighbour would. I've regretted it ever since. Barra, you see, really is the most boring person in the world. He repeats just about everything. Everything. I would like to strangle him, but sheer lethargy would take over my muscles two seconds after he opened his mouth to speak, which he does without asking permission.

I think his real name is Barry, short for god knows what. But he pronounces it Barra: according to him it comes from the Irish Finnbarr, some mythical figure, who, if Irish mythology is like any other, probably means something like "the big man who slaughtered the giant pixies who lived over the hill and deserved to be slaughtered because they were giant pixies, lived over the hill, and picked their noses in public." Could be worse. He might have called himself Bazza. Though there's another word that rhymes with that which would have fitted.

Personally I reckon they didn't know what to call him because he was so boring. I can imagine his parents having a discussion:

"Well, let's name it after the place it was conceived. Where was that?"

"The Barra ferry."

"Right, that's what we'll call it then."

"What, Ferry?"

I call him Barra Coulder, because he's always telling me how he could have been this, he could have done that, but somehow never did nor was. The first time someone tells you they could have been regional sub-manager isn't that interesting. The tenth time feels like the seventh circle of hell.

Barra, of course, will never recognise my description of him in a hundred years, however many times he reads it. I'm not sure we'll be that lucky with most of the individuals involved in the court case, so we're really going to have to go to town in giving them new identities. Postie's just left the place opposite. That was quick, maybe he was just delivering something.

Or maybe things aren't as innocent as they might seem.

Why didn't he ring the bell?

Mmmmm.

Bugger off Beazeley.

...

I do like those things.

...

And breathe.

It's either that or throttle Beazeley.

Still haven't said the X-word. Not going to. No matter what Beazeley does or says.

You can put money on that.

Trust me.

No, sirree.

Okay, let's give person A and person B, the plaintiff and defendant, some names and faces which don't fit. Let's say that the defendant – the one who allegedly wrote the book – was female, thirty-five to

forty, a redhead, slim but not skinny, good looking, about five-five, five-six. Green eyes. Freckles. Smart dresser. Everything about her spoke of money, but also style, the kind of woman who can wear a lime-green/avocado matching skirt, blouse and shoes and make it look the height of expensive fashion, though in a conservative lady-of-the-manor way. Looks after herself, you know? But, oh, what the hell, let's give her one drawback in the looks department – let's say she had the most incredibly large nose ever seen on the otherwise stunningly attractive face of a green-eyed, freckle-faced, red-headed smart-dressed defendant. And I mean big. A whopper of a snoz. Humungous. Forget Cyrano de Bergerac, this is Guinness Book of Records stuff, and more. The size of whales. Let's call her Melody Mary. Just because it's so unlike a witch's name. Not that I'm saying she was a witch, of course. Or that her name was Mary. It's possible that she was a witch, I'm just not saying that. It's also possible that she spoke with a voice that seemed to come from somewhere else, another planet, or the spiritual world, or the sound just bounced up the walls and played along the ceiling. Maybe she was a ventriloquist in another life.

Oh, sod it. We all knew her as Norah The Nose. Let's stick with that. It wasn't her real name, so we should get away with that. Go away, Beazeley.

Or was it fish-paste?

No, sure it was fish fingers.

Norah. We've just done Norah.

She had red hair. Why didn't we call her Flaming Norah? I would have.

Hmmmm. Good question.

I wonder if I can wangle getting 'Flaming Norah' in later.

I'll have to have a ponder on that one.

Now the plaintiff. Okay, let's forget that nonsense about a mousey-haired chap with the wispy moustache and a limp in his left leg. Let's make him slim, slightly taller than average, dark eyes with a hint of amusement, black hair, a languid air, wears very smart, very expensive double-breasted suits. Holds himself well, the type of man who can easily win the confidence of honest, trusting people, though they might leave his company wondering why they kept thinking of eels and oil and estate agents. And let's give him longish hair – to cover the most enormous ears you ever saw, ears that could act as wings for an elephant. He kept the ears pinned back with something – he continually smoothed them back, as if worried that they had suddenly sprung open, which they did from time to time on an individual basis. Every time he uttered a lie, that is.

Did I say he did continually smooth them back? Well, he might have. Or might not have. From here on in, take it for granted that when I say something happened, or describe someone's appearance, well, yes, maybe, and no, possibly. Just use a little injunction.

Look, Beazeley, a sturgeon!

(But they didn't half make a funny pinging sound when they sprang open. I think he was using paperclips somehow.)

Remind you of anyone you know? No? Good.

Now to the judge. Let's go for a little bit of stereotyping here. Let's say he was old – ancient, in fact – desiccated, tall, his grey wig covering most of his face so that only his beaked nose pointing out told you that this wasn't some strange Grim Reaper you were facing. And what a beaked nose. Roman, with an edge you could shave with, if the urge to shave with a judge's nose ever crossed your mind.

Oh, and he was somewhat deaf. And wore a red robe with white piping.

Let's see, chuck a bit more stereotyping in: he kept falling asleep. And he'd never heard of the Rolling Stones. Right, that should do it for the judge.

Coconut.

Next, the lawyers. The counsel for the prosecution was the tallest man I have ever seen. About nine feet tall, or that's what it seemed like, looking down on him from the gallery. To compensate for his vertical growth his horizontal growth had reversed itself. I have to presume that there was space left there for such a thing as a skeleton, but not much, even given the fact that his black robe staying upright made it appear as if there had to be something supporting it. A hat-stand, possibly. A very, very tall and thin hat-stand on a starvation diet. He resembled an elongated and starving vulture. His hooded eyes weren't made for his face – possibly a transplant gone badly wrong. They started around about where his ears ended, as if the ears hadn't quite finished, and were fighting for space. One lazy blink would have given an eagle a heart attack. Perhaps he was born with them, and couldn't afford corrective surgery, but that did not excuse his wig; I've seen a number of judicial wigs in my time, and his was the tiniest I can recall. And while some legal wigs turn a faded yellowish-cream-off-brown kind of colour with age, his had turned bright yellow, possibly an accident in the washing machine. It perched precariously on top of a completely bald head as if it were a confused budgie. I expected it to suddenly go "cheep" at any time, and fly off to freedom.

To complete the picture, he had two speech impediments, or to be more accurate, one speech impediment and one verbal habit. Firstly he had a lisp, and secondly he prefixed every word with "h", except those words which start with h. "Your honour" kept coming out as "H'your onour".

Happy, Beazeley? Can't see anyone recognising – whatsisname – from that description.

Whoever made the prosecuting counsel used a different model for the defence. And whoever brought them together in the same court either had a very strange sense of humour, or was certifiably mad. Where the prosecution – let's call him Mr Crane, Mr Hector Crane – was tall, the defence – shall we say, Mr Horace Ball? – was short, at most four foot. (I later learnt that he was four foot and one inch in his boots, which had a four-inch sole and padded socks.) Where Mr Crane was thin to the point of invisibility, Mr Ball in his own black robe – well, he was so rotund that if he spread any further, he'd burst. One more mint and he was history, all over the court, splatter-splat-splat-splat.

Splat.

....

Apparently he wasn't a great eater, which would have been just as well, for there was no more room for him in his little dock.

And I think he had Mr Crane's wig. He had a fat, round head on top of his enormously wide body, and it was covered by a wig about ten times too large, a wig the colour you could describe as a brighter shade of blue-rinse. It would have come down to his waist if his girth hadn't interrupted its downward flow. The only reason it did not close entirely around the front of his face, as the judge's did, was that he wore amazingly large, thick-rimmed spectacles, from behind which two furiously blinking eyes looked out, making him resemble a confused owl hiding in a mass of light-blue wool. Somehow I just knew that he would have a tiny, squeaky voice.

But of course things weren't that simple, oh no. Oh, no, they never are. He had taken elocution lessons, hadn't he, and, when in control, had the most booming voice you could ever expect to come out of his cubicle. It was when he became excited that the boom turned into a kind of squeak-squeak-squeak, very quick, very high pitched. Being in the gallery I could see him. To anyone at the side of his dock he would have been hidden behind the wall. Any such person, hearing his squeaky tone, could only have presumed that there were a small family of strange furry creatures ferreting around behind the panelling.

Normally Mr Ball was accompanied by an orange crate, some ancient wooden thing he had discovered from the days when, presumably, oranges were transported in wooden crates. It made an ideal stand for him to step on so that he could peer over the top of his little dock. Unfortunately, that Monday morning, this familiar friend had either been hijacked, temporarily lost or decided to take a break from its onerous duties. In somewhat of a flustered panic he had ordered the court usher to immediately procure for him another orange crate.

The court usher was a thin, underfed, pony-tailed youth of about fifty-five; let's call him Harry. He had been a thin, underfed, long-haired youth of about seventeen in the days when flower power was on the wane, and had waned with it. He had also picked up an indulgence in smoking what was then probably called "grass" or "pot", and he now spent most of his working day quietly inhaling in a shady nook near the court, what could be termed as his niche in life.

And then there was the recorder. In this case acting as both recorder and part-time usher, someone had to make up for the many absences of Harry The Aged Hippy. The recorder was what might politely be termed as petite. When on her chair she sat on three editions of what I originally presumed to be the enlarged version of War And Peace, but which turned out to be the full telephone directory for the UK and Europe (including Western Germany and Important Numbers in Poland), 1975. She even had a little set of steps to allow her to climb onto her raised directories.

Let's say, just for argument, that she was Asian, more specifically, Indian. Now, with all due respect to the sub-continent of India, and I have met many wonderful people from there, but they do seem to breed some aggressive women. I have no doubt that they also have demure women, docile women, happy women, confident women, you name it. It's just the ones who make you think of a slim, tanned, younger, probably teenaged version of good old Queen Victoria in one of her less-obliging moments that stick in the memory – with the exception that Queen Victoria would get someone else to do the garrotting while this one would do it herself and enjoy every moment. And just because she wore an extremely bright and fetching midnight-blue sari with matching shawl, headscarf and light blue top, once you looked into her eyes – or she looked into yours – you no longer thought of her as a woman, not even as human, but as a

...

Force.

It's difficult to describe, but think of it this way: you've wandered out of your comfortable-if-dated-and-cluttered room at ye Olde Englande local inn, mildly contemplating how long it will take you to negotiate the hundred miles of different corridors which appear to have attached themselves to the dear old building before you get to the bar, and suddenly a child appears in the gloom before you as if from nowhere, a child wearing a midnight-blue sari, matching shawl and light blue top.

And just as suddenly it isn't a child.

Or, to put it another way, one minute you're strolling along in an English country town, all flower-pots and hurzel-wurzel top-o-the-day to you milord, the next you're looking into deep dark eyes which take you immediately to the more painful mysteries of the Orient, black magic, secret potions and poisons, sharpened stiletto knives slinking from cheerfully bright folds of clothing, blood red as the lipstick on smooth lips, the vast open space of the night desert as you wait for sunrise with your body buried up to the neck by a passing band of Bedouin, direct descendants of Ghengis Khan, led by the little assassin with the deep, dark eyes, and she didn't like the look you gave one of her camels, that sort of thing. And you hope that dear old Sherlock Holmes has finished that messy business on the Reichenbach Falls and is at that moment speeding his way towards you to sort things out and prove how elementary it all is. And dig you out just in time.

Just before the scorpions begin using your head as an extended breakfast.

A little of an over-exaggeration and geographical confusion, some people might say. All I can say to such people is, if you'd looked into those deep dark eyes you'd know better.

Okay, before I get back to the orange crate, let me describe the jury – a possible jury, on that first day. Calm down Beazeley, take an aspirin – or get yourself a drink, there's some brandy in the sideboard, there's a good lad.

Have a toilet roll with it while you're about it.

We can afford to splurge.

Now what did I do with those peaches? They aren't there anymore.

Must have given them away to someone.

If you find any left, Beaze old boy, fill your boots.

He would, too, you know. Squelch, squelch, squelch.

I think I might just stretch my legs before getting on to the jury. And my eyes. How people can sit in front of a computer screen all day tapping away at the keyboard beats me. I've hardly started and my eyes are beginning to feel it. I think I'll do some rolling-eyeball exercises at Beazeley.

Now there's a thought. Maybe I could give one of the jury a twitch in their eyes. Yes, a tic. You know, I know exactly which one it's going to be.

...

I'll probably make them vegan, too, that'll grind their socks.

.....

Even better, I'll make them a French vegan.

....

With a hiccough.

....

Chapter III. The Jury

Eye exercises over – I even got Beazeley doing them. I convinced him that he needs to do them once every hour.

I should have called him Pike, from that episode of Dads' Army where he keeps rolling his eyes, the stupid boy. He'll be frightening the horses over the next few days.

Still, it gave me something to do while wondering how to create a distinctive and unrealistic jury. I've realised that it's not going to be easy as I first thought. Imagine that you have witnessed an absolutely brilliant goal at a soccer match. If you aren't into soccer, think of tennis, or snooker, or ballet, flower arranging, whatever makes your boat rock, or float, or fly, or whatever your boat does. Now imagine that you have to describe this goal – let's say it was kicked from forty yards out, aimed to deflect off a passing bee, snick a defender's elbow, hit the cross bar at a thirty-degree angle precisely, bounce off the back of the goalie's head, and then trickle just into the net before another defender got to it. All deliberate. And you're so excited about the person who created this goal to beat all goals you want him to have someone's babies and you just have to tell the others about it down the pub, or at the tea party, or the Church social, or wherever. Only you aren't allowed to describe it as it happened. You have to paint it as a – well, a walk in the park. Or Charlie Chaplin not falling off a log. Or Boring Barra describing the post-room. That's more or less the problem we're facing here. I have to create a jury, the members of which have to appear as over the top, based on a jury who were totally over the top in real life. It's a problem. But hold my hand while I take you through it and we'll get there.

No, not you, Beazeley! Let go of my hand you – idiot.

I don't know. Think of all the genius-sidekick setups in history. Sherlock Holmes and Watson. Hercule Poirot and Hastings. That other bloke and the girl – Dr Who, I think.

Me? I get Beazeley. Beazeley, for crying in a wet bucket.

Watson was a Doctor. Hastings was a Captain. Miss Marple always had Chief Inspectors and Senior Commissioners and god knows what. Even Clouseau had Cato, a trained killer. Me? I get a pesky Tarian. And he's proud of it.

I was a Gemini yesterday.

I think I'll be a Taurus today.

Because I choose so.

Complete nonsense.

Oh, dear, he's got that "I'm about to cry" look in his eyes.

Tissues.

Best press on with the jury before he starts blubbering.

Let's see, we'll have to make them each as different as possible otherwise I'll be forgetting which is which or who is whom.

I know:

Taking the back row, starting from the end nearest the judge. Let's have an old woman, weather-beaten, flushed face, beaming red, faded old navy-blue coat buttoned up to the neck, greying hair, funny little battered, faded grey hat with a half veil you might have seen in the roaring twenties, looking as if it were part of a damaged fishnet stocking. She got there early, surrounded by plastic bags of various requirements to get her through the day. Let's call her Mrs Baggs. Very cheerful, keeps saying things like "This is fun, ducks, innit?" every so often. Don't worry too much about her, she won't be around long. But she is almost central, pivotal, to what happened. She just didn't know about it. She never would.

What might have happened.

Thinking about it, "what should have happened but didn't" might be more accurate, but things are getting confusing enough as it is. Just remember there are at least three elements to this: what really did happen, what I have to tell you happened, and what I originally meant to happen. There's at least a fourth involving hedgehogs, but I've decided to leave that bit out, it's just too painful.

Underpants.

Right. On with the jury. Next to Mrs Baggs, The Major. You could tell he was a major, he was wearing a uniform. He'd done his best to make it appear like civilian dress: a fawn-brown suit, dull-yellow-brown shirt, brown tie, polished but dull brown shoes, but you could see the bits on the jacket shoulders where the pips had been, relatively unworn compared to the rest.

We'll give him a faded-tan face with first blushes of red and a slight brown moustache looking embarrassed for itself. Had it been in earlier years you would have presumed him a retired major from some minor Indian regiment, looking back to the glorious days of the Raj when he had appeared in starched khaki uniform, including creased shorts, thin legs and knobbly knees, on the parade ground to review the troops before retiring for a bracing snifter to face the day's paperwork. Now all that was left to him was to meet like-minded, empty-minded souls in each others' houses, bungalows, or council flats, to share a large bottle of cheap red wine and abysmal excuses for Asian food from the local curry take-away while agreeing that the world had gone to the devil and that the only answer was to bring back hanging, flogging and National Service.

They'll never recognise Percy from that description, now will they, Beazeley?

Oh, dear, Beazeley's really got stuck into the brandy. Better push on before he reads this.

Good thing it's the cheap stuff.

Note to self: check how many toilet rolls are left at the end of the day.

Okay. Next to the Major we'll have a Prim Maiden Aunt. Tall, sitting upright, very flat chest. Grey hair in two buns. Why two buns? No doubt there was a reason. Actually, there was a reason, as I was to find out, but I'd rather forget until the appropriate time comes to mention it. Grey cardigan, grey skirt, grey blouse, grey face, eyes cast sternly downwards, ready to see all the evils of the world cast before her feet without looking at them. And thin lips. I hate thin lips. I accept that some people have them, and it doesn't necessarily make them one of the bad guys, but some people develop thin lips at the same time they develop their thin minds. You'd have to Botox their brains at the same time as their lips.

I used to go out with a girl with thin lips.

She left me for a cheesemaker.

I used to love cheese.

Gorgonzola.

We'll give her the tic. Prim Maiden Aunts never have a tic, so that should fit in nicely.

Can you have a tic in both eyes?

Go on then, she had a tic in both eyes, one at a time, like it was playing ping pong across her nose.

Next to her. Miss F. Short for Feminist. With a Capital F. Seventeen, looking about thirteen, she was a university student who had reached that stage where having a pet grievance is all the rage. She had just started on the feminists of the Sixties and Seventies. She was wearing a light-blue boob-tube which just covered her late-developing chest, leaving her thin shoulders and midriff bare, and skin-tight powder blue trousers, slacks I suppose they would have been called once, which were meant to emphasize her figure but only revealed an embarrassingly thin backside which could have done with the calories provided by a few cheese burgers. She had gone to town on the make-up front: scarlet lipstick, blue eye-shadow, mascara, everything she could find to turn herself into Miss Sexy. Most fathers would be thinking, "God, if she were my daughter I'd give her a slap, tell her to take the rubbish off and go play in the mud in the garden like any normal thirteen year old." To complete the ensemble she was wearing bright, sparkly flip-flops on her feet, the kind a ten-year-old girl might fall in love with. Altogether a skinny bag of contradictions to be avoided.

Her mother, of course, would tell her father that she was just being a normal little girl and to stop being silly.

You won't believe this (wake up in the back row, you're not supposed to believe this, go away Beazeley, you lay another finger on this keyboard and – oh, go have another brandy), but the juror alongside her was indeed her mother. Only she wasn't actually a juror, of course, she was there because her daughter was technically a minor, and needed a chaperone.

It's a pity, really, that we can't spend more time on Miss F's Mother, because I think she could be really interesting. On the surface she appeared to be your typical middle-class mum. Looked after her appearance and figure, probably had some of her daughter's boyfriends looking at her respectable cleavage thinking naughty thoughts which they didn't understand, spent her time apparently trying to work out whether to take Miss F to gymkhana first and pick up little Davy later, or pick up little Davy first and then take Miss F to gymkhana, what was going to be for dinner that evening, that sort of thing.

The thing about the respectable Miss F's Mothers of this world is that you never know what's going on behind that veneer of Women's Institute mildness. I could easily see Miss F's Mother as an eighteen-year-old teenager having a wild fling with an Arab Prince or French

Marquis, before setting off on a six-month grand tour of Europe with an assorted group of free-thinkers, anarchists and general dissolutes, whereafter she would return home and settle down as your ideal housewife and respectable mother, only occasionally having discreet affairs with interesting men who wouldn't stay around too long. But she would only do so when sure that no-one would find out. Until, after she had gone to a Better World, they read the diaries she had meticulously compiled and kept securely hidden. Her funeral would have a lot of people looking at each other wondering whether the other person was the "P" mentioned, or the "SG", and also whether either was male or female, and was that position really in the karma sutra? And wasn't it a pity they were no longer in a state to do that sort of thing? And where had they left their bus pass?

Her husband, naturally, having politely pre-deceased her some years before, of course. One has to have propriety in these matters.

Maybe another time. She looked an interesting woman. At the moment we'll have to press on with the rest of the jury.

(Miss F, by that time a mature and respectable mother herself, would be highly incensed that her mother hadn't confided in her, otherwise she would never have called her a boring old fuddy-duddy, and she, Miss F, would have started her own life-experiences much earlier.)

Next to the Miss F's Mother, on the end of the back row – what name could I give to him other than Mr Windy? You could call him Farmer Giles – pleasant claret-infused face, the suggestion of ripe red apples, a healthy paunch, dark brown corduroy jacket, unaccustomed waist-coat of cross-checked yellow, pipe hanging out of his mouth (unlit of course, don't want to get banned in public spaces), old-fashioned gaiters replacing the normal Wellington boots as if he were dressed for Sunday service.

But, unfortunately, and much as I would like to bypass this issue, it has to be said, without beating about the bush ... that he ... well, the truth is ...

He broke wind regularly and effusively. Every so often it sounded like a fog horn had gone off in the court room, and everyone would put their gas masks on.

Okay, we really don't want to read about that sort of thing every other page, so let's say – let's say he fell asleep a lot and snored loudly on the odd occasion. No, let's not call him Mr Windy, let's call him Mr Sleepy.

Right, let's move rapidly on. There are enough of the peppermints floating around, they're getting confusing. It's going to be difficult enough as it is remembering which one wasn't whom. Or have I already said that? Nope, no time at the moment to check, crack on, crack on.

Peppermints? I meant varmints. Creatures. Critters. People. Thingies. Humans. The ones the Little People call The Big Jobs. Hoobly-blooblies. Those things.

Humbugs.

At the start of the front row just in front of Mrs Baggs, Mrs Plum, a plump, middle-aged (i.e. above sixty-five these days) grandmotherly figure, white hair, staid lavender dress, white blouse, matching lavender cardigan, cheerful, knitting away with the biggest knitting needles I've ever seen. Sparkling steel, about two feet long, and easily two inches wide at the widest point, but looking sharp as anything at the business end. Not knowing anything about knitting, it never struck me at the time that there was something inherently wrong with those knitting needles. It was fortunate that she was in the front row and at one end, otherwise those needles would have taking someone's eye out, or even their arm off, in a sudden frenzy of plain-one purl-one. As it was, she was able to turn sideways and knit contentedly away over the side of the jury box.

Next, let's have a vicar, in front of the Prim Maiden Aunt. A smiling vicar wearing his uniform of black. Vicar Preachy. A beneficent vicar. Mostly bald, but with two Devil's horns of hair, sandy-going-white, sprouting out from just behind his ears, long tufts that managed, somehow, to reach above his massive dome, and that's quite an achievement. To call him an egghead would be to misconstrue even the largest ostrich egg in existence. Try dinosaur size. Big dinosaur size. As a thoughtful and thinking parson he rarely looked in people's eyes, preferring to gaze upon the middle distance as if he were gazing upon the very mysteries of Life. Which was just as well, since, just as many male interlocutors allegedly gaze at a female's mammary attributes during converse, anyone initially meeting the vicar could hardly take their eyes off a shining expense of domed head which was suggestive of a pale-pinky-brown version of the type of moon base you see in Sci-Fi magazines. The worst thing was his habit of stroking this bald protrusion as if it were still covered with hair. He had the longest and thinnest fingers I have ever seen, a bit like some of the aliens you see in movies. He could scratch his left ear with his index finger while his thumb was doing the same to the right ear.

There was a strange symmetry to his face, bald dome and all. He had these large sandy-white tufted eyebrows which turned up exactly in alignment with the Devil's horns of hair rising from behind his ears.

Oh, and this vicar was wearing a dog collar. A real dog collar. He had forgotten his normal collar at home and, realising the necessity of appearing properly dressed as a minister of the one and only real faith, had borrowed a collar and lead from a sleeping dog. It was white (the collar, not the dog, that was an Alsatian) which matched the requirement. The steel studs did not show too much, and the lead hung down Vicar Preachy's back, largely hidden by his black jacket, apart from about a foot or so which could be seen trailing when viewed from behind.

Then we come to someone I dubbed "The Quiet American". Five hundred gallon Stetson hat with "Jakes Auto Spares" on the front. Lurid yellow and green Hawaiian shirt. Light-brown, knee-length shorts. White socks peeking out from the top of cowboy boots. A white moustache and goatee which might make one think of fried chicken, and his ample girth was certainly suggestive of too many doodle burgers with extra cola and suicide sauce. White hair longer than the norm flowing out from beneath the Stetson.

And a pair of six-guns in holsters hanging from a belt around his huge paunch. Not real guns, of course. After all, they wouldn't allow those in an English court of law. But, since he was of American origin, and would have been, in his country of birth, more used to carry firearms or a small tactical nuclear device in a court, he was allowed toy guns – water pistols, one a transparent blue, the other a transparent green, both with red nozzles.

(They probably aren't allowed to openly carry guns in American courts of law, the lawyers and judge perhaps, but not the average jury member. Though it's easy to believe any story that comes out of that place.)

(You know, thinking about it, I'm sure, if you look long enough, you'll find somewhere in the States they allow jurors to wander around all tooled up. Alaska, probably. They can see Russia from there, so I'm told. On a clear day.)

What next? How about a "Nun With Guitar"? A young nun with an old-fashioned acoustic guitar, honest, helpful, innocent face staring brightly from underneath her wimple. But, just in case that might remind you of someone, this Nun With Guitar was wearing a tiny white wimple, had jet black hair, pale, almost luminous skin, a suggestion of Slavic cheekbones, white makeup with thick black mascara and black lipstick, and her honey-shot eyes glowed as if a lightning storm was softly playing within them. And because we already have Vicar Preachy in black, we need a bit of colour, so this nun was wearing nun's clothes mostly cut in the old-fashioned style, but they were tight and very light blue, with a shimmering effect, almost as if covered by hundreds and thousands of tiny sequins, little blinking, winking dots of light which shimmied and shimmered and shivered as her body parts moved. Let's just say it was a habit of hers. (Beazeley's just asked me to explain that last sentence. Have another brandy, Beazeley.)

Yes, okay, I admit it was a pretty weak joke, but you try explaining it to Beazeley if you have the misfortune to meet him.

Quickly scroll down while he's getting his next brandy so he won't read that.

Hmm.

I've just re-read that description of the Nun With Guitar. I'm not sure whether the word "innocent" is the right one to use. In fact I'm pretty sure it isn't. I think it's an automatic concept that pops into your mind along with the word "nun". Vicar Preachy might have been an innocent, almost naive person, the Nun With Guitar certainly wasn't. If I had known how much trouble she was going to cause me – ah, well, I suppose I would still have made the same mistakes.

I just would have enjoyed them more.

And had them build in sprinklers.

Original sin, yeah ...

Blinking, winking wittle dots ...

She had deep dark twinkling, sparkling, lightning-shot eyes that could welcome you to heaven or hell with added mayonnaise ...

I will never forget how ...

Anyway, enough of that, you don't want to know that. How many have we got so far – nine, excluding Miss F's mother. Right, tenth member of the jury, sitting in front of Miss F's Mother. Let's go for a little pipsqueak of a person. A bit like that blasted cheesemaker. One of those really annoying people who thinks he is always right and you are always wrong. Someone with a superior inferiority complex. (Or should that be an inferior superiority complex?) Sitting with his knees clenched together, his mind clenched together, his nose and mouth reeking of righteousness. And because he's such an irritating, obnoxious, odious specimen we'll make him a right little runt of a person. Think of someone who looks like a schoolboy in a suit, and will always look like a schoolboy in a suit, with pens sticking out of the front breast pocket, even when he's got to the age of overweight as this one had. The schoolboy that sneaked on all the others – the one everyone wanted to beat up, but couldn't, because he was teacher's pet. A dusty-black suit which looked embarrassed for itself, and even more so by being worn by him.

He really did remind me of that cheesemaker.

You could see that he was actually proud of that suit. It was probably the first one his mother hadn't bought for him, twenty years before. He was wearing dark glasses, and holding one of those white walking sticks those with impaired vision use. For absolutely no other reason than that I feel like it, we'll call him Hugo. If you don't like the name, just scrub it out and use whatever you prefer. I've never met anyone called Hugo, so there's less likelihood of mixing him up with anyone from real life. Remember, if you know a Hugo, this isn't him.

Probably.

Finally, in the front row, we come to the juror originally mentioned in the preface, Miss Strawberry Mousse, our statuesque blonde. Bouffant blonde hair, bright pink lipstick, magenta eye shadow which, when she blinked, flashed like strobes, pink jacket, white blouse, pink skirt, pink and white shoes, a long, white, silk scarf which she threw over her shoulder when irritated, or wished to make a point. End of blonde hair dyed deep pink. She had a large, firm bosom, but not the type you might see on the cover of a lads' magazine. Hers was the heavy artillery of the bosom brigade. The only bed it might make you think of would be those in a hospital, commanded by a stiff, starched matron who thought the Puritans were a frivolous bunch, a Nurse Shark as it were. Our Miss Strawberry Mousse would only vaguely make you think of Marilyn Monroe. Miss Strawberry Mousse had a figure that said she was definitely a woman, but a look in her eyes that said you were history if that gave you any thoughts. If she ever asked you if you fancied a good time she'd mean that she was the one going to have a good time, and you'd be the one ending up searching for your internal organs.

And the external ones.

Now, with all twelve seats occupied – and the jury box was originally constructed to take twelve, and only twelve members of the jury, and the damage it had since incurred meaning that any more and it would tip over – it might appear that said jury was complete. However Miss F's mother, it must be remembered, was Miss F's chaperone, and not a member of the jury. Which leaves one over. And for a reason, there were actually two left over. Two clowns.

Greasepaint is very effective in disguising a face, they tell me.

(I'm not making this up, you know.)

(Well, okay, I am, but not really, if you see what I mean.)

(Beazeley, pass me that brandy. Hold the toilet roll. Ta.)

Mmmm.

That tastes better than I thought. I must get more of it more often.

Or perhaps they were mimes. They never spoke in court, but they were dressed as clowns: Master Clown, let's call him, a young man with a huge, red, happy mouth painted on his face, but the original lips so turned down you might think he was about to burst into tears. He was dressed in baggy white clothes with red pom-poms down the front of his white top, as was his companion, who we shall call, for the moment, Miss Clown – we'll get to their real names in a minute or two.

Miss Clown's painted mouth was turned down in the fashion of someone who has just learnt that their pet hamster, the only friend they had ever had in a long, painful and orphaned life, had accidentally been turned into the stew she had just consumed as lunch. Her real lips, however, never stopped smiling, and her eyes had a gay and happy shine to them, constantly looking up at her partner, devotedly, the look of a young woman deeply, desperately, heart-achingly, totally, irremediably, in

....

* * * Love * * *

....

The type of look that might make a jealous reporter of the situation wish to paint the object of her feelings as either ugly or stupid, possibly both, but unfortunately he was what some women, I would imagine, for some reason, think of as sort of good looking in a way, if you like that sort of thing, and need your eyesight tested, I suppose.

Now I give this description as a fair and accurate portrayal (within the bounds already described) of these two, but the fact is that they were not actually that visible to the rest of the court. Being the last to arrive they had been told to sit on the floor in the well of the court, below the jury box, so that most of the time you could only see Master Clown's coned white hat – topped off with a red pom-pom – and Miss Clown's expanding white feather headdress, a bit as if it were a white peacock's feathers – also topped with a red pom-pom – and guess from the movement of these what the pair were thinking or doing. Fortunately I had two advantages, firstly of being able to lean over the edge of the gallery to get a better look, and secondly, of having with me a small mirror which I could, from time to time, use to see people and places not immediately in the direct line of vision. Why I had the mirror is a story for another time.

Let's just say I touch up my make-up quiet often. Okay?

Sometimes you don't ask questions. Because you might not like the answers. They might contain the X-word. And we aren't going to use the X-word.

I blame Beazeley.

Everybody blame Beazeley.

Good.

Poppers.

Right, so that more or less sorts out the relevant dramatis personae. Another cuppa and let's get back to the start of the Monday morning and Mr Ball's missing orange box. Now we can really let things rip.

Beazeley, it's time for your eye exercises. I suggest you do them looking out of the lounge window. Practise staring up and down the street for a while. Just try not to stare at the young lady across the road, it's rude.

Blow me down if she isn't washing her front windows again.

I wonder if those things are called shorts. They seem a bit on the skimpy side.

Note to self: do not let youself get distraxted by good-loojing young wiman acrodd the rosd.

Kinda reminfs me of the Young Nun With Guitar in a way. The legs especially.

And the high heels.

....

Dots. I'll never forget those dots.

As her body shivered and shimmied and suppled ...

... 13 ...

Okay, let's let the good times roll again.

Lots and lots of lanky little dots and a body made in Heaven...

... and some spare parts made Elsewhere ...

Chapter IV. The Ruling

Oh, dear, you have to laugh. A couple of schoolkids walking past saw Beazeley and thought he was making faces at them so they returned the compliment. He thought they were also doing eye exercises, and carried on. The sight of a grown man making faces – well, it's not something you see every day.

Note to self: grow up sometime. In about five or ten years should do nicely.

xxxxxx

The bad news is that the young woman across the street came out into her little front garden to pick some flowers while this was going on, and thought it quite funny. If anyone is going to make that lady laugh it will be me. After all, she is my neighbour, not Beazeley's. And I don't know for sure whether she is married, after all, I haven't actually seen her husband. And I am currently single.

Why is it that, when you're trying not to think of something that happened to you, you tend to hit the Enter key a few times for absolutely no reason?

Or even something that didn't happen but could have and would have been very nice?

Must be just me then.

Ah, well, back to that Monday in court. The time comes, as they say, to speak of things such as vultures, assassins, orange crates and silly rulings.

And washing powder.

It was just before the case began and the fifty-five-year-old youth, Harry the Aged Hippy, was in the well of the dock to prove that he existed, normally a five-minute presence which would ensure the continuation of his salary, before disappearing in a puff of smoke for the day. He heard a squeaky voice demanding a box of oranges coming from the defence dock. He couldn't see anyone in there, but something must be in there, and that something was asking for a box of oranges. He looked up to Mr Crane for advice. Mr Crane extended and retracted his neck in a gesture that was supposed to be a nod, but resembled more the action of a vulture approaching a rather dubious carcase. The usher scratched his pony-tail and looked back through a fog of confusion and years of whacky-baccy.

'Ha bokth h-of h-orangeth h-for h-the h-defenthe!' ordered the vulture for the prosecution.

Well, I don't care how doped-up and worn out a man's brain may be, when a vulture with a lisp and a careless approach to his h's orders a box of oranges for the defence even the dullest usher will obey. Happy Harry didn't stop to ask how large or how many. All he wanted was to get to his niche in life, light up, and drop out. So he hurried out to the local greengrocer and told him to send a box of oranges to the court. And the greengrocer, baffled by Happy Harry's less than clear communication skills, and afraid that somehow, should he raise even the slightest objection, he might end up in the court himself, immediately sent a box of his finest Seville oranges. The usher, deciding that his duty was completed for the morning retired to his niche and lit up a peace pipe. Mr Ball put the box of oranges in front of him, ready to climb upon it when his turn came to speak. He had an eager look on his pudgy face, almost comical in contrast with the more serious and world-weary look of the vulture in the dock next to him

The tiny, midnight-blue sari-, headscarf- and shawl-clad homicidal court usher climbed up her little steps and popped herself on her telephone directories. Then she pressed a button on her desk as the judge was about to enter the court, and a recorded voice announced:

"All rise for the presiding judge. All rise. All rise. For the presiding judge. Mind the gap."

There was silence. The court rose. The jury box swayed. The judge entered.

'H'Permithin h'to h'approach h'the h'benth, m'lud,' requested the Vulture once the Beak had seated himself, his nose and his wig, and the jury and the rest of the court had sat down to watch play kicking off.

The nose poking out from the wig nodded briefly. And slowly. Strangely the wig did not move at all.

The Vulture and Mr Ball opened the doors to their docks and stepped down into the well of the court. Mr Ball took a cap from his pocket and placed it on top of his blue-rinsed wig. At first sight it was a normal New York Yankees cap, but it had an extendible radio aerial poking upwards, with a small blue triangle of cloth attached, flapping along as he walked. This, it transpired, was to let the judge know where he was, as he was too short to be seen from the bench.

'Mr Ball, Mr Crane,' Judge Beak's nose nodded. Slowly. As if it hurt. His head leaned forward as if it were a mechanical toy.

'H'm'lud,' said Mr Crane, his large eyes looking up at the nose peeking out from the wig above and in front of him.

'Mr Crane?'

'H'm'lud, h'thith h'cathe h'ith h'a h'cathe h'of h'public h'intereth.'

'Public interest.' Slowly. 'I see.' A pause. 'Do you agree, Mr Ball?'

'PUBLIC INTEREST,' boomed Mr Ball from the floor and the little blue flag nodded strenuous agreement, the aerial making a twanging sound.

'I see.'

Mr Beak was silent for a few minutes as he contemplated this, or possibly fell asleep.

'We will have to declare it *sub judice*, if it is a question of the public interest,' he finally decided. You agree, Mr Crane?'

'H'very h'muth h'tho, h'm'lud.'

'Mr Ball?'

'DEFINITELY, YOUR HONOUR. *SUB JUDICE.*'

The judge's nose nodded slowly. His head and wig still didn't move.

'I shall so rule,' he ruled.

(Which is where we came in. I wasn't too worried at the time, expecting the *sub judice* ruling to only last as long as the trial. If only I had known what was coming.)

The two lawyers returned to their docks and the trial began in earnest. Mr Ball sat down and removed his cap. Mr Crane stood up and flapped his black wings before tucking his hands underneath his armpits, elbows sticking out.

'H'ladieth h'and h'thentleman h'of h'the h'thury,' he began, 'h'during h'the h'courthe h'of h'thith h'trial h'you h'will ere h'many h'thrange h'and h'unuthual h'claimth h'from h'the h'defenth. H'all h'contained h'in h'thith h'book.'

He nodded meaningfully at the jury, his budgie-wig scuttling around his bald bonce, while he held up a luridly covered book between the tips of a thumb and finger, as if it were some revolting object he would have preferred not to have to handle. The statement had different effects on the ladies and gentlemen of the jury.

'This is fun, ducks, innit,' said Mrs Baggs cheerfully. Mrs Plum wrinkled her nose and smiled at her knitting, suggesting that she had now lost count, but had no intention of getting angry with such sweet knitting. The Major glared disapproval at introducing a book into the matter. He knew what books were, and they had never done the world any good. Best keep them locked up somewhere. The Prim Maiden Aunt stared at the ground disapprovingly. And hiccoughed. Strawberry Mousse tossed her head as if to say, "So? I've read a book before. I know what a book is." Then she tossed the end of her scarf over her shoulder. It landed on Mr Sleepy's face. Mr Sleepy, head backwards, carried on snoring, the end of the scarf levitating with every exhalation.

Vicar Preachy bowed his bald dome and said a quiet prayer hoping that he would not have to read the book, since it looked like the kind of book he had once accidentally read without realising what kind of book it was, or what effect it would have on him, which had resulted in Mrs Preachy ejecting him from the matrimonial bedroom, to which he had ever since been refused re-admittance.

Then he scratched his left ear with his right hand.

The Nun With Guitar, on the other hand, looked as if she hoped it was that sort of book, and was looking forward to perusing it in detail. She licked her black lipsticked lips. Her guitar made a sudden, short, plinking sound. She had an inviting half-smile on her lips, just slightly apart.

Miss F leaned forward and tried to read the author's name. If it was written by a man she was prepared to give her verdict right there and then. Miss F's mother pulled Miss F back before she fell over The Nun With Guitar in front of her. The Quiet American nodded slowly. And stayed Quiet. Hugo's face remained impassive behind his dark glasses, mouth and knees tightly shut.

Boy Clown sat on the floor looking down, as if he were the one on trial, and the book evidence of his crimes. Miss Clown rested her head on Master Clown's shoulder and looked up into his face with wide, innocent white eyes. He kissed her forehead gently and stroked her blonde hair.

(I forgot to mention: he had boy-next-door hair, she had shiny-princess-could-be-a-sex-kitten-if-she-knew-what-not-to-wear   (i.e. fewer and tighter clothes with a good cleavage for a start) hair.)

Mr Crane continued.

'H'now h'the h'counthel h'for h'the h'defenth h'will h'claim h'that h'it h'ith h'merely h'a h'work h'of h'ficthin. H'but h'it h'ith h'a h'Pack h'Of h'Lies. H'yeth, h'a h'complete h'a h'Pack h'Of h'Lies, h'ladies h'and h'gentlemen. H'indeed, h'you h'will ear h'evidenthe h'which h'will h'thow h'clearly h'that h'it h'identifieth h'my h'client. H'intimate h'evidenthe.'

I think the suggestion of "intimate evidence" was designed to catch the attention of the jury. It certainly made Vicar Preachy cross his legs, and the Nun With Guitar licked her black lips again. Licked her lips very slowly. And then looked up at me and smiled. And licked her lips again. Slowly.

Of all the cases in all the courts in the world she had to walk into mine...

I concentrated on Mr Crane the Vulture. I could handle the guitar. But suggestive looks from a Gothic Nun – well, think about it.

No, you're right, better not to think about it.

'H'thorieth h'of h'affairth,' Mr Crane was saying. 'H'grotethque h'thorieth.   H'black   h'magthic.   H'defrocked   h'nunth. H'accuthathionth h'of h'murder. H'insects. 'Alibut.'

Was it my imagination, or did The Nun With Guitar suddenly look down, avoiding Mr Crane's eyes?

Mr Crane again nodded at the jury meaningfully, and, having finished his introduction, sat down.

Beazeley's just told me that trials don't work that way. Keep up, Beazeley, keep up.

Did you know, a Firkin used to be a small cask used to hold things like beer or fish? I mention that because I'm thinking of converting a Firkin to an adverb or adjective. Or possibly a lethal weapon.

Right, where was I?

Firkin doofus.

Vultures.

Budgies.

Ah, yes. Right.

Once Mr Crane had finished his oration Mr Ball stood up. He mounted the box of oranges and put his plump little hands on the ledge in front of him.

'LADIES AND GENTLEMEN OF THE JURY,' he boomed in such a deep and loud voice that the entire jury blinked and sat up straight, apart from the two clowns on the floor, Mrs Plum who had attention only for her knitting, and Mr Sleepy, who continued the rise and fall of Strawberry Mousse's scarf.

'This is fun, ducks, innit,' said Mrs Baggs cheerfully once she had recovered.

'Oh, dear, now I've missed a stitch,' sighed Mrs Plum. Mr Sleepy burped.

It was then that Mr Ball began to realise the difference between an orange box of the old-fashioned type made out of wood, a solid crate, and a modern box of oranges made of cardboard, tissue paper and oranges. The former can take a lot of pressure. The latter tends to slowly surrender to a short but heavy weight, which is what this one now began to do.

'THIS CASE IS A VERY SIMPLE ONE,' he continued as the jury, apart from Mrs Plum, looked on, fascinated, as he slowly sank from view.

'E's deflating,' Mrs Baggs said with great satisfaction.

'THE WORK IN QUESTION' – his nose level with the dock – 'IS NOTHING MORE THAN' – now his eyes – 'A WORK OF' – as he lost sight of the jury his carefully controlled boom escaped him, and he ended with a squeak – 'fiction!'

Mr Crane opened his large eyes with a start and blinked slowly, twice. He looked around and realised that Mr Ball, apart from two pudgy hands holding on to the dock, appeared to have vanished. He leaned over the panel dividing them and peered down at Mr Ball, wrinkling his nose at an unexpected smell of orange juice.

'H'a h'problem, h'Mr h'Ball?'

'Me oranges are squashed,' Mr Ball squeaked.

Mr Crane, noticing the state of the box of oranges underneath Mr Ball's feet, nodded understanding.

'H'I h'thall h'athk h'for h'an h'adjournment.'

'Please, please do, Hector,' squeaked Mr Ball.

'H'your onour,' Mr Crane said, turning to the bench. This was met with silence. Mr Crane paused before trying again.

'H'your onour?' Another silence.

'What's happening?' squeaked Mr Ball.

'H'I h'think e'th h'fallen h'athleep h'again. H'you'll' ave h'to h'wake im. H'give h'your h'I h'demand h'thpeeth.'

Mr Ball's "I demand" speech was a technique they normally used when Judge Beak fell asleep. It consisted of Mr Ball booming "I DEMAND!" once or twice.

'I demand!' he squeaked from his pit.

'H'louder, h'Mithter h'Ball.'

'I can't do it,' squeaked Mr Ball. 'I can't do it when I can't see anybody. You'll have to go over and tweak his nose.'

'H'I h'can't h'tweak eth h'nothe. H'the h'latht h'time h'I h'tweaked eth h'nothe e h'found h'againtht h'me.'

The recorder, who had been looking up at the judge anxiously during this exchange, stepped down from her chair and telephone directories and went up to the bench to try to wake the sleeping judge. Unfortunately the bench was a good five feet taller than her upraised hands, and despite jumping up and waving her arms in front of him Judge Beak's nose remained solidly and silently asleep.

'American ingenuity,' cried a voice from the jury. The Quiet American had stood up and was twirling his water pistols, the other jurists holding on precariously as the jury box wobbled and swayed with intent. He took quick aim, fired, slipped the water pistols back into their holsters, and sat down again as if nothing had happened. Two spurts of water shot across the court and hit Judge Beak's nose dead on, splattering themselves into multiple droplets as they made contact with the bone. Everyone, apart from the clowns and Mrs Plum, held their breaths to see how Judge Beak would react. There was only the smallest of starts, and a droplet of water fell off his nose.

'Mr Crane. Mr Ball,' he said after a few moments, 'I perceive that it has begun to rain. It might be best if we call off play. And since the members of the jury have still to acquaint themselves with their lodging, I suggest we adjourn for the day. Do you agree, Mr Crane?'

Indeed, Mr Crane, h'did.

'Mr Ball?

The little blue flag waved sad agreement above the defence's dock.

'Until tomorrow.' The recorder pressed a button on her little desk.

'All rise for the judge,' came a metallic order. The judge left quickly, carrying a set of golf clubs and a golfing umbrella, preceded by his nose.

I have to confess to a little feeling of irritation as I watched the jury file out, climbing against the camber of the leaning and wobbling jury box. The trial had had five days allotted, and day one was effectively over without anything to show for it, apart from one crushed box of oranges. At the same time I noticed the nice pair of silk-clad legs the Nun With Guitar showed as she stepped out of the jury box. I'm not au fait with the clothing fashions of modern day nuns, but it was the first time I had seen one with slits in her habit running from the bottom to half way up her thigh.

And her legs were quite

....

'That's a bit of a nuisance,' said a voice next to me. It was the MI5 agent. I was going to call him Mr MI5, but that voice spoke of something other than a mister. It was the sort of low voice which suggested that it was either a woman in man's clothing or a man in man's clothing pretending to be a woman in man's clothing or ...

'Why do you have MI5 written all over you?' I asked, deciding to go for the blunt approach. The moustache bristled, the way false moustaches glued on with hallucinogenic glue do when the wearer takes a deep breath through the nose.

'What makes you think I'm not an MI5 agent?' it asked. I looked into two eyes which looked back with a woman's view. They were wearing mascara.

The light red lipstick was also a little confusing.

'The fact that you look precisely like the idea of an MI5 agent which someone who had never seen one would have,' I replied. It sniffed again and pushed past me. Brushed past me. The sort of close physical encounter a member of the opposite sex might use to erotic advantage. Not the sort you'd want with a moustache. I decided I'd have to keep an eye on it.

Right, Beazeley, time for lunch. I'll have a ... No, on second thoughts, I'll make it myself. Last time Beazeley made anything it was fish salad with live piranhas.

I don't know who was more surprised, me or them.

I know who moved faster, though.

Beazeley keeps pointing out that my motives for being there were not exactly altruistic. So? Did I ever say they were?

Lawyers.

Fish soup. That's what I'll make him. A fish-soup sandwich.

He'll like that.

Not a lot.

.....

Chapter V. A Trip Around the Railway Tavern

Beazeley's gone to lie down because he was "feeling a little faint". Feeling the effects of cheap brandy on an empty stomach, more like it. He's lost his appetite for some reason. Thinks I'm going to write something which will give the game away. Well, just for him, I will – when he's around, peering over my shoulder.

Note to self: for god's sake, remember to delete it afterwards!

Extra note to self: keep away from exclamation marks, they're too melodramatic.

Right, where were we?

Ah, yes, the jury and their lodgings.

I remember the first and only time we walked into a restaurant together. Beazeley and me. He suddenly said, "See, food!" Of course I could see food, it was a flipping restaurant. What did he think we would see, a flying saucer? Vampires? Morris dancers? Bottles of medical samples?

Poor chap's a little off his head.

A lot off his chump.

Lodgings.

Judge Beak's comment about the jury's lodging might need a little further explanation: due to the nature of the trial everyone involved had been booked into a local hotel – let's call it the Railway Tavern.

Now, let's see ... how shall we invent this Railway Tavern ... a Railway Tavern ...

Let's say it's one of those typical old English hotels, the original part built about a thousand years ago, with parts falling off and other parts being built on over the centuries, so that in the end it resembles nothing more than a collection of disparate rooms of varying shapes, sizes and styles, connected by a maze of corridors which can suddenly go up a flight of stairs, or down, or go up or down without the stairs, or even more suddenly curve left or right as the fancy takes them. It's the type of hotel that issues guests with maps based on the same idea that underpins the design of the London Underground map, namely, for someone in the dark, they don't need to know exactly where they are, just where the next station is and what its name is. And dark is the word: outside the sun shone and summer sang, whereas the Railway Tavern was built by various generations who believed that, if you couldn't get blackened oak beams or panelling, paint things deep maroon or chocolate brown. They weren't much interested in lights either, they could make one twenty-five watt bulb last an entire corridor. And don't, they appeared to have instructed the architects, get carried away with windows, the government will just start taxing them again.

And alcoves. Deep alcoves with curtains, alcoves just made for someone who likes standing in the shadows in order not to be seen. Heavy, dusty, red velvet curtains with faded gold trimming. Possibly because the few windows there were, were in the alcoves, and the heavy velvet curtains helped keep nasty things out, such as bright sunshine and fresh air.

Mirrors at the end of each corridor. The type of mirrors that antique collectors go ga-ga over. "Ooh, look, a Fronzi Bonzi 1721 reverse mirror with curlique side splats." Only problem is that they aren't very good as mirrors anymore. The ones that do reflect anything other than a vague, amorphous blob, reflect things the same way those weird mirrors at carnivals do.

It's the type of hotel where, to get to the basement, you have to go up to the first floor, turn right, turn right, turn right, down a few steps, thirty yards up an incline, and you're there, next to the basement boiler which is actually on the fifth floor.

The type of hotel in which using a satellite navigation device is a bad move. The last person to try that in the Railway Tavern disappeared and was never found again. One theory is that he's stuck in a room that was lost from the map in 1848. More popular is the idea that he opened one of the doors on the fourth floor which open directly onto the outside without a compensating balcony, tumbled over into the back of a refuse-collection truck, and was crushed and fed into the incinerator.

It's just not as romantic as the first idea.

And the fourth floor is actually the attic. On that part of the hotel that has an attic.

(Why is it that that type of hotel always has Teasmades in every room which never quite work properly when you try to use them when you wake up, but when you complain the maid or whoever switches it on and it works every time?)

Oh, they have a ghost, of course. All old English Railway Taverns have a ghost, it's mandatory under the Trades Descriptions Act. Unfortunately no-one had seen their ghost for some years, so they were thinking of getting in a fresh one. (Okay, I made that last bit up.)

Anyway. Back to Monday.

I'd cased the joint earlier – dear me, I seem to be lapsing into Americanisms again. Note to self: tidy this up later.

Thinking of it, after Beazeley's comment you might be wondering now what my interest in the case was. Let's just say I'm a nosey-parker. (Which is a lot closer to the truth than some of the things the others were going to come up with.)

Okay, I'll be straight with you. I can't say why, but I will say how. I had one Plan A and one Plan B. Plan A was to make sure the jury came to the right verdict. But, just in case Edgar The Ears was successful and Judge Beak ruled against the book being published Plan B was to get a copy. I was going to make sure that at least one copy got smuggled out of the country. I didn't have much faith in the legal system, and filching a copy as insurance would be, I thought, a stroll in the park.

The trouble with something that's a stroll in the park is that there are parks, and there are parks. And for some you say "Parks", and others you use "Pox". And you don't want to go for a stroll in the Pox.

Why, you might ask, was I so desperate to see Edgar The Ears get his come-uppance? Since you ask again, as an objective observer of events I can't make any prejudicial comments about the slimeball, I can only state that I wished to see justice done and have the world read the truth about the double-dealing low-life little rat.

Nothing personal, of course.

And I really don't see any point in using the word "fixated".

Anyway, I'd cased the joint earlier, and had become pretty familiar with the place. And the receptionist. Ever notice how that sort of hotel always has a rather strange receptionist who seems to be permanently on duty? This one – okay, Beazeley, calm down, get yourself another brandy – good boy – silly sod can't even have a lie down properly – this receptionist wore the staff uniform of the hotel, canary yellow skirt, maroon top, little dark green apron, almost large enough to be a bikini, purple polka-dotted scarf tucked into the maroon top and high-heeled pale-blue toe-pincher shoes. Her name tag said "Mildred". That didn't help much, all their name tags said "Mildred", I think the owner got a discount on a bulk used set. So let's call her Mildred One. She had the appearance of someone who had gone to the hairdressers and changed her mind half way through. The left side was long, below the shoulder, straight blonde. The other was bouffant, hennaed, and tinted with electric blue glitter. To balance this she wore blue eyeliner on the left and yellow on the right. I had never heard her say anything apart from "Heyick".

Where would I find the dining room?

"Heyick," with a toss of the head in the direction of the dining room. Straight blonde hair flies over bouffant section, hanging off like a desiccated octopus's tentacles.

Is there a pub close by?

"Heyick." Yes there is. Toss of head towards the entrance. It's out there. Straight blonde hair back in position.

Would you like to have my children?

"Heyick." Get stuffed. With a hippopotamus.

And so it was when I returned from the court and walked into reception that day.

'Afternoon, Mildred One. Everything happy with the world?'

'Heyick.' Sod off, I'm busy doing my fingernails. She was. She was painting them white.

Now most hotels, if they are going to have some form of music in reception, would have some softly piped muzak. Not the Railway Tavern. They had five mournful Italian cellists in reception, hidden behind an aspidistra, next to the ancient suit of armour holding a pike.

Hmm, that might be a problem, introducing five Italian cellists, it's too close to reality. Too easy to identify.

Okay, I know, let's make it just one.

And, it wasn't a cello, let's say it was very similar but different ... I know, a Jello.

Right, so they had a mournful Italian Jellist.

Okay, better not to call him Italian. Let's make him Czechoslovakian.

Beazeley has just politely pointed out, as is his want, that Czechoslovakia no longer exists, so he'd have to be either Czech or Slovak.

Thank you Beazeley.

Pollock.

Beazeley, for your information, this Czechoslovakian left the country before it divided into two. That's why he's still here. He doesn't know who he is. He has a split identity.

Actually, I felt sorry for the Jellist. It must be pretty soul-destroying to have to play hidden behind an aspidistra. So, that lunch time, just to cheer him up and make him feel appreciated I decided to compliment him.

'Nice piece,' I said, turning around and parting the branches. 'I've always thought you can never get enough of Beethoven.'

He gave me a sour look through the leaves.

'Heyick,' said Mildred One behind me.

Translation: That wasn't Beethoven. He was just tuning his Jello. Plonker.

There's just no pleasing some people.

(Actually the word Mildred One used wasn't plonker, but something beginning with "b" and not sounding totally unlike plonker if you took the "l" out, but I probably shouldn't mention that.)

Well that more or less describes the Railway Tavern and Mildred One – and the Czechoslovakian Jellist. It's a bit all over the place, but I am working both from some notes I made at the time plus what I can reliably remember. And then I have to filter it all through a lens to distort it, sufficiently so to keep the lawyers at bay, while still keeping that core of fact. This afternoon I'll concentrate on what happened between myself and the Clowns that Monday afternoon, because that's when I first got the inkling.

Beazeley doesn't like inklings. He doesn't like the word, that is.

I think I shall use it more often.

Who's a nasty bar steward, then?

All I can say in my defence is, that if you knew Beazeley, like I know Beazeley, oh, oh, you'd want to thump him too.

. . . 13 . . .

He was also at the trial. Keeps saying things such as "it didn't happen that way".

Good grief.

Meatballs.

Chapter VI. The Secret of the Clowns

Page break. New chapter. Chapter – six, chapter six it is.

This isn't as easy as I thought it would be. I thought writers just sat down there and churned the words out as their muse hovered around looking – musy, I suppose. And I have an advantage, because I was there when it happened, I've got the facts to work with, I don't have to invent something unbelievable out of thin air. It's not as if I'm suddenly going to face writer's block, not knowing what happens next. I've got my tattered little notebook from that week in front of me – it survived accidentally going into the wash down at the laundromat. I've even got Beazeley, who was also there, to remind me of any little detail I might have forgotten so that he can tell me not to include it.

The one thing I wish I did have was better shorthand. I'm not sure whether this page starts "dandelions for lunch" or "train delayed". What do you think, Beaze?

Right. He thinks it's "sunset serenade", fat lot of good he is.

Never mind. I can see everything as clearly in my mind's eye as if I had a video of it running on the telly in front of me. A huge, ceiling-high, wide-screen, panoramic telly. With surround-sound and three-D effects. The Nun With Guitar's deep, jet-black eyes looking directly into mine, with more than a suggestion of ...

Whoah, down boy. One thing at a time.

....

Oooh, whoopy.

....

It's either those things or the pills again.

Beazeley's just mentioned that the young woman across the street has just come out. I do wish he wouldn't keep interrupting.

Looks like she's off to do some shopping. On foot. Down to the local corner shop, I would imagine.

She doesn't look married.

I shall have to find an excuse to say hello to her.

Do you need an excuse to say hello to your very attractive young neighbour?

Where was I?

Ah, down here.

Monday afternoon. Back at the Railway Tavern. Yes, that's it ...

There was a convention in town that week. Now, we have to be careful with this one. Too easy to make it obvious. If I said it was a Freemason bachelors' party someone might put two and two together and get three. And if I said it was a Taiwanese monks' naturist gathering, well, that might give them four. So ....

I know, let's call it, well, a shy singles' rabbit costume convention. That's right, a meeting of various very shy single people who have to dress up in bunny costumes to protect their identities and prevent embarrassment, pink for the girls, blue for the boys, and I'll leave you to your imagination if you think of any other colours. In addition to the bunny outfits they had a fancy-dress theme, so a cape would suggest a swashbuckler, a cape and an eye-mask a highwayman, a flouncing dress with tiara a queen or princess, and so on.

(If you prefer, imagine them as, I don't know, marmosets, or mastodons, or menhirs, or marshmallows. Hell, make them wumpets from Wibblywobblywangly World if you want. I'm going to go with the bunnies.)

As I ambled apparently aimlessly along one of the corridors two of them lolloped past me, holding paws and looking very smug. In the world of the shy bunny, those who can get past their inhibitions far enough to hold paws with another are king. And queen, I suppose.

One who wasn't either opened her door and peeked out as I passed it. I had the chance, before she saw me, squeaked and dived back into her room, to notice that she was a small, very attractive looking bunny with a healthy pink nose, white and pale pink fur, bright eyed and bushy tailed, no doubt a great catch for any blue bunny who might get past her demure reserve. That was unlikely to be the one I spotted hiding in an alcove watching her door like a love-lost teenager staring at the window of an unreachable girl he'd be prepared to die for if only being dead didn't involve being dead afterwards. His whiskers drooped, his fur was dull and matted faded-blue, and I was willing to bet a bob or two that his eyes were mournful behind the large and wonky dark glasses he was wearing. On the spur of the moment I decided to call him Sad Sid and the pale pink one Matilda. After all, even the shyest bunny deserves a name, and I felt just a little sorry for them.

Walking past the next alcove I realised that shyness was likely to be the least of Sad Sid's problems. Almost blended into the shadows so that an untrained eye would miss him was what I immediately termed Bunny Evil. He was wearing dark glasses and a velvet 4-am-in-the-morning-blue costume, so dark as to be almost black. A sleek, slim body which made you think of a wild cat – a lithe cougar, perhaps – rather than a bunny. A feral hunter wearing a veneer of civilisation, with sophistication bent towards the deeds of the night. Behind the dark glasses his close-slit eyes were firmly locked on Sad Sid's alcove, watching, waiting. If he was a shy bunny I was a flying hippopotamus.

Fortunately it had nothing to do with me, nor why I was there. Sometimes you can get involved in other peoples' problems and do some good. Most of the time people enjoy sorting out other peoples' problems merely to avoid concentrating on their own. The bunnies had exactly zero relevance as far as I was concerned – or so I thought at the time.

However relevant or irrelevant they were, I realised that they did had the potential to be a nuisance as I approached the door I had been looking for, to find a huge mound of electric-blue fur lying stretched out across the corridor carpet, clutching an empty vodka bottle and snoring like a conveyor belt with a cog missing and loopback on. That's one of the things about these shy singles' gatherings. Half of them are teetotal, the other half are normally plastered by lunchtime. Understandable, I suppose, for people who are so shy they need a double whisky before they have the courage to switch on the television in the morning, just in case the news presenter can see them.

The good thing about Snoring Beauty was that his noise covered any I made. The door I sought was ajar – at least it was after I had picked the lock and given it a slight push. I opened it further, wide enough to slip in and close it behind me, ready to announce that I was hotel security, or just someone who had mistakenly entered the wrong room, or, as in this case, not to say anything at all until the occupant or occupants, if there were any, which there were, said anything.

'Who are you?' asked Master Clown from the jury. He and the Miss Clown had taken off their costumes and makeup and looked like any clean, eager, helpful, well brought up youngsters, the sort you find in books as opposed to the ones in real life. The ones in real life either belong to the local Fascists and go to church every day, or listen to extremely loud and offensive music while setting fire to your car. Sometimes both.

Now, in case you're wondering why I had slipped into the Clowns' room, it was, as mentioned, the first step in ensuring the jury came up with the right verdict. I wasn't going to interfere with anything, I wanted to get to know each one so that I would have a fair idea of how they were going to vote, and perhaps put a little pressure on them to vote the right way. That's not interfering, it's just making sure the world goes the right way.

Okay, it is interfering, but if you had been in my shoes I wouldn't have been wearing them.

What's that raw Japanese fish stuff called?

Anyhow, there was something very interesting about these two without their clown costumes or makeup: previously the boy had a smile painted on his face, while his own mouth had been turned down so far it resembled an inverted U, whereas the girl had been the reverse. Now, sans makeup, the boy was cheerful, while the girl looked like Ophelia about to commit suicide. The boy had been trying to comfort her, both sitting on a couch, his arm around her shoulders, when I appeared.

'So it is you,' I said in response to his query.

I didn't know them from Eve and Adam, but you'd be amazed at what people will fall for. Try it with some stranger sometime: start off with something like "My goodness! It's been ages! How are you?" Ninety-nine percent of people will presume that they should know who you are but can't remember, and are too embarrassed to admit it. On average you can chat to someone that way for ten minutes, and then leave them firmly convinced that they should know who you are. My best was an hour and a half on a train journey once. She still sends me Christmas cards every year, though she addresses them to 'Peter' for some reason.

'You recognised us?' the boy asked.

'I told you he did,' cried the girl, her eyes red, looking at me in fear.

Hey, I'm not that ugly.

'What do you intend to do about it?' asked the boy, rising threateningly, looking like your typical good-natured kid who thinks he might have to thump someone and isn't quite sure how to start.

'Relax, kid, you don't have to worry about me,' I said. 'Here, have a cigar.'

He took the cigar, a look of surprise in his eyes. It's another trick that hardly ever fails. People seem to have something in their collective cultural consciousness that says a cigar is good. It speaks of celebrations and good news. Slip it across smoothly enough and even the most hardened anti-smoking zealot will happily accept, and take five minutes to work out that it's a, yuk!, cigar.

'So, come on kid,' I said, going into Marlon Brando mode, 'spill the beans.'

'I'm not a kid, I'm twenty-one. And I don't have any beans.'

'Yeah, well, that's just a figure of speech, kid, don't worry about it.'

'Here, you're Liverpudlian, aren't you?'

'Wastchesutchenan, East Tennessee, kid.'

I'd spent a lot of time getting the pronunciation of that right. (I live in fear of one finding out that there really is a Wastchesutchenan, East Tennessee. It sounds like the sort of place they lynch strangers for being strangers.)

'No, you're not, you're from Liverpool,' said Master Clown.

Well, sometimes you have to let them think they're in control.

'Okay, I was born in Toxteth. So what. You a racist or summat? I'm the only thing standing between you and something nasty. So, give.'

'You won't hand us in, will you?' asked the girl.

'Not if you come clean, hon.'

'Her name isn't hon.'

It was round about then that I began to realise that these two, open, honest-looking youngsters were going to be the types who take what you say literally. You have to be really, really careful around people like that. Fortunately these two didn't look entirely stupid, but I've known some who, if you told them to check a room out and make sure there was space to swing a cat in it – well, you can guess the rest. One severely extremely not-very-happy cat. And hopefully the literal interpreter covered in scratches.

'Okay, kid, tell me your real names then,' I said, as slowly as possible without appearing to treat them as half-wits.

'Clyde and Bonnie. I'm Bonnie, this is Clyde,' replied Master Clown.

I nodded. I could tell those weren't their real names. If they were their parents must have got their genders mixed up. But, as Shakespeare once said, what's in a name? A rose will smell as sweet even if it's called a septic tank. It just gets confusing when ordering stuff from the florist's over the phone. In this case you have to remember that Bonnie was the boy and Clyde the girl, otherwise your brain might develop a mental knot when I mention Clyde wearing a dress or putting lipstick on. Bonnie going to the gents. That sort of thing.

'Well,' the kid – Bonnie – began, 'it all started when we ran away from our grandfather. We wanted to get married, you see.'

'Whoah! You ran away from your grandfather? You're related?'

'Well, we're brother and sister, in a way.'

'In the "you have the same mother and father" way?'

'Well, not exactly. You see, we're orphans.'

I sat down. It sounded like this could take a long time. And I had a feeling I wouldn't even understand it when the kid had finished.

'We were adopted,' Clyde put in quickly, casting a worried glance at Bonnie. 'Bonnie was adopted first, when he was one year old, and then I was adopted three years later, just after I'd been born. We were adopted by the same parents. But we're not actually related biologically. So there's no reason we can't get married.'

'Apart from your grandfather.'

'Yes.'

I waited for an explanation. I waited a long time. Several days went by. Eventually I gave up.

'How does he come into this?' I asked, very slowly.

'Ah, well, when our parents died he became our legal guardian, you see.'

'Our adoptive parents,' Bonny said in clarification.

'Yes, he isn't our real grandfather.'

'He's our adoptive grandfather, as it were.'

'Though we do think of him as being our real grandfather.'

'And he said we'd have to wait until Clyde turns twenty-one.'

'But we were in a hurry. The clock is ticking.'

I decided it was time to get some facts out of them. Anything that I could latch on to as making sense. Anything to stop them wittering on. Preferably avoiding any questions asking them whether they knew of the age limit at which an individual might decide to get married without needing the permission of their legal guardian. Mainly because I was afraid the answers might make just enough sense to give me a headache.

Another headache.

'How old are you?' I asked.

'I'm twenty-two, Clyde is almost eighteen – she'll be eighteen on Friday.'

'We'll have to throw a party,' I said, somewhat sarcastically. Very sarcastically, actually.

'Thank you,' Clyde said, totally missing it.

They were those sort of kids.

'The thing is,' Bonnie said, 'our parents – adoptive parents – left us a legacy in their will which we get when Clyde turns eighteen. But we only receive it under certain conditions. One of them is that neither of us must have a criminal record at that time.'

'We need the money if we're going to have a family,' Clyde said. 'We both want a family, as many children as possible.'

'We're planning on having four sets of twins.'

'One set of boy twins. One girls. And two mixed.'

'I'm going to get a job as a clerk or something, and then work my way up to senior manager or something.'

'And I'm going to be a housewife. I'll teach the girls to sew and to knit.'

'I'll come back in the evening and read them bedtime stories.'

'And we'll have a big garden where they boys can play rough and tumble.'

They smiled at each other, looking deeply into each other's eyes. I felt sorry for them. They were living in a dream world. A long-lost, never-existed, fantasy dream world, where the sun always shone. Except in the winter nights, when the family would be clustered around a blazing fire toasting marshmallows and singing songs about love, happy families and Charlie the Cherubic Chopper. They were the type of people who would go to their local little church, where everyone knew each other and baked cakes for the school fete, and sang happy, cheerful songs about Christ being crucified without thinking it in the slightest strange.

'But,' continued Clyde, 'Bonnie won't get paid very well as a clerk, and without the legacy we'd have to live in poverty until he becomes senior manager. And poverty wouldn't be good for the children, would it?'

I would imagine most people would agree that poverty isn't good for children, or even for adults, come to it. And at least it showed that Clyde was keeping one toe in the real world. But things were becoming clearer.

'And you've done something that could land you in chookee?' I suggested, hoping they wouldn't stop to wonder why I was asking that question if I had, as I was supposed to have, recognised them. Fortunately I was in luck. They looked at each other. Bonnie turned back to me.

'You remember the Tonalard Missing Envelope case?' he asked.

'Of course. I –'

Suddenly the penny dropped. But first I need to explain about the Tonalard case. Herpes Tonalard (not his real name) was an important minister in the government at the time – let's say he was Minister for Toy Trains and Christmas Tree Regulations. Anyway, there had been rumours floating around that he was in the habit of wandering down to the more rosy parts of Soho, London, UK, receiving large sums of cash and free service in exchange for going easy on Christmas tree regulations and making sure toy train companies could reduce their services while still getting government subsidy. Everyone knew that this was true, but without evidence you had to use the word "alleged" a lot of the time, and even though Herpes Tonalard weighed about thirty stone, and looked as if he would never fit through an average doorway, he was very good at disappearing before any nasty photographers could take shots of him doing anything naughty, like taking bribes in little (or large) brown envelopes.

(I would like to point out here the total lack of similarity between Eric the Ears and Herpes Tonalard. Two, totally, totally different individuals. Is that clear? Oh, dear, Beazeley's having conniptions.)

So, Herpes Tonalard remained to public gaze a rather over-weight saint. (With big ears.) Until one day a year or so before the trial I was attending. He had just come out of an establishment – let's call it "Lady Erotica's House Of Fun And Massage If You Really Want It" – with a brown envelope sticking out of his pocket. It was an unusually careless mistake to make. Before he knew what had happened, two enormous thugs ran past him. It wasn't until they were out of sight that he realised that the envelope was gone. He immediately reported the theft to the police, but to the date of the trial no-one had been arrested.

Now the interesting thing is that the very same day he was accused in public of accepting brown envelopes in exchange for political favours. Someone had finally got a snapshot of him caught red-handed, a brown envelope in his pocket. His career should have gone down the swanny. But not our Edgar. I mean Herpes.

He stood up in Parliament with a copy of the police docket and pointed out that the police themselves had noted that he had had no brown envelope on him when he went to see them. Not surprising, since the reason he was there was to report its theft, but politicians have a slightly different concept of reality to the rest of us, and he was duly cheered to the rafters by his party colleagues, most of whom hated his guts.

Of course, had the police quickly recovered the envelope he would have had a small problem. But so long after the affair the only thing the media and people remember was that Herpes Tonalard had once been accused of accepting brown envelopes and been acquitted. So long as the envelope did not reappear.

'So you were the two enormous thugs,' I suggested to Clyde and Bonnie. Bonnie nodded. No wonder the police had never tracked down the desperate duo. Clyde was a very attractive young woman, and Bonnie made one immediately think of the word "slim". A bit tall to be a scrum-half, if you're a rugby fan. Not tall enough to be a tennis pro. But not the basis of your average enormous thug.

'It was a spur of a moment thing,' Bonnie said. 'And we needed the money.'

'We would have repaid it after we came into our legacy,' Clyde insisted.

'I wouldn't worry too much about that,' I replied. 'How much was there?'

'Ten thousand pounds and some photographs of medical experiments.'

I decided not to enquire further about the photographs. I don't think, if they came from Lady Erotica's House of Fun, that they had anything to do with medical experiments.

'You won't tell anyone, will you?' pleaded Clyde.

'Not a chance,' I replied, quite honestly. I would have loved to have seen Edgar-I-mean-Herpes Tonalard publicly humiliated and voted out of his fat office – after all, that was the very reason I was there – but you know how these things work. The kids would be locked up for theft, Edgar-I-mean-Tonalard would get his money and photographs back, and should anyone accuse him of receiving the envelope he would point out that the only proof was the word of two criminals, and the reason fighting crime was so difficult was because of the namby-pamby liberal approach of his accusers who obviously supported the criminal fraternity rather than the innocent victim.

That might sound the result of a fanciful and overactive imagination, but it's been done before. Believe me.

No, I decided, I was going to see Edgar-I-mean-Herpes got what he deserved – if I died in the attempt I was going to make sure that that happened – but not at the expense of these two kids.

It was time to go. I had the information I needed from those two. If they felt inclined to vote the wrong way, and didn't look like they might succumb to reasonable persuasion I had the tool of blackmail at hand. I hoped I wouldn't have to use it, they were a really likeable couple of innocent kids. I certainly hoped that they would, if it came to it, be too innocent to realise that I would never actually reveal their secret.

'You're the only one who knows about this apart from our grandfather,' Clyde said as I turned towards the door.

Have you ever heard someone say something and known that that was precisely the moment to reply "Oh? Really? Amazing. My goodness, is that the time? Must go, I'm late for a session with my psychoanalyst", before getting the hell on out of there?

No?

Oh, well, must just be me then.

Anyway, I had this out-of-the-body experience, hearing my mouth say:

'But I thought you'd run away from your grandfather because you wanted to get married? I thought that's why you needed the money? How come he knows about it?'

'Well,' said Clyde, 'you see, when we realised what we'd done we decided we needed help, and granddad was the only person we knew we could trust so we went back to him.' From the look on Bonnie's face I guessed that he had not shared that sentiment of trust, but had gone through with it for Clyde's peace of mind.

'He told us that he would have to turn us in to the police,' the boy said. 'He went on for hours about his standing in the community, his position, his responsibilities.'

'But he said he would take his time about it,' Clyde added gaily. 'That, so long as we disappeared until my eighteenth birthday, they wouldn't be able to try us. Which meant not getting a criminal record. Apparently getting a criminal record afterwards doesn't make a difference.'

'And after that we'll be able to pay the money back,' Bonnie concluded. 'Anonymously,' he added, just in case I thought he was stupid enough to imagine that a person such as Herpes Tonalard the Ears would say "Oh, well, so long as I've got the money back, nothing else matters, no need to send those two scrotes to jail for ten or fifteen years."

And disappearing in a place like Wellbury made sense – if you kept low you'd have to have extremely bad luck to be discovered. Not because it's such a big place, he hastily added in case anyone might take that as a hint, but because no-one ever goes there. And Wellburians tend not to give a fig for anything that goes on outside Wellbury. Apart from football.

Now, as I've mentioned, Eric the Ears and Herpes Tonalard were obviously two totally different people. (Koff.) I just thought it a curious co-incidence that Clyde and Bonnie should turn up as jury-members at that trial. Still, we've all seen stranger coincidences, so, at the time I decided to leave Clyde and Bonnie with their secret and go snooping somewhere else. Eric the Ears would probably never recognise them. The best thing seemed to be to ignore the connection. I had no reason to turn them in at that moment. All in all, that sort of thing would just complicate matters.

'So,' I said purely as a parting sociality, 'what's with the clown costumes?'

'They're a disguise,' said Bonnie. 'We can't take the risk of being identified.'

'I wouldn't have thought that likely,' I replied mildly. 'Not here. Not when no-one has your description. You hardly resemble two big thugs.'

'Well, the thing is ...' Bonnie said slowly. They looked at other. Clyde turned back to me.

'The thing is,' she said, 'Judge Beak is our grandfather.'

Right, time for a break, I think. I need a cup of tea and a stretch of the legs. This is taking me a lot longer than I thought. It's almost evening and I'm not even at the end of the Monday. Having Beazeley hovering doesn't help. I'll suggest he comes for a walk as well. Maybe push him into the canal or something.

Now there's a thought.

God, the power! Just one short sentence – or maybe a couple – and Beazeley ends up being slowly eaten by termites on acid in a bath of baked beans.

Start placing your bets as to whether Beazeley survives. My money's against.

....

Chapter VII. Encounter With the Ghost

Going for a walk with Beazeley was a bad idea. He wanted to discuss the book, but without being overheard. So he'd say something in a whisper and then tell me to hush when I replied in a normal voice. Eejit. As if anyone walking along wants to listen in to our conversation, or would even understand it if they did. It wasn't as if we were talking on mobile phones after all.

I couldn't get him to agree to a walk along the canal, so we strolled up the High Street and I bumped him into the traffic a few times instead. How he didn't get run over I don't know. He has the luck of the devil. Either that or the drivers realised that he was a lawyer and didn't want to take the chance of being sued. I did manage to get him run over once, but that was by a woman pushing a pram, so I don't think it counts.

She wasn't too amused, I must say. Dreadful language. The kid in the pram was just as bad.

Beazeley's in the kitchen at the moment, making himself a cup of black coffee. His hands are shaking so much that he's having trouble getting a teaspoon of granules into a mug. (He complains that I don't have "real" coffee – that stuff you have to put through a machine for half an hour before throwing it down the drain because it tastes so godawful.) The last I saw he'd gone through half a bottle of coffee without succeeding in getting a teaspoon into the mug, and had lined up all the mugs I possess next to each other, in the hope that he'd hit one sooner or later. Gives me a chance to get on without interference. So, full speed ahead: Monday evening.

Right, consult notebook first.

Now where's the damn thing gone?

Let's see, I took it with me when we went for a walk, we popped into the corner shop to pick up some beers, I put it into the bag ... Ah, that means it must be in the fridge with the beers. I'll get it out just now, I don't need it for this bit.

God, it was funny, in the corner shop. I said "Evening all," the Ethiopian bloke behind the counter who knows me said "Good evening, you are well?" and Beazeley stammers, "What precisely do you mean when you refer to 'Good'?" Poor Ethiopian bloke has to deal with all sorts, but he'd never encountered Beazeley before.

Monday evening.

After dinner that evening I made my way to the residents' lounge. As I expected, there weren't many occupants. The shy bunnies had their own private lounge, they weren't likely to sit watching telly with humans who had such little self-respect they appeared dressed only in clothes. Judge Beak and the lawyers would keep well clear for fear of having to exchange social chit-chat with members of the jury while avoiding any mention of the trial, something pretty much impossible. So instead I was there to get them to discuss the trial, on my terms. With a little prompting in the right direction they would be galloping towards the correct conclusion by the end of the evening without even knowing why.

Mrs Plum was there, as was Vicar Preachy and his domed head, the Prim Maiden Aunt, Miss F, Miss F's Mother, Strawberry Mousse and the Major. They all had their eyes glued to the television, apart from Miss F's Mother, whose attention was continually diverted to her daughter, stroking her hair into place, pulling a crease out of her clothes, the sort of things a mother like that does because she loves her darling daughter and still thinks of her as a little girl. Miss F acted as though she didn't notice, but I guessed she was more than happy with the attention. I think there was quite a big part of her not-very-large frame which wanted to stay a little girl and I couldn't say I blamed her.

They were watching the television news, which surprised me. I would have expected a soap opera or some gardening programme. Or perhaps that baking show or the dancing one. Either way they had the looks of people who would not welcome a diversion, such as the one I had planned.

'Evening, all,' I said sociably, only to be hushed by the Major.

'There's a siege on in Bognor Regis, it's live,' said Strawberry Mousse, ignoring the glares the Major threw at her. 'Two bank robbers were being chased by the police. They've taken three hostages in a house, a poodle and two stray cats. So far a pizza delivery boy has been shot by mistake, and one policeman has fallen off a wall he was climbing. Oh, and their spokesperson is quite drunk. She slurs all the time. And she keeps saying things like, "David, if you're watching this I want you to know that you're a total bleep, creep, son of a bleep, and I want the world to know that you're an impotent bleep and have a very small bleep."'

There was a strange sort of lack of emotion in them, as if they were watching something not real, some show created for their benefit, where the actors would all get up afterwards and give a bow.

'Sounds like she's having a bad time,' I said. 'Man trouble. A bit like Norah The Nose, when you think about it.'

'There was a four-car pile-up earlier,' Miss F – to whom my comment had been subliminally aimed – said with the childish enjoyment teenagers sometimes show when they forget to be obstreperous for a few seconds. 'Caught on CCTV live, like that OJ chase. They were cutting bodies out of cars. I wanted to stay watching, but the vicar said it made him feel ill.'

'I had an Audi just like the one involved,' explained Vicar Preachy. 'It was very dear to me.' He paused for a nano-second. 'Have I told you about my garden?'

'Edgar The Ears has three cars, I understand,' I commented quickly with a fixed smile, one so fixed I think it was beginning to look glued on. 'An extremely wealthy person, so rumour has it. I've always wondered whether a person can become really rich by purely honest means. Take our group, for instance, now –'

'Damn adverts,' muttered the Major as a tube of toothpaste filled the screen. 'They always do that – they always do that – go to commercials just as things become interesting. It's to make you not change channels. They're trying to stop you changing channels, you see.'

The Prim Maiden Aunt wagged a finger as if about to make a declaration. A tic went ping — pong across her nose. And she hiccoughed.

Miss F was already changing channels with the fervour of the devoted. Mrs Plum's attention had gone to the bag she carried with her, the one containing her knitting. A Mary Poppins bag – you just knew that Mrs Plum would find anything in there. At that moment she was muttering sweetly to herself as she extracted items in a search for something. First out was a well-thumbed 1983 railway timetable for somewhere or other. In my job I get to ask a lot of questions, so I know which to ask – and which not to ask. Such as "Why are you carrying a well-thumbed 1983 railway timetable around with you?"

And right at that moment I had run out of the right questions to ask. Trying to get that lot to concentrate and follow my prompting to the right conclusion was apparently going to be harder than I expected. The phrase "herding cats" came to mind.

Next out of the bag came a chocolate teapot.

(It really was a chocolate teapot, honestly. A variation on a chocolate Easter egg of some sort. You think you'll never be surprised at the silly ideas companies can come up for new stuff to flog to the public, and then you are.)

Last out onto the table was a single, large, chrome knitting needle covered in knitting plus attached ball of lavender-coloured wool.

'Oh, dear,' she murmured. 'Oh, dear, dear.'

'You okay, Mrs Plum?' asked Strawberry Mousse.

'How very strange,' Mrs Plum said, speaking into the bag. An echo returned.

'What's the problem, Mrs Plum?'

'Well, I seem to have mislaid one of my knitting needles,' replied the good lady, turning the bag upside down as proof. I half expected something else to drop out. A telephone box, sewing machine, portable sun-bed, electrical hair curlers, something like that, but nothing did. How you could mislay one of those needles was another question. Two feet long and two inches across at the wide end?

I just hoped no-one would sit on it by accident.

Someone like me for a start.

'Where did you have it last, Mrs P?' asked Strawberry Mousse.

'Now, let me see ... I'm sure I had it just before dinner, you know, that bread and butter pudding was lovely. Very filling, though. I suppose Mrs Baggs has gone to lie down, poor thing, she had three helpings.'

I think we all recognised the moment. That awful moment when a sweet-natured old woman is just cranking up to discuss all the meaningless trivia of the day. If you don't get out before she gets to "You know, I remember when" you've had it.

'Perhaps it fell down behind the couch,' suggested Strawberry Mousse, standing up and going to check in the way people do when desperate to shut up sweet old ladies.

'She was obviously somewhat hungry, poor thing,' Mrs Plum continued.

'Or maybe it's fallen between the cushions,' suggested Miss F's mother, another person who realised that the only way to stop Mrs

Plum going on was to find her knitting needle. I had no doubt it was a tried and tested strategy Mrs Plum employed on such occasions. 'Stand up, Miss F, let's see if we can't find it.'

Miss F stood sufficiently to allow her mother to search between and underneath the cushions, but kept her attention on the television.

'Now I had a custard tart,' Mrs Plum continued, 'with Devonshire cream. Though you know, I remember when ...'

I quickly made my excuses and left. There's a well-known adage about the man who runs away being able to sweet-talk a jury into the right decision another day. I wasn't really worried at that stage about getting the result I wanted. I thought I had plenty of time.

Hah! If only I'd known.

Right then I left with the Major and Vicar Preachy hard on my heels, going somewhere else fast. Sweet little old ladies who can't remember whether they had bread and butter pudding or a custard tart for dessert obviously appealed to them as much as to me. As I left Mrs Plum was saying, 'Take Marjorie Hortense at school, now, she was head of the hockey team. Or was that Calamity Caroline? No, wait a moment, it wasn't the hockey team, it was the rugby squad. Oh, dear, what on earth am I thinking of, of course we didn't play rugby, it was ...'

The Major and Vicar Preachy rapidly headed off their separate ways before I could stop one of them for a man to man chat about how evil Edgar The Ears was. So I wandered along the hotel corridors, going nowhere specific, just ambling around hoping to see or overhear something I wasn't supposed to. Pressing my ear to certain chosen doors just in case the occupant or occupants were discussing matters of interest a little too loudly. There wasn't much happening. The couple in the honeymoon suite were having the first argument of their married life. Or I presumed that it was the first. Maybe they'd been arguing since finishing off the "I do" bit.

That was actually a mistake, the honeymoon suite. I had thought it was Mr Crane's room. It was only when the horse-shoe fell from the lintel and almost cracked my head open that I realised. The horse-shoe had a message attached: "To Cynthia and Cyril. May every day of your married life be better than the last". The way those two had started that wouldn't be difficult. I put it back where it belonged, hoping that it wouldn't drop on one of their heads as they left the room, and sauntered casually onwards. Or sauntered as casually as a man can who has begun to realise that instead of facing a bunch of easy-going, well-mannered Brits willing to listen to reason, he is facing a disparate group of individuals not particularly interested in what he had to say.

Still, I fully believed that they'd come around to my way of thinking. I believed it so much I kept repeating it to myself like a mantra.

As I strolled down one of the corridors on the third floor I noticed a curtain in one of the alcoves sway slightly. I slipped in. Standing there, leaning against the wall while looking out of an open window was the last person I expected to see.

Let's say it was the hotel ghost. Having a fag. Puffing the smoke out of the open window. He was a grey sort of ghost. Translucent, that sort of thing. You know, the way ghosts normally are.

'Bad for your health, those things,' I said mildly, mainly to strike up conversation. His mouth curled up in a tired sneer.

'I'm a ghost,' he said. 'Hardly likely to do me much damage.'

'Good point,' I said. He went back to looking out the window and puffing on his cigarette.

There was a pause as I tried to think of something slightly more intelligent to say.

'Been a ghost long?' I enquired.

It's not easy to strike up idle chit-chat with a ghost. They tend not to share the same interests as we might.

'Ever since bleeding 1067,' he replied. He spun the cigarette out of the window and immediately lit another. 'You have no idea how boring it is.'

'Good point. Um, someone told me that you haven't been seen recently.'

'I've been on strike. It gave me something different to do.'

I nodded in a friendly fashion to show that I sympathised. He sneered again to show that he had already seen through me. And he wasn't even looking at me. I hate people who can do that sort of thing. They seem to have eyes in the back of their heads. Though, considering this was a ghost, he probably could see out of the back of his head.

'Right,' I said. He carried on saying nothing.

'Anything serious, then?' I asked. 'Your dying, that is.'

'Serious?'

'I meant, well, it wasn't too painful, was it?'

'I was murdered. What do you think?'

'Ah.'

I almost asked, "Friend of yours, was it?" but caught myself just in time.

We passed a few seconds in silence.

'If you're from so long ago, shouldn't you be saying "thee" and "thou" and that sort of stuff?' I asked, trying to keep the conversation going.

Talk about hard work.

'If thou didst prefer, I shalt. But actually I'd be speaking a mixture of Anglo-Saxon or Norman you wouldn't be able to understand, thou bawdy bottom's buttonhole.'

I had to admit he had a point. And I read somewhere that the language of those times was earthier than we might use today. Or maybe he was just that type of ghost.

'Point,' I said. 'Perhaps we'll stick with the modern version.'

There was no reply to that, so I carried on. There were ways in which the Ghost could be extremely useful.

'You couldn't do me a favour, could you?' I asked. 'Seeing as how you're at a loose end?'

'Favour?' he replied angrily. 'Why should I do anyone any favours? What favours has the world ever done me?'

'Ah, come on, you can hardly hold it against me, not something that happened a thousand years ago.'

'Why not?'

I could see that this was going to a be a difficult ghost.

'I wasn't around then, was I?' I pointed out.

'It was one of your ancestors. Blood shall rest upon the children's children's children.'

That didn't make any sense at all. I decided to try logic instead. I counted quickly on my fingers.

'That only takes us to about thirteen hundred,' I said. 'That's long gone.'

'You're human. That's enough for me.'

'So were you, once.'

'No I wasn't.'

That was when I realised that there was something not quite right about the Ghost. In the semi-darkness he could have passed as a human ghost. But a sudden beam of moonlight struck his hand as the clouds scudded overhead. It was hairy. And looked vaguely cloven.

'I was a fawn,' he explained in an embarrassed voice, backing into the darkness.

'A fawn?'

'Yes. A gambolling, innocent, wide-eyed little baby fawn. Until one of your came and put an arrow through me. William the Conqueror's page-boy! Not even the illegitimate Norman horse son himself! His page-boy!'

The question was so obvious I didn't want to ask it. He lit another cigarette and shot the old one out of the window, which is when I realised that I couldn't smell the cigarette smoke, which makes sense if you think about it. Ghosts and ghosts' cigarettes just don't smell. No aroma, no bouquet. Not to us, anyway. Maybe a ghost can detect another ghost's BO, or, in their case, GO, but to us, not a whiff.

'Because – Have you ever wondered what effect a ghostly fawn has?' he asked, answering the question I had decided not to ask. 'Have you? People laugh. That's why I have to pretend to be a human ghost.'

He lit another cigarette, almost unconscious of the one already in his left hand.

Hoof.

'Most of my lot aren't even that lucky. The best they can manage is coming back as a ghostly hunk of venison. Imagine how frightening that must be to humans. They just lick their lips and presume they're dreaming.'

'Not easy,' I said. Purely to humour him. Apart from that I was trying not to lick my own lips. A nice flame-grilled haunch of venison sounded rather appealing. Roast spuds, gravy, broccoli in cheese sauce ...

Parsley.

'They're not real rabbits, you know,' he said suddenly. 'That lot walking around. I used to have some good friends who were real rabbits. Used to romp around in the heather together.' He noticed that he had two cigarettes on the go and tucked one behind his ear, backwards. It was still smoking.

'No,' I agreed, 'it's just a disguise they're wearing.'

'They're humans underneath. Disgusting,' he said, lighting another cigarette and tucking that behind the other ear.

'I, ah, suppose you must see things differently. So to say. If I can put it that way. If you know what I mean.'

The sneer increased.

'I do,' he said. 'That Nun With Guitar. She was having a shower half an hour ago. I watched. She couldn't see me.'

I could see that he was trying to contort his face into a leer. It was a good effort, but it didn't quite work.

'She's young,' he said. 'Looked pretty cute, with the water running off her naked body. Nubile. That's the word, isn't it?'

'Is it?'

'I don't bleeding know, do I?' He lit two new cigarettes from the old and threw the old out of the window. I just hoped no-one was walking around down there. 'You humans go around sizing each other up all the time. I'm just a dead little fawn who wouldn't understand that sort of thing if you gave me a manual to read, which I can't. You don't want to know what it's like watching your television and not being able to understand why people are laughing, those double entendre things. As for naked women, sheeze, give me a break. What's that supposed to mean to me? For all I know she could have a bow and arrow hidden somewhere.'

His hand trembled as he took another puff. I had a suspicion that he'd built up his hard-man image from old black and white movies on the lounge television in the early hours of the morning. It would explain the constant smoking. I expected that any moment he was going to be speaking of "dames" and "broads". But he didn't. He tried to hide in the shadows, but I could see a little tear gleam and shiver below those long eyelashes.

'She knew I was there,' he whispered, more to himself than to me. 'She knew I was watching her. She was – she knew I was really just a fawn, she was giving me the chance to amble up and be stroked. I would have done, I would have, but ...'

His voice choked.

'So long! So long!' he cried.

It was probably a trick of the hotel. The idea of the Nun With Guitar stroking with those slim fingers of hers – somehow the floorboards seemed to sway just a little.

Just a lot, in fact.

But the Nun With Guitar was just another sensually beguiling woman in a world of sensually beguiling women. You meet one, she turns your brains into scrambled eggs with a dash of sage, you see another, same thing, perhaps with coriander. In the end you decide you'll have to learn to live with it. Splosh, get over it, splosh, get over with it. Maybe one day you make it and live happily ever after, otherwise it's just splosh, splosh, splosh until it don't matter no more.

I had a job to do. A job I'd promised myself and my memories to do. The Nun With Guitar – Strawberry Mousse, Miss F's Mother, whoever – could splosh my brains as much as they wanted. I was on a mission.

I Am On A Mission, I told myself, just in case I'd forgotten the point. Then I repeated it to myself, twice, trying to put the emphasis on the various words to see if it sounded different.

'That's an interesting point you have there,' I said, giving up on the words and deciding to nudge things in the right direction. 'You know the trial that started in the courthouse today?'

'Course I do. You think all I do is walk around this stupid hotel with a sign saying "One out, all out. Strike for ghosts now on"?'

'Of course not. I'm sure you get to see – things which others don't.'

'And you want me to tell you about them? Hah!'

'Look,' I said, my self-control weakening in the face of the truculent and bloody-minded ghost, never mind the other thoughts involving habits hovering at the wilderness edges of my mind – a lack of a habit, to be technically correct – 'if we can get proof that what's in that book is true it could be dynamite. All you have to do is take a peek and let me know what you find out. I'll do the rest.'

He shook his head at my stupidity. Then he tossed the last two cigarettes out of the window. He closed the window.

'You're forgetting something, friend,' he said. 'I'm a freaking fawn, I can't freaking read, can I, you dipschitz? Haven't I already told you that?'

Then he turned and walked through the window and out into the night air, the cigarettes behind his ears leaving a kind of twin contrail.

I couldn't believe it. I've been in some tough spots. There have been times when all I've had for evidence was a bent safety-pin and a dab of butter, and I've managed to do what's required. Now, here I was, with a ghost who could go anywhere and see anything, and he was refusing to co-operate! Just my luck. Other people get Caspar, I get the ghost of a fawn with a chip on his shoulder.

A jury most of whose members appeared uninterested in the only important game in town. An obdurate Ghost. A bunch of bunnies. I almost began to despair of finding anyone vaguely sane in that place.

I nearly said the X-word.

Of course, when things appear bleak and desperate that can be a good sign. Like the football team trailing three to minus four suddenly popping out of nowhere and scoring ten goals in the last five minutes. Only this time the score was nil-all, and I was already getting the feeling that I would have all the advantages on paper, and absolutely none when push really came to shove.

And then it happened for the first time.

As I stood there the haunting notes of Ave Maria came floating from somewhere. Accompanied by guitar. A woman's voice.

A young nun's voice.

The beautiful voice of a beautiful young nun. Whose habit had a slit in it which revealed the calf and part of a thigh which would drive a sane man mad, and an insane man off a cliff.

And stiletto heels, stiletto heels ...

The best thing to do in situations like this – the only intelligent thing – is to go to bed and hold the pillows over your head to stop hearing the voice.

Did I do that? Of course not, would you? If you were me, that is. I suppose a woman – Miss F's Mother, for example – would have been able to ignore it.

Come to think of it, I think Miss F's Mother would have done exactly what I did. Especially when considering later events.

I strolled swiftly (also called the "Me? Hurrying? Of course not" walk) to the end of the corridor and turned left. Within a few paces I realised that the song was coming from behind me, somewhat to the right and above. So, up a flight of stairs, and hurry on.

I should have known. In the Railway Tavern sound never comes from the same place twice. In this case the Nun With Guitar's voice was now coming from below, to the left. As soon as I went down another flight of stairs it had moved above again. Which is when I bumped into the Major on his way to his room.

'Can you tell where that song is coming from?' I asked. He gave me a very strange look.

'What song?' he asked. 'I can't hear a song. What song are you talking about? Eh, what song? I can't hear a song.'

I listened. The voice had gone. But he must have heard it. Except the look in his eyes showed that he thought I was two woofs away from barking mad.

And if that were his estimate, I can't honestly say that I was far from disagreeing with him. When you're living in a place such as the Old Railway Tavern it's not too difficult to wonder whether you've turned up in a strange world which you don't understand, but one which understands you only too well and is about to do something to your life you aren't going to enjoy.

'Must be the old tinnitus playing up again,' I said, giving him the strongest weak smile I could summon up. He nodded rapidly twice, slipped quickly past me and headed for his room at speed, giving two last concerned looks back at me as he disappeared around a corner. I decided to have what would be for me an early night.

Sometime later, as I lay in bed trying to get to sleep while concocting my strategy for the following morning – a detailed yet fruitless strategy as I was to discover in less than twelve hours – I heard a voice going past.

'But, you know, it has to be real Devonshire cream. So difficult to get these days. And of course you must be sure that it's fresh. I remember once ...'

I opened one eye and looked at the ceiling. I didn't need to be psychic to know that the missing knitting needle hadn't been located. But by god I would do everything in my power to find it. To keep her quiet. A week of Mrs Plum nattering on – I shuddered at the thought. I still shudder at the thought. Even now when I know how it all turned out. Which is why I shall put this to rest for the evening and relax with a drink. Get rid of Beazeley, vacuum up the coffee granules in the kitchen, pour myself a whiskey, put my feet up and watch a movie.

And try not to think.

But the question kept running through my head, keeping sleep at bay. It's that itch you can't help but scratch.

What had the Nun With Guitar looked like while she was having a shower?

For the first time in my pursuit of Edgar The Ears, the phrase "mixing pleasure with business" came to my mind.

But, with a nun? A Nun With Guitar?

On the other hand, why not?

Because it's not the done thing, not with a Nun.

Certainly not With A Guitar.

As I drifted into a light sleep I had this vision of myself and the Nun With Guitar checking out of the hotel together at the end of the week, walking out hand in hand. We'd find ourselves a little cottage in the country and live happily ever after. And we'd keep little baby fawns in the garden.

It felt not only perfectly normal, but also extremely agreeable.

I don't know why, but it felt as if I was coming home.

The young woman across the road has switched her lounge lights on. She hasn't drawn the curtains. I hate it when people do that, it's very distracting.

She's got an aquarium in the corner. Maybe that's what the postman delivered.

She's doing some sort of exercises with little dumbbells, wearing one of those miniscule tops which are apparently designed for a gym. Can't say they do much for me.

Still, it might help take my mind off the Nun With Guitar with a slit in her habit. Or two slits in her habit.

Actually, it was three.

Whiskey. Double. And now.

I might even line up a few glasses to make sure I hit one of them.

But I'll never forget the memories.

...

Chapter VIII. A Horrible Discovery

I think Beazeley was worried that I wouldn't let him in today. (I might well not have, come to that.) He turned up at the crack of dawn this morning pretending to be a Polish plumber. That's all I need, that idiot wandering around playing with the waterworks, which is exactly what he would do. Five minutes and it would be like a domestic version of Niagara Falls. And the really irritating thing is that I've been waiting for a plumber for weeks.

I don't think I've ever been closer to using the X-word.

Instead I upended a bowl of cold porridge on his head and slammed the door on him. That'll teach him.

It was only as I slammed the door shut that I realised that the young lady opposite had been watching, wearing a negligee. (She really should learn to close the curtains.) The good point is that she was laughing. The bad point is that, supposing I do manage to strike up a conversation with her, and she does turn out to be single and available, and is willing to view me as potential partner material, sooner or later she will bring the subject of tipping bowls of porridge over visitors' heads, and what will I be able to reply?

Odds are that, if I say that I thought the knocker was a Jehovah's Witness, she'll turn out to be one herself.

Then again, if that's the case, does it matter? What person in their right mind would go out with a Jehovah's Witness, no matter how short the shorts she wore?

It was a white negligee, by the way. Or rather see-through-going-on-white.

That reminds me, I need to visit the optician. I think I might need glasses.

Anyway. Tuesday morning.

Now, how can I put this ... ? I could say that you aren't going to believe this, but that doesn't matter because I know you aren't going to believe this. So, let me put it this way ...

I woke up early. I opened my eyes to find a mouse sitting on top of the counterpane on my chest, looking at me, its nose and whiskers wrinkling as if it were sniffing to determine whether I was animal, vegetable or mineral.

'Shoo,' I said.

'Shoo yourself,' it replied.

Well, okay, of course it didn't actually say that, but from the expression on its face it really looked as if that's what it would have said if it could have.

Okay, okay, for the purpose of this, let's say our meta-follicle mouse could actually speak.

'Got any cheese?' it asked.

'No, sorry. It gives me nightmares.'

'Doesn't matter. I don't really like cheese anyway. I prefer blackberry pie. But I have to pretend I like cheese. Otherwise people feel cheated for some reason.'

'I suppose they would,' I replied.

'Oh, well, better be off, the missus is waiting for me. She has this strange phobia about being stepped on. Ta-ta.'

'Ta-ta,' I replied, watching it scamper away.

Now most people would have an infarct if they woke up in a strange hotel to find an even stranger mouse sitting on them, watching them. I have to admit that normally I would have flung the bedclothes away and quite possibly emitted one or two blasphemous incantations, possibly even used the words "Holy mackerel!" once or twice. But for some reason it just seemed entirely normal and acceptable that morning in that hotel. When you're surrounded by clowns, vultures, ghostly fawns, pink and blue bunnies and the rest, a talking mouse with a preference for blackberry pie isn't really that much out of place.

I'm normally an early riser when I'm on my own. Straight out of bed, into the shower, shave, that sort of thing. Check to confirm the Teasmade doesn't work, etc. I've never been able to do the turn-over-and-get-another-forty-winks-in lark. Waking up to find a mouse on your chest looking at you is also an experience which encourages getting up. There's a suspicion that if you roll over and fall asleep again he'll be back to tell you off. So I was already up, shaved, dressed and ready for a brand new day when I heard the scream. A woman's scream. The sort of scream that isn't going to take no for an answer. The sort of scream that isn't interested in the question in the first place.

The sort of scream that Dracula would appreciate as a novelty alarm clock.

It certainly acted as an alarm clock for the hotel residents. Usually I would ignore such a scream based on the facts that (a) someone screaming normally indicates trouble, and you don't need to go looking for that, and (b) there were other people far more qualified than I to handle whatever problem it was – it was in a hotel with trained staff, after all – but that morning, before I realised what I was doing, I was out the room and running like hell towards the sound. As I raced down the corridors doors were opening, people asking, through various layers of sleep and odd clothing, what was going on, was the hotel on fire, and in the case of an elderly gent, whether the Germans were invading.

There's always one.

I was glad that I was fully awake. There was one door just open which revealed a pink bunny wearing some very suggestive deep purple lingerie. As I passed she squeaked embarrassment and quickly shut the door. Another open door showed a pale brown bunny wearing a sparkling blue dressing gown, smoking a pipe, demanding to know who was making that awful racket. And the same bunny from the previous day, Bunny Bacchus in electric-blue costume, (I presume it was the same) was lying in the middle of a corridor, fast asleep, vodka bottle in paw. I had to hurdle that one. It's not the sort of thing you want to do when half asleep, as the cries of people following and falling over the supine lapin told me. Or "freakin rabbit!" as I heard someone term it, shortly before the noise of a body falling and a head hitting a wall full on, followed by that "Thump-thump-thump-ooh-ooh-ooh" sound a person makes in such situations as they bounce down a flight of stairs on their backside.

(You'd think it would be "Thump-ooh-thump-ooh-thump-ooh", but for some reason it rarely is.)

Now I've already described trying to locate the Nun With Guitar's singing the night before, so you won't be surprised when I say that trying to tell the direction of a scream coming from something which sounds as if it's being slowly and very badly garrotted with a chain of blunt razorblades is just as difficult. I heard it coming from upstairs and took said stairs two at a time. I paused to listen, and found that it now came from two floors below, from the north.

As I stood there breathing heavily a bedroom door opened. It was Judge Beak, in a red dressing gown with white piping, wearing his wig with just the nose showing. The really strange thing was that I could have sworn a black eye was peeking out from between the folds of the red dressing gown at about waist level. The lethal black eye of an assassin.

And a tiny, curly, brightly coloured, pointed slipper just peeping out from below the judge's dressing gown. The sort you associate with turbans, nasty knives and silent death in the night.

From behind the judge came the sound of "I Can't Get No Satisfaction".

There wasn't time for questions. I hurtled downstairs, two flights, heading northwards, before pausing again. This time it came from one flight above, to the east.

And blow me down sideways, but this door opens and it's the judge again, red dressing gown with white piping, wig, beak showing, and the hint of an oriental eye looking at me at about waist level.

With "Goodbye Ruby Tuesday" playing in the background. "Still gonna miss ya."

No time to stop. Up a flight, head east young man. Pause. Now it was coming from the ground floor, south.

And then this door opens and it's the judge again. Dressing gown. Wig. Evil eye.

"You Can't Always Get What You Want" mocking me.

Which is when I decide, sod this for a game of soldiers, I've have enough of this malarkey, it's too early, I'm not as fit as I used to be, even then I wasn't exactly Mr Marathon Man, and I need a coffee. Whoever's being murdered will have to find something else to do for five minutes while I get some caffeine in me. Let someone else play the hero, I've never had the training.

Anyway, I like to think of myself as more the villain type.

It's a man thing.

So I stumble down towards the dining room. Down towards the dining room, the scent of freshly made coffee exciting every corpuscle in my blood, the smell of frying bacon making me famished for want of a bacon butty, bringing the strange image of a haunch of venison to my mind, steaming, the fat slowly dribbling past the ingrained herbs and spices.

And then I realise that the scream is coming from inside the dining room.

As in, there is coffee inside there, caffeine, coffee, my morning deity. But also a scream. And it's very off-putting if you're sipping the gods' nectar of the first cup of lovely instant when someone is screaming in your ear. I've always thought that very rude in a civilised society.

I had a girlfriend once who used to do that.

There are a number of ways to approach this type of situation. You can pretend it isn't happening. You can make yourself scarce before anyone official turns up. You can take four paces back and then charge the door with your shoulder. (Don't bother with that one, it only works in books and movies. In real life all you achieve is a broken shoulder, believe me, I've tried it.) You can quietly open the door and slip inside, hoping no-one will notice you until you've finished at least one cup of coffee. You can open the door quite openly and demand to know, excuse me for interrupting, but what exactly is all the noise about, could they keep it down, because Aunty Agnetha has a headache, thank you very much. I chose the "slip inside and grab a cup of coffee" approach. It might not sound heroic, but jeez, I need that first cup.

I spotted her straight away. Not difficult, not with that scream going on. Mildred Two. One of the hotel staff dressed in the staff uniform of canary yellow skirt, maroon top, dark green apron and black leggings. Polka dotted scarf. High-heeled pale blue toe-pinchers. Hair dyed purple to show that she was an Individual, not just a very strangely-dressed waitress. Staring at something on the floor next to the breakfast counter, screaming one continuous wail, hands tearing at her hair, but not too much in case it became disarranged.

Lavender eye-shadow. I'd never seen that before. Not with vanilla lipstick.

I must have moved too quickly because she turned and spotted me before I could make it to the espresso machine. As she saw me enter she ended her scream in a gurgling noise and fell down in a faint, or, in her case, a swoon. If she'd waited a few seconds more I could have caught her. As it was her head caught the edge of a table before hitting the floor with a rather interesting crunching sound.

I took in the scene at a glance: tables set for breakfast; side tables holding sealed Tupperware containers of various breakfast cereals, organic, inorganic and plain cardboard; jugs of orange juice and milk freshly put out; a rather interesting mixture of milk, orange and other assorted juices and glass on the carpet which the waitress must have dropped. And next to the table, with Mildred Two out of the way, I could see the body of Mrs Baggs, her face looking strangely happy, a shiny chrome knitting needle through her chest. A knitting needle which had last been seen in the hands of Mrs Plum, and which had apparently disappeared some time the day before.

Just then another of the pretty hotel staff (Mildred Three) wearing the distinctive uniform entered the dining room in a skippy-dippy-dancing fashion. She had dyed her hair bright green.

'Mildred Two? Where is that girl?' she asked, 'I thought I heard her singing.'

If that scream resembled Mildred Two's singing, I might be eating out in future. And sleeping out. And living out.

'Mildred Two?' she asked, noticing her colleague's comatose body and running up to share in the excitement, 'not another fainting fit, Mildred Two! You haven't lost Mister Moppy again, have you?'

Just then Mildred Three saw Mrs Baggs' body and she promptly – after the appropriate and regulatory scream – fainted on top of Mildred Two. At least she had the sense not to bounce her bonce. And she had a softer landing.

The MI5 agent came crashing through the swing doors of the kitchen.

'Stop,' I called. 'Go back and phone the police.'

She came up to have a look. Typical MI5 agent, they never do what you tell them to.

'Yuk!' she said, leaning over the body.

'Don't touch anything,' I warned.

'Good point. I'll just take a few photographs.' She took a compact camera from her pocket. I'd had my suspicions. That only confirmed them.

'Which newspaper?' I asked.

'I'm not a journalist, I'm from MI5,' she said, deepening her voice.

'And I'm Rudolph the red-nosed reindeer.'

'How do you do, Rudolph.'

'Very funny. I don't think they'd be as amused if I called them and told them a journalist was pretending to be one of their people. What newspaper?'

She paused in taking her pictures to give me a pleading look which said, "Please don't, you so and so."

'The Daily Trifle,' she said finally.

'The Daily Trifle is a carpentry magazine. Since when did they give a damn about the dead?'

'Er ... We're doing a special section on coffins this month?' she suggested as she took the photographs.

'Nope, null points for that one.'

'Er ... We've decided to branch out?'

'Oh, please.'

'Okay, okay, the truth is that I want to get a decent job, something on one of the tabloids. The editor of the Daily Excess promised me something if I could come up with a scoop. This could well be it.'

A number of questions plopped into my head. How could she get a scoop out of a trial which so many others were following? A trial that was currently *sub-judice*? Okay, photographs of the dead Mrs Baggs might go for something, but not a lot. After all, it was unlikely that Mrs Baggs would turn out to be the long lost love child of Prince Theobald the Randy or anything like that. And did she – Julia the

Journalist, let's call her, it's better than Mary the MI5 Moustache –
really understand what an editor might mean in promising
"something"?

She turned to me.

'Look, I'm desperate. I'll do anything to get a proper job. Anything.'

That was said with the arch look which does not speak of doing the
washing up. I wasn't buying. That type of relationship – you think
you're in for a bit of how's your father, you end up discovering that
the "anything" she was thinking of was actually dropping your dead
body into a fast-flowing river. Or even a stagnant one. People don't
tend to be picky in situations like that.

'Well, if you've taken enough photos,' I said, 'would you be so kind
as to go telephone for the police? Or do you need a kick up the
backside as encouragement?'

She left, giving me a very ladylike look which stated plainly that a kick
up the backside, even the suggestion, was not one that she was
accustomed to, not in her society. Even her moustache looked
ladylike.

Just a pity about the moustache. She would have been quite attractive
otherwise.

I sat down and looked at the body of Mrs Baggs.

She looked quite cheerful for someone who had been murdered,
lying there amidst her bags, next to a supermarket trolley. I hadn't
noticed the trolley the day before. I presume that it had been hidden
somewhere – she could hardly have fitted it into the jury box.
Thoughts tumbled through my head as I sat. Mrs Baggs had been a
bag lady. She couldn't have been a real member of the jury. Unless
she was pretending to be a bag lady. But if she wasn't, what reason
could anyone have to kill her?

'I've phoned the police,' Julia the Journalist said, interrupting the whirlwind in my head. 'Tell me something. Do you mind if I ask you something personal?'

'Ask away,' I replied, not adding "But you won't get any answers."

'Do you normally sit on a pile of waitresses?'

I looked down. In my deep state of cogitation I had sat on the nearest available object, which now turned out to be Mildred Two and Mildred Three.

'Not normally,' I said, standing up quickly and giving the somnolent bodies a quick dust as you do. 'We'd better get them out of here. They'll only faint again if they come to and see Mrs Baggs' body again.'

'Much easier if we wake them up,' said Julia the Journalist, picking up a jug of iced water and pouring it over Mildreds Two and Three. It certainly worked. They sat up, shook their wet heads, their faces now dyed respectively purple and bright green, looked at the body of Mrs Baggs, checked to make sure that someone else was in the room to appreciate their acting, said "Oooh!" and fainted again in very stylistic and suggestive poses, bouncing their heads off each other in the process.

'Come on,' I said, taking Mildred Three's feet, 'we'll have to drag them out.'

Julia the Journalist took Mildred Two's feet and between us we dragged the waitresses into the corridor, stacking them neatly in an alcove to avoid a Health and Safety violation. Just then Mildred One appeared. I wondered whether she had a twin on the reception desk. I just knew that, if I went down to reception at that moment, I would find her sitting there painting her nails white.

'Heyick?' she asked. I nodded towards the alcove. She looked in, shook her head irritably.

'Heyick!' she called.

The Hunchback of Notre Dame appeared out of nowhere. I had listed every single person in that hotel, and had not spotted him anywhere. Beetle-browed, obviously nervous of us, his massive shoulder muscles cringing, hands which, if they weren't wringing, would have been dragging along the floor.

'Heyick,' Mildred One ordered him, tossing her head towards the alcove. He disappeared into the alcove before re-appearing with the bodies of Mildreds Two and Three, one underneath each arm. Mildred One led him and his baggage away towards the kitchen.

'He's quite cute,' said Julia the Journalist.

'Cute? Have you had an eye test lately?'

She laughed, her fake moustache pirouetting across her upper lip.

'I think you're jealous,' she said.

'Hah!' I sneered, dismissing such a ridiculous idea. I wasn't jealous. Just a little confused about feeling an attraction to someone wearing a moustache and dressed up as a man from MI5. I think it's called sexual ambiguity.

Then again, how would I feel about a gorgeous woman from MI5 who had been trained to kill with one blow from her little finger? Unless she was lying about being a journalist from the Daily Trifle. Maybe she was a trained MI5 killer pretending to be a journalist disguised as a trained MI5 killer? Maybe she was a trained male MI5 killer pretending to be a woman disguised as a journalist disguised as a trained female MI5 killer?

Of course, she wasn't. Or, if it was a he, he wasn't.

I was getting another headache just thinking about it.

Anyway, I was rubbing my jaw, trying to look as if I were deep in thought about our next step when a man suddenly appeared.

'Detective Inspector Summers,' he introduced himself, showing a warrant card with the title "Detective Inspector F Summers". I looked at him. Smartly dressed. Polished shoes. Loud tie. Handsome,

I would imagine many women might think. At least Julia the Journalist stiffened when she saw him. Whether because she fancied him or because he might ask difficult questions I wasn't sure, but I guessed the former.

He had a look in his eyes which stated that he was more than ready to be sociable and friendly if you were, but if you weren't he would just as happily put your head in a vice and tighten it until you confessed or your head split open and your brains spattered themselves around the floor and walls and ceiling like so much spare grey matter. Though not, I would imagine, on his smart suit.

There was something strangely familiar about Summers. As if I knew him from somewhere. He had a leather jacket draped over his shoulder, almost as if, having put his suit on, he hadn't been sure whether it was required. There was a kitten in one of the capacious pockets. I looked at it. It looked back as if to say, "You are a strange person."

Now that was darn unfair. I've faced pretty much everything. Plods with Pitbulls. Coppers with Cocker Spaniels. Bobbies with bloodhounds. Bluebottles with Bassett Hounds. Rottweilers with rozzers. Dobermans with Detectives. R Soles with Alsations. Jerks with German Shepherds. You name it. You accept that. It's part of the game. So maybe you end up eviscerated, you take your chances. It's life. But a kitten? That's just playing downright dirty.

'And this is special constable Squishy,' Summers said.

I decided not to make a comment. Things were bad enough without having coppers with kittens wandering all over the place. Besides which, these sort of things happen in the best of families.

'You were the person who found the body?' asked Summers.

'No, I was the person who found the person who found the body.'

'Ah. Not to worry, that sort of thing happens in the best of families.'

I gave a weak smile. I suppose that's what passes as humour in the police ranks these days.

'Who found the body?' he asked.

'A waitress. She's in the kitchen, being revived with smelling salts.'

'Smelling salts?' he asked, intrigued. 'Do they still use them?'

'It's a euphemism. In this case I would imagine the smelling salts are a couple of bottles of cooking brandy.'

'Ah, pity. Smelling salts sounded much more interesting I've never seen smelling salts. Oh, well, I'd better get to the kitchen. They might even have some fish, what do you say to that, Squish?'

Squish looked up at him and miaowed a "Well, what are we doing here, then?" at him.

That was one intelligent kitten. Cute, too.

I watched them walk away. Or I watched him walk away, that little Squish in his pocket, looking back at me, still with the "You are a strange person, do you have any fish?" look. I decided it was time to see how the others were getting on.

'I'm going to go to my room and have a little snooze,' I told Julia the Journalist. It was an attempt to throw her off the scent.

'Can I come too?' she asked. There was a funny look in her eyes which suggested that it could be my lucky day, and it wouldn't involve snoozing. It was a terrible temptation, but somehow that moustache, fedora, tie and Macintosh made me uneasy.

'We can't both snooze at the same time,' I said. 'One of us has to stay alert. You go up to the attic and see if you can find a place to keep an eye on what's going on in the street.'

She gave me a hurt look.

'I'll do it because you've asked me, not because I want to,' she said. Then she turned and walked away, giving one last tearful look back at me before turning the corner.

I didn't feel good about it. But it would take her about three weeks to find the attic. Keeping her out of the picture not only kept her out of my hair, but also meant that I could concentrate on clearing up the murder before it took over the trial. Much as I felt sorry for Mrs Baggs, the trial – the book – was the important thing. Magazines like the Daily Trifle tended to get hooked on the trivia, ignoring the larger picture.

Once Julia the Journalist had gone I returned to my room to pick up my notebook and to have a think about things. I had presumed that the Clowns' appearance at the trial had merely been one of those strange coincidences which crop up all the time and cause most people to take up religion to make sense of the world. But now we had a murder on our hands, and that seemed far too much of a coincidence. It was time to sit down and list the facts.

After about half an hour of heavy sitting down, deep cogitation and listing the facts I had one: someone had done Mrs Baggs in. Two, if you counted the knitting needle as the murder weapon, which I wasn't prepared to do at that point. Too often you make such a presumption and it turns out that she was already dead at the time, poisoned by the butler or someone. Possibly strangled and the knitting needle used as a weak attempt to hide the fact. Hell, she could have died of a heart attack while doing something unmentionable in a family context, and her partner had decided to attempt to cover it up. It didn't blinking matter whether she'd died in a tombola orgy or some bizarre bag ladies' religious ritual. What mattered was in clearing it up so that we could proceed with the important business, i.e. Edgar The Ears' come-uppance.

She probably, almost definitely, wasn't a real member of the jury. But that didn't make a difference. Someone might have thought she was, which would have been good enough for them. Which could have been a motive. Or maybe, whoever it was, had known that she wasn't, which could have been a motive too. What for, I don't know. Making space in the jury box?

Or perhaps she knew something and someone wanted her kept quiet. Even if she might not know that she knew something that someone didn't want her telling anyone else.

See how it goes? Good old Occam's Razor. You come up with one theory to explain something and the next minute you've made leaps of logic and you end up concluding that the three-headed toad of Jumpijora is behind it all. In the end I decided to set off in search of the jury. They were going to turn out to be the clue to Mrs Baggs getting the chop, I was sure of it. Besides which, it was high time I got back to the business of piloting their thoughts in the right direction vis-a-vis a certain trial.

While I had been in my room cogitating the dining room had been sealed off so the plods could peruse the probable scene of crime. (In case Mrs Baggs had met her end somewhere else and her body dumped in the dining room, as so often happens in these cases. Summers had apparently even said that suicide could not be ruled out, though I suspect that was just his warped sense of humour.) Temporary arrangements had been made to convert the lounge into a breakfast room. Due to staff and space constraints the love bunnies had to share the same room. They had appropriated a couple of coffee tables, dragging them into a corner where they could sit separately. The bunnies now sat on the floor, nibbling at carrots from a pile on a tea-tray, looking suspiciously at everyone else.

Mrs Plum, Vicar Preachy, Miss F and Miss F's Mother sat at a rickety card table. Miss F was consuming a bowl of cereal while simultaneously ordering a Full English breakfast, I was glad to hear. I guessed that, in about six months or a year she would turn out to be a perfectly normal human being, whatever one of those is.

Vicar Preachy was steadily consuming a huge bowl of prunes and porridge. It wasn't a pretty sight. Mrs Plum was bemoaning Detective Inspector Summers' inability to understand the finer points of needlework.

'He's a very nice young man, and I'm sure he's very efficient, but –' she sighed. 'I suppose you can hardly expect him to understand the finer points of needlework.'

Mrs Baggs had certainly understood one of them, at the end, anyway. At least she had got the point.

I'll explain that to Beazeley later.

'He said they couldn't take the knitting needle out of the body until their investigations were complete,' Mrs Plum carried on, 'but if I could use it where it was now he had no objections.'

'That would be rather difficult, I would imagine,' said Vicar Preachy, spitting out a prune pit into his tea cup. It made a kind of "plop" sound.

'Extremely unhygienic,' contributed Miss F's mother.

'I wanted to see the body,' countered Miss F, with the emphasis on "I", 'but they wouldn't let me.'

'Just as well, my dear,' her mother replied. 'Seeing dead bodies at your age? It would never have happened in my day.'

Now that, I thought, was absolute bunkum. Miss F's Mother had probably seen more dead bodies by the time she was Miss F's age than the average person has had haggis. She was that sort of woman. But she had to put a pretence on for her daughter's sake. A pretence that the real world is pretty humdrum, and Miss F shouldn't expect too much in the way of fairy tales coming true.

'How old do I have to be to see a dead body?' asked Miss F with that deadly logic that teenagers often have.

'Now, my dear, just eat your Choc-pops and we'll discuss it later,' replied her mother with the delaying tactics most parents end up resorting to. Miss F made a face which told everyone exactly what she thought about the respective attractions of dead bodies and Choc-pops.

'Was there a lot of blood?' she asked me.

'About what you'd expect, under the circumstances,' I replied, my eye on Hugo, sitting on a sofa, happily consuming cornflakes soaked in guava juice in a way no blind man would do. It was a neat trick, using guava juice. As if he couldn't see what was in the jug and had poured it onto his cornflakes by mistake. Hugo, I decided, merited a little attention.

'Poor thing,' said Mrs Plum, noticing the direction of my gaze. 'He didn't realise that it wasn't milk.'

'How much is what you'd expect?' demanded Miss F of me, determined not to let go of such a satisfying topic. 'Was there a pool of blood?'

'Miss F, eat your Choc-pops,' admonished her mother.

'Oh, chuck the Choc-pops,' Miss F exclaimed, the way teenagers are wont to do. The way her mother didn't turn a hair suggested to me that she was used to this behaviour. I rather suspect she was thinking of a day when she had used similar language to her mother – "Sizzle the sausages!" or something similar. And her mother might well have responded, "Yes, my dear, but only one or the other, and I think eating them is the best bet at the moment. Though I might take breakfast in bed tomorrow."

'I suppose you could say it was a pool of blood,' I said.

'I try to keep blood out of my sermons,' Vicar Preachy noted, spitting out another prune pit. 'It sounds just too – Catholic.'

'I knew a Catholic once,' Strawberry Mousse mused. 'She had strange tastes. Liked the whip for some reason. I don't mind my male customers who like the whip, but it's unusual in the female.'

'Did you -' started Miss F, her lust for blood overtaken by this confession from Strawberry Mousse. 'Did you – well, you know? With her?'

'In my business you have to take the rough with the smooth,' Strawberry Mousse replied.

'So many similarities,' said Vicar Preachy. 'People tend to distinguish, but I find that it is quite incredible the similarities between our various callings. Taking the rough with the smooth is just one example. My wife, I am afraid to say, finds the concept difficult to understand. But then her attention has turned towards breeding stud hyenas. I find it dangerous even entering the vegetable patch these days.' He sighed as deeply as a man of religion would under such trying circumstances, but not long enough to allow anyone else to take the opportunity to talk. 'I do hope she remembers to water the prickly pears while I'm away. They've got a good chance of winning first at the harvest fair. No-one else has gone in for prickly pears this year. They're very good for you, you know, full of polyphenols and betalains. You just have to remember to peel them properly to get rid of the glochids otherwise they can get stuck in your throat. Very unpleasant.'

'So,' said Miss F, moving next to Strawberry Mousse, 'what's it like – doing it with a woman?'

Strawberry Mousse gave an explicit and detailed description. But I'm not going to repeat it here. Any reader interested can find it in the Appendix. This is not because I'm a prude, but because I know Beazeley will read this and will break his buns until he can find out what Strawberry Mousse is going to say.

Yes, I know, I'm a cruel and heartless son of a gun. Someone has to be with Beazeley.

Bombay Duck. He likes that. I'll get some, it might keep him quiet for an hour or two.

I'm kind that way.

God knows why.

I had it once. Tasted rubbery. More like chicken than duck.

Where was I?

Ah, yes. Explicit description.

While Strawberry Mousse was giving Miss F a graphic description of female erogenous zones rarely found outside scientific research I wandered over to Hugo.

'Everything okay?' I asked. It's not a question I resort to if I can avoid it. You end up sounding like one of those obnoxious waiters who interrupt your obvious enjoyment of a meal in order to enquire if you're enjoying it.

'Needs more garlic,' he commented. I looked at his bowl. Cornflakes, guava juice and raw garlic cloves.

'So what's with the dark glasses and the white stick?' I asked, sitting down next to him, but not too close. I said it in a manner which plainly said I didn't buy the "poor blind person" smaltz.

He paused. Chewed on a clove of garlic thoughtfully, looking straight ahead.

'I think I can trust you,' he said suddenly, turning towards me. I tried not to recoil too much from the wave upon wave assault of airborne garlic, a carpet-bombing of the nasal senses.

'I'm not blind. I see that you've spotted that. In fact the glasses and stick were my grandmother's. I carry them in memory of her.'

'Your grandmother died before you were born,' I replied. I didn't know that. But either it's true or it isn't. If so he would be forced to respond one way or another.

'I have a very long memory,' he said, after some thought. 'I was only a three-month foetus, but I remember the funeral well. People in my profession are well known for having extraordinarily long memories.'

'Nice try,' I said. One of those meaningless phrases designed to get a response.

'I can see you don't believe me.'

I stayed silent.

'Very well,' he said, lifting the glasses slightly, letting me see his eyes, 'the truth is, I'm an accountant. I didn't want anyone to know.'

I nodded. I suspected something of the sort. I had noticed how careful he had been with his money. And the pens sticking out of his top pocket were a bit of a give-away. I just knew the lump in his jacket pocket would be a calculator.

'I understand,' I said. After all, if I was an accountant I'd also be too embarrassed to tell anyone.

'Yes,' he continued, 'it's the inferiority problem.'

'Just so.'

'Understandable, though. Just unfortunate.'

'Yes, I can see that.'

'It does make social intercourse quite difficult.'

'Yes, yes, I suppose it would.'

'One minute you're chatting to someone as their equal, you mention that you're an accountant, and then they act as if they aren't worthy to be in your company. They realise they're talking to someone special.'

'Eh?'

'Of course you do need a certain amount of intelligence to be an accountant – much higher than the norm, and a very sharp understanding of figures. The average layman finds it difficult to converse normally in the company of someone his intellectual superior.'

'Eh?'

'So I'd be most grateful if you could keep it a secret just between the two of us.'

I think by that stage my eyes weren't far from popping out of their sockets.

'Not at all. Your secret's safe with me,' I assured him, standing up as fast as I could, getting a dizzy feeling in the process, ready to leave. More than ready to leave. The further away I could get from Hugo the better, and not just because of the garlic. As I left I overheard a number of conversations.

'Is it true that you're a Miss Hand Wrist?' – Miss F.

'Darling, eat your Choc-pops, they're becoming soggy' – Miss F's Mother.

'Of course, the Resurrection is one of the most difficult areas in my experience' – Vicar Preachy.

'Poor, poor man. Blind and an accountant' – Mrs Plum.

They were one weird lot, that jury.

An hour later or so I discovered that my chief worry – that the murder of Mrs Baggs might delay the trial – was not to be fulfilled. Judge Beak ruled that the police would have to continue their enquiries around the trial. Which was both fortunate and unfortunate, as it turned out.

Beazeley's just turned up. It looks as if that that pretend Polish plumber was a real Polish plumber, the one I've been waiting for.

Butter.

I wonder whether I can convince the Polish plumber that pouring cold porridge over someone's head is an ancient English tradition showing that they are welcome.

You know, that might just work.

That and slinging him a couple of bottles of Slivovitz.

Still, Beazeley's asked to see what I've written so far, so I gave him a copy of Ulysses. At this moment he's sitting on the couch in the lounge scratching his head and making despairing legalistic groans.

He'll probably end up being one of the very few people I know who has actually managed to finish it.

Time for break, a cuppa, and then on with the start of day two of the trial.

That postman has just walked out of the front door opposite. In broad daylight. Either the young woman gets a lot of heavy parcels or something funny is going on.

None of my business, really.

Unless she is single and gets a lot of heavy parcels.

In which case maybe she would welcome a hand with them.

No, sod it, concentrate on the story. Try not to get involved with strange women yet again. For all I know those parcels could contain the bodies of her previous lovers, and I had enough bodies lying around that week to keep me going for a while.

Why would she post the bodies of her previous lovers to herself?

Forget it. A cup of tea and then

It's apple box time.

Chapter IX. Apple Box Time

Right, back again. Beazeley's had to pop out to buy some more notebooks for the notes he's making on Ulysses, so we'll be left in peace for at least half an hour or so, more if he follows the directions I gave him for the local newsagent. Maybe he'll realise he's going the wrong way when he gets to the canal on the other side of town. Knowing how difficult it is for him to alter track I wouldn't be surprised if he tries swimming across. Poor lad.

Right, Tuesday morning, let the trial re-commence.

Now I know this is going to sound surreal. I found it difficult to believe my own eyes. If I could describe accurately what actually happened you wouldn't believe me. I don't think I'd believe myself either.

Judge Beak, having spent Monday afternoon on the golf course, decided on Tuesday morning that enough time had been wasted, and if the trial was to be concluded by the Friday they would have to get straight on. Inspector Summers was told that he could interview whoever he felt necessary, but that it would have to be done as the trial was taking place. So while the lawyers were speaking Summers was sitting on the leaning edge of the jury box interviewing the jurors. Next to him was a small but full-busted young blonde woman who I learnt was his detective constable. She took notes as he interviewed. Though she kept shooting filthy looks at Strawberry Mousse as if she thought the other woman's attributes owed more to medical science than nature. The battle of the busts, I suppose.

The Prim Maiden Aunt was allergic to cats – a dodgy sign, I've often thought, whatever your feelings about certain animals might be, becoming allergic to them seems a step too far – so the kitten Squishy was given to the clowns to look after. Clyde was more than delighted. I doubt she heard a single word the lawyers said, playing with the kitten, or stroking it as it lay asleep in her lap. Bonnie was obviously happy that Clyde was happy. He even had an occasional smile on his face. A sad smile, admittedly, but a real one.

Mrs Plum had had no time to find a replacement for her knitting needle, so she was using Vicar Preachy's middle finger as a temporary replacement. He seemed quite happy for her to do so, holding his arm out as he concentrated on the trial. Though I must admit Mrs Plum kept giving Hugo's white stick many sharp looks, as if sizing it up as a replacement.

Julia the Journalist was absent, probably still looking for the hotel attic. The Major was wearing brown again, I noticed. I had a feeling that he had seven sets of exactly the same outfit, one for each day of the week. Seven fawn-brown suits, seven dull-yellow shirts, seven brown ties, seven pairs of polished brown shoes.

Miss F was the opposite. She was the "different outfit as often as possible" type. That morning she was wearing a short, red mini-skirt and a red-striped man's shirt a couple of sizes too large for her, knotted at the waist. The ensemble was topped off with red-framed dark glasses, the outfit slightly marred by the same sparkly little-girl flip-flops and a lollipop sticking out of her mouth. Her mother sat next to her, attired in a light mauve jacket, tight-fitting white t-shirt and jeans, with matching light-mauve shoes, still managing to look stylish. She was idly flicking through a magazine. If it wasn't for her mild and detached manner a cynic might have thought she was sending out a message: "Not bad for a woman who has a seventeen-year-old daughter and a boy named little Davy, what do you think? And no cosmetic surgery either, it's all natural."

The Quiet American was dressed the same, apart from the loud Hawaiian shirt, which that day was largely orange and gold. The Nun With Guitar had changed her shimmering light blue habit for a shimmering light yellow habit, little yellow sequins, dots of light rippling with ever move she made. Strangely enough it went quite well with the black makeup. I also noticed something I had missed the day before, unless it hadn't been there with the previous outfit: if you watched carefully when she moved you could see a slit down part of the front, a kind of partial cleavage as it were. Very odd.

Even more odd. No sign of any undergarment.

There are certain questions in this world you do not ask. Not if you want to stay vaguely sane. I decided to push such questions right out of my mind – hold my nose and squeeze them out of my ears, as it were – and concentrate on what I was there for, the trial.

The legal teams of vulture and ball were back in their little docks waiting for the kick-off. Mr Ball had told the court usher that a box of oranges was too soft and something more substantial was required. Some confusion arose somewhere between that statement and the usher's brain, and he had ordered a box of apples, premium Granny Smiths. Once the trial began Norah The Nose was called to the witness box. Mr Crane stood up, fluffed his feathers, and picked up the loudly coloured book with two disgusted fingers.

'H'now, h'Mitherth h'Nothe, h'let'th h'turn h'to h'page h'fifty-three h'in h'thith h'novel h'of h'yourth. H'allegthed h'novel, h'I h'thould h'thay.'

Mrs Nose looked back down upon him, imperturbable, a lady of style, grace, poise, and a whopping big nose.

'H'on h'page h'fifty-three, h'Mitherth h'Nothe, h'you h'dethcribe h'the h'main h'protagonitht'th h'buthineth h'partner h'ath h'a h'Japanethe h'gentleman, h'do h'you h'not?'

'That is correct.'

'H'but h'you h'ex-huthband'th h'buthineth h'partner h'wath h'American, h'not h'tho?'

'That is correct.'

The Quiet American appeared to have suddenly lost any interest. He was carefully cleaning his six-spurters. I just hoped they weren't loaded. "I was cleaning it and it went off" wouldn't be much consolation for anyone who copped it.

'H'ith h'it h'not h'remarkable ow h'clothe h'the h'dethcription h'of h'the h'Japanethe h'gentleman h'ith h'to h'your h'ex-huthband'th h'American h'buthineth h'partner?'

Mrs Nose snorted with laughter. With a nose like that she could really snort. A cross between a donkey braying and an air-raid siren going off. The noise rebounded off the walls of the court like an oral pinball hitting top score. Almost all of the heads of the jury shot back as if suddenly and violently assaulted. When she had recovered Strawberry Mousse shook hers as if to clear it, and indignantly threw her scarf over her shoulder, where it came once more to rest, hovering over Mr Sleepy's sleeping face.

'If you think there can be any comparison you must have an extremely good imagination,' Norah The Nose said once completely finished braying.

'Hit h'ith ardly h'a h'laughing h'matter, h'Mitherth h'Nothe.'

'Hi think it is.'

Judge Beak rapped his gavel, cried "Order! Order!" and went back to sleep.

'H'I h'think h'you h'will h'be h'laughing h'out h'of h'the h'other h'thide h'of h'your h'nothe h'ath h'time h'goeth h'on, h'Mitherth h'Nothe. H'let h'uth h'look h'at h'page h'thirty-one. H'and h'I h'quote: "H'Thethil ad h'theveral h'mithtreththeth, h'alwayth h'on h'the h'go h'at h'the h'thame h'time. H'thith h'rethulted h'in h'a h'great h'deal h'of h'jealouthy h'among h'them". H'now, h'Mrth h'Nothe, h'your h'ex-uthband ath h'never h'been h'convicted h'of aving h'mithtreththeth, ath e?'

'I'm not aware that having mistresses was something you could be convicted for.'

'H'ah, h'the h'rethort h'to h'nit-picking. H'take h'note, h'memberth h'of h'the h'jury, h'take h'note! H'Mitherth h'Nothe h'refutheth h'to h'anthwer h'a h'thtraight h'quethtion. H'inthtead h'the rethorth h'to h'nit-picking! H'I h'thall leave you h'to h'draw h'your h'own h'concluthionth.'

With that he sat down with a great deal of smirk on his face. Or, in his case, thmirk. Taking his cue Mr Ball struggled to his feet enthusiastically and mounted his box of apples.

'MRS NOSE! THIS NOVEL –' he held it up in case the jurors or Norah The Nose had never seen it before '– IS A WORK OF FICTION, IS IT NOT? IT STATES SO AT THE BEGINNING, DOES IT NOT?'

'Precisely,' Mrs Nose replied quickly as the box of apples began to give way and Mr Ball began to slowly slide from view.

'IT ALSO CONTAINS' – chin level with balustrade, crunchy sound of apple cider in the making – 'THE STATUTORY DISCLAIMER' – nose dropping from sight – 'IN THE FRONT' – eyes open wide as he lost sight of Mrs Nose – 'thatallsuchworksdo?'

'Of course,' said Mrs Nose, leaning forward to catch a final glimpse as Mr Ball's blue wig finally sank below the parapet. There was a pause as Mr Ball vainly tried to find an unsquashed apple to stand on before it was disturbed by the sound of a fat little lawyer slipping on apple pulp.

'No further questions,' he squeaked finally. I could see him slumped on his back, tears coursing down what little could be seen of his cheeks. The acidic tang of squashed apples floated slowly up to the gallery. It isn't easy to feel sorry for lawyers, but I think almost everyone in that court was beginning to do so for Mr Ball.

Besides which he was messing up his chances of nailing Edgar The Ears, which was especially infuriating. Here I was, prepared to go to almost any limit to ensure that Mr Ball won the case, and he was messing about in apple juice! At that rate the only verdict the jury could possibly bring in would be the wrong one.

Fruit salad.

'Unusual trial,' said a voice next to me. It was Summers with his sidekick. I hadn't even noticed that he'd left the jury box. A disturbing man.

The sidekick had recovered Squishy and was holding the kitten in her arms. Squishy was back at the "You are a strange person" looking game. A disturbing kitten.

Summers sat down on my right, and his sidekick took the seat to my left. He sat with his hands in his pockets, legs out, relaxed. Had I not known that he was a copper I might have taken him for a cricket fan relaxing, watching his side bat against a far inferior team. A dangerous man.

'Who's winning?' he asked.

'Prosecution ahead on points, I would say,' I replied, trying to keep my voice neutral. He nodded.

'He'll be in trouble once the defence get their oranges and apples sorted,' he noted. I was surprised. I hadn't seen him pay any attention to the case. As Mr Ball sank into his apples Summers had merely continued his chat – it looked more chat than interview – with Strawberry Mousse.

'H'Mr H'Ball?' asked Mr Crane with some concern, looking into his dock.

'Call for an adjournment, Hector,' cried Mr Ball. 'Please, please call for an adjournment.'

'Ah, well, fascinating though it is, I suppose I have to earn my salary,' Summers said, a lazy smile on his face. 'Care to tell me your story since you got here?'

It was said so languidly another man might have supposed that Summers wasn't taking the business seriously. I wasn't about to make that mistake. I told him exactly what had happened. Well, perhaps not all of it.

'H'you onour, h'we h'would h'rethpectfully h'call h'for h'an h'adjournment,' Mr Crane said as I recounted most of what I knew to Summers.

'H'your onour?' Mr Crane asked, no reply coming from the bench.

I could have sworn that Summers wasn't listening to me. He had leaned forward and was watching in fascination as the little recorder jumped up and down in front of the sleeping Judge Beak, waving her thin hands and arms to wake him up.

Innocent, brown, thin little hands and arms that could kill a man silently as he slept the sleep of the blissfully unaware. And the last time he'd ever party in the land of Nod.

'Mr Quiet American,' said Mr Crane, 'would you do the honours?'

'Sure will, pardner,' replied the Quiet American, drawing his water pistols and taking a bead on the judge. He paused.

'Shucks, that's too easy,' he said. He turned around, bent over, and aimed between his legs. A perfect shot hit Judge Beak on his beak.

'Good shot!' murmured Summers. 'I wonder if he'd lend them to me next time.'

'Frank!' admonished his busty sidekick.

'I see that it is almost time for lunch,' Judge Beak said slowly, wiping his nose with a handkerchief. 'Mr Ball, Mr Crane, I suggest we adjourn for lunch. Do you agree?'

Mr Crane nodded, his budgie skidding around his head. Mr Ball waved his sad little blue flag.

'All rise for the judge,' came the metallic announcement. All rose, apart from Summers, who had returned to his "watching my cricket team" pose.

'Interesting, isn't it?' he asked as I sat down again, watching the jury sway out of their rocking box. I tried to look as if I hadn't noticed the Nun With Guitar smile slowly up at us and wink at me as she left, one lovely leg showing as her habit moved.

'In what way?' I asked. I knew what he meant. I just wasn't going to admit it.

He smiled. I was beginning to hate that smile.

Correction. I already hated that smile.

The thing is, he knew the tricks as well as I did. Or perhaps better. Leave a silence for the other person to fill. Say something ambiguous and watch the mark to see which way he or she would interpret it. Pretend to know something when you're guessing.

So we both sat there in silence, waiting for the other to break it.

After half an hour I decided that he had won.

'Lunch time,' I said. 'If you don't have any more questions I'm off to grab a bite of something. I expect Squishy is hungry too. Aren't you, Squish? Tuna?'

Little Squishy miaowed plaintively: "You are a strange person, but for tuna I'll overlook anything."

Summers smiled at me. He took a relaxed draw on his cigarillo and blew a languid jet of smoke out.

Okay, he didn't. He still had his hands in his pockets. But he looked at me as if he was languidly blowing smoke at me.

I even coughed.

Not a man to play poker with.

He nodded slowly, smiling. The game was one point each. I had broken the silence. But I had got to Squish. He would have to feed

120

her now. He couldn't stay there sitting silently forever. Squish was miaowing at him, saying "Come on, it's lunch time."

'Any time you want to tell me the truth, you know where to find me,' he said, standing up.

There were two lies. First about telling the truth. He didn't know if what I'd told him was the truth or not, he was guessing that it wasn't. And secondly I didn't know where to find him.

If I'd known how much trouble Summers was going to be, I'd never have met him in the first place.

Beazeley says that that doesn't make any sense. Jeez! Critics!

Good thing he's gone to make coffee or I'd make him into something.

Gorgonzola surprise! perhaps.

Bouillabaisse!

There are those exclamation marks again. A sign that I'm getting tired. Time to break for a snack. And then onto Tuesday lunchtime and Hugo's story.

I should at least pretend to feel sorry for Hugo, after what's going to happen to him.

I won't feel sorry for Beazeley when something nasty happens to him. He met the young woman from across the road on his way back from the newsagents. Apparently they had a lovely chat for about fifteen minutes. And you know the only thing he found out about her? She doesn't like football. I mean, for crying in a bucket, there are so many obvious things he could have found out. Rough age bracket. Whether or not she's a religious or other freak. Partnership status. Sexual orientation. If she's interested in a deep and meaningful relationship between the hours of midday and two o'clock on Tuesdays and Thursdays. That sort of thing. And all he can come up with is that she doesn't like football. So what? The Nun With Guitar wasn't into football either.

It was her only flaw.
Black Forest Gateau.

.

Chapter X. Hugo Almost Spills the Beans

Beazeley's been trying to talk me into replacing Vicar Preachy with a shepherdess. Complete with crook, floral skirt showing white-stockinged ankles, a bonnet with a blue strap, holding a cute little lamb. The shepherdess holding the cute little lamb, not the bonnet. I suggested that we change Mrs Baggs into a cute little shepherdess with cute little lamb. That way we can have the lamb skewered at the same time as the cute little shepherdess aka Mrs Baggs. Just think, cute little lamb chops for dinner. Maybe even kebabs.

Yum yums.

He didn't like that idea for some reason. He's gone for another lie down.

One of these days I'm going to start charging him rent.

What's the name of that raw fish stuff the Japanese eat? Sake? Sushi? Something like that.

Anyway, back to the Tuesday. I remember walking back into the Railway Tavern reception, one of those silly things that just stick in your mind for some reason. Alberto was tuning up again behind the aspidistra. I was determined to make up for the gaffe of the previous day.

'Tuning again, Alberto?' I asked. 'Keep up the good work.'

He gave me a sour look.

'Heyick,' said Mildred One behind me. "That was Chopin's *6th symphony for string in G major with minor variations for flute in C minor with added clefts and things.* Berk."

'Ah, yes, of course,' I said, giving her one of those smiles you come up with when you realise you've just put your foot in it again. 'Of course, of course. Lovely stuff. Er, any post for me?'

'Heyick.' "Stupid question. I'd have given it to you if there was. Anyway, who in their right mind would want to write to you? Even someone in their wrong mind."

'Right, right. I'll be on my way. Nice hairdo, by the way, Mildred One. Cheerio, Alberto.'

'Heyick.'

(I won't translate that last one. It wasn't very nice. It was almost as bad as the X-word.)

I looked around the dim-lit reception and decided that I wasn't in the mood for aimlessly wandering around darkened corridors at that moment. I strolled back outside into the sun and found a bench to sit on opposite the hotel, watching the wisteria-covered entrance. There was something that was starting to bother me. I was beginning to wonder whether everyone in that jury had a connection with Edward the Ears. The Nun With Guitar. The Quiet American. The Clowns. I had a hunch that, as the trial continued, the book would contain details about Strawberry Mousse and the others. Probably not all of them, though. At least one, maybe two, would turn out to have nothing to do with him. The trick was to work out who did have an interest. And then pump them for information.

Now, if you're looking for a weak point in a case, go for the accountant. Firstly they're the ones who know – should know – what money has gone where, and there's almost always money involved. Secondly, they're almost invariably in love with themselves. They think that figures rule the world, and they rule the figures. They're totally blind to the idea that someone may be outwitting them. Which makes it easy to do. And Hugo was even more full of himself than any other accountant I'd ever met. (It's easy to slag off bean counters in a book, because they never read books. Books cost money.)

There was no guarantee that Hugo was involved in any way. But he was the easiest target. And, as Sherlock Holmes once said, once you eliminate the impossible, whatever remains, no matter how improbable, must be the something-something-something. (I can never remember how that quotation ends. Note to self: check it out.) So even if he weren't involved I would have to, to use a phrase, eliminate him sooner or later. From my enquiries.

As I sat there wondering how to corner Hugo, who should slip out of the hotel tapping his stick in front of him. He was wearing a silly peaked cap, with something hidden underneath his jacket? Hugo, bless him. So I followed him. He didn't even look around to see if he had a tail. Then again, a supposedly blind man checking around him for a tail would look a little suspicious. I was about ten feet behind him when he got to his destination, a dark, dingy little bar which had a sign saying "Eff Off" written in front of it. It wasn't a pub. Pubs are welcoming places. This was a bar, the type of place furtive people go to.

I needed two things before following him in. Firstly to disguise myself so that he wouldn't recognise me. Secondly, some sign by which he would think I too was a fellow figure-fixated nerd. I popped into a news agent and bought a box of different coloured pens and a large blue plastic toy calculator, the type you give to two-year-olds to break, or eat. The pens went into my top pocket, the calculator jammed into a side pocket with just enough to show a suggestion of calculator. Then some thick dark glasses of the kind that would have been considered fashionable around about 1952 for a week or so. And a silly peaked cap.

I gave it another five minutes before entering. I ordered myself a Scotch and pretended to be surprised to see Hugo sitting in a dark corner. He was tapping into a laptop, which explained what had been underneath his coat.

I briefly wondered whether they had asked him proof that he was old enough to drink, this short, aged little schoolboy with his feet hardly touching the floor. I doubted it. People don't ask questions in pubs like that. Anyway, they probably took one look and decided to ignore him as far as possible. Unfortunately I didn't have that option.

'Busy man,' I commented, sitting down next to him, looking at a screen crowded with numbers in all colours. He was so engrossed in his figures he didn't even seem surprised that a stranger should suddenly start chatting to him. 'Nice spreadsheet.'

'It's the Fullbrights' final quarter,' he said, without looking at me. 'I'm the only one who understands these spreadsheets. If it wasn't for me the figures would never be ready in time.'

I nodded in sympathy, as if I were a fellow-spreadsheet fixated nerd. In truth I'd struggle to switch a spreadsheet on if my life depended on it. Fortunately I only need to be able to sound as if I know what a spreadsheet is.

'Strange how these computer people can never come up with software which does what you need,' I said. 'I know people in that line, and somehow they always come up with a package which falls short in significant areas.'

Strangely enough, that bit was more or less true, if you look at it from the computer peoples' point of view: for them, no matter how good a system they design, an accountant will always find a problem with it. I won't repeat the description one of them gave me about accountants. Apparently she had come up with some software which provided everything everyone from the managing director to the lowliest clerk agreed was just what they needed. There was just one problem. The accountants always disagree, she said. They carry on creating spreadsheets which make no sense to anyone else.

'Exactly,' replied Hugo. 'People just do not understand the complexities of accounting. The managing director of Fullbrights' insisted on buying a software package which just doesn't do everything that we need.'

Thought so.

'He probably spoke to some lowly clerk who didn't know what they were talking about.'

'You know, that's exactly true.'

Bait taken. Here comes your next cue, Hugo me mate:

'Which means that you have to spend time you don't have on spreadsheets to make up the lack.'

'I can see that you've worked in accountancy. You know exactly how it is.'

Nope, but I can recognise a dipswitch when I see one.

'Oh, yes, I've been there, as they say. Been there, done that, didn't bother buying the t-shirt.'

'Eh?'

Whoops. Slight mistake. I'd forgotten that people like Hugo speak their own language and don't understand anyone else's.

'I mean, you end up a martyr to your job. Such as bringing it along here while you're –' I almost said "a member of the jury", but coughed that into 'should be on your lunch break.'

'I can't count the number of lunch breaks I've missed due to having to get the right figures through on time,' he said.

I just resisted the temptation to suggest that an accountant who couldn't count must be a pretty useless accountant.

You have to humour pillocks like that. They seriously believe that what they're doing is of crucial importance to mankind. They take themselves so seriously that you feel they would be better off locked up in a padded room. But it was time to get a little closer to the nub of things.

'It is a tough job, isn't it?' I said, humouring him. 'Just the same with the work you did for Edgar The Ears, I suppose.'

He stiffened suddenly.

'Who told you that I did any work for Edgar The Ears?' he asked.

'Oh, it's general knowledge, isn't it? In the trade.'

He paused before replying.

'I never discuss clients. Confidentiality is key to my reputation.' Said looking down his nose at me, which, since he was a head shorter, didn't really work.

'Of course,' I said. I nodded towards the screen in front of him. 'It's an art, really, isn't it?' If he wasn't going to discuss Edgar The Ears directly, I would have to try to get him to do so sideways.

'It is,' said in such a patronising manner I almost thumped him. 'Take the heliollating discumtotal waddy woo-waa here,' he said, tapping a part of the screen. ("Heliollating discumtotal waddy woo-waa" wasn't exactly what he said, but whatever it was he did say meant as much to me.) 'It shows quite clearly that Fullbrights are spending too much in various areas – paper and ink especially. They could save up to twenty-percent if they cut down by just fourteen point three nine percent per annum.'

'Wow, that's a lot. What do they do? Fullbrights?'

'They're a publishing company. Now here too, the number of agents they're using for advertising needs to be reduced ...'

He waffled on. I listened with half an ear. I would have listened with no ear if I could have gotten away with it. Only someone like Hugo could come to the conclusion that a printing company could economise by doing less printing.

You know how your mind tends to wander when you're stuck having to pretend to be listening to someone? Like being in local town hall during a really, really boring meet-your-council public do? And you start to wonder what the woman in the green dress looks like naked, just to keep yourself awake. Or you wonder whether the head councillor would be improved by having an affair with that really ugly old woman sitting next to him. Or maybe he is having an affair with the really ugly old woman sitting next to him. And then that gets boring, so you pretend that the Battle of Britain is being re-enacted around his head, little Messerschmitt and Spitfires whizzing past his ears, tiny little bursts of fire almost singing his hair.

That's what happened then. Hugo the accountant was droning on in a manner that, if it could be harnessed, would make a terrifying military weapon. He'd just need to open his mouth and the enemy would be keeling over in droves. Trouble is he'd probably be shot by his own side before he could open his mouth. I was tempted to slip a knife into his side myself, a scientific experiment to see if he would change register. Probably not. He'd just carry on droning, droning, droning ...

'Of course, I used a slightly different approach for Edgar The Ears,' he said in his monotonous, monotonous, droning tone. I wondered if he were married. It seemed an incredible, hilariously impossible notion. But stranger things happen at sea, so I've heard.

'His wife wanted it in a different colour ...'

If Hugo was married, his wife would be big, I imagined. Huge. The size of an ocean-going liner. Wears pearl twinsets and strict lavender jacket-skirt combinations.

'Numb numb numb numb numb ... '

He'd be henpecked. He'd have to wear an apron and do the dusting. As a special treat he'd be allowed half a glass of sherry on special occasions. Such as when she was away for a few days visiting her gargantuan mother.

I wondered what the Nun With Guitar was doing with her Guitar.

'Numb numb numb numb numb ...'

I wondered what it would be like to stroke those dots.

'Numb numb numb numb numb ...'

Those lovely, lovely little dots.

It was some five or ten minutes before I realised that Hugo and his laptop had left and I was listening to the sound of a refrigerator somewhere arguing with itself.

So Hugo turned out to be a damp squid , a complete dead end. I decided that I would just have to see whether any of the others could come up with some solid information. One of them had to have something I could use. Anything. Just so long as it were true. Or roughly in the same universe as true.

I wonder if I should pop across the road and borrow a cup of sugar.

I wonder if there ever was a time when people popped next door to borrow a cup of sugar. Sounds like an urban myth to me.

Or perhaps there was a day when they didn't have corner shops open all hours.

That postman's back. Another large parcel.

Hmmm.

Tea bags.

Chapter XI. Now it's Soap Boxes

Beazeley says that a trial would never have happened this way. Well, Beaze, isn't that the effect you wanted? Do keep up old boy.

Poor chap, he does live in cloud-cuckoo land sometimes.

Sometimes I don't know whether to feel sorry for him or beat him to death with a boiled cabbage.

Whatever.

It's Tuesday afternoon now, and it was Tuesday afternoon then. It's strange. It's almost as if I'm writing this in some time parallel to then. Sitting here, tapping away, it feels as if I were back there, instead of here, present tense. Almost as if I'm back in the Old Railway Tavern, sitting in a corridor, Sleeping Beauty Bacchus at my side as I type. It's a weird feeling.

Note to self: do not let your imagination run away with you.

!

Extra note to self: get rid of the pesky exclamation marks. They just look silly. Do a global search-and-replace with something like #.

Tuesday afternoon.

Sashimi, that's what the stuff is called.

Right, Tuesday afternoon – then. The court had re-assembled. The Judge was back on his bench, asleep, as usual. The jury – the main body of the jury – were back in their place, one place empty, no-one seemed in a hurry to claim Mrs Baggs's seat. I wasn't sure whether that was superstition or just the good old 'I've got my seat and I am not going to change it for anyone' mentality. The clowns were in the well of the court, practising being unseen, Clyde playing with Squishy, Bonnie behind her, an arm around her waist. No sign of Summers or his sidekick. I presumed he was interviewing the hotel staff and the bunnies.

Norah The Nose was in the witness box again. There was a rumour that Edward the Ears would appear the following day. His job as Minister for Toy Trains kept him busy, so there was no guarantee he would find the time to turn up on time. There was also the question of security: his appointments were kept secret up to the last minute, to prevent any possible assassin pre-planning his demise. Quite a few people would have liked to have seen him have an unfortunate and terminal accident, including most of his best friends.

The court usher had been sent to get a soap box for Mr Ball. A "large one". Yup, you guessed it. Mr Ball returned to his little dock to find a five-kilogramme box of SudsForMuds, or whatever it was called. The usher was sent back out with an order to find one twice the size. As he couldn't he returned with another two of the same size before disappearing as fast as he could back to his niche and a rollup. The three boxes of soap were stacked up in front of Mr Ball. They looked fairly solid from where I was sitting. At the same time I had a feeling that their appearance was a little misleading. Especially compared to Mr Ball. He didn't look solid. But he did look heavy.

Mr Crane the vulture had stood up to continue questioning. He gave his usual neck-stretch, flapped his black wings, and held up the book between his thumb and finger. I have to admit that I looked at it with the same sort of face you see in illustrations of Dickensian orphans peering through the window of a sweet shop. I won't say I would have killed to get a copy of that book. But it would have been a close run thing. I was tempted to creep up to his dock in the absurd hope that no-one would notice, and quickly whip it away from him before doing a runner. I even felt my muscles tense up in readiness. Then I got a strange feeling, and noticed the Nun With Guitar observing me without looking at me. I relaxed and leaned back. Sometimes it's not nice to be noticed.

But as it was her, okay, no problem.

'H'now, h'Mrth h'Nothe, h'in h'thith' – he waved it in the air, just below the ceiling – 'h'book h'of h'yourth, h'the h'principal h'antagonitht'th h'name h'ith h'Thelley Ope, h'not h'tho?'

'No, it's Shelley Hope.'

'H'that h'ith h'what h'I h'thaid, h'Thelley Ope.'

'No, Shelley Hope.'

Either Mr Crane was a quick thinker, or he had experience of that sort of thing. He quickly gave up what was going to be a losing battle. 'H'and h'your h'ex-huthband'th h'name h'ithn't h'Thelley Ope, h'ith h'it, h'Mrth h'Nose?'

'No, of course not. It's Edgar The Ears.'

'H'tho, h'you h'admit h'that h'you h'dithguithed ith h'name.'

'Not at all. The character in my novel is named Shelley Hope. My ex-husband's name is Edgar The Ears. There's no similarity whatsoever. If I wanted to disguise him I would have called him Donkey Breath.'

'H'oh, h'come, h'Mitherth h'Nothe, h'pleathe h'don't h'try h'to h'deny h'that h'thith -' he waved the lurid cover in the air again '- h'ith h'not h'jutht h'a h'thinly h'dithguithed h'tithue h'of h'lieth.'

'It's a work of fiction. By definition it can't be a tissue of lies.'

'H'you h'inthitht h'on h'claiming h'that h'thith h'ith h'true?'

'No, I insist on claiming that it's a work of fiction.'

Mr Crane nodded slowly, as if to say to the jury, "See, I've given her every chance and she refuses to admit that it's all lies."

'H'let h'uth h'turn h'to h'page h'one undred h'and h'three,' he continued.

It was then that something struck me. None of the jury had a copy of the novel. I had presumed that each would receive one. But obviously they were taking security seriously. They weren't taking the chance of some light fingered lad lifting a careless juror's copy. Which was a distinct nuisance, since that, of course, had been my backup strategy.

(Beazeley has asked me not to admit that. According to him, these days you can get locked up just for contemplating committing a crime, even if you don't carry it out. Can you imagine a country like that? The jails would be full. Who would be that stupid?)

'H'on h'page h'one undred h'and h'three h'you h'write: "H'Thelley h'felt h'a and h'upon ith h'knee. H'it h'wath h'the h'Major'th and." H'in h'other h'wordth, h'Mitherth h'Nothe, h'you h'are h'thuggethting h'that h'my h'client h'ith h'not eterothexthual?'

I glanced at the Major. he was looking down, a hand across his mouth and cheek as if deep in concentration. Nobody else appeared to notice, but I could tell that he had gone the colour normally called puce. Hello, hello, I thought. So the Major's involved somewhere. Now how would he find himself in the circles Edgar The Ears travelled in?

Actually, Edgar The Ears didn't travel in circles, he travelled in corkscrews.

'I'm not saying anything of the sort,' Norah The Nose said. 'Both Shelley Hope and the Major are invented characters. In that paragraph I was exploring the possibility that either one of both might have homosexual leanings. In the end it turned out that they were just discussing cavalry twill.'

'H'cavalry h'twill? H'Mitherth h'Nothe, h'do h'you h'really h'exthpect h'thith h'court, h'thith thury, h'to h'believe h'that?'

'No, I don't.'

'Ey?'

'I said I don't expect them to believe it. It's a work of fiction. Do you believe that every novel you read is true? Little Nell never really existed, you know.'

That seemed to stun the vulture for a few seconds, as if he had hopped over to a rather tasty looking corpse only to find it selling him a life assurance policy and asking him to sign just where the crosses were. He stretched his neck to recover. His bright yellow budgie-wig bounced a few times on top of his bald head.

'H'the h'truth h'ith, h'Mitherth h'Nothe, h'that h'that h'thene h'wath h'merely h'a h'thinly h'diguithed h'vertion h'of h'thome h'ugly, h'ugly h'rumourth h'thpread h'by ith h'political h'opponenth. Ith h'enemieth. H'that h'ith h'the h'the h'truth h'of h'the h'matter, h'ladieth h'and h'gentlemen h'of h'the thury. H'pure h'and h'thimple. H'remember h'that, h'ladieth h'and h'gentlemen.'

He sat down, a smirking vulture with huge eyes and a budgie on his head, confident that he had proved yet another point. Lawyers do that, you know. A bit like politicians. They have to appear confident, even when it's quite clear the walls are coming down and no-one believes a word they're saying. Even Mr Ball looked confident as he struggled onto his boxes of soap powder. But like most fat men he was unsurprisingly heavy on his soap boxes.

'NOW, MRS EARS,' he began.

'It's Mrs Nose, Mr Ball, Mrs Norah The Nose.'

'Ah, yes, of course, of course. NOW, MRS NOSE, WE RETURN TO THIS WORK OF FICTION.' He held it up as if it were a favourite book of classical poetry. 'THIS WAS INSPIRED BY OTHER WORKS OF FICTION, WAS IT NOT?'

'Quite so.'

'NONE OF THE CHARACTERS RESEMBLE ANYONE IN REAL LIFE, DO THEY?'

'I think you'd have to be rather a strange type of person to remotely imagine that they resembled anyone in real life. Certainly not anyone I have ever met. But then I've never been a state school teacher.'

'A state school teacher?' squeaked Mr Ball in surprise. I think he sensed that more than the conversation was shifting against him. The boxes of soap powder had begun to leak. The bottom one was spurting a fine spray of powder across his little dock.

'I'm told that state school teachers have to deal with children whose behaviour can be beyond imagination. Or unimaginable.' Mr Ball blinked. Suddenly his left side seemed to drop half an inch.

'Ah, yes, I see. HOWEVER' – a quick glance down: soap powder was beginning to fly around his dock, a mini-blizzard, and the boxes were groaning – 'HOWEVER, AND THIS IS THE CRUCIAL POINT, LADIES AND GENTLEMEN OF THE JURY' – the bottom box burst and Mr Ball sank by another inch (2.5 cm.) – 'THE CRUCIAL POINT, ER, THE CRUCIAL POINT' – box number two collapsed in a puff of scented soap powder: Mr Ball was sinking fast, Norah The Nose sliding from his view – 'crucial, crucial ... oh, bugger#'

The last box slid sideways in the way flattened soap boxes do when a fat little man has been standing on them for too long. Mr Ball slipped into a fragrant winter wonderland. With added conditioner.

'A suitable point on which to conclude for the day,' Judge Beak announced suddenly, having just woken up and realised that there was a puzzling silence in court. 'You agree, Mr Crane?'

'H'er, h'ath h'your onour h'witheth,' Mr Crane said, unbending himself and standing up.

'Mr Ball?'

The little blue flag gave a slow, sad, negative shake as Mr Ball sat on the remains of his SudsForMuds, tears streaming down his cheeks and into the folds of his wig.

I felt sorry for Horace Ball. I glanced up to find that The Nun With Guitar was also looking at him sympathetically. Then she looked up at me and shook her head slowly and sadly, a wry smile on her face.

And then she winked at me. And drew a black-painted nail slowly down her chest as if she had an itch.

Just where she didn't have an undergarment.

I knew she was one of those I had to speak to. I didn't want to. I wanted to keep her an idea, a beautiful image. I had this fear that once she spoke to me she would turn out to be just a normal human being, someone with unexpected flaws, a bit like finding out that the gorgeous girl you worshipped when you were growing up farts in bed.

Mentally I put her at the bottom of the list. I put the list in my pocket.

I didn't realise that it was upside down.

Horlicks.

Chapter XII. First Encounter With the Nun With Guitar

I walked around for a while after leaving the court. I needed some time to think, away from the others. The Major was my next obvious target, but also not so for the same reason. After the mention of a major in the court room he'd be on his guard. He'd think twice about any question someone asked him, even perfectly innocent ones such as "Have you got the time?"

(Thinking about it, that question could definitely be interpreted the wrong way.)

I meandered along in the afternoon sun, browsing shop windows. I find it a handy way of letting the brain cells get on with their job while I do as little as possible. While in this vacant state I noticed a little bakery tucked in-between two other shops. On impulse I popped in. The entrance was deceptive: the shop stretched away for quite a distance, gleaming shelves holding – almost groaning under – a selection of cream cakes, buns, chocolate eclairs such as would make any child's eyes pop out of their head in wonder. Behind the barriers of children's delights stood a smiling, rosy-cheeked woman, straight out of an advert for Mother's Apple Pie.

'I'd like a blackberry pie,' I said. 'A small one will do.'

'Will that be for Charlie the Mouse?' she asked. For a moment I wasn't sure what to say.

'Yes, for Charlie the Mouse,' I agreed eventually.

'Ah, such a sweet little thing. A real ladies' man. And would you be wanting the coconut ice for his little wife?'

'Um, yes, good idea.'

'He is devoted to her,' Beaming Apple Pie said, taking out two of the smallest boxes I have ever seen – about a tenth of the size of a match box – and carefully placing in one a tiny but perfectly made blackberry pie and a tiny, perfectly made slice of coconut ice in the other. She tied a little blue ribbon around one, and a little pink ribbon around the other. I slipped the two boxes into my jacket pocket and paid for them before quickly leaving.

Had I just bought a tiny little blackberry pie for a mouse? And a tiny little wedge of coconut ice for his missus?

I shook my head to clear it. And then turned to see if the shop still existed. I had this horrible feeling travelling up and down my spine that it would no longer be there. It would have turned into a firm of undertakers, with a grinning skull over the front entrance.

But it was. Still there. Along with rosy-cheeked woman serving a mother and her young son. He was wearing grey shorts and a red-striped school blazer. With a red-striped cap. His grey socks were down, his black shoes scuffed. He had his hands jammed into his trouser pockets and a scowl on his face.

Somehow I just knew that, if I asked, his name would turn out to be William. Just William.

I hurried away as fast as I could. I needed a drink. A solid drink that would tell me that this was the real world, and I wasn't about to meet Alice, a Queen and a Mad Hatter at a tea party around the corner.

Just then a picture of the Mad Hatter popped into my head. A white rabbit wearing a top hat, waistcoat and fob watch: Vicar Preachy dressed up as a rabbit to marry a shy couple of bunnies. I was seriously beginning to wonder if I wasn't going mad, one part of me re-assuring the other that only sane people would think that, the other unhelpfully suggesting that many mad people realise that they are insane, they just can't do anything about it.

There was no doubt about it. I really needed that strong drink.

I walked into the pub next to the hotel, the good old Baby's Arms. And back into reality, thank god. The shy bunnies were assembled in a group at the furtherest, darkest end. There was a bunny ordering drinks for them, a bunny I automatically named Bunny Blue, the perfect Bunny true, the sort who would get on with everyone. Handsome without being too overly good looking; intelligent without being too smart; witty, but not the court jester; well off but not stinking rich.

It's one of the distinctive traits of the species: the least shy will be elected to do most of the getting and gathering where humans are involved. But the way Bunny Blue was chatting to the barmaid I rather suspected that there was something not kosher about him. He just didn't look like a real shy bunny.

'So, how's the convention going?' I asked casually, sitting on a bar stool next to him, trying not to get caught on a cactus in a miniature rock garden on the counter, some theme of the week or other, or a subliminal message put there to make people think of the desert and feel thirsty.

'Great. Couldn't be better,' he replied easily. Too easily for the ultra shy.

'You aren't really a bunny, are you?' I asked. Underneath those buck teeth I could sense a broad grin.

'No, I'm not, actually. This is just a disguise.'

'Let me guess. You're infiltrating the group for a reason. They're a secret terrorist cell?'

Again, that grin. The kind of easy-going grin which makes people like the man underneath. The bunny underneath. An honest grin. The kind of grin that could be lethal in the wrong hands, but I had a hunch that Bunny Blue was on the level.

'Not at all,' he said. 'They're exactly what they claim to be, just a bunch of very shy single people on a dating meet. Which is why I'm here.'

He winked.

Bunny winks take quite a while. They've got a distance to travel.

'It's not totally a ruse. The thing is, I'm single and on the lookout myself. But I realised, after I broke up with my last girlfriend, that I prefer the shy, retiring type. Demure, you know? And where better to find someone like that than here?'

He had a point. A straight going out with a shy bunny. It would probably work.

'Good luck,' I said, as he picked up the tray of drinks.

'Cheers. I think I've already met The One – that Significant Other.'

'Bunny Pale Pink?' I asked. I'd already noticed her amongst the others, sitting quietly, her lovely bright open bunny eyes locked on Bunny Blue. Matilda was sitting next to her as many shy girls do, seeking comfort in numbers. Sad Sid was sitting alone at a table nearby, pretending to be reading a book, sneaking glances at Matilda. He was so engrossed he hadn't noticed Bunny Evil merging into the shadows not too far behind him. I don't think any of them had. He had a glass in his hand. He wasn't drinking from it.

It was knife shaped.

'That's the one,' Bunny Blue said. 'Cute, isn't she?'

'Cutest bunny I ever did see,' I agreed.

'That she is. See you later.'

I ordered a whisky on the rocks and watched him as he returned to the group, sitting down next to the deliciously cute Bunny Pale Pink, her eyes fluttering at him as he sat down. After the barmaid had poured the whisky over the rocks in the little cactus garden I explained that what I had meant was whisky and ice, not all over the miniature gardens. She told me that I should have said so, and poured me a fresh one, charging me for both.

So, I thought, that old trick. Pretending to be some hick pub, but waiting for some big-city sucker to ask for something such as "double whisky on the rocks". One double quickly poured over the rocks and, sorry, sir, that is what you requested. Innocent rural waitress takes orders literally. It's done every night somewhere in the world.

Just as well I hadn't asked for a chaser.

I told her that I'd complain to the management as I passed a dud twenty pound note. I always do that when I'm passing a forged note. They forget to check. I was about to check my change when I noticed the Nun With Guitar sitting quietly in a nook, reading what looked like a breviary, a glass of tomato juice in front of her. White face, black eyeshadow, black lipstick, shimmering yellow and white habit. I downed my whiskey and ordered another. It was as good a time as any other to have a word. Then I downed that whiskey and ordered another. It was as good a time as any other to have a word. So I downed that one and ordered another. By then it was an excellent time to have a word.

'Afternoon, sister,' I said, approaching. 'Could I offer to buy you a drink?'

'Bloody Mary,' she said, not looking up. 'Vit zelery. Make it double.'

She spoke with a Russian accent. One of those deep, husky, yet soft female accents which would have any red-blooded man signing up for the first course in Marx he could find. Well, in the good old days, before the wall came down, when we all knew where we stood, and all female Russian agents were beautiful, and could make "Da, komrade" sound like it should be wrapped in plastic and kept only on the top shelf, well above the magazines for better homes and cuter curtains.

I got her drink and sat down next to her. The way she was holding her book pulled the slit in the top part of her shimmering yellow habit slightly apart, straining against her chest in a way no Nun With Guitar should be allowed to get away with.

'Are you really a nun?' I asked, deciding that straight talking and keeping my eyes away from her bosom was the best option.

'Ve are all none,' she replied, still reading, or at least looking at her breviary in the way women do while they wait for you to say something worth looking up for. I put my thumb to my nose and waggled my fingers at her.

'Az Zartre zaid,' she added.

Great. All I needed was a philosophical Goth nun. Suddenly she put the book down. I noticed the title: "Jiggle those attributes: How to make a fortune from topless dancing. By John Jones".

(Not the real title to the book she was reading, in case you wondered. And actually it was a magazine about motorbikes, but Beazeley won't let me say so.)

'Zomeone vunz zaid zat nudding iz real,' she said, turning her eyes on me. 'Doz dod mean zat nudding iz, or everyting iz nod?'

Boy, those eyes# A man could get lost in those eyes and never want to come out again. I experienced a feeling which I encountered once years before and have spent much time since looking for a word to describe it. You see a person who you think is sexy as hell. But it's not just physical, it's – it is as if the other person is your other half, as if you could merge to form the perfect individual. The closest I've come to a single word to describe it is "triple-euphoria-on-toast-with-anchovies". "And-hot-melting-butter". "Not-margarine,-butter". And even that doesn't do it.

And now I was feeling toast for a Nun With Guitar. As if I didn't have enough problems.

I decided to concentrate on her question. Keep things platonic. Not let her see the strange feelings I could feel coursing through my veins, especially the ones around the belly button which seem to develop a life of their own under certain circumstances.

"Someone once said that nothing is real" she had said. Focus on that. Nothing is real. Fortunately it was a question I had often pondered over during the early hours of the morning after the urban foxes had woken me up by knocking over the dustbins.

'You have a problem with foxes where you live too?' I asked.

'Yez. Zey are ze nuizance. I uzed a zhotgun on zem vunz, but ze neighbourz made ze complaint.'

'Should have used the shotgun on the neighbours first,' I suggested, saying the first silly thing that came into my head, feeling the same way I had years before when trying to chat up Leonie Leftfield at school. Like a total prat, in other words.

She looked at me, the sort of look some women have, inwardly calm and tranquil but very alert, trying to figure something out about you, confident that they will eventually get there. My mother used to look at me that way a lot. She would flex her fingers while doing so, as if her hand had suddenly gone numb.

She raised her glass.

'Za lyoo-bóf', she said.

'Zlooey boff to you too,' I responded, clinking glasses.

We looked into each other's eyes for a few seconds. The world around us had disappeared.

'Vot iz your mizzion?' the Nun With Guitar asked, taking a sip of her Bloody Mary, her eyes still locked on mine.

When I try that I always end up dribbling down my shirt. Not this nun.

'My mission?'

'Vy are you here?'

'I'm just doing a job like everyone else. You know.'

She took another sip, quite plainly disbelieving me. My mother would have been reaching for the large wooden spoon at that point. More exercise.

'I like you,' she decided. 'I zhall kall you Viktor.'

After saying that she liked me she could have called me anything she wanted, but I thought I'd risk putting the record straight.

'Or E,' she added, before I could.

'My name's Irene,' I said. 'Call me the happiness fairy. I go wherever there's unhappiness and wave my delicate wand. It doesn't always work, mind, but it's worth a shot. I have these fragile green, diaphanous wings, and stardust in my hair.'

She chuckled in Russian. The sort of chuckle that makes you tingle all over.

'But, Viktor, or E, you are called Zhirley, you veigh twenty-two ztone and only zhave every tird week,' she said.

That puzzled me.

'No I'm not,' I said after a reasonable pause to indicate my confusion. 'I look after myself. Perhaps not as fit as I could be, but I do my best.'

'Ah, Viktor, Or E, but you vill be in zis book,' she said.

'Ah, good point.'

I scratched my head. She was right. I can hardly describe myself accurately when everyone else is disguised. But twenty-two stone and shave only every third week?

'I tell you what,' I said, 'we'll compromise. I'll be tall and slim and shave every fifth day, how's that?'

Another look. Another intriguing half-smile.

'Very, vell, Viktor, Or E. Zere is zomething aboud a man of ztubble zat exzites me. Bud ve muzt eggzplore ze man zat iz you a lidddle further, I tink.'

She took another sip of her Bloody Mary, the stick of celery sliding slowly across her cheek. For a moment I was envious of that stick of celery. I wanted to grab it and lick it all over.

But I believe you can be arrested for that sort of thing.

'Are you human?' she asked. Twenty questions, and this was number two.

'As human as anyone else. Cut me, do I not bleed? Smack me with a wet kipper, do I not smell of fish for days afterwards?'

'I'm not,' she said.

'Not what?'

'A fizh.'

We looked at each other with understanding. We both understood that neither of us knew what the other was talking about. It felt like the beginning of a great relationship.

But a forbidden great relationship.

Or a great forbidden relationship.

'Vat vere you born vor?' she asked.

'I don't know, I don't think my parents kept the receipt.'

She smiled. Her eyes were deeply alight.

'I, Viktor, or E, voz born to roam. Vere you? Ve could go togedder.'

Suddenly I felt I had to get out of there. Any more time in her company and I could well forget my original mission in favour of ....

'I've got to go,' I said, finishing my drink. 'I'll see you later. Good luck with the topless dancing.'

'Room Zerteen,' she said, picking up her book. 'Do nod be lade. I do nod like ztaying up avter eleven.'

I nodded and left. I knew there was no room 13. Believe me. There never is in places like the Railway Tavern. It's that superstition thing. The Chinese don't like it. The numbers go 11 ...12... 14...15...

I knew she had been too good to be true.

Unless it was some sort of challenge she was setting me.

No, give up the wishful thinking, I thought.

No, there is no 13. Believe me. There never is, no matter what they tell you.

Though I have stayed in a hotel where the numbers went 11...12...00...14...15... The 00 was for special people only. God, I'll never forget that weekend.

....

Miss Young Lovely across the street is clipping her front hedge. She's using a silly little pair of shears. Secateurs, I think they're called. The sort an attractive young woman might use to attract some fit young person to pop over and offer to do the job with his electric hedge trimmer, it won't take long and the gorgeous young woman would take forever with those little clippers, and yes, a cup of tea would be lovely, thank you.

Any other time I'd be over there like a shot. The memory of the Nun With Guitar ... well, now just doesn't feel like the time.

Anyway, the hedge trimmers have never worked since Barra Coulder borrowed them.

You love, you lose. It's the story of our lives.

Well, perhaps not this story, because some loved and won.

Only I can't tell you who.

So they didn't.

Baskets.

Chapter XIV. The Major and the Exploding Bully Beef

I've just realised something interesting. Well, strange, anyway. Beazeley – he's making himself another brandy, so I'll get this in sharpish – Beazeley's nitpicked about every single character bar one. "The Vulture's not tall enough." Not tall enough? Nine feet tall? Any taller and his head would have gone through the blasted ceiling.

"You haven't made Mr Ball fat enough." Okay, Beaze, he was fifteen feet around at the smallest point, his neck. Happy?

"Mr Sleepy doesn't snore as much as he did." Beazeley, I've got him snoring right the way through, apart from the one time, okay?

"Strawberry Mousse's – things – were never that big." Jeez, Beaze, give me a break. Whine, whine, whinge, whinge.

If he's not careful I'll get him some Fugu liver.

That'll make him jump the snark.

I wonder where that phrase comes from.

But the thing is, everyone gets the critical treatment – the Major's moustache is wrong, Vicar Preachy's dog collar was actually cerise, the ghost doesn't fit, etcetera, etcetera, et-blasted-cetera until doomsday and a good couple of years beyond. Moan, moan moan. Carp, carp, carp. Whinge, whinge, whinge. Apart from one character. The Nun With Guitar.

It's strange that. At the time, as I've mentioned, she hit my psyche like a ton of hormonal bricks on speed. I suppose she could be quite disquieting to others, for different reasons. You can criticise a vicar, question a prelate, argue over a bishop, even caricature a Mother Superior (though not to her face, of course, not unless you want to die young and horribly). But somehow a nun, even a Goth nun with stunning eyes and a figure which gave a different interpretation of the meaning of the word "heaven" – well, it's just not done, is it? And I kept getting this image of her in the shower popping into my head.

Unfortunately the glass was frosted.

I had decided that the next time I saw that ghost I'd barbecue him for putting that thought into my mind. Venison a-la-petrol-or-the-nearest-inflammable-substance. But that only raised the question of how you barbecue a ghost. Or solve the problem of a Nun With Guitar.

That evening I had a cold shower before dinner. Personally I hate cold showers, but I needed to keep my mind on the job. I didn't have the time to let myself get carried away. In fact I didn't have time to have dinner, so I called room service and had them send up a selection of sandwiches which I multi-tasked by eating while I was having the cold shower. Then I went outside and sat in the early evening twilight on the bench that faced the hotel entrance, admiring the rose creepers that surrounded the entrance, wondering if they changed the plants each day and what tomorrow's would be. I wasn't sure who was going to pop out for a quiet early-evening stroll on their own – I wasn't even sure that anyone would, though I knew for certain that someone would.

Beazeley has just wafted into the room having returned from Planet Nervous and read that without a comment. I think he might be coming down with something. Am I concerned about Beazeley's health? Damn right I am, it could be catching.

Where was I? Ah, yes, sitting watching the hotel entrance, drinking in the sweet smell of the blossoming rose creepers.

I noticed the Major slipping out, sauntering in the way some people do when they're anxious not to attract attention. He looked ridiculous trying to do it: when you've spent your entire life cultivating a ramrod stiff back you can't suddenly slouch around with your hands in your pockets, you'll do yourself an injury.

Hello, I thought to myself, and where might you be going in such a casual fashion? Out for a stroll and a breath of fresh air? I decided to follow his example and follow him. He didn't go far. Just down to one of those alleyways of dusty little shops. Dusty book shops, dusty pet shops, dusty barber shops. And a dusty little pub which the Major was headed for. The type of pub a man goes to when he wants to be able to sit on his own with a drink, staring into nowhere, bitterly remembering all the slings and arrows life had thrown at him. And then, having had a few drinks, going out to find the type of pub where you can get seriously sozzled and tell a complete stranger your entire life story, ending up with the classic "crying into your beer" trick. I didn't want to hear the Major's entire life story. But I suspected there was a section of it that could prove useful. First I had to make sure that I appeared as someone he could trust. A sympathetic brother soldier. There was a dusty fancy dress emporium in the alley. They're always emporia when they're that small. And they always have these unintelligible notices in the window.

"Go as Gorgon the Gorilla – Hilarious#"; "Surprise them with Ghandi's loincloth# (discount available depending on size)"; "Sorry no bunny costumes left#".

I wandered in. Behind the dusty counter a dusty old man in a dusty old cardigan was re-reading a dusty old newspaper which I guessed was about ten, if not fifty, years old. He looked up in surprise.

'Sorry,' he said, 'we're all out of bunny costumes.'

'Yes, I know,' I replied. 'I saw the notice. Actually I'm not the bunny type. I'm looking for a soldier's uniform. Colonel would do nicely.'

'Gestapo or Wafffen SS?' he asked.

'Well, no, British uniform. Modern day.'

'Ah, I see. That's unusual. Most people want jackboots for some reason. I had a Nun With Guitar asking for them today. Just as well you don't. I'm afraid they're all out. Miss Marple took the last one yesterday. She looked ... interesting. But I think I have a British uniform. Colonel, you say?'

'Colonel would do nicely. Major, if you don't have the higher rank.'

'Ah, now I'm sure I have a major somewhere. Give me a moment.'

I looked around as he shuffled off in carpet slippers to a room at the back. There were a few mannequins dressed with the most popular costumes. Mandatory Marie Antoinette, desperately needing dry-cleaning. British bobby, circa 1900, complete with wooden truncheon, ditto. Wild West fringed outfit, from its shape presumably supposed to represent Annie Oakley with deep cleavage. Butler's uniform, Art Deco period – Jeeves, I would imagine. Battered old bowler and black jacket – Charlie Chaplin? As the jacket was hanging on the stool the old man had been sitting on, and the bowler on the counter, I had to presume they were his. He came shuffling back, blowing dust off a box.

'You're in luck,' he said, coughing. 'British Army major's uniform. Pristine condition. Never been worn before.'

He opened the box to prove the point. My luck was in. It was probably outdated, but sealed in waxpaper, with just a hint of must and mothballs. It even had the red tabs and red band around the cap of a general staff officer.

'Swagger stick?' I asked.

'Of course.'

'Little moustache?' I suggested, not hopefully. I won't say that the moustache was crucial, but it was the defining part. The little moustache army officers grow when they realise they've reached the height of promotion and aren't going any further. Just like the one the Major had developed.

'Of course,' repeated cardigan man.

Oh, yes# My lucky day.

(Okay, these #'s are becoming irritating. The !'s are a bit of a turn-off, but not as much as the #'s. Let's go back to using the !'s. If you prefer the #'s just overwrite the !'s with #'s. You can't overwrite a #

with an !, but you can do it the other way round, and even play noughts and crosses with them. Now, where was I?)

'Could I try it on?' I asked.

'Certainly,' he said. 'There's a changing room at the back.'

He returned to his newspaper as I shot into the changing room. Ten minutes later I emerged as Major Arthur Arbuckle with silly little moustache and swagger stick.

'A very good fit,' noted cardigan man.

I couldn't agree more. A uniform suits me. Think of some old black and white movie star. Or the early colours. One of the big ones of the golden era. David Niven. Richard Burton. Elisabeth Taylor. Clint Eastwood. James Bond.

Not Marilyn Monroe.

Okay, perhaps MM in a uniform.

'Perfect fit,' I said. 'I'll need it for about an hour.'

His eyebrows raised slightly, but he nodded.

'I'll give you a discount then. I normally charge by the day, but competition is fierce these days. Try not to get it dirty.'

'I won't,' I promised, rather ambiguously to my mind, but he returned to his out-of-date newspaper without comment. I slipped across to the dusty pub, made sure the cap was on straight, swagger stick under arm, stiffened my back, and sauntered into the pub as if I either owned it or didn't care who did. Just the way they do in cartoons.

'Two pink gins,' I said to the barman, a hefty chap reading last week's Racing Post, a sour and cynical look on his face as he looked up. 'Make them doubles. I'll be sitting over there.'

I nodded to the table where the major was sitting, back ramrod straight, looking into nowhere, his face a combination of sadness and anger. I marched over and slipped into the chair opposite. I dropped my peaked cap casually onto the table, along with the swagger stick.

'Drinking alone, old boy?' I asked. 'Not good, not good at all. Nothing wrong with a snifter, but not alone, old boy, not alone.'

He gave me a bitter look and took a sip of his drink. The barman came up and banged the pink gins on the table, then walked away, flicking a tea-towel at some dust, just to remind it of who was boss. Then he sneezed and carried on.

'None of your business,' the Major said. 'Not any longer. Not anymore. I'm a civilian now. Not your business any more. Civilian. That's what I am now. Civilian.'

I gave him a slow, confident style, took a sip of foul pink gin and crossed my right leg over the left, polished brown shoe swinging nonchalantly.

I don't know who originally came up with the idea of a pink gin, but they were definitely masochistic. Absolutely horrible stuff.

Used drain cleaner.

Ugh triple time.

'Now I'm not sure that's strictly true,' I said. He gave me a sudden agonised look, the type that sees a light at the end of the tunnel, but knows that it's an illusion.

'They're re-opening the case?' he asked, plaintively.

'Unlikely, I'm afraid, old boy. I'm just trying to tie up some loose ends. I've read the file, but I'd like to hear your side of things.'

Needless to say I hadn't read any file, but with the army you know there's going to be a file, quite probably several, in triplicate. I know some people in Military Intelligence. They store everything on computer files. And then print it out in case the computer gets taken out by a nuclear strike.

'What's the use?' he asked. 'No damned use at all. That's the point. Isn't any use, is there?'

Oh, great. One of the "what's the use?" brigade. About as much help as a – a – paper tepee in a thunderstorm.

'Sometimes it helps to speak to a brother officer,' I replied. 'Get it out of your system. I know there's no going back, but – well, worth a try, I would say, wouldn't you, old boy?'

He nodded at the pips on my shoulders.

'Took me twenty years to make major,' he said. 'Twenty hard years. And then they throw me out on my ear. Threw me out. On my ear. All because of that damned politician. Damned politician!'

Here we go, I thought, paydirt!

'Never trust a politician,' I said.

The only person who would disagree with that would be a politician. And they'd be lying.

'Twenty years,' he repeated, his drink shaking in his hand. He pressed it down on the table to control it. Left handed, I noticed. That was important. Not that it suggested anything sinister. Just that it helps to remember which is the main arm if you end up having punches thrown at you. And it isn't unusual for the punching bit to happen just before the crying-in-the-beer bit.

'Twenty years,' he repeated, making me wonder how long this conversation was going to take to get anywhere interesting. 'You know, they wouldn't take me at first. When I first applied to join officer school. Said I didn't have the qualifications. No qualifications, they said. Not enough, not the type they needed. I could be a private if I wanted. Not officer material.'

He paused and glared at me again.

'The truth is that they'd all been to Eton and Harrow, places like that,' he continued. 'I had to settle for Lower Piddlington Bog Standard Comprehensive For Poor Peasants. But I was determined. I went to night school for six years. Six damned years. They couldn't refuse me after I'd been awarded my Diploma in War Games. Only a third, but it was still mine. They didn't like it, but they had no choice. But it didn't stop them from making it difficult for me to get promotion. But I got it. It took twenty years, but I got there. And then it happened.'

'Why don't you start from the beginning?' I suggested. 'I mean when it happened,' I added hastily, in case he thought I was asking him to tell me his life story starting from his first memory of his childhood and his feelings for his mother.

'Why? You've read about it. The official version. All in the files, isn't it? Their damned official version. Their files.'

"The official version" said with so much scorn he was almost spitting.

'That's just it,' I replied as easily and confidently as I could. 'It's the official version. I want the unofficial, unexpurgated, un-filleted version. Look, I know there's not much we can do for you. But we can be better prepared for the next time Johnny Politician comes knocking on the door.' He gave me a trembling sneer.

'Why should I help? None of the others did anything for me at the time. Nothing. Not a thing. Brother officers? Brothers in arms? Hah! More like brother damned Judases, they were. Judases. Damned Judases.'

'Don't worry, we've got the others in our sights too. If I can get the right evidence there are one or two people with a shock in store.' There was a gleam in his eye. A weak point. He wanted revenge.

'Can't talk in here,' he said, casting a glance at the barman. 'Too many civilian ears wagging.'

Mine, for a start.

'I think we're quite safe. There's only the barman, and he can't hear us.'

'I tell you what,' the Major said, leaning forward. 'I'll use code, how's that?'

Please don't I thought

'You know I was chief procurements officer for – let's say bully beef.'

156

'Bully beef? Ah, yes, of course, bully beef.'

'Yes, the exploding kind of bully beef.'

I nodded empathetically. Exploding bully beef? The man was off his rocker.

'Now I'd been working on a deal for an upgraded version of the XK Mark Three. Now you know the Mark Three – can of bully beef.'

'Not quite my area of expertise,' I coughed. 'Tell me all about it.'

'Well, exploding – bully beef – can make quite a mess, you know. Of course, a professional can bring down a thirty-metre bridge with a single can. Half a can if it's a wooden bridge. The Mark Three's good, one of the best we've ever had, but it's a bit dated. After all we've been using it since the last war.'

For "the last war", read World War Two. To people like the Major other conflicts don't count. They're the types who think that the reason the Yanks lost Vietnam is because the Brits weren't there to show them how to do the job properly.

'Now I had a contract almost signed, sealed and delivered for a long range version of the Mark Three. It could go much further, and faster. It was going to be a real feather in my cap. Once that was done they couldn't refuse me promotion. For once I had found a challenge I knew I could pull off. I know I wasn't perhaps the best major around. Not that good at getting people to march around properly, that sort of thing. At least not if there was a cliff nearby. But I was good on the contracts side, and the new Mark Three – the Mark IV, as I called it – was going to prove it.'

'Something you could get your teeth into?' I suggested.

'Precisely. The Mark IV – tin had – let's say, added gravy.'

'Could make a right stew of things?'

'Exactly! I can see you understand.'

He paused to take a sip of his pink gin and the bitter look returned. I wasn't sure whether that was because of his memories or the absolutely foul taste of the drink.

'Then along came the – let's call the evil Minister for Weapons of Minor Destruction. A junior minister. I wouldn't have trusted him to tie his shoe laces properly. But he was friends with the Minister for Toy Trains and Christmas Tree Regulations. And he had a contact in a different company who were also trying to sell us a new version of the Mark Three. Except that theirs was nowhere near as good as even the old Mark Three. Let's say that theirs contained too much – fat. Quite often the cans exploded when they weren't supposed to. They were a damned health hazard. Handle them the wrong way and you'd have egg all over your face.'

'But minor minister wasn't interested in quality?' I suggested. 'He was going to get a nice little backhander from the dodgy – bully beef company.'

'Exactly. His only problem was me. I had the figures to prove everything. The tests we had run. The company I was talking to were even prepared to discuss meeting the other company's price, or close to it.' He shook his head at the memory. 'The worst thing was that the other company was Argentinian. Can you believe that? Politicians prepared to go to the Argentinians for – bully beef.'

'That is low,' I agreed. 'Buying bully beef from Argentina. Very low.'

'I was naive. I thought I had all the cards. I didn't realise that Edgar The Ears was playing with a stacked deck.' Now it was out! He'd used Edgar The Ears's name. All I had to do was to get him to tell me what the "bully beef" really was.

But I mean, really, "stacked deck"? Oh, dear. He really did use the phrase.

'He began spreading rumours,' the Major continued before I could say anything. 'Got his odious little friends to suggest that I was

. . . 13 . . .

playing for the other side. And you know what happens when your fellow officers start believing that you're playing for the other side. Disgusting! I would never have played for the other side. Just because I'm not married doesn't mean anything. Look at Monty. Brilliant Field Marshal. He was married. But they still spread rumours. Only after he had gone, though. They couldn't stand the fact that he was better than them.'

I suddenly realised what he was on about. Little touches in the locker room. A friendship in the field just a tadge too close for comfort. The hesitant touch on cavalry twill, just as the book said.

'Of course they never say it out straight,' the Major continued. 'Innuendo. Gossip behind your back. I couldn't believe my fellow officers could believe a politician's lies. Fellow damned officers, hah! Judases.'

He downed his pink gin, looking into the glass in his hand afterwards as if seeking enlightenment there.

'I know I wasn't much good at being a soldier,' he told the glass. 'I knew my limitations. I regretted them. But I had to live with them. Most of all I wanted to see live combat. Face the bullets. Go into the action armed with the latest exploding bully beef. Bomb real bridges in real battle. See if I really had what it takes. But they never sent me anywhere where I could prove myself – or not, as the case might be. You don't know how soul-destroying that is.'

'I think I do,' I said, quite honestly.

'Do you?' he asked, empty glass still in hand. He looked into my eyes. I looked into his. For a moment it was as if we connected on some mental plane. He probably didn't realise it, but the look in my eyes was one of admiration and sympathy. I didn't share his urge to be shot at to prove himself, but just as I have no urge to go trainspotting I can understand that some people do, and it means a lot to them. A lot of people support their football clubs even though none of the

159

players come from their area or even country. Passion rarely makes sense. The Major was passionate. I could empathise with that. I had presumed him to be a prejudiced, narrow-minded clot of an officer. He had turned out to be more complex than I expected. I had the feeling that he knew what a miserable figure he looked as he put on the same type of brown suit and dull yellow shirt every morning. No wonder he looked for places like that dingy pub, somewhere to drown the world out. The world and himself. Because he hated himself.

'And that was that,' he said. 'Offered a transfer to the – Catering Corps. Suggested I might fit in better with them. Damn silly slur on them, I've known some fine cooks. You don't mix with them, of course, but some damn fine cooks. But there's the rub. If I accepted it would be an admission of guilt. I had no option but to resign. That's how they do it, you see. The army. Make it impossible for you to stay. At least in civvy street they have the honesty to fire you to your face. The army just make it impossible for you to stay.'

He obviously didn't know civvy street that well. He finally put his empty glass down.

'And that was that,' he concluded. 'End of story. End of twenty years hard slog. Story over. Finished. End of story.'

End of story? Whoah, Major, we haven't even started yet.

He stood up.

'You were right, you know. It does feel better now that I've spoken to a fellow officer. I don't feel that bad about it any more. I'm sure you'll pass the truth on to those who matter. Major, I salute you.'

And he did. Ramrod straight, crisply executed. A perfect salute. And then turned on his heel and strode out. I waved a vague salute after him. The barman came over, flicking his towel.

'Poor bloke,' he said. 'You'd think they was all mates, them officers together. My son's in the army. He can't speak highly enough of his officers.'

I was about to make the classic mistake of saying something the character I was pretending to be wouldn't say. Bad mistake. You must always shift the conversation back to the other person.

'You must be proud of your lad,' I said instead.

'Oh, I am that, sir. Very proud.'

'It's the women who find it difficult, I would imagine,' I suggested. 'His mother must be continually fretting about him.'

'Oh, no, sir. Never knew who his mother was. Neither did I. She was just a fly-by-night. Left me and 'im. Just the two of us. Still, better that way. Just us together.'

I think I must have put a hand to my head trying to understand that. The next thing his voice was full of sympathy.

'Another pink gin, sir? On the house. I can see how you're tired. Never stops, does it, sir? A free pink gin, double, on the house, as I said, sir.'

I shivered. The very idea of another of that vile drink had me reaching for the telephone directory, the Temperance section.

'No, thanks, but no,' I said, standing up, putting the peaked cap on and picking up the swagger stick. 'I have things I must get done.'

'I understand, your honour. Still, offer's still open when you get a chance to pop in again. I'll tell the daughter.'

I kind of guessed the daughter's mother had disappeared in the same fashion as his son's, leaving only the three of them. All together on their own.

'Very kind,' I said. 'Arthur Arbuckle's the name. Major Arthur Arbuckle.'

I went back to the fancy dress shop to return the costume.

'Good party, sir?' asked cardigan man as I placed the major's outfit on the counter.

'I think the others enjoyed it more than I did,' I remarked.

'It often happens that way. Perhaps a bunny costume would have been better.'

He scratched his ear with a pencil, scoring a grey mark across his earlobe.

'Though we're all out of bunny costumes at the moment.'

I think he was Beazeley's father.

Chapter XV. The Recorder in the Dumb Waiter

Miss Lovely Legs across the road has her lights on again, curtains undrawn. It reminds me of that film by Alfred Hitchcock, *Rear Window*. I'm expecting some man – her husband, boyfriend, whatever – to come in and start a fight with her. I'd have to be James Stewart in that scenario, I suppose. Fortunately no-one has ever suggested that I look anything like James Stewart, so I won't have to play the hero role.

Anyway, she's just sitting there watching television.

Looks a bit like Grace Kelly, mind.

I wonder what she does for a living.

Someone a couple of houses down has started playing the Saxophone. Funnily enough no-one ever calls the police to complain about the noise. Whoever it is is quite good, actually.

Bass.

Just as well it isn't a bassoon. I might call the police myself.

Oh, well, je ne regrette rien, as Edith Piaf used to sing. I do, but let's pretend I don't and carry on.

I'll bet she did, too.

In the early hours.

Before the sunrise.

Ho hum.

That evening back in – what did I call it? Wellbury. That summer's evening.

Later that evening I was going for a walk along the corridors to get some exercise, doing the occasional push up against a door as I passed, having listened for any internal presence. It's the sort of habit you get into that keeps you fit. I hadn't found anything interesting, such as the sound of a Nun With Guitar singing Ave Maria, and was about to give up for the evening when an alcove psst at me.

'Psst!'

A shy bunny, I presumed. I slipped into the alcove to find Bonnie out of costume.

'Taking a chance, aren't you?' I suggested. 'Out of your room with no costume?'

'I've been looking for you,' he said. 'The recorder's stuck in the dumb waiter.'

I looked at him. I've heard some incredible statements in my time, but a recorder stuck in a dumb waiter was a new one on me.

'We've got to hurry,' he said. 'Clyde's keeping her company, and she's not wearing her clown costume either. She could be discovered at any time.'

He pulled me by my sleeve and I followed him, trotting along behind him, downstairs, upstairs, leftstairs, rightstairs, until we came to the dumb waiter close to their room. Clyde was sitting next to the dumb waiter hatch, holding the recorder's tiny little hand sticking out from a gap.

'He'll look after her now,' Bonnie said to Clyde. 'Let's get back to the room.'

'Will you be okay, Minti?' asked Clyde. A muffled reply indicated that she would, so long as I held her hand, which I did.

I've been in tough situations before. But I've never held the hand of a trained killer sitting in a dumb waiter. A soft little hand. Clutching. Clutching at mine. My spine shivered at the thought of what her other soft little hand might be holding.

Razorblades.

The Clowns scuttled back to their room, leaving me alone with a trained killer. I peered into the gap. Two dark, shining eyes looked back at me. The two dark, shining eyes of someone for whom a human life was merely a job to get out of the way. Two dark, shining eyes with a hint of tears in them.

Very confusing.

'The hatch has jammed the dumb waiter,' I said, probably not too helpfully. The same two dark eyes blinked slowly from the darkness, and the soft little hand pressed harder.

I felt along the hatch. The top part of it had pushed inwards, preventing the dumb waiter from moving up or down. I gave it a tug. Nothing. I gave it a more powerful tug. Still nothing. I braced myself and pulled with all my strength while still holding the recorder's hand. Not a millimetre. Not even a perception of a millimetre. Which, thinking about it, was probably just as well. The moment that hatch came loose the dumb waiter was going to be going somewhere, and at that moment I still had my hand in the gap. It would have been the equivalent of slamming a car door on it. Or worse, a guillotine.

'I'll go down to reception and see if they can get a handyman or something,' I said. This was rewarded with a voluble and frightened flow of words in some foreign language which I did not understand, but took to mean "No! Please don't leave me here on my own!" It was either that or "You leave me and I'll cut you into small little pieces and feed each to my pet tiger while you're still alive, pigface." Her grip tightened to the point of becoming painful.

'Okay, okay, I won't,' I reassured her, scratching my head with my free hand. I could call Clyde and ask her to keep the recorder company while I went down to reception, but I couldn't see Bonnie agreeing to that, he was paranoid enough as it was of Judge Beak recognising either of them. Clyde staying with the recorder – without her clown costume – while Bonnie came to find me must have been agonising enough for both of them. To my relief Mildred Two and Mildred Three appeared, whistling to themselves, each carrying a basket of laundry, and wearing, for no apparent reason, silver party hats on their heads.

'Mildred Two! Mildred Three!' I called. 'Over here. This hatch is stuck, and the recorder's trapped inside.'

Mildreds Two and Three danced across, eyes wide, lipsticked mouths open.

'Oh dear, it always does that,' said Mildred Two. 'Hello, Minti, are you in there? The claustrophobia not getting to you, is it?'

A noise from inside suggested that the recorder was only just holding on.

'Just a tick, love,' said Mildred Three, handing me her basket of washing to hold in my free arm. She took a shoe off, took aim at a specific part of the hatch and gave it a firm whack. 'Try it now, love.'

There was a sudden whirring, a noise from the recorder which presumably translated as "Thanks, I don't have to kill him right now after all! Byee!", and she was on her way upwards – at least I presumed it was upwards. I only just got my hand out in time.

'It always sticks like that,' Mildred Two said. 'You have to know just the right place to hit it. Still, no time to chat, busy, busy, busy, must get on with work.'

They danced away again, Mildred Three doing so at an angle, carrying her shoe. I decided to have a word with The Clowns. Perhaps find out why it was the recorder insisted on travelling in the dumb waiter, out of sight of everyone. I was increasingly getting a feeling that there was more to the recorder than met the eye, and there was enough of that as it was, even given how small she was.

When I knocked at their door, Bonnie opened it a crack before peeking out, and then opening it for me to enter, and then quickly closing it again.

'Did she get out okay?' asked Clyde.

'Yes, yes, she's fine.'

'Put your laundry down, take a seat,' offered Bonnie.

I looked at the laundry basket under my arm. Both Mildred Three and I had forgotten about it. I put it to one side and sat down.

'So, tell, me any idea why the recorder travels by dumb waiter?' I asked.

'She finds it much easier to get around,' Clyde replied. 'It's just right for her size. And she has a problem climbing stairs, and these old hotels never have lifts.'

'You have to admire her, though,' Bonnie added, 'she told us she suffers terribly from claustrophobia. She's okay when it's moving, but when it stopped she almost died of a panic attack.'

'But she has a wonderful sense of humour,' said Clyde. 'I think that's what helps her get through.'

'You speak Hindu?' I asked, surprised.

'Hindu?' asked Clyde, also surprised. 'No. I don't think anyone speaks Hindu, do they? Can you? Don't you mean-'

'I can't. What about you? Any Oriental or Asian language?'

'I don't know anyone who speaks any Oriental or Asian language,' Clyde replied, looking at Bonnie as if to see whether he knew what I was talking about. Bonnie caught the look and misinterpreted it.

'Yes, I think we can tell him,' he said. He turned to me. 'We're breaking out of here at first light tomorrow. It's too dangerous to stick around.'

'Breaking out?'

'Just before five. We'll leave in our clown costumes, out the back way. I've worked it out. We should get to the train station for the first train. We've got the train timetable. If we blend in with the other passengers people will presume we're just normal commuters. We'll take seats away from each other, that way if one of us gets caught the other still has a chance. And we'll buy newspapers to hide behind. We'll buy tickets to London but get off before we get there, to throw them off the track.'

I refrained from pointing out that, if they were on a train, anyone on the track wouldn't need throwing off, they'd need their little bits and pieces pieced together again.

'I thought we should stay together,' Clyde said. 'I'd rather be taken with Bonnie. But he's right. If I get caught I don't want him taken with me if he can get away. What do you think?'

They looked at me with such innocent, trusting faces I didn't have the heart to tell them that it was a high risk gamble. Your average British commuter would be far too polite to comment on two clowns sitting apart, each reading a newspaper, but they'd definitely notice them and remember them. Instead I just smiled and said 'Good luck. Be careful now,' as I stood up.

'We will,' Bonnie said.

'Don't forget your washing,' Clyde added helpfully.

What worried me was that if the clowns did manage to get out without being spotted there would only be ten members of the jury left, and the trial would have to be restarted at some later date. Had it been anyone else I might have thought about shopping them before they could do anything. But Clyde and Bonnie were just so naively young and enthusiastic about the ideal family they were going to have I just couldn't help but hope that it would all come true for them.

It was one of the most difficult and easiest decisions I had ever come to. I decided that I'd just have to rely on getting a copy of the book if it came to it. And good luck to the Clowns. I hoped I'd meet them again one day when they had settled down in freedom. They'd probably be living in a twee, vomit-inducing little house with their twee, vomit inducing offspring, but, hey, each to their own.

I took the laundry down to the laundry room. Mildred Three was ecstatic. She and Mildred Two had been searching all over the laundry room for it.

'I knew I had it when I came in,' Mildred Three said, in total contradiction of all the facts. 'So clever of you.'

I muttered something about it being a pleasure and left them to it. I wandered up to the lounge to find the usual suspects watching television – Mrs Plum, Vicar Preachy, the Prim Maiden Aunt, Miss F, Miss F's mother, Strawberry Mousse and the Major. By that stage I wasn't really looking for anything apart from a bit of company.

'What's on the menu tonight?' I asked, taking a seat.

'Menu?' asked Vicar Preachy. 'We've already eaten, thanks.'

'I think he means what's on television,' interpreted Miss F's Mother.

'Funny, I thought he could speak English,' commented Vicar Preachy.

'Not much,' said Miss F. 'There was a shoot-out in a store in Kansas, but they have them every day over there.'

'I much prefer the British stuff,' said Strawberry Mousse. 'The Americans never seem to get it right.'

The Prim Maiden Aunt wagged a finger as if about to make a declaration. A tic went ping — pong across her nose. And she hiccoughed.

'Too many channels,' the Major put in. 'They make up any old rubbish these days just to fill the time. Far too many channels, you see.'

'There's a good Dracula on later,' Miss F said, making a sucking sound with her lips. 'Lots of blood and young peasant girls being –'

'Yes, my dear, but you don't want to stay up too late,' interrupted Miss F's Mother.

'Is it in black and white or colour?' asked Strawberry Mousse.

'Black and white. One of the old ones.'

'Ah, good,' said Strawberry Mousse, 'I might watch that. The colour ones just seem wrong somehow.'

'It's the quality,' said the Major. 'Same as television. When it was black and white they saw it as an art. An art, you see. Once colour came in it became cheaper and any Tom, Dick or Harry could make a film. What they called films, anyway. No quality, that's the thing.'

'*Opuntia*,' said Vicar Preachy.

'Bless you,' replied Miss F's Mother.

'No, *Opuntia*. I've been trying to remember that all day. It's the scientific name for Nopales, which, as you know, is what is more commonly known as a prickly pear.'

'My goodness,' said Miss F's Mother, and you could almost believe she gave a fig's leaf for prickly pears.

'It's an interesting question,' I said, deciding that it was time to steer things in the right direction or die of boredom, with a hopelessly optimistic feeling that I could still retrieve something from the ruins of the day. 'The trial, for example. One side claims the book's fiction, the other that it's a pack of lies. Difficult one to call, really. Unless you know what's inside, of course.'

I didn't expect anyone to actually answer. What I was looking for were the tell-tale signs of sudden stiffness, pretend lack of interest, anything that would indicate who else was involved. The Major, as I expected, developed an interest in his fingernails.

'Oh, dear, not the other one,' came an echo from the couch. It was Mrs Plum with her head in her bag. On the coffee table in front of her were a portable iron, a camping gas stove, five rolls of wool, assorted sweet wrappers and a pair of winter warmers.

And some chocolate logs, the small ones.

'How very strange,' she said, taking her head out of the bag and turning it upside down. 'First the left one, now the right one's gone. I wonder where on earth I could have left it?'

We looked at each other. Someone would have to say something. Whoever it was was going to trigger Mrs Plum off. No-one wanted that.

'Maybe it's in your room?' suggested Miss F's Mother tentatively. A good try. It might get Mrs Plum off to her room.

'No, no, my dear, I'm quite sure it can't be there. I had it at the court this afternoon, and I haven't been up to my room since then. I'm sure it was in my bag at dinner. Yes, I remember looking at poor Mr Hugo and thinking what a shame it was, having to wear those glasses and find his way with that stick.'

'Let's check the couch, it might have fallen behind the cushions,' Miss F's Mother said quickly, jumping up.

'He had ice-cream and garlic for dessert, you know,' Mrs Plum said. 'It reminds me of the time during the war, we just couldn't get garlic for love or money.'

'I'll check underneath the couch,' Strawberry Mousse put in, diving down.

'I'll search the pub,' the Major offered, heading for the door at the quick-step.

'I'll give you a hand,' said Vicar Preachy, his dog collar trailing two steps behind as his bald head flew after the Major.

'Of course not many people ate garlic in those days,' Mrs Plum was remembering, 'but we had all the poor French refugees, and they loved their garlic and snails. Now what was it they called them? It wasn't gateau, no, that's French for sugar, isn't it? Wait a minute, it'll come back to me.'

I slipped out, my last image being a tableau of Miss F half-standing to let her mother search the cushions while hopping channels, and Strawberry Mousse's white-clad legs and pink derriere sticking out from underneath the couch. It could have been an erotic sight had it not been for Mrs Plum holding her bag and describing the snails the

French refugees had apparently been so fond of. I headed rapidly upwards on the theory that the Mrs Plums of the world only go upstairs when it's absolutely essential, such as bed time. And on the other theory that the Nuns With Guitar of the world tend to go straight to their rooms after dinner, in which case I might accidentally find out which was her real room. All I had to do was listen for someone playing a guitar.

As I was strolling along with both ears alert I heard someone coming down the corridor and quickly ducked into an alcove just in case it was Mrs Plum retiring early. I stood there in darkness for a few seconds increasingly getting a strange sensation that I was not alone. The hairs on my neck rose. My shoulder blades tightened. I waited until my eyes had sufficiently adjusted to the darkness and then whipped around, crouching, my hands in the attack position.

The Ghost was hovering in the corner, happily chewing on a chicken leg. I stood up slowly and took a deep breath.

'You seem cheerful,' I noted, deciding not to comment on the appropriateness of a ghost fawn chewing a chicken leg. I guessed he'd just been around humans for too long. He looked back and smiled.

'First time I've had company in over a hundred years. No, more like two hundred.'

I confess I was puzzled. Then I heard a voice coming from another part of the alcove.

'This is fun, ducks, innit?'

'Mrs Baggs?' I asked, backing away just slightly. I didn't have a problem with The Ghost. Meeting the ghost of someone you had known – more or less – when alive just sounded, well – well, you wouldn't mention it in polite company, would you?

'She can't hear you,' The Ghost said. 'She's still finding her voice.'

'This is fun, ducks, innit.'

'Sounds like she's found her voice.'

'No, she's just repeating automatically something she would have said when alive. It'll take her a few weeks to become accustomed to being dead.'

Great. If only I could have asked her who her murderer was I could have told the police. That would have cleared the decks for the more important business, the trial. Just how I would explain it to the coppers was another story. I wasn't prepared to worry about that at that stage.

A thought struck me.

'You can talk to her, though? Can't you?'

'Of course I can.'

'Thank god for that. Listen, ask her who murdered her.'

'Mrs Baggs,' said The Ghost, addressing himself to the chicken leg, 'who murdered you?'

'This is fun, ducks, innit?'

The Ghost shrugged his shoulders, as if to say "Told you so".

'You said you could talk to her,' I pointed out.

'I didn't say she'd understand me.'

'Very funny.'

'You asked me a question. I answered you.'

I glared at him. The only thing that stopped me thumping him one was the respect I had been taught to have for the dead. That, and the brick wall behind him that I would have been punching. He noticed the glare and sniffed.

'Well, I know when I'm not wanted,' he said, tossing the chicken leg over his shoulder, or in his case, through his head. 'Anyway, I have some haunting to do. Can't float around here the whole night.'

And then he disappeared through the wall and I was alone in the alcove.

'This is fun, ducks, innit?'

Sort of alone.

I pushed my way through the curtains, back into the corridor. As I did so Bunny Matilda was passing. She squeaked in surprise and jumped away.

'Sorry, didn't mean to startle you. Keep getting lost in this place.'

'This is fun, ducks, innit?'

I looked at Bunny Matilda in the manner of a man who doesn't have a dead bag lady speaking into his ear.

'Well, best be off to bed then. Goodnight. Sleep tight.'

She squeaked a goodnight back at me and carried on. I walked away as swiftly as I could trying not to look as if I were in a hurry. I had spotted Sad Sid's snout peeking from another alcove, and I knew he'd be desperate for me to disappear so that he could continue his love-lorn shadowing of Bunny Matilda. I stopped at the end of the corridor and looked back. As I'd expected, he was lolloping on after her. I felt sorry for them. They were made for each other. All they needed was a small introduction and to be left alone together for half an hour or so, and they'd probably end up spending the rest of their lives together. But it's a tough world, and the other bunnies weren't likely to give them a break. Least of all Bunny Evil who had slipped out from his own alcove and was sliding along the wall doing a great impression of a very nasty and almost invisible stalker.

For a moment I was tempted to follow Bunny Evil quietly until I got a chance to shove him out of a window, but the chances seemed slim. And the greater probability was that I'd manage to get almost within finger distance of his back, he'd tense as he realised someone was behind him, and then next thing he'd be trying to get his teeth into my neck and I'd be fighting for my life. Those bunnies have amazingly good hearing, and when they get violent they get seriously violent.

I was about to head for bed when I heard the singing again. Ave Maria, hauntingly sung to the accompaniment of a guitar. Somewhere the Nun With Guitar was calling to me. Mockingly. From a room that didn't exist.

There is no 13. There never is. The numbers go 11 ...12... 14...15... . Believe me. There just isn't a ... 13 ... .

I checked my watch. It was just after eleven. I don't like staying up after eleven, she had said. Presumably she was singing her night-time prayers.

I paused in the way the hero does in a movie to indicate that he is about to do something extremely brave but rewarding, or to take the irretrievable step that will lead to disaster.

What, I thought, if the Nun With Guitar was dyslexic? She would be in room 31!

I paused only to pop into my room to put on my James Bond evening gear – tuxedo and bow tie – before shooting out to room 31.

As I approached the Nun's voice became more distinct.

And then less distinct.

And then more distinct.

And as I stood in front of No 31 it faded out entirely.

I hesitated for a second. What, exactly was I going to say? What was I hoping for? A family of Happy Families?

I decided that I'd play it by ear.

I took a breath, smoothed down my lapels.

And knocked on No 31.

The door opened.

Two women looked out. And down. Two tall women. Twins in ruffles with dainty handbags. They must have been in their eighties, if not nineties.

'Yes, young lady?' asked the one.

For a split second I thought I had accidentally put the wrong disguise on.

'Er, sorry?' I asked.

The one twin slowly put a hand into her reticule and took out a pair of thick-glassed lorgnettes. She put them to her face and her eyes turned into massive magnifying glasses.

'It's a man thing, Martha,' she said, and handed the lorgnettes to her sister.

'My goodness, Mabel,' said her sister, now the one with the huge eyes. 'So it is. What does it want?'

Her sister took the lorgnettes back and peered down at me.

'What do you want?' she asked.

That had me stumped. I had been wondering how the Nun With Guitar would react to my presence. There was always the possibility she would ask, 'What do you want?' I hadn't expected it to be two nonagenarian twins asking that question. The answers wouldn't have been the same.

'Room 41?' I asked in a sudden flash of creativity.

The two looked at each other.

Then they looked at the number 31 on the door.

Mabel with the lorgnettes peered closely at it.

She handed the lorgnettes to her sister.

Martha with the lorgnettes peered closely at it.

They stepped back and pointed at it.

'What does that say, young man?' they asked.

I leaned forward and peered at it.

'Can I borrow your lorgnettes?' I asked.

Martha handed them over. I used them to peer at the '31'.

'My goodness,' I said, '51. I'm a floor too high. Sorry about that. Oh, well, soonest mended, must rush, many thanks.' I handed the lorgnettes back and hurried back to the stairs.

'Poor thing,' I heard. 'They probably don't let their staff wear glasses. In case they fall in the soup. Like Gerald.'

By then the hotel was as quiet as the grave. The Nun With Guitar had obviously finished he nocturnal devotions. I decided that I had been silly enough for one night, and to give up any idea of pursuing a relationship with a nun of whom I knew less than little.

So I muttered my own night-time prayer and went to my own bed. I wasn't going to get caught by that "it's coming from here", "no, it's coming from there" trick again.

At the same time I made a note to see if there was a room 113. One of the ones could have fallen of. It's an easy mistake to make.

So that was Tuesday evening. It's evening here now, time to wrap up for the day. Tomorrow I'll begin to tell you what happened on the Wednesday morning. It involves – well, no, can't give hints, that would be unfair.

I think I'll have a whiskey before dinner. I've got a little of the good stuff left. They say you shouldn't drink alone. I don't know who "they" are, but if they'd gone through a week like that they'd join me in drinking alone.

Right, click on "Save", "Close" – What's this? "Do you wish to save your changes?" I just have, you stupid blinking machine. Why the hell do you have to – Oh, sod it, okay, click on "Yes". And shutdown.

Note to self: buy new laptop.

She's fallen asleep, the young woman across the road. And that postman has turned up. He let himself in with a key, which looks well dubious.

I think tonight I shall sleep with one ear open. But I think there might be something good about to come round the corner.

Shark fin soup.

Chapter XVI. Screaming Déjà Vu

Oh, happy days! Beazeley's taken to bed. He sent his sister Jennifer around to pass on his apologies (I've unplugged the telephone). Talk about opposites. She's an actor. She's about five-six, bobbed black hair, a cheeky little nose, and light blue eyes full of mischief. The minute I opened the door to find her on the doorstep I had that funny sort of reaction where your brain forgets to send out signals such as telling the heart to carry on pumping or telling the knees not to collapse. The reaction where your lungs are also having a look, forgetting that they're there to breath, not to fall in love. And somewhere in your self-defence mechanism a voice is shouting "Whoah! This is what the Nun With Guitar did to you, and remember what came of that!"

I invited her in, excusing my floundering by telling her that I'd been working on this quite hard, and how draining it can be, just by yourself. She said she knew exactly how I felt, how absolutely spent she felt after just one performance. Then, for some unknown reason, we got chatting about Beazeley. Honestly, he'll get in anywhere, even if he's not there.

Apparently Beazeley was a promising, if perhaps too earnest, young man with everything before him. In another universe he might have become the life and sole of the party. Well, a quiet, restrained party, anyway. With only a few, selected guests. He'd just got his degree, top of the class, his only choice seemingly whether to be a great white in a pond or a minnow in the Goby Sea. But then he actually began practising law. He thought he was arguing about truth. Instead he found his opponents were arguing about perception. As an actor his sister can't be bothered with the difference between the two, she says she'd go bonkers if she even tried. As she put it, when she's Joan of

Arc she has to be Joan of Arc, otherwise how would the audience believe she was Joan of Arc?

Jennifer. It's a nice name. I like it. And I like Jennifer. She likes what I've written so far, so how could I fail not to like her? (She giggles every time she reads the Beazeley bits.) (I made sure I removed anything mentioning the woman across the street before I showed it to Jennifer, don't want her thinking I'm ogling my neighbour all day.) (Remind me to change the neighbour's gender or age or something at some stage. And a few other things.)

Besides which, she has a very nice derriere. And she wears such tight jeans, if they were on a bloke it would bring tears to your eyes. And shiny brown boots with high heels which emphasise her lovely calves. And a loose, Russian-peasant style smock which occasionally tightens against the bits that matter. Stylish to the nth degree. And apparently it's all "just something I picked up at Oxfam". I could have sworn that it would be by that bloke Amardi, or Jacuzzi, or Givenchy, or whatever they're called. Just goes to show.

I've always thought that there is something appealing when a woman giggles at your jokes. It's more intimate than an outright laugh, almost as if you're sharing something private. A laugh is public, a chuckle is friendly, a giggle is personal.

Something like that.

But Beazeley's sister? You like someone. You go out with them. You stay in with them. Things get serious. Maybe you get engaged. Get married. And then you wake up one morning to discover that Beazeley is your brother-in-law.

I shall have to think about that one.

And I won't show her the last few lines.

Anyway. Wednesday.

You know that awful feeling you get when some idiot says "Things can't get worse", and you just know fate is floating around listening for stupid remarks like that to prove them false? That morning I woke to find Charlie the mouse sitting on my chest again, whiskers twitching as if trying to decide about something.

'Thanks for the blackberry pie,' he said. 'Would you like to know who murdered Mrs Baggs?'

'What I'd really like is to get a good look at that book,' I replied.

'I've had a good look at the book. But I can't tell you what's inside.'

'Why not?'

'Cause I'm a mouse, dummy. Whoever heard of a mouse that could read? But I will tell you something.'

I sighed. A ghost who can go anywhere. A mouse who can creep around unseen. And both completely and utterly useless.

'Go on then,' I said, 'what is it you're going to tell me?'

Just then there was a scream. Just like the day before. Bouncing around in the corridors, rolling up and down staircases, battering at the walls, screeching for a way out. Flying into my head and then racing around looking for a way out. And not finding one.

'Too late,' said Charlie, 'I think you're going to find out. I'd better get this back to the missus before the other guests start charging around. When humans get excited they just don't think about where they put their feet.'

'I thought your missus was the one with the phobia about being stepped on?'

'Just because you're paranoid doesn't mean they aren't out to get you.'

'The old ones are the best,' I called after him.

'They have to be to survive, think about it,' he called back. And then he was gone, a last flash of the little box of coconut ice hanging from one paw by the tiny pink tape, the box of blackberry pie from another with the blue. But the scream stayed.

I shot out of bed, threw on a dressing gown and raced out. If there's one thing I hate it's having to run around in a dressing gown and slippers. Firstly the slippers shoot off and there's no time to stop for them – mine disappeared at high speed somewhere or other before the first corner – and secondly the dressing gown always flaps around in a way that can look either highly comical or deeply melodramatic on the screen, but it's a real pain in real life. You just know that sooner or later it's going to be trapped in something. A passing harvester or thresher, something dangerous like that. You have to block out the common-sense thought that expecting a harvester or thresher to pop up in the corridors of a hotel is a silly idea, because even if it isn't a harvester or thresher it will be something, and you won't find out what it really is until it's too late.

This time the scream came from one of the corridors. I raced upstairs, almost falling over Bunny Bacchus who has decided to fall asleep just around a corner, just managed to hurdle him, came to a skidding halt to listen whether I'm going in the right direction.

(Coming to a skidding halt in your bare feet on a carpet is a painful business. Don't try it at home.)

A door opened. Judge Beak's nose appeared, surrounded by legal wig. Same red dressing gown. Same dark assassin's eye looking at me from waist-height.

Though this time the eye looked at me with less coldness. If I had the time to think about it I might have even described it as interested, or even curious.

"Love don't come easy" coming from behind Judge Beak.

'That's not the Rolling Stones, it's Phil Collins,' I pointed out, before turning back downstairs. The scream was now coming from below. I ran past more doors opening, people asking what was going on, images of various degrees of nightwear which I'd rather forget. I came to another stop to get my bearings. A door began opening. I pulled it shut, slamming it. I knew who was behind it. I had caught the first strains of "You're just another brick in the wall".

'Stick to the Stones,' I muttered under my breath, what little breath I had left. After all, what's the country coming to when a judge begins enjoying Pink Floyd? The beginning of the end of civilisation as we know it.

And then on. Left, left, left, left again until I was in a totally new corridor, dizzy as hell. An open bedroom door. Inside there's the same girl from the day before, Mildred Two, in her staff uniform of canary yellow skirt, maroon top, polka-dotted scarf, dark green apron and high-heeled pale blue toe-pinchers, screaming at the top of her lungs, just like the day before. And just like the day before, the instant she sees me, that's it, gurgle, gargle and out like a light on the bedroom carpet. This time she bounced her head off the wall, caught it on a bedside table and then expired with a happy sigh. I stepped in carefully and took in the scene. Bed, one. Coverlet thrown back, one. Dead accountant, one. Shiny, chrome, two-foot long knitting needle, one.

Pushed through one ear into his brain. And out the other ear. There could be no doubt about it. Hugo would never spread another sheet in this world again.

Whoever had done it had broken some keys from his laptop and tied them to either side of the knitting needle, leaving them dangling like earrings. On the left was "Pip" and on the right "Squeak".

(And, Beazeley, when you come to read this, as I know you will, I know a keyboard only has one P key. Beaze, old boy, the second p was a q turned around, okay?)

Right ...

....

Bananas.

As I stood there another of the staff came running in. Mildred Three. Exactly the same as the day before. And faints in exactly the same way as the day before, falling on top of her colleague. So now we're in Groundhog Day. I leaned against the wall, and sure as eggs is eggs, here comes Julia the Journalist aka Miss MI5 With Moustache.

'Hurry up with the pictures and then call the police,' says I. She takes the scene in with one glance, takes her pictures and is about to leave when she looks at me.

'Bit of a coincidence,' she says. 'You discovering a second body.'

'Yes, but at least I remembered not to sit on the staff this time.'

She looked at the slumbering staff.

'Another coincidence,' she says. 'Same two waitresses.'

'They were taken off breakfast duties because of trauma,' I said. 'Apparently they've developed a phobia about guava juice. You'd better get along and call the police.'

She left to make the phone call. I had no intention of staying in the same room as ex-Hugo, I had seen more than I wanted to. I was tempted to close the door on him and the sleeping beauties, but if they woke up to find themselves locked in the same room as a body they'd probably end up freaking off the walls. I dragged the first one to the door, threw her into the corridor, and followed her up with the other. Once I'd closed the door I stacked them more tidily to make it easier for people to pass. Igor the Hunchback of Notre Dame appeared suddenly and silently. I could have sworn that he must have been hiding in one of the alcoves. Otherwise I would have heard his knuckles dragging along the floor. He motioned towards the two Mildreds with his beetled brow.

'Ug?'

'Yes, Igor, you can take them away.'

'Ug,' he said, knuckling his forehead in thanks. He lifted a Mildred under each arm as if they were feather pillows and ambled away. Miss MI5 With Moustache passed him on her way back.

'Hello, sexy,' she said, ruffling his greasy hair. He went beetroot red and scuttled away.

'Sweet,' she said as came up to me, watching the massive back of Igor and dangling legs of the Mildreds disappear around a corner. She turned to me, absent-mindedly wiping her hand on my sleeve.

'No, I am not going up to the attic,' she said. 'You conned me that way yesterday. I was lost the whole day. I'm not falling for it today.'

'I didn't ask you to go up to the attic,' I replied. 'There's something else I need you to do.'

'What's that?' she asked, the bright light of suspicion shining out of her eyes.

'Guard this door until the police arrive,' I said, pointing a thumb at the door in case she got the wrong one. 'I've got to get dressed. Can't stand around in a dressing gown the whole day.'

She managed "But –" before I was gone. I moved along the corridors as swiftly as I could, dodging the various hotel residents racing around, demanding or squeaking to know what was wrong. The place was in an uproar, anonymous Mildreds bouncing off bunnies and vice versa. Halfway to my room another door opened and Strawberry Mousse appeared, wearing a pink and white striped dressing robe, open to the point where you could almost see the artillery.

If I had had a white flag with me I would have surrendered immediately.

'What's going on?' she asked.

'Would you believe me if I said that Elvis had been sighted in the bar having a toasted banana and peanut butter sandwich?' I asked.

A bunny hopping quickly past stopped suddenly, looked at me and squeaked 'Elvis!' before racing on. She – it was pink, so I presume it was a she – almost bumped into a knot of bunnies coming in the opposite direction.

'Elvis! In the bar! With a toasted peanut butter and banana sandwich!'

The other bunnies immediately turned around and raced after her.

I scratched my head.

'They didn't really fall for that one, did they?' I asked, half to myself.

'They'll fall for almost anything,' Strawberry Mousse said. 'Those Bunnies are like that. So what's really going on?'

'Would you believe me if I told you that Hugo the Accountant was murdered – with Mrs Plum's other knitting needle?'

She nodded.

'I was expecting something like that,' she said. 'As soon as the other needle went missing I knew someone else was going to get it.'

That was much more than I had expected. I hadn't even considered the significance, apart from the affect it had on Mrs Plum's ramblings. I had presumed that Mrs Baggs's murder was a one-off irritation which would be side-lined by the trial.

'You weren't worried it might be you?' I asked, merely out of curiosity.

'We slept together for safety,' said Miss F, poking her head out underneath Strawberry Mousse's left arm.

'Ah,' I said. "Ah" was about the only thing that came to mind with the combination of those two.

'Safety in numbers,' said Miss F's Mother, poking her head out underneath Strawberry Mousse's other arm. 'And we're armed,' she added, showing a rather sharp and nasty looking kitchen knife. The kind that tends to get over-used in horror movies.

'Ah,' I said. I was getting good at it. Try it sometime. Just say 'Ah'.

'Ah.'

'And I've got the bread knife,' said Miss F, displaying a serrated knife. 'Though I still don't understand why it's called a bread knife. It's not made of bread.'

Her mother shook her head sadly underneath Strawberry Mousse's arm.

'She thinks bread is made sliced,' she explained. 'We're hoping to go for a stroll at lunchtime and see if we can find a shop that sells unsliced bread to show her.'

'Ri-i-i-ght,' I said slowly. I was tempted to ask Miss F if she knew where milk came from, but it's not the sort of question you ask a teenager such as Miss F before the first mug of coffee. Especially not when her head is so close to the means of production. 'I'd best be along, have to shower and get dressed before the police turn up.'

'Why, are you going to wash off the bloodstains?' asked Miss F, giving my dressing gown a careful and intimate inspection.

I hurried quickly away. If I answered "yes" she would have believed me. If I had answered "no" she wouldn't have believed me. Behind me I could hear her mother remonstrating mildly.

'Now, Miss F, that's not the sort of question you ask a gentleman in a dressing gown.'

'Would it be okay if he wasn't wearing a dressing gown? What if he was stark naked?'

'Miss F! Really, I don't know what they teach you at that university.'

Same sort of thing her mother would have learned at school, I presumed. There's so much more of it to learn these days they have to postpone some of it.

I turned to look back as I came to a corner. They were still underneath Strawberry Mousse's arms, calmly carrying on their chat across her bosom. Strawberry Mousse was looking from one to the other as she followed the conversation. I hurried on. There had been too many strange sights before the first dose of caffeine.

I had a long, hot shower, using both shampoo and conditioner. (It's better than a headache tablet, and your hair comes out looking soft and shiny, especially if you use the herbal stuff.) It had been a long time since I had been in the habit of taking an early morning jog (and that had only lasted three days) and now, two days in a row, I'd been racing up and down hotel stairs, in and out of corridors, and my muscles were just beginning to wake up to the fact, and they weren't best pleased.

Apart from easing the muscle tension the long shower gave me time to think. The problem with the hectic pace of modern living is that it's just too easy to forget the important things and end up concentrating on the trivia. You're driving along in a new car, up comes a billboard showing a busty blonde wearing only a bra, you lose your concentration, think, damn, almost forgot the girlfriend's birthday, then, wham, you've wrapped the car around a lamppost. Which means you've just totalled your brand new car and can't afford to buy your girlfriend a birthday present. So she leaves you for someone with more money and with weaker eyesight.

In this case the billboard was a number of billboards. The murders. The ghost. And Charlie the mouse. The road, which is what I should have been concentrating on, was the trial, or more specifically, that book. How to get a copy of the book, that was the question. Having said that, the best method is not always to ignore the billboards. Sometimes it's better to pull over, park the car, have a good leer, and then carry on – preferably chopping the billboard down first to get it out of the way. Using that analogy, the first thing was to sort out Charlie the mouse. Charlie the mouse could not exist. There was no way a hotel such as the Railway Tavern would have mice scampering around in the early hours looking for blackberry pie.

They'd be looking for cheese. Charlie was clearly lying.

So, the simplest method of eliminating Charlie – in a manner of speaking – was to get someone to tell me that he couldn't exist. Once I'd finished showering, shaving and getting dressed I went up and down to reception. Mildred One was on duty again, strangely enough. I decided to approach her.

'Did you know there's a mouse running around upstairs?' I asked.

'Heyick.' – "No, but if you hum a few bars I might pick it up."

'I'm being serious, Mildred One. He was sitting on my chest watching me when I woke up.'

'Heyick.' – "That's Charlie. He must like you, though I can't understand why. He's normally got much better taste. I suppose he got out of the kitchen again. I've told Mildred Two a hundred times to keep an eye on him. He likes to wander. It just upsets his little wife. Typical man."

'Right,' I replied. 'Good. I'll bring him down if I see him again, shall I?'

After all, what would you say?

Though, to be honest, I was interpreting Mildred One's answers. After all, with someone who only ever says "Heyick", you have to. For all I know it was quite possible she had just called me a whinging Southern softie tosser, and invited me to make whoopee with a yak. Or a penguin. Who knows? Sometimes you have to see things in a positive way.

Just then there was a scrape of strings behind me. I knew it was Alberto, and I knew he was doing it deliberately. I could feel his dark Latin, Czechoslovakian eyes boring into my back. I could almost feel his lust for revenge. He was trying to tempt me into saying something silly which Mildred One would only Heyick at. I sighed and went through to the temporary breakfast room cum lounge for a cup of coffee. I might not have managed to get Charlie the mouse out of the equation, but I was damned if I was going to let Alberto force his way into it.

Coffee.

The lounge was deserted when I walked in. I guessed everyone was either getting dressed or searching the bar for Elvis. That suited me. I made myself the strongest cup of coffee I could and wandered over to the window, looking out in a pose that suggested deep thoughtfulness. Though in reality thought was the last thing my brain was doing. Actually, I think my brain had packed its bags and gone on holiday. The only thought running through my mind was that I had to get a copy of that book. Hugo had been Edgar The Ears's accountant, and now Hugo had been posted in the deficit column of life, he wouldn't be around to spill any beans, let alone count them. The way things were going the only evidence left would be in the book. The trouble was that, after that logical step had been processed, my mind shut down.

'Detective Inspector Summers,' someone said at my side, interrupting that blissful state of nothingness. I looked around. "Inspector F Summers" said the warrant card.

Smartly dressed. Good looking. Very good looking. A look in the eyes that said that thumbscrews, nailing of heads to planks and other assorted torture was the preferred option, but if you insisted on being friendly and sociable and telling the truth, the whole truth and only the truth, well, there would unfortunately be no other option but to treat you as if you were vaguely related to the human race.

Leather jacket hanging off shoulder. Kitten in pocket.

'And this is special constable Squishy,' Summers said.

Special constable Squishy returned my look with one that said "You're still a very strange person, got any fish?"

It was déjà vu with a difference. Detective Inspector Summers wore a navy blue skirt-suit, and I instinctively knew the skirt would have a slit in the back, showing very nice legs. The trouble was that Inspector Summers had turned into an extremely attractive woman, a fact that some men might have found confusing, at the least what might be termed a sexual anomaly.

She also had a look that was decidedly lacking in that well-known balm, a sense of humour. She obviously hadn't gone to the School of Service With a Smile, even if the service involved unsharpened truncheons.

I decided not to mention it. These sort of things happen in the best of families. Besides which, I was increasingly beginning to wonder whether the mushrooms in garlic I had had as a starter the previous evening hadn't been the breed which normally has the prefix "magic". If I started saying Heyick any time soon I'd know.

'You were the person who found the body?' asked Mrs Inspector Summers.

Mz Inspector Summers.

Ma'am.

Boss.

Sir.

'No, I was the person who found the person who found the body,' I replied, trying not to blink. I could have sworn I had had the exact same conversation a day before with the same person when she was still a he.

'Ah. Not to worry, that sort of thing happens in the best of families,' Summers said.

I tried a feeble grin. It seemed the right thing to do under the circumstances. And I'm good at feeble grins. I get a lot of practice.

'Who did find the body?' she asked.

'Mildred Two. I was in bed speaking with Charlie when I heard her scream.'

Whoops. That was a mistake.

'Charlie? And who is Charlie?'

'Um, well ... would you believe that Charlie is a mouse? A mouse who likes blackberry pie? You see ...'

I trailed off. It was either that or gabble. And it was too early in the morning for gabbling. Besides which little Squishy was showing far too much interest in the mention of Charlie the mouse. I'm not sure that they would have got on together that well. I suspected Squish was a Libra, and I was pretty sure Charlie was Aquarius. They never hit it off well. Besides which, Charlie would be a very bad influence on little Squishy. He'd probably lead her into all sorts of mischief.

'You were in bed with a mouse called Charlie,' Mrs Inspector Summers said slowly.

'Well, no, I was in the bed, Charlie was sitting on the counterpane on my chest ... Look, Charlie doesn't exist, of course, haha, of course not, it's a, um, a, an um, a, er, mental mouse.'

'Charlie is mental?'

'An imaginary mouse. Haha. Haha. Of course. It's a morning exercise I learnt when I was in, ah, in Burma, many years ago. It develops the neck muscles and also exercises the mental facilities first thing in the morning. It's very good, you should try it sometime. The monks recommend it.'

I think I preferred Summers when she had been a man. At least the man Summers would smile as if sharing a joke, even if you got the feeling that the joke was on you. Summers as a woman gave me a slow look which didn't bother suggesting anything. It told you that you were quite plainly several hampers short of a picnic, and the sooner you were thrown into a padded cell the better.

Or an unpadded one. She probably enjoyed the sound of things going clunk.

'O-k-a-y,' she said, dragging the letters out as if they were suspects and she had got to the coshing-them-over-head part and took pride in doing her job very slowly and very well. 'So you were doing your morning mental exercises. What happened then?'

'Well, I heard a scream.'

'The same as yesterday.'

No. Of course not, I thought. Yesterday was yesterday. Today feels like being – some other day. Perhaps tomorrow. Definitely not yesterday. Yesterday I wasn't having a conversation with a mouse when I woke up. Definitely no.

Or was I?

'Yes,' I said. 'I put my dressing gown on and ran to find out what the problem was. I found Mildred Two screaming in Hugo the Accountant's bedroom. He had Mrs Plum's shiny chrome knitting needle through his ears. Mildred One fainted when I got into the bedroom. Mildred Two then ran in and also fainted. No sorry it was Mildred Two and Mildred Three. Or Four or Five. Or one of them, anyway. I mean two of them. I dragged them out and shut the door. Igor came along and took them away. Miss MI5 With Moustache appeared and I sent her to call your lot. When she came back I left her on guard while I took a shower. Then I came down here, which is where you found me.'

Okay, yes, I was gabbling by then. But I did leave out the bit with Strawberry Mousse, Miss F and Miss F's Mother. And the Elvis thing. Apart from not clouding things with too much detail, I wasn't sure how a woman who had been a man the day before would react to the image of Miss F and Miss F's Mother underneath Strawberry Mousse's arms. Especially not the bit about the knives.

Summers lit the Corona in the corner of her mouth, slowly waved the match out and flipped it casually into an ashtray behind me, her eyes creased against the smoke, her mouth a hint of Clint Eastwood about to call someone "punk".

Well, she didn't, of course, but it was the same trick of appearing to do so he – she – had done the day before.

'I'd better go have a word with the Mildreds, then,' she said. 'Oh, you know what they say about the first person to come across a murder victim?'

'No, what do they say about the first person to come across a murder victim?'

'They say that they're usually the one who found the body.'

I practised the feeble smile again. Police humour obviously hadn't improved in the past twenty-four hours.

And then she and Squish were gone. Not before Squish had a chance to give me another look. "Very, very strange man, are you sure you don't have any Tuna?" it said. I sank down onto a couch and sipped my coffee. It was not so much a feeling that the billboards were multiplying, more like they were multiplying and fighting back. Dozens of billboards showing young women wearing only underwear and making suggestive comments. Apart from the one carrying a Department of Roads warning: "Looking at this sign could kill you".

Just then the door opened and someone floated in. To my relief it was the Nun With Guitar. I felt I could talk to her. Not understand her, mind. But at least talk to her. She smiled at me, poured herself a cup of coffee and came over, sitting down opposite me. That morning she had chosen shimmering orange and white for the day, more little sequins all over, thicker in some places, rippling with movement, like one of those shoals of fish which suddenly change shape as a shark dives in. I made sure I didn't look where it might be considered impolite. But there was definitely a slit there. And no sign of an undergarment.

Snuggle. The word popped into my head. I wanted to snuggle up with her. Was that so wrong?

'Ve live in inderezding dimez, id appearz, Viktor, or E,' she said in her soft, husky, shall-we-have-an-early-night-and-I'm-not-talking-about-sleep Russian accent.

'Amen to that, sister,' I replied.

Okay, not original, but how would you feel after having just been dragged through the mental ringer by a man who had become a woman overnight? And then find yourself talking to a Nun With Guitar who made your heart thump, your knees go weak, and your brain shrivel up as if it were a droplet of water on a hot stove?

'I zought I vould be zpending a quied veek addending a boring drial ov liddle inderezd,' she continued. 'Inzdead I vind myzelf in ze middle ov murder, having med ze man ov my live.'

I smiled and put my mug down on the coffee table between us. I had picked up on the tiny slip she had made. At last, my brain was working again!

"Boring drial ov liddle inderezd"? I don't think so, Zister.

'So,' I asked her, deciding to go for broke, 'how did you get involved with our friend Edgar The Ears?'

She looked at me. Strummed a few chords on her guitar. Looked at me. Didn't strum a few chords on her guitar. Picked up her coffee. Looked at me. Took a sip. Put it down. Didn't take a sip. Finally she nodded slowly, in the way that Nuns With Guitars do when reaching a decision to trust someone.

'You are do dell no-vun zis,' she said.

"No-vun". The word strummed the chords of my heart, singing it softly. I felt like a little puppy. If she'd thrown a stick I would have run off to fetch it before bringing it back and looking at her hoping she would pet me.

'Cross my heart and hope to die,' I said instead. She nodded. The look in her eyes suggested she was taking the second part of that as guaranteed.

'Let uz zay zad vunz upon a dime I vas vorking in an orvanage. Tink of it as a metavor.'

Damn, I thought, I don't need a metavor. I've got metavors coming out of my ears. What I need is some concrete facts.

Not coming out of my ears.

That would be painful.

'Ven I ztarted zere id vas a very happy plaze. Ze children vere happy. Ze ztaff vere happy. Everyvun vas happy. Id zeemed az iv every day ze zun vas zhining.'

She paused to take a sip of coffee. I'd never dreamed before that I might want to become a coffee mug in the next life.

'And zen vun day ve heard zat ze company vich owned ze orvanage vas about to be daken ofer by a privade equidy kompany. You know zem?'

I nodded. Whenever I hear the phrase "private equity" the phrase "asset stripping" comes to mind.

She moved slightly, sufficient to make the word "stripping" leave me breathless.

'Ve knew vat vould happen. Halv ze ztaff vould be vired. Zen ze orvans vould be zold orv. Zen ze rest ov ze ztaff vould be vired. Ze building orgzioned orv. Zey vould make a good provid. Land and buildingz make good money.'

She looked into my eyes. I only just managed not to fall off the couch.

'Dell me, Viktor, or E,' she asked, 'do you tink id iz money zat makez men bat, or iz id juzt bat men who make money?'

She was asking my opinion? Couldn't I just lick her toes instead?

'Difficult question,' I said slowly, trying to give the impression of a serious man who had thought about these things. I had, but all previous rational deliberations appeared to be locked away in a file marked "Currently Unavailable".

My brain was 404.

File not found.

Invalid address.

No-one at home.

'Not all rich men are bad,' my mouth said. 'Not all poor people are good. In fact I'd say that poverty is more likely to make people go sour than money is.'

She nodded.

'Perhapz id iz a queztion orv doo much and doo liddle. However. Ze orvanage. Ve needed money do buy ze orvanage ourzelvez. Much money. Ve did all ze uzual tingz. Fêtez. Collecting boxez. Cake zalez. Jumble zalez. Ann Zummerz partiez. Ztrip Zhowz. Naked calendarz. Ze local people vere very good. Zey vere nod wealty, bud zey vere prout ov ze vork ve did in ze orvanage. Liddle by liddle by liddle ve kollected. But vun mond bevore ve needed ze money ve vere ztill zhort of many dousands ov money. And zen I med Edgar Vit Ze Big Earz. He vas on ze board orv ze privade equidy company.'

'I hope you aren't going to tell me anything good about him? He didn't agree not to carry out the bid? Agreed that the orphanage was a worthwhile project? I'd hate to hear that he might have a heart.'

She smiled.

'Ze good zing about Edgar Vit Ze Big Earz iz zat you kan truzd him.'

She took a sip of her Bloody Mary while keeping her eyes on mine.

Oy Vey.

She was now drinking a Bloody Mary at breakfast time?

Where did that come from?

Double Oy Vey.

'You kan truzd him becauze zere iz only vun perzon in hiz live and zat iz himzelf. Zuch men are nod likeable, but zey are reliable. Vortunately he did nod know I vaz vorking in ze orvanage. I dold him I vaz on holiday vrom my konvend in Rome.'

She smiled. I almost fell off the couch again. Women who smile like that should be locked up for the public good.

Okay, I did fall off the couch. I pretended I was looking for my lighter.

'And I vound oud his veaknezz.'

'He has a veaknezz?' I asked, feeling, for the first and hopefully last time, a strange sort of empathy with Edgar.

'Led uz juzt zay zat he collectz ... guidarz. I dold him I had vound a zpecial vun at ze convend in ze Eternal Zity. A very zpecial vun. Ve arranged a dranzaction, Edgar Vit Ze Big Earz and myzelf. No-vun knew ze guidar vaz zpecial. No-vun vaz hurd. No-vun needz do know. Ze amound he paid vaz juzt ze amound ve needed. And ze really vunny zing iz zat he paid vid money vrom ze company drying to buy ze orvanage. Vich I believe iz illegal. Or vaz. Until zey changed ze law.'

'What was special about the – guitar?' I asked. 'Purely out of interest, of course.'

She smiled again. There was a wicked twinkle in her eye. God, I could have dissolved in those eyes!

'I told him zat id vaz zanctified by ze Pope.'

'Sanctified by the Pope?'

'Well ... id vaz nod zat guidar, but anoder I left lying around. Ze Pope tripped over id and broke his noze. When he ztood up he azked, "Who ownz zad blezzed guitar."'

'Well, that sounds sanctified to me.'

'But, ze one I zold him ... Ze zpecial zing aboud zat guitar vas zat I knew it wazn't zpecial and he didn't.'

'You mean –'

'Vat I mean iz zad he paid a lod of money vor zomething he could have bought on ze Internet vor about vive of ze quid. Or vound in ze zkip vor vree.'

I couldn't resist a chuckle. Edgar The Ears having one put over him. That didn't happen too often.

'Do not tell anybody, Victor, or E,' she said, a sudden concerned look on her face. 'If he vound out id vould be veeding nunz to ze vizhiez dime.'

'Don't worry, sister,' I re-assured her, 'my lips are sealed.'

She looked back and licked her black lips. Slowly.

'My lipz are unzealed vor a very zpezial perzon,' she said.

I wondered who the lucky bloke was. Probably the big J.C. himself. No use trying to compete with that sort of competition.

'I had bedder go, ze trial iz about do reztart,' she said, standing up.

'Before you go – why are you here?'

She rested a slim hand on the back of the chair.

'Victor, or E, vere I kome vrom ve have a zaying: ze Volf iz nod dead undil id iz killed.'

'Yes, we have something similar, only it's about egg stains.'

'I zee.' She looked at me. 'Zere vaz alzo zomething – vun ov ze orvans vaz named Nell. Zhe vaz deaf, poor zing. I told her zat everyzing vould be okay, zat I would look avter her.'

Lucky Nell.

'But – zhe didn't make it. Ze ztrain, ze worry ... Zhe became ill. Zhe choked. Zhe died.'

'The deaf Nell?'

'Prezizely. Zo you zee, ze Volf ztill owez. Dogether ve kan make him pay.'

'Now that's a dance I'll happily join in, Sister. I'll even try the twirly bits with the hands.'

She paused and smiled her black smile.

'Number 13, Victor, or E,' she said. 'Perhapz you kould make id during ze lunzh break.'

I watched her go, hips swaying in a way that a Nun With Guitar's hips shouldn't.

Hips swaying a way they shouldn't. A number 13 which didn't exist.

There is no 13. Believe me, there never is.

And I'd checked number 31.

I made a mental note to check for number 131. The last "1" might have fallen off.

The billboards were definitely multiplying. And ganging up on me.

But sometimes there's a billboard you wouldn't mind spending more time with.

Strangely enough, it rarely contains underwear.

Chapter XVII. Take Down The Clowns

You know, it's strange. That young woman across the street is now washing the inside of her windows. You would think that that would be distracting, especially when she reaches up for the bits at the top, but it isn't. I think that's because Jenny is pootling around my place, looking into all the nooks and crannies as most women I've known like doing in other peoples' houses. She asked if I minded, which I don't, it's quite comforting in a way, knowing she's just a couple of rooms away. I was worried that she'd just dropped in to let me know of Beazeley being poorly and would then disappear out of my life, but she's resting, as they say in her world, and quite happy to spend a morning investigating a bachelor pad. She sings to herself every so often as she pootles, which I think is quite sweet. It's probably not politically correct to describe a young woman as "sweet" these days, but, sod it, I don't care, she is sweet, and she has a lovely singing voice.

To be honest, I was even ready to give up today's work – if this ends suddenly in the middle of a sentence, you'll know who to blame – but she insisted she wouldn't hear of bothering me or my not cracking on with things. So, let's crack on. Jenny insists on wanting to read the morning's work as soon as it's finished. I'll just make sure this paragraph isn't included. First impressions are important, and the last thing I want Jen to think is that I sit here daydreaming most of the time, especially not about the young woman washing her front windows.

Carpe Diem, that's my motto.

That morning. The morning the Nun With Guitar had tickled my funny bone and achieved the same effect on my heart as a defibrillator. Walked away with my soul in her hands, as it were, mocking it with her number 13 nonsense.

Come fly with me to nowhere, on a non-existent plane to a non-existent place.

Thanks, sister, maybe next week.

After I've done the dishes, anyway.

I finished my coffee and headed off to the court. It was still a little early, but I was determined to empty my mind of all those distractions. Concentrate on the trial. Work out how I was going to filch a copy of that book. I wasn't sure how I would use it once I had got my hands on it – that would depend on what was in it, and how far the contents could be interpreted to reflect reality, or misinterpreted if necessary – and the particular laws of whatever country I chose to publish it in – but if I didn't come up with a failsafe plan for nicking a copy I might as well have gone home right then. So I was in the public gallery when the jury filed into their rocking box. Most of them. I noticed that The Clowns were missing. I said a silent prayer, wishing them bon chance. I didn't think they had done the right thing, but good luck to them. It would be the end of the trial, but – what the hell. At least Clyde and Bonnie would have got something out of it. I'd just have to find another little trial in another little courthouse in another little town, as the saying goes. And since I had failed to work out my book-heist strategy it was a pretty academic question anyway.

The rest of the jury were there. Miss F and Miss F's Mother were almost colour-co-ordinated. Miss F was wearing a faded denim dungaree dress with lumberjack shirt, her mother had opted for a denim jacket, denim skirt and the same type of lumberjack shirt. Miss F's Mother had even decided to wear the same spangly flip-flops as her daughter.

The Nun With Guitar smiled at me and gave a slight wave. Those sequins. A shimmering haze of little dots of light. There was no doubt about that parting in the top. I don't know which denomination she thought she belonged to, but it would give any Mother Superior a heart attack. What it might do to any passing priest I don't even want to think of.

The Quiet American had decided to go for a light blue and peach coloured Hawaiian shirt, with real peaches. The Prim Maiden Aunt was in her usual grey, jumping slightly and making little "ick" noises at regular intervals, the Major was in his usual brown. Mrs Plum was happily knitting away, wearing almost the same lavender combination she always did, but the colour was sufficiently different to ensure that no-one would make the mistake of thinking she wore the same clothes every day.

Once what remained of the jury were ready the recorder pressed the button on her desk and the metallic voice called for the court to rise. Judge Beak took his chair and everyone sat down.

'There has been an interruption to this trial,' he announced. I thought calling the murder of a juryman "an interruption" somewhat lacking in feeling, but it turned out he wasn't talking about that.

'We must perforce attend to a different trial,' he continued. 'Officer, bring in the prisoners.'

There was a gasp as the prisoners were pushed up into the dock.

Clyde and Bonnie hadn't made it after all.

The Clowns were on trial.

'Ladies and gentlemen of the jury,' Judge Beak said, 'this will be a short trial, as the facts are quite plain. The defendants are charged with begging. Sergeant Johns, are you there?'

'Yes, sir,' replied a portly police sergeant, standing below the dock.

'Sergeant Johns arrested the miscreants at five o'clock this morning,' Judge Beak said. 'An open and shut case of flagrant begging while dressed as Clowns, at a most heinous hour of the morning, and, to make matters worse, at the rear of the hotel. Mr Crane has agreed to appear for the prosecution, Mr Ball for the defence.'

'Yoh honour, might Ah ask something?' asked The Quiet American, standing up in the jury box. The other jury members held on desperately as the jury box tilted forward.

Judge Beak's nose frowned.

'Very well, if you must, Quiet American. Go ahead.'

'Whal, where Ah come from a jury has to be twelve men and true – or women, and true, ahf course. But, whal, we seem to only be ten, now.'

Judge Beak's nose nodded slowly up and down as he counted and came to ten.

I wasn't going to tell him that Miss F's Mother wasn't a juror.

Mr Crane stood up.

'H'your onour, h'I h'would h'point h'out h'that h'the h'prithonerth h'at h'the h'bar h'are h'still h'technically h'memberth h'of h'the h'jury.'

Judge Beak thought about this for a few moments and then his nose moved briefly.

'Correct, Mr Crane. Therefore we still have enough members of the jury. Carry on, Mr Crane.'

The Quiet American sat down, a look of mild surprise on his face, as if to say "Whal, guess they do things differently over here".

(Warning. Beazeley's just turned up, looking pale. Bugger.)

(Must have been something he ate.)

(Quick, feed him some more of that.)

'H'call Thergeant h'Eric h'Johnth h'to h'the h'thtand,' Mr Crane called out. The portly policemen disappeared from below the prisoners' dock and reappeared, fifteen minutes later, puffing, in the witness stand.

'H'Thergeant h'Johnth, h'you h'arrethted h'the h'Clownth h'you h'thee h'before h'you h'earlier h'thith h'morning, h'did h'you h'not?'

The sergeant hesitated. His physique and lack of fitness made it obvious that anyone he tried to arrest would be able to escape at a casual saunter.

'I was on desk duty when they were brought in,' he said carefully. 'I took down their statements.' He took out a notebook. '"You have got us bang to rights," the prisoners said. Whereupon I immediately charged them under the Terrorism Act.'

(See, Beazeley, no-one will ever believe that one.)

(Oh, dear, Beazeley's fainted. Too much coffee, probably.)

'H'Thank h'you, h'Thergeant, h'that h'ith h'all,' Mr Crane said, sitting down.

Mr Ball got to his feet. He stepped as gently as he could on to the latest contraption designed to give him added height: a set of collapsible steps.

You know, there's an advert for wood varnish or something where the tag-line is, "Does exactly what is says on the tin", or words to that effect. I can only presume that Mr Ball had never seen it.

There was a creaking sound.

'SERGEANT JONES.'

Another creaking sound. Louder.

'Er, that's Johns, sir.'

This time the creaking sound had an added melodramatic squeal of metal about to protest very loudly.

'VERY WELL, SERGEANT JOHNS. YOU CLAIM THAT this young couple ... arrggh!'

The jury leaned forward as the collapsible steps lived up to their name and Mr Ball disappeared suddenly from view, his blue wig following him a second later. The sound of creaking metal hung around for a few moments, and then there was silence, apart from a low moan. The jury turned to the judge. He appeared to have gone to sleep again.

'H'your onour,' called Mr Crane.

No response.

'Ith onour'th aving h'a h'thnoothe h'again,' Mr Crane said mournfully.

'Tweak his nose! Tweak his nose!' groaned Mr Ball from the depths.

'H'and h'lothe h'the h'cathe? Mithter h'Quiet h'American, h'could h'you h'do h'the onourth?'

'Sure can, pardner,' replied The Quiet American, twirling his water pistols before letting rip with a squirt which bounced straight off Judge Beak's nose and shot up the gap in his wig.

'Harrumph, quite so,' exclaimed Beak, taking out a handkerchief and wiping the end of his nose. 'Mr Ball, you have finished?'

A sad blue flag waved defeat. It was about then that I realised that it wasn't just waving defeat for Mr Ball. It was waving defeat for the Clowns. And me.

'Members of the jury,' said Judge Beak's nose, 'you have heard the evidence. Obviously a straight-forward case. What is your verdict?'

'Ah, whal, we haven't had a chance to vote, your lordship,' said The Quiet American, standing up.

'A vote?' asked the judge, as if he considered this a novel and not too welcome concept. 'I suppose that's what they do where you come from. Very well, hurry up and find them guilty then.'

There were muttered murmurings as the members of the jury discussed the issue with each other. The Quiet American noted each vote on a piece of paper. When they had finished he looked across to the prisoner's dock and scratched his head. He leaned down to the recorder.

'Er, Missy?' he called in a loud whisper. 'Missy! Could you ask The Clowns for their verdict? Missy?'

She remained seated with her back to him, apparently deaf. Mr Crane stood up and addressed The Clowns.

'H'the h'thairman h'of h'the h'jury h'witheth h'to h'know h'your h'verdict.'

The Clowns shook their heads in mute sadness, looking at the ground.

'H'ith h'that h'guilty h'or h'not h'guilty?'

Another sad shake.

'H'I h'thee. H'guilty.'

He sat down. The Quiet American scratched his jaw and turned to the judge.

'Yo worship, we find the defendants not guilty by a vote of ten to two.'

'Ten to two?' asked the judge, checking his watch. 'I make it ten o'clock.'

'H'that'th h'the h'jury'th h'verdict,' Mr Crane interpreted.

'What, not guilty?' exclaimed the judge. 'Ridiculous! A perverse verdict if I ever saw one. I shall so rule later on. Take the prisoners down.'

The recorder pressed a button.

'Take the prisoners down to the cells,' came the metallic recording.

'No, no, take them down into the well of the court,' said the judge. 'They still have to hear the case involving public interest. They are still jurors, after all.'

The two sad Clowns were taken down into the well on the court, and sat there miserably, her head on his chest, his arm around her, both looking down. Only the Quiet American amongst them looked surprised at what had just passed.

'Are you ready to continue with the case of public interest, Mr Crane, Mr Ball?' asked the judge.

'H'I h'think h'Mr h'Ball h'needth h'a h'new h'box h'of h'orangeth,' said Mr Crane. 'H'or h'thumpthing.'

A little blue flag waved agreement.

'Very well. We will adjourn until after lunch.'

And so will I, now, I think. Jenny's told me that she's made a toasted sandwich for me for lunch. I don't know what it is, but it smells good. She's good looking, has a great sense of humour, is an actress, can cook, and has cooked me lunch without being asked. Call me a male chauvinist pig if you want, but women don't come much better than that.

Anyway, I can cook too, and I do. I've just been busy recently.

I do a very nice Halibut Surprise.

Who am I arguing with? I think it must be me.

Note to self: get out more often.

As soon as I've finished this. And finish it I am going to do. Oh yes I am.

Without the X-word.

It's the Quiet American next.

Yee-Ha.

!

Chapter XVIII. The Quiet American and the —s

I must be mad. Here I am, eating a toasted chicken and mayonnaise sandwich – with loads of mushroom and garlic, yummy – while tapping away. (If any vegetarian is reading this, pretend it's a toasted snail and green-pepper sandwich.) It's a lovely toasted sandwich, not a lot of it, but what there is is perfect. But eating and working at the same time? I promised myself to stop that sort of nonsense after the heart attack at work, the "I'm-so-busy-I-have-to-work-through-lunch" nonsense.

Okay, okay, it wasn't a heart attack, but I had to pretend it was. It was the only way I could explain why I threw my computer screen at the head of marketing. I told them I was trying to attract attention to my having a heart attack.

The real reason I threw the computer screen at him? Well, firstly, he was an idiot, and secondly, the blinking computer was playing up again.

That job didn't last.

Anyway, here I am, working extra hard, eating a toasted cheese and ham sandwich (I changed it because I was worried about that vegetarian reader, let's face it, toasted snail and green-pepper? Yuk), thinking back to that other Wednesday lunchtime.

That blasted Czechoslovakian Jellist had begun following me. I'm all for music, especially the Jello, especially Beethoven, but to have it shadowing you throughout the day?

You can always tell when things are getting dodgy for someone in the movies. The Jellos start up. Look what happened in Jaws. Innocent young little-town lady goes for a quiet midnight dip in the nude, the Jellos start up, there's a Finn scything through the water, next thing you know it's shark-bait time.

A new billboard. This time a dodgy Czechoslovakian called Alberto haunting me along the corridors. I didn't see him, but I could hear him. And with the corridors in that hotel, well, as you've realised by now, trying to trace a sound is a matter of hit or miss. And I had my attention on something totally different. The Quiet American. I had my eyes on him for the next interrogation. I was lucky enough to overhear him saying that he was going to skip lunch to visit one of the local tourist attractions. So I decided to follow him.

Now I knew that he would recognise me unless I disguised myself, he must have seen me in the gallery, and he'd have to be an idiot not to think it a bit too much of a coincidence if he saw me behind him. I had to make myself blend into the crowd. And what would a Quiet American regard as just another innocent soul going about his daily toil in Wellbury? Simple. Pin-striped suit, three-piece. Polished shoes. Bowler hat. Black umbrella in one hand. Copy of the Times underneath the other. Regimental looking tie. Paper packet containing home-made Marmite sandwiches. Five minutes in my hotel room and then I was out after him, umbrella swinging, bowler hat at slightly jaunty angle, strolling along just as if I was any other office worker out for lunch. All I was missing was Purdey.

Following him was easy to begin with. Let's just say that Wellbury was having one of its annual festivals – call it the Annual Summer Harvest Festival.

Beazeley (yeah, he's woken up, unfortunately) has just pointed out that you can't have a summer harvest. Harvests take place in autumn. I'm thinking of harvesting Beazeley. And not waiting until autumn.

Beazeley, I wrote you into this story, believe me I can write you out of it. Painfully.

Anyway. Festival. We'll have Morris dancers, maypoles and maidens. Rosy cheeked maidens with full figures, none of your cat-walk insect stick creature nonsense here. Blonde hair in braids. Oh, sod it. And brunettes, redheads, you name it. After all we can afford it. And just in case the gender lot complain, we'll throw in a cartload of senior female executives. Baby in one hand, briefcase in the other. One smoking a cigar. Another in blue jeans smoking a corncob pipe and singing Old Man Ribber.

(Okay, finding a whole cartload of senior female executives might be a bit beyond anyone's imagination, but try.)

(Anyway, they'll really be actors, in reality.)

And to add that little touch that defines a quintessentially English festival, there was a float with a group of Rastafarian actors doing Midsummer Night's Dream in rhyming gangsta rap.

It wasn't difficult to follow the Quiet American. You don't get many people dressed up as a cowboy at Wellbury summer harvest festivals. Not ones in shorts, Stetson hat, loud Hawaiian shirt, cowboy boots and armed to the paunch with water pistols. He climbed aboard a number 23 bus, double decker, red. There were two other number 23 buses directly behind. I boarded the third, to keep out of sight. I went to the top, and could see him quite clearly. Fortunately the bus he had boarded was one of the tourist type, open topped. I watched as he glanced around, totally oblivious to his tail.

The biggest problem with buses, I've found, is that they seem to go everywhere without actually getting anywhere, if you know what I mean. These three went around the suburbs, endlessly stopping and starting, it seemed. The first one would stop to let an old woman off. Another old woman at the same stop would decide that she wanted to catch the second bus. Why, I don't know. They were all on the same route. All going in the same direction of nowhere very much. Maybe she knew the driver. I was worried that our bus would overtake the others and I would lose sight of the Quiet American. Fortunately at most stops someone would turn up late and hail our bus, or there would be someone wanting to get off, so the three buses stayed in convoy.

Up until we reached open country, that is. Flowing fields of green, hills, blue sky. Sunshine and the scent of summer blooms. It was glorious. The sun was coming in on my side. I loosened the military style tie and basked in the warmth. It was so nice to be able to relax for a change that I almost dozed off. In fact I think I might have, for a few seconds, because I suddenly started and realised that the front bus had a worrying lack of Quiet American. I rushed downstairs and asked the driver to let me off. He refused, saying that he wasn't allowed to let people off other than at designated stops. I promised not to tell anyone. He said he could be reported. I pointed out that there was no-one else on the bus. He said there was – a university student just out of the pub, asleep at the back. I went to check. He was right. I came back and pointed out that the student was fast asleep. The driver still refused. He whispered that they had installed cameras. Finally I gave up. I hit the emergency release on the door, jumped out and landed, rolling, in the grass. Just like they do in the movies.

Why is it that, in the movies, they never sprain an ankle? Or have to spend ten minutes retrieving an umbrella, bowler, packet of lunch sandwiches and a copy of the Times?

Once I had found the umbrella, bowler, packet of lunch sandwiches and Times I hobbled back to the previous stop, dusting off various pieces of straw and grass. There was a path leading up the hill. I took the only option and followed it. If the Quiet American wasn't up there somewhere, it would be too late anyway. By a stroke of luck he was. I found him standing in the woods outside the remains of a little old chapel, reading a plaque. I straightened my tie and hobbled jauntily forward, the original city gent on an innocent lunchtime stroll. I paused as I reached the plaque.

"In memory of the bombing of 6th May 1943" it read. The Quiet American looked up at me and nodded in a friendly fashion.

'You Brits sure went through something during the Blitz,' he said. 'A man has to admire you for that.'

'That wasn't during the Blitz,' I pointed out politely. 'The Blitz was Forty to Forty-one. There was a baby Blitz in Forty-four. Anyway, it wasn't the Germans who bombed the chapel.'

His eyebrows rose.

'Not the French?' he asked.

'No, your lot – the Yanks. A Liberator dumped its load here by accident. They were lost. They thought they were over the Channel.'

'Heck. Sorry about that.'

'Not exactly your fault.'

'Not – not too many injuries?'

'Depends on what you see as too many. In this case there weren't any. The chapel just received a few more holes than it already had.'

He scratched his head.

'So, why the plaque?'

'The local council were responsible for repairing existing damage,' I explained. 'They didn't want to spend the money. When it was bombed they declared it a war monument and stuck the plaque up. Meant they didn't need to repair it. Thought it would be cheaper that way.'

'It wasn't?'

'The plaque maker was one of the councillors' buddies. Fiddled the account. Cost them a quarter of a billion in the end.'

He whistled softly, with just a touch of admiration for the fiddler.

'Funny, meeting you here,' I said nonchalantly. 'You remind me of someone I used to know. He was also American, strangely enough. Worked in the — industry.'

'The — industry?' he asked, his eyes narrowing slightly under the brim of his five hundred gallon hat. I kept mine innocent as the driven snow under my bowler.

'Yes, the — industry,' I remarked casually, as if it were perfectly acceptable for anyone to work in the — industry. 'Happened quite a few years ago. An unfortunate tale, sad to relate.'

'How so?' he asked, looking directly into my eyes, thinly disguising his suspicion. I turned to look down at the plaque, pushing the bowler up with the handle of my umbrella. His hand hung lazily down his side, a bit too close to his pistol for my liking.

'Careful,' I said, 'you Yanks have a bad habit of making mistakes with those things.'

It's one of my failings. I tend to say things some other people misunderstand. Or sometimes understand perfectly.

'Yeah?' he shot back. 'Know what? If it wasn't for us Yanks you Brits would be speaking German.'

Oh, great, that old one. You know, they really believe that sort of thing, some of them?

'Yeah,' I replied, letting myself get a little irritated, a silly thing to do, 'and if it wasn't for the Brits you Yanks would be speaking Deutsch. Anyway, I'm not a Brit,' I said, 'I'm Welsh.'

He blinked his eyes, trying to make sense of that. I couldn't blame him. It didn't make any sense to me either.

'America is a light upon a hill,' he said slowly, as if repeating a mantra, 'a beacon for the free world.'

Ah, one of those Americans.

'Just such a pity the fuse blows every so often,' I commented, unable to resist the urge to wind him up just a wee tadge. 'Or you forget to pay the electric. Now, shall we forget the platitudes and get back to the — industry?'

'Ah've always thought we shoulda stuck to gas,' he said, as if lost in some private memory. 'But, go on, pardner, tell me about this American you once knew.'

'He was young,' I began. The Quiet American nodded, a sudden wry smile twisting his mouth to one side.

'He didn't have a paunch in those days,' he suggested.

'No, he didn't. He was a fresh-faced kid, just out of college. Eager to see the world. And make a fortune, the good old American way. The good old American Dream.'

'Don't knock it till you've tried it, buddy.'

'I have. They put too much chilli pepper on it. Anyway, back to our young friend. He landed up in England after a series of adventures, including a French mistress who carried a blue-dyed poodle everywhere she went, a fight with a Corsican pirate, the rescue of a millionaire's daughter from Bedouin tribesman, the sinking of a freighter carrying illegal Barbie dolls, and being the first person to swim across the Mediterranean naked while singing Yankee Doodle Dandy and holding a rose in his mouth.'

This time the Quiet American gave a lonesome grin.

'I kinda wish I had been him. He must have fond memories. Good days.'

'I would imagine he does. Of those times. Not, perhaps, of later times.'

The suspicion was back.

'I guess he made some kinda mistake. Innocent young men eager for the American Dream sometimes do.'

'Yes, they do,' I agreed. 'In his case it was —s. Of course —s are perfectly legal. You don't mention them in respectable company, but they are perfectly legal, and everyone knows they're out there.'

'I hear your government are planning to illegalise them,' he commented. It didn't fool me. I wasn't about to be side-tracked.

'They'll make anything illegal these days. But that's bye the bye. Let's get back to our American Dreamer. He didn't know much about —s. He wasn't worried about what people get up to in the privacy of their own homes. But he did know that there was a demand for —s. And where there's a demand a young man can make a few bucks. Honest bucks.'

He took his hat off and wiped his brow thoughtfully. He could have been a farmer taking a brief pause during honest toil. Apart from the fact that his wig of white hair was sticking to the hat. Underneath he was quite bald.

'Different days,' he commented.

'Oh, I agree. Different days entirely.' I looked around the rolling green hills. 'But I expect there's always been a time when a young man gets duped by an older man. Because that's what happened, isn't it?'

'Your story,' he said. 'You make it go the way you want to.'

'Thank you, I will. I'll make it the devious-Limey-two-timer-cons-innocent-American-abroad story, shall I? Innocent young American college boy.' I prodded a leaf with the end of the umbrella, hooked it and brought it up, looking at it thoughtfully.

'So, back to the —s,' I said. 'Our nasty Englishman lets slip to our naive American boy that they could make a fortune out of —s. Tells him that he's just finished getting a degree at Oxford – or perhaps Cambridge, but I expect he'd say Oxford – he's just finished getting a First, and is eager to make a pile. The Oxford issue is purely for verisimilitude, of course.'

'He said it was Oxbridge. I've often wondered whether he did go to Oxbridge. Or was that a low-down lie?'

I was pretty sure he hadn't been to Oxbridge. But that wasn't going to stop me making something up.

'Oh, he went to Oxbridge. But he didn't get a degree there. He bought a one-day cheap return to Oxbridge so that he could honestly say that he'd been there.'

The Quiet American shook his head in both disgust at the Englishman and sadness at the naivety of the American youth.

'So our naughty Englishman talks our sweet American into joining him in a venture in selling —s. And boy, did they do well. The money came rolling in. It was champagne, caviar and limousines all the way. Until one day the reporters turned up. Newshounds. Eager for a story. The police couldn't do anything – everything was totally legit – but that didn't mean the newspapers couldn't have a public trial in print. Trial by media.'

'Newshounds,' he said slowly, rolling the word around his mouth. 'More like – what's that animal you have here? Ferrets? Weasels? Sharks one and all.'

'Those are the ones. Yes, along came the ferrets, weasels and stoats, carrying cameras, and with fat wallets to tempt anyone willing to pass on the lurid details. And they found one straight away. The company secretary. Two seconds and she was blabbing away quite merrily.'

That was a pun. The girl's name had been Merry. The Quiet American didn't seem to catch it. His jaw was set and he looked angry. Really, really angry.

'The amount we – the amount she was paid she should have known better to keep her mouth shut,' he said grimly. Then he added: 'Well, that's what it sounds like, from what you say.'

'Oh, I don't think we can blame her,' I said. 'She was also young. She wanted to be a celebrity. Get her name in the papers. A lot of people at that age do. She just didn't realise what was coming. She was as naive as he was, really. That's where the Dream goes wrong. You find out that other people's Dreams are your Nightmares.'

He turned away to look at the hills.

'Very sad, really,' I said. 'The young American Dreamer was in love with her. He was about to declare himself when the walls came crashing down. Ironic, wasn't it?'

'Ironic?' He turned back to me. 'In what way?'

'The news first appeared in The Trumpeter. The walls came crashing down. Jericho, that sort of thing.'

'Jericho? Never been there. Never been north of the Watford Gap. Until now.'

'No? Well, never mind. Back to our American youngster. One moment he's the ideal entrepreneur, making his fortune. Next thing his face is across every newspaper in the land, exposed as being the — baron. Yes, it's legal to sell —s, but is it acceptable? No! No! howled the tabloids. Send him home, the pernicious Yank, corrupting our youth, abusing our country. Questions were asked in the Houses of Parliament. Petitions were signed. Demands made. Hysteria in the media. Lock up your sons and daughters!'

The Quiet American had gone quieter than usual. I began a game of noughts and crosses in the earth with the point of the umbrella.

'Worse was to come, of course,' I continued as I played. 'It always does in such cases. Firstly, the Dreamer's business pardner disappeared, our nasty Englishman did a runner, along with all that lovely lolly.'

'Lolly?'

'Money, in English. His business colleague disappears, he can't do much about it because the mob are baying for his blood and he's too busy just trying to keep from a lynching. Then, secondly, his pappy hears the news. The unbelievable happens. A story from little old England winds up in the New York Blatherer and our young lad's father just happens to see a copy. The trouble is, our lad's dad is a respectable senator. He's got a reputation to uphold. He wuz hoping to be president. So the next thing our Dreamer knows is a telegram lands on his desk saying "Get your little butt back here right away or I'm coming to shoot it off".'

I paused to let him say something. Noticing the silence he interrupted his looking wistfully into nowhere.

'If you put a nought there you win,' he said, pointing at the ground.

'Ah, yes, thanks.' I made the nought and drew a line through the three. 'Anyway, our young American Dreamer. He left. Quickly. Economy class on the first bucket with wings. Wearing dark glasses, no doubt. And a false beard, perhaps.'

'Don't see how anyone could blame him,' the Quiet American said softly.

'No. No, he was young, he didn't realise what he was getting into. He was an idealist at heart.' I rubbed my jaw thoughtfully. 'You know, I've often wondered how the story ended. I have this idea that our young Dreamer went to work incognito on his pappy's ranch. As a lowly cowhand. Paid for his sins and found his salvation in hard work.'

'Ah kinda like that version,' he said. 'It's better than ending up as a slop boy cleaning the leftovers from bowls of clam chowder in a diner in Wastchesutchenan, East Tennessee. It's the sort of place they lynch strangers for being strangers.'

He put his hat back on. Suddenly he was the white-haired Quiet American again.

'It don't matter a hill of beans no more,' he said. 'All happened a long time ago. Nobody remembers.'

'Oh, I think it might matter a little bean or two,' I replied, turning directly towards him. 'I think it matters quite a few beans when that young American Dreamer turns up at the trial of a book about the man who conned him all those years ago.'

The look in his eyes told me that I had been right. I didn't know what the real —s had been, but I was definitely on track. And by now he thought I knew everything. It wouldn't take much to steer him towards a slip of the tongue, revealing exactly what the —s had been. After that it would just be a simple question of research to get the facts I needed.

'I guess,' he said, 'that if that young man did return like you say, I guess maybe he was thinking of revenge. Maybe he heard about the trial, used his life savings to get over here and bribe his way into the jury. Maybe he visited all his old haunts. And maybe he took a little time out and realised that he'd spent a lot of time in a hot diner sweating out his soul, and revenge wasn't worth it.'

'Maybe,' I agreed. I wasn't sure what I was agreeing with, because I wasn't sure if he was telling the truth or not.

He looked at his watch

'Best we be making tracks back to the court,' he said. 'Be bad manners to keep them waiting.'

'Er, just a sec,' I said, limping after him, 'about the —s ...'

'I made a promise to ma pappy never to mention the word again,' he replied, moving quite quickly.

'You could whisper it in my ear, I won't tell anybody.'

He stopped suddenly and turned around.

'You don't know what they were, do you?' he asked. 'You were making it all up, weren't you?'

Thankfully there was just a tinge of admiration in his voice. It gave me the hope that we weren't about to re-enact the shoot-out at Gulch City. I'd be the one with the handicap of not being able to fire back.

'Well, part of it,' I admitted.

'Which part?'

'I suppose you could say, the part that starts at the beginning and goes on until the end.'

He chuckled and shook his head.

'Nice try, pardner,' he said. 'Better luck next time.'

'Oh, come on, now, just a tiny clue? Be fair.'

'Only when hell freezes over, pardner,' he replied, not unkindly. In fact he even burst into a guffaw of laughter. 'Must say you had me going with that outfit. Thought you was just another British gent out for a lunchtime stroll.'

He paused and looked me in the eye.

'Ya know that little casino on the edge of town?' he asked.

'Not really.'

'I was thinking of doing some gambling there, poker, something like that. They tell me the chips are looked after by the monks from the local monastery. They're called the chip monks. You reckon that's true?'

I think his real question was, 'Just how stupid do you limeys think I look?'

'I doubt it,' I said. 'The monasteries were closed down by Henry VIII. It was called the Great Dissolution, if I remember correctly.'

He smiled thinly, as if to say I'd passed his test.

Then he turned and we ambled away. Or he ambled and I limped.

We must have looked a curious pair. A paunched old cowboy wearing a Stetson and shorts, a tall city gent in pinstripes with umbrella. And a limp. But it seemed perfectly normal at the time.

'What happened to Marlene?' he asked suddenly, as we approached the bus stop.

Marlene. The girl that blabbed. Merry Marlene. The girl that the American Dreamer was in love with.

'She took up missionary work,' I said. 'Went out to Africa.'

Actually, she died of a drug overdose in Soho four years after the Dreamer had left. But I wasn't going to tell him that.

'That's good,' he said. 'I've thought of her almost every day since the last time I saw her. You have her address?'

'I understand she works in a village cut off from civilisation for nine months of the year. I don't know the name, I'm afraid.'

'That's alright, pal. I couldn't afford to get there anyway. Still, it's nice to know things turned out okay for her.'

So that was the Quiet American done. Another cul-de-sac. Another failed attempt. I had dreamed of the day I would confront Edgar The Ears with the truth. At that moment all I would be able to say is "I know all about the exploding bully beef and the —s." He'd think I was Dagenham. Two stops beyond Barking. There was nothing for it. I would just have to go with the original plan. I would get that book. How was a question I was going to ignore. It was going to be a case of just do it.

Jennifer and Beazeley are having a discussion about the morality of telling white lies. It's a bit off-putting because she's in the kitchen and he's in here. He's trying to have the conversation in a low voice while attempting to read what I'm typing, whereas she's shouting back and using sibling language. Well, let's put it this way, it's the sort of language a sibling might get away with using. Try it with a stranger in a pub and you'll have a faceful of glass before you can say

Sherry.

Beazeley's view of life could be summed up as a cod philosophy.

Jennifer's is more full speed ahead and damn the torpedoes.

And the young woman across the street is washing her front windows again, probably for the third time. I can't help but wonder if she's trying to tell me something.

Or perhaps it's Beazeley's attention she's trying to attract.

Oh, God, I hope that isn't true. I know there's nothing stranger than why some couples get together – I tend to put it down to Darwinism – or alcohol – but Beazeley and the gorgeous young lady across the street? Beazeley and any woman, come to think of it.

Perhaps that isn't fair.

I'm sure his mother loves him.

Probably.

But I can promise you something, he didn't score while we were at the trial. If he had I would have created a scene where he gets tied naked to his bed by Mildreds One, Two and Three, who then proceed to strip off in front of him, very slowly.

You know, in a way I wish he had scored. It would be worth it for that scene.

Now Jen has called to tell us that lunch is ready. I thought I'd already had lunch. I'm pretty sure I didn't imagine it, I can see the crumbs in the keyboard. Or are those from yesterday?

Oh well, better go find out what she's on about, and then crack on into Wednesday afternoon. Because that's when Edgar The Ears comes to life.

Plum pudding.

Chapter XIX. Edgar The Ears Makes His Appearance

Why is it that food always tastes better when someone else has cooked it? Okay, that's a bit of a generalisation, I had a girlfriend once – we split up because I didn't take the tablets every day like they said, talk about a real bean counter. Anyway, she couldn't cook for toffee. Where does that expression come from? Must look it up. Anyway, all she could do was baked beans on toast, and then she burnt the toast half the time. She claimed that it was because of my doing things like creeping up behind her and shouting "Hippopotamus" every so often.

Well, what's wrong with that? Doesn't everyone do that sort of thing?
....

Jen and I discussed such issues over a late lunch – I thought the toasted sandwich was lunch, but that was just to keep me going while she made the real lunch. She says I shouldn't spend lunch with a sandwich sitting over a keyboard, and how right she is. We had everything, scrambled eggs with cheese and onion, sausages, mushrooms in garlic, bacon, toast and sweetcorn in cream. That might not sound like everyone's cup of tea, but it was more or less a mixture of everything that was left in the fridge and cupboards. Haven't had a chance to stock up recently. Jen said she'd pick up a few things since I was too busy. I gave her fifty quid, which she says is plenty if you know where to shop and what to buy. Apparently canned food is a no-no, it has to be fresh. I was tempted to point out that pizza deliveries are always fresh, but sometimes it's better not to try to be too clever. Jennifer is a woman to be wooed, not patronised by smart-alec comments, and a-wooing I intend to go. Hopefully, by the end of this saga, I will be able to report success. Keep your fingers crossed.

So, that's how it stands at the moment. Jenny's out shopping and I'm back on the case. And she's taken Beazeley with her. And the woman across the road is entertaining the postie again, so now I've got at least an hour of peace and quiet to get on with that afternoon.

....

Wednesday afternoon is when it happened. I was in the public gallery with Miss MI5 With Moustache. She wasn't talking to me for some reason, which was just as well, since I wasn't listening. My concentration was on the person in the witness box. Edgar The Ears had arrived.

His mien, considering that the jury included some of his worst enemies, was surprisingly confident. And it was a mien. We plebs would be happy to have an appearance that didn't come across as too tatty, he had a mien. I don't know whether he bought it, borrowed it or stole it, but it was definitely a mien. He even gave the jury his politician's smile. Most of them returned it with a blank, wooden look. Apart from the Clowns, who were back in the well of the dock, looking much happier about life. Clyde was playing with the kitten Squish, and Bonnie was looking at her with the proprietary smile of a young man deeply in love, a young man whose happiness is always one step happier when his girlfriend is happy.

Those Clowns were strange. They were the soppy type that normally my first reaction would be to pour a vat of five-day-old custard over them. But they had taken soppiness to the end and out the other side. It would be like dumping custard over a pair of puppies. Except the puppies would actually notice the custard. And probably enjoy it. The Clowns would just carry on looking into each other's eyes. Soppily.

"Dahling?"

"Yes, dahling?"

"You've got custard in your hair, dahling."

"Have I, dahling?"

"I love you, dahling. And your custard."

"I love you too, dahling. And your custard."

Yuk.

Mrs Plum was smiling at her knitting as usual, needles clicking away. The needles now consisting of two wire coat hangers opened up – I could see that they were unsatisfactory, she kept talking to herself in a low monotone, about bread pudding and snails, I guessed. Miss F was reading a Mills and Boone romance. Miss F's mother was also reading the novel, her arm around her daughter's shoulders. Miss F had to wait until her mother had finished before she could turn the page, but she seemed happy enough to do so.

They were wearing matching reading glasses.

Mr Sleepy was sleeping. Strawberry Mousse had flicked her scarf over her shoulder when Edgar The Ears had smiled at them, and it had resumed its levitational position two inches above Mr Sleepy's face. The Prim Maiden Aunt was looking down at the floor in a disapproving manner, as was her wont. The way that makes you wonder whether the cleaners hadn't done a proper job. The Quiet American, the Nun With Guitar and the Major all had the wooden looks. The wooden looks of people who hated Edgar The Ears' guts.

The most interesting look of all was on Judge Beak's nose when he sat down and saw Edgar The Ears. It twitched. It definitely twitched. As usual you couldn't see anything else of him, but it was a very expressive twitch.

Hello, I thought. Why is it you don't like Edgar The Ears?

Before I could follow that train of thought the Vulture had stood up. He flapped his black wings again and looked up at Edgar above him.

'H'you h'are h'Mithter h'Edgar h'the h'Earth, h'O-h'B-h'Ney?' he asked, in the most servile manner a nine-foot tall vulture with a yellow budgie on his head can aspire to.

That came as somewhat or a surprise to me – that Edgar The Ears had been awarded the OBE. Not that he might have been awarded it, just that I hadn't heard about it.

Edgar The Ears smoothed an ear to check that it was in place, and to give him a few seconds to test the question to see whether it contained anything dangerous, such as needing a direct answer.

'I am,' he replied eventually, giving the impression that, by admitting his name, he was conferring – magnanimously – an honour upon the wide-eyed vulture.

'H'you h'are h'the h'Minithter h'for h'Toy h'trainth h'and h'Chrithmath h'Tree h'Regulathinth?'

'I am.'

'H'a h'rethponthible h'pothition, h'one h'whith h'would h'only h'be h'given h'to h'thomeone h'of h'great h'reliability h'and h'trutht?'

'I believe that is the general feeling, yes.'

'H'thomeone h'of h'impeccable h'character?'

'I would like to think so, yes.'

'H'not h'thomeone h'thuthch h'ath h'dethcribed h'in h'thith – h'thith h'thing?'

Mr Crane held up the lurid cover. Edgar The Ears' left ear pinged open. He smoothed it back.

'A complete tissue of lies,' he smiled. 'A veritable farrago.'

'H'the h'lollipop h'lady h'on h'page h'fourteen?'

The right ear pinged open. He smoothed it back.

'Utter fabrication. I have never spoken to a lollipop lady in my life. Although I appreciate, of course, the crucial work they do in the community. And, of course, some of my finest friends have spoken to lollipop ladies.'

'H'the h'New h'Zealand h'butter h'inthident h'on h'page h'thixty?'

The left ear quivered. His hand got to it in time.

'Absolute nonsense. No one who knows me would ever believe I could even contemplate such a thing. I only ever order British butter, from Harrods of course. I believe in supporting our honest British farmers and British businesses.'

'H'thank h'you, h'Mither h'Earth, h'that h'will h'be h'all.'

Mr Crane sat down, a confident smile playing on his lips.

The court waited for the Beak to say something. There was utter silence for a few moments as we all slowly realised that the Beak was again fast asleep. The Quiet American raised an eyebrow at Mr Crane, who shook his head. He stood up and leaned over the partition into Mr Ball's cubicle.

'H'Mithter h'Ball, h'it h'appearth h'that h'Mithter h'Beak ath ... h'dothed h'off. H'perhapth h'you h'thould h'continue h'without im?'

Mr Ball stood up. I could see in his eyes that he was looking forward to this. I could also see the reason why. He had been given a chair to stand on, an office chair. That surely would not collapse underneath him. He could now make up for lost time. He clambered onto the chair, a determined smile on his face.

I said an internal prayer of thanks, given along with a deep internal sigh of relief. With Mr Ball on form there was a pretty good chance of his winning the case. We were back on track to victory.

'MR EARS,' he began, followed by 'arrgh!'

The problem with the chair was the wheels. The chair had gone one way, and Mr Ball the other. He was now holding on to the balustrade in front of him, chin just over, with the rest of his body at an angle. He slowly pulled the chair back with his feet until he was upright. Then he took a firm grip on the balustrade.

'MR EARS,' he began again, much more slowly this time, not as loud, and with a careful glance at the chair beneath him. 'MR EARS, YOU AGREE THAT THIS BOOK DOES NOT DESCRIBE YOU IN ANY WAY at all arrgh!'

The chair had gone the other way this time. Once again Mr Ball pulled it slowly back. This time he knelt on it, presumably feeling that this gave him more control. Unfortunately it left only his eyes showing above the balustrade. Edgar The Ears must have been looking at the top of a massive light-blue wig and a large pair of spectacles which I suspect rather resembled the head of a mad owl.

'Well, Mr Ears?' squeaked Mr Ball.

'Er, well what?' asked Edgar The Ears, looking, for the only time I have ever seen, slightly less than a hundred percent confident.

'What is the answer to my question?' the top of the owl demanded in a squeaky voice.

'Er, which question?'

Now it was the owl who looked confused. He ducked down, retrieved a piece of paper, read it quickly, and then his eyes and wig re-appeared, a pudgy fist next to it holding the notes.

'MR EARS, you agree that THIS BOOK does not describe you IN ANY WAY at all?' he asked, his voice going up and down as he desperately tried to regain control while half his attention was on the treacherous mobile chair beneath him.

'It's a complete distortion of the facts,' Edgar The Ears replied, holding firmly onto both ears. 'A complete pack of lies.'

'A work of FICTION, in other WORDS?' prompted Mr Ball.

'It pretends to be a work of fiction,' Edgar The Ears said, his head beginning to vibrate with the effort of holding his ears in check.

'No-one would EVER recognise the central character as yourself, WOULD THEY, MR EARS?'

'Ha! That's what they'd like everyone to think.'

'That is what everyone WOULD think. THAT'S the truth of it, ISN'T IT, Mr Ears?'

'There is no truth in it, I've already said so.'

'PRECISELY. Take page four hundred and three. THE CASE OF PERUVIAN PAWPAWS. You have never taken a bribe of PERUVIAN ... PAWPAWS, have you, Mr Ears?'

For a moment his ears seemed to relax. He knew he could answer that one truthfully.

'I wouldn't recognise a Peruvian pawpaw if you showed me one. I can also honestly state quite categorically that none of my colleagues have ever been involved with Peruvian paw paws. However I cannot say the same for the party opposite. I mean the party in opposition.'

It hadn't been Peruvian paw paws, of course. Norah The Nose would never have made the mistake of stating exactly what the bribe had been. She was hardly that stupid. I had a hunch that it might have something to do with the Major's exploding Argentinian bully beef. I glanced at the Major's face, but it retained its wooden appearance, giving me no clue.

'OR PAGE SEVENTY-FIVE, where the main protagonist is found STAGGERING IN HYDE PARK wearing only a feather boa while SINGING A SEA SHANTY at the top of his voice. You never did that, DID YOU, Mr Ears?'

His face twitched just ever so, ever so slightly.

'Of course not.'

As it happens it had been in Trafalgar Square in the early hours of the morning. Some of his friends had made sure it had been hushed up. And it had been a leather thong, not a feather boa.

Even now the image of Edgar The Ears wearing just a leather thong makes me feel queasy.

'So, Mr Ears,' Mr Ball said, very slowly as he began carefully standing upright, getting prepared for the killer blow, 'the only POSSIBLE CONCLUSION ANY SENSIBLE JURY COULD COME TO IS THAT THIS WORK IS INDEED arrrgggh!'

There was a crash as the chair went backwards. Mr Ball went over, this time failing to get a grip on the balustrade. He bounced around the cubicle a couple of times before ending up lying on his back, surrounded by the remains of the office chair. One of the wheels skittered around, making a plinking sound before giving up its escape attempt. Then silence. The jury leaned forward to get a better view. The jury box creaked and shifted. The jury slowly leaned back very slowly and very carefully until it stopped.

'Just so,' said Judge beak. Everyone turned to him. 'A suitable juncture to end for the day. We shall continue at nine o'clock tomorrow morning. You agree, Mr Crane, Mr Ball?'

'H'if h'your onour h'so h'witheth,' Mr Crane said.

The little blue flag waved above Mr Ball's cubicle. It seemed smaller and more pathetic than ever. The recorder pressed a button and the metallic order to rise rang around the court. Everyone stood up awkwardly and the judge disappeared into his chambers. The jury looked at each other. They shrugged their shoulders, stood up and began filing out against the camber of their box.

I leaned forward and put my chin in my hands, watching them go. For the first time in my life I regretted not having done carpentry at school. I would have stolen into the courtroom at night and built Mr Ball an orange crate that not even a tank could crush.

But the way my luck was going at that stage I probably would have built it into Mr Crane's dock by mistake, so better I left that option well alone.

The Nun With Guitar looked up at me and winked. She strummed a few bars on her guitar, singing softly to me. Once again I felt that strange attraction, almost as if there were an invisible bond connecting us together across the crowded courtroom.

Miss MI5 With Moustache noticed the wink. I could sense a struggle in her between not talking to me and not finding out what the wink meant.

'Often have nuns winking at you?' she asked casually.

'All the time.'

'That looked like a special wink to me.'

'Was it? What did it say?'

'You're not telling me you don't know?'

'She's a nun. I'm not. I don't even have enough belief or disbelief to qualify as an agnostic. We speak a different language.'

She shook her head.

'Are you for real?' she asked.

'No, please,' I said, 'I've already had that discussion with the Nun With Guitar and I couldn't understand a word she was saying.'

'I just don't believe you,' she said. 'I've known bats that can see more than you can.'

'Bats aren't actually blind, you know.'

She sighed and stood up to go.

'Before you go, tell me something,' I said. 'I didn't know that Edgar The Ears had the OBE. What did he get it for?'

She looked at me, puzzled.

'It's not the OBE,' she said, 'it's the OBN. Some people just pronounce it sideways so that it sounds like the OBE. I thought everyone knew that.'

'OBN? Order of the British – Numpire?'

She took a copy of Private Eye from her pocket.

'You're joking! Order of the Brown Nose?'

She nodded.

'And he's proud of it?'

'I doubt whether he gives a monkey's bottom. It just allows him to claim to have been awarded the O-B-Neh, which comes out as the OBE if you don't listen too carefully.'

'But why? Surely sooner or later someone is going to pull him up on it?'

'Pull him up on what? That he's making a joke? Everybody in the know knows he's making a joke. They aren't bothered about anyone not in the know falling for it. Nobody in the know ever worries about the opinion of anybody not in the know. It's well known.'

By the time she finished that I had one eye closed, the other one was twitching dementedly and I was getting a thumping headache.

'But – what if, I don't know, say the American ambassador isn't in the know and falls for it? Surely it could create a diplomatic incident if he found out that the bloke he has been treating as an OBE is actually an OBN?'

'Think about it. Firstly you'd have to be incredibly stupid to fall for it – that is, if you travel in those sort of circles – and countries don't normally appoint idiots as diplomats to other countries. Well, not all the time. And if you did get taken in, would you admit it? You'd end up a laughing stock.'

She had a point. It was a typical Edgar The Ears move. I had a distinct feeling that Edgar The Ears was way ahead on points. It would be nice to think that he had engineered Mr Ball's verticality problems, but I suspect that that had been merely coincidental. Edgar The Ears's weapons were words: gossip, rumour, innuendo, a politician's swords and pistols. The physicality of fiddling with boxes of oranges and chairs with wheels attached would never have occurred to him.

A thought occurred to me which slightly brightened my outlook. If others also felt that he was winning, certain others on the jury for

234

example, it was distinctly possible that they might want to balance the scales by having a word with someone nasty.

Like me.

They might not know it was me they were looking for, but if not they'd be looking for another kind of me. All I had to do was stroll around the hotel corridors until they realised it was me they were looking for. So that lunchtime I dressed up as a waiter, stuck on glasses and a thick moustache, got myself a tray and champagne bottle, and strolled around the corridors looking like a waiter to most people, but also just like me would look if someone was looking for me. It wasn't long before I noticed Strawberry Mousse in an alcove, apparently idly doing her makeup. It didn't fool me for a second. She was waiting for me, and we both knew it. Or at least I knew that I knew it. I'm pretty sure that she knew it too.

Hugo was a zero. The Major was ineffectual. The Quiet American was too set on repentance rather than revenge. Miss Strawberry Mousse was a different question altogether. She had that quiet look of a woman determined on doing something, a woman who would let nothing get in her way. With her on my side Edgar The Ears had as much chance as that well known snowflake in the infernal regions.

I might not, as the saying goes, be cooking with gas.

But I felt that I had, at last, found the stove.

Chapter XX. Strawberry Mousse Reveals her Recipe

Jen and Beazeley are back from shopping. They're in the kitchen unpacking the goodies, which is strange for Beazeley. Normally he's straight in here for his latest heart attack, masochistically eager to read whatever I pretend is my latest chapter. I overheard part of their conversation, which doesn't augur well. Actually it doesn't augur, it sounds like a death knell.

"You can't go out with him," Beazeley said. "He's a total – total – he's downright evil. He's made my life hell."

"Now, now, Harold, swearing."

Harold? His name's Alfred. And who is it that Jennifer wants to go out with?

"Jenny, he's a total – total – he's evil. Evil! He pretends to be nice when you're around, but believe me, he's a total and utter – You know! Thing!"

That's when my heart did the famous sinking-through-the-floor feeling. Jenny has found some bloke she fancies, and he's one of those Rhett Butler characters. All smooth and moustache on the outside, a right vicious summer beach on the inside. I couldn't help but hope that it wasn't Edgar The Ears, but unfortunately Beazeley's description fits too well. Edgar The Ears's philandering is widely known. Why women fall for him God alone knows, but they do.

And it would explain why Jennifer is here. "I've heard that someone is writing a book about that silly trial," he would say. "Be a love and have a look around. Find out what he's up to."

And the sort of woman he attracts would reply, "Of course, darling. Anything for you, darling."

Or am I letting my imagination get carried away?

Fact: Jenny has met someone she fancies who Beazeley thinks is total evil, and if Beazeley thinks that the person must be bad he must be bad, Beazeley just doesn't normally use language like that.

Question: Is it Edgar The Ears?

Answer: Unlikely. Possible, but unlikely.

But possible.

Why else would she hang around here?

You have to hold on to certain things when your world is falling apart. I kept to my mission when the Nun With Guitar was singing me softly dead, I will keep to this while Jenny breaks my heart.

Though it has to be said that Jenny is very real, whereas the Nun With Guitar was wholly ethereal.

Strawberry Mousse.

Not even thinking of the X-word.

The postie has just left the house opposite.

Oh, woman, thy name is frailty!

Stop being an idiot and get on with the story.

Strawberry Mousse and the heavy artillery ...

'So, Mizz Mousse,' I said, slipping into the alcove, 'how did you get involved with Edgar The Ears?'

She gave me the look of a woman who knows men well, is used to dealing with them, a woman who looks upon men as unfortunate necessities in life, the same as septic tanks and dustbins. A woman who has spent her life trying to work out a way to teach a dustbin to mow the lawn.

'Why should I have got involved with Edgar The Ears?' she asked. She was applying pink lipstick to her lips as she spoke. In another woman it might have appeared provocative. Alluring, even. The way Strawberry Mousse did it made you keep your distance. Those lips weren't designed for kissing a man. What they were designed for I can't say.

(It's covered by the Official Secrets Act. Also, I really don't want to think about what they were designed for. I'd end up like Beazeley if I did.)

I nodded and pretended to be confident and unconcerned.

'Let me tell you a story,' I said, 'and you can tell me how true it is.'

She didn't say "Go on" or anything like that. She just carried on applying lipstick. She had a layer about half an inch thick by that stage.

'There was once a woman who owned a bakery shop,' I began. 'She lived in a town where running a bakery shop was legal, but frowned upon. People who used her bakery shop – they were all men. There was a quiet side entrance where they could slip in without been seen. Now the top people – the aristocrats, shall we say – were continually telling the people and peasants that bakery had to be permitted, but that it was a bad thing to go to a bakers. Which was a bit hypocritical, because they had their own personal bakers in their mansions which the people never got to see.'

I paused. I was finding it hard to keep up the analogy. Any minute now there'd be mention of tea and cream and jam and cake and I'd really be skating on thin ice slippery as an eel at the birthing hour.

'How am I doing so far?' I asked.

'It's your story,' she said, shrugging her shoulders. I could tell by that shrug that I was getting to her. It was the sort of shrug a woman like Strawberry Mousse makes which emphasises her bosom in order to distract you. You look down, next thing her fist is in your teeth. I wasn't going to get caught by that one. I continued quickly, looking directly into her eyeliner.

'Let's say there was a special aristocrat. A man who had bought himself into the aristocracy. With money he had made on the backs of the peasants – and by nasty little things like blackmail. Now this aristocrat didn't like spending money on a full time baker, so he was one of the few aristocrats who used the baker's services. The baker was a pretty shrewd woman. She made sure her clients didn't accidentally meet in the patisserie section by mistake. She knew which of her clients preferred macaroons, ginger bread men, Battenberg, that sort of thing. So she made sure each had their own little room where they could indulge in their own illicit desires. Or is the phrase "illicit desires" too close to the truth?'

'It's an interesting story,' she said, putting the lipstick away and starting with the pink eyeshadow. One of those little paint tins containing about half a litre of pink paint, and an artist's large paintbrush.

'Let's say our dodgy aristocrat is worried that the baker might try to blackmail him. He knows the form, he's done it to plenty of other people. So he decides to get in first. He discovers that the baker is also selling marzipan to the womenfolk. Now if it's unacceptable to supply the menfolk with their sweet fantasies, selling marzipan to the womenfolk is just so way beyond the pale the baker's likely to get torn to pieces if anyone finds out. So he takes a few photographs of the baker handing over the goodies to the Lord Mayor's wife, shows them to the baker and says, "You give me any trouble and these appear in the Daily Liar, capisch?" So what do you think the baker replies?'

'I wouldn't have a clue,' Strawberry Mousse replied. 'But I think you're going to tell me.' She was pretending lack of interest. The way she was applying pink eyeliner to her eyes told me that all her attention was on me.

'She doesn't have a choice. She's got a pretty good business, she doesn't want to leave town. And even if she started up somewhere else the aristocrat will find her. So she has to agree. No word about the aristocrat's attending her bakery, and he can have free meringue for the rest of his life.' I paused. 'Personally I feel sorry for the baker.

I think she was the heroine of the story. She fought for her own freedom against the hypocrisy of the state. I often wonder why she didn't poison the aristocrat's meringues.'

She snapped the tin of eyeliner closed, slipped it into her handbag and gave me a direct look.

'It wasn't meringues,' she said, 'it was profiteroles.'

'Profiteroles. I like profiteroles.'

'Some were made with French butter.'

'Ah.'

'Others with extra-virgin olive oil.'

'Ooh.'

'Double cream.'

'Yum.'

'But all with an added soupçon of cyanide.'

'Oh.'

' Or sometimes soup spoon of cyanide.'

'Eek.'

'Unfortunately the aristocrat didn't die. He just got very ill. But he never went back to the baker ever again.'

I nodded slowly. Thoughtfully. And put my tongue back in my mouth in case she had any leftovers on her.

'I like happy endings,' I said. 'What I can't understand is why the baker is still after the aristocrat.'

'To finish off the job. To rid society of a pustulous sore. To cleanse the social body. I would imagine.'

'And for a little revenge?'

'Just a smidgeon. It's the vital ingredient in the recipe of life.'

I paused. There was something I wanted to ask her, but it was a delicate subject. You can ask a world-famous cricketer what inspired him to go into the game. You can even interview a politician as to his decision to enter such a foul profession.

It isn't that easy with bakers.

'Tell me if I'm intruding into a personal affair,' I said, slowly, 'but, do you mind if I ask you why you – why she became a baker? It isn't the profession that you expect many people to choose.'

She gave me one of those looks people do when debating whether to answer your question or just smack you around the head a few times to teach you better manners. Finally she nodded.

'I don't hate men per se,' she said, which was a little bit of relief to me. 'But it's an unfortunate fact of life that men have easier choices when it comes to earning a living. Women, whatever they say, effectively have a choice between a career or bringing up a family. I chose the family. I mean, she chose her family. She thought she had a loving husband, but it turned out that he was an alcoholic. He left her with a young son to bring up on her own. She couldn't manage the son and earn a living. She tried. She didn't have any qualifications so she took any job going, cleaning, working in cheap restaurants, stacking shelves. But the hours were long, she was kept away from her child, and despite all her efforts the money just wasn't enough. In the end she had to give the son up for adoption, just before his first birthday.'

She didn't say it, but I could tell in her eyes what an emotional battle it must have been. Keep your child with you in poverty or give him up in the hope he would have a better life elsewhere?

'And then,' she continued, her voice hardening, 'her husband returned, apparently cured. She was so desperate she took him back in. In a short while she was pregnant again. A baby girl. She dreamt of getting her son back, of restarting their family. He would have been three years old then.'

She took a tissue from her handbag and looked at it. She wiped her nose delicately. It was done in the manner of someone who had learnt long ago to control her emotions, but they still beat heavy at her heart.

'The husband wasn't cured. He went back to the booze. The baker was left alone again. The trauma was too much for the baker. She had a nervous breakdown. Her baby was taken into care. While she was undergoing treatment they talked her into giving that daughter up for adoption.'

Despite her control I could see her eyes were moist.

'When she recovered she made a decision. If she couldn't have a family she would have a business. Be independent. Be free, as far as she could. There aren't many choices for a woman in this world without qualifications. Not if she wants the freedom money can buy. So she chose the age-old route. Baking. Not the sort of thing most women would prefer, but when life has dumped a ton of manure on you twice you realise that the only thing to do is get a shovel out and sell it at a profit.'

I nodded slowly. Hopefully showing my understanding. She was twisting the tissue into pieces. I wished there was something I can say. Unfortunately it was one of those times when there was just nothing to say. Or nothing for me to say. Finally she shoved the tissue back into her handbag, gave me a brief nod of acknowledgement and then was gone.

She didn't even leave her business card. I had been hoping to add it to my collection as a novelty. I only had one vaguely similar in the collection, and that had been given to me by an aunt when I was eleven.

No doubt her mind hadn't been on business right at that moment. Anyway ...

I parked my butt on the windowsill to think. Strawberry Mousse had told me all I needed to know. Only trouble was, there was nothing I could use. I could hardly go to the major newspapers and say "Hey,

I've got this brilliant story about a baker." Never mind how they'd react if I mentioned the exploding bully beef and —s. They'd think I was a right fruitcake.

Still, as far as Strawberry Mousse went, it was probably purely my fault. I should have got her tell her story her way. Though god knows what she would have used instead of a baker.

'This is fun, ducks, innit?' said a voice next to me.

'I wouldn't quite put it that way, Mrs Baggs,' I said. 'You don't happen to remember who murdered you, do you?'

I wasn't that interested, to be honest, but one tries to be polite.

'This is fun, ducks, innit?'

'No, I didn't think so. Well, time I was moving on. Look after yourself.'

'This is fun, ducks, innit?'

'Still not found your voice, then?'

'This is fun, ducks, innit?'

'It'll take a few more days at least,' said the Fawn Ghost, materialising outside the window. 'You don't have a fag on you, do you?'

'No, sorry.'

'Doesn't matter. I can't smoke the real things anyway. Oh, well, can't stop, must get on.'

'You're in a hurry?'

'Yeah. That other bloke you sent over, the accountant, he's driving me crazy. He keeps – oh, bugger, there he is now. I'm off.'

I looked up to where the Fawn Ghost had pointed before he disappeared. An outline of Hugo with knitting needle through head was looking around.

'Looks like you've got company, Mrs Baggs.'

'This is fun, ducks, innit?'

I left quickly. Time was running out. The older members of the jury were obviously too street-wise to give me anything usable. However there was one member of the jury who was open to being conned. I mean, who would be more honest. One member of the jury who, strangely enough, made no sense. Miss F. Miss F was really too young to have had anything to do with Edgar The Ears. Was she just what she appeared to be, an innocent young member of the jury, there just by chance? Or did she have some information, did she know something I could use as concrete evidence? There was only one way to find out. First of all I had to find her. Away from Miss F's Mother, preferably.

It wasn't easy. I tried all the obvious haunts. The television room. The games arcades outside. The music shops where youngsters often congregate. I finally found her in a Milk Bar playing with a Sundae Surprise.

Beazeley has just interrupted to add his widow's mite to the general effort. He has pointed out that Milk Bars are American and that you wouldn't find one in modern Wellbury. Maybe in the 1950s, perhaps, but not these days.

Well, Beazeley, this is a special one I had flown in for the occasion, okay? It's your typical 1960's Milk Bar, all chromium and imitation red leather. And the waitresses are all would-be actresses, young, wearing tight-fitting white tops and skimpy little red mini-skirts. They get around on roller-skates, skating around with their trays of ice-cream sundaes and knickerbocker glories. They're also the cheerleaders for the local football team on Saturday games, the well-known Wellbury Redskins.

Beazeley? Beazeley?

Damn.

I'd forgotten he had a thing about young cheerleaders with tight-fitting white tops and tiny little mini-skirts. His eyeballs are spinning around in their sockets like pinballs on speed, and steam is starting to come from his ears. He's not allowed to watch American football in case they show the cheerleaders.

Okay, Beazeley, I was lying about the waitresses. They were actually all old crones in black. With warts and moustaches. And they cackled a lot.

Nope, too late, he's gone.

Oh, well, let's get on. Beazeley will just have to catch up when he returns from whatever private planet he's orbiting at the moment.

So, Milk Bar and Miss F.

Chapter XXI. Miss F and the Lime and Mint Treble

I spotted Miss F through the window of the Milk Bar. She was sitting idly consuming her milkshake, kicking her legs and looking bored. She'd changed into a red polka-dotted halter top and frilly yellow skirt, but kept the spangly flip-flops. She looked as if she were a young girl wondering when the boys would turn up so that she could ignore them. There weren't any boys around, so she'd just have to do with me for the moment.

I knew that I had to act quickly, before her mother turned up. I turned my collar up, put on a pair of reflective dark glasses, retrieved a battered Homburg hat from a nearby dustbin, hurried into the Milk Bar and slipped into the seat opposite her. She slurped on her straw and looked at me with that blank look teenagers give adults they don't expect to find very interesting.

'Any good?' I asked as something to break the ice. She shrugged her little shoulders and went back to her milkshake.

'Okay,' I said, pushing the salt and pepper shakers to one side and leaning my arms on the able, 'I won't beat about the bush. What do you know about Edgar The Ears?'

Another shrug.

'Why don't we start with when you first met him?' I suggested.

Another shrug. I sighed and reached for the menu.

'I see, it's bribery time,' I said. 'Okay, what about a Chocolate Double Thick? Vanilla With Organic Pods? Peach Triple Boat with biscuits shaped like zoo animals?'

No response. I leaned forward again.

'Or I could ask for the Lime and Mint Treble?' I whispered. That got her attention. Everyone had heard about the Lime and Mint Treble. Only adults over a certain age were allowed to order it. Miss F wasn't.

I could get five years for ordering one for her. A severe ticking off at the least.

'With Smarties?' she whispered back, eyes wide.

'With Smarties,' I agreed, 'green ones. As many as you want.'

'Wow,' she whispered, awed.

I raised my hand for a waitress, not taking my eyes off Miss F's. A passing old crone hammered her tray down on it, her roller-skates squeaking. She sped off, cackling.

'Fffftt!' I screamed as quietly as I could, nursing my battered hand under the opposite armpit. I'd forgotten how vicious those old waitresses could be. Once the pain in my hand had moderated to a burning thumping I looked around and raised my eyebrows at one of the old women who had been watching me with some amusement. She skated over slowly, black dress flapping.

'Lime and Mint Treble?' she asked, sneering. I nodded.

'With green Smarties?' I nodded again.

'Just for yourself, sir?' I nodded again. The "sir" came out as an insult. She sneered again and roller-skated away.

'Now,' I said to Miss F. 'Edgar The Ears. When did you first meet him?'

She pouted and looked back in silence. Then she folded her thin little arms across her flat little chest. I could read the body language. "Only when I have a Lime and Mint Treble in my sticky little paws" it said. "Until then you can just go –"

She did have a very expressive little face.

Fortunately the waitress returned almost immediately. She must have known what was coming. She didn't even pretend that it was for me. She placed it in front of Miss F. Miss F got stuck in before the waitress had even turned her skates around. She had her spoon in that bilious green concoction before you could say "Yuk".

'Okay, now tell me about Edgar The Ears. What happened?'

She sucked her spoon and looked at me. She was already a quarter-way through the Lime and Mint Treble. The good thing about those are that they slow you down very quickly. Very few people have been known to finish a full one without throwing up.

'He got me drunk and seduced me when I was fifteen,' she said in that offhand way such girls do when they are deliberately trying to impress someone but don't want to appear as if they were. I smiled back at her. A cold, thin smile. A cold, thin smile that said "You're a lying little brat, aren't you?" Edgar The Ears was a swine. He was a crook. A swindler. An adulterer. Hypocrite. Double-dealing, black-hearted, immoral, big-eared, downright heel.

Allegedly.

What he wasn't was a school-girl seducer.

Oh, he had loads of affairs, even if you discounted the dodgy rumours. But his affairs were almost always with women in their thirties. Women who knew what they were doing. Women who knew it wasn't likely to be kisses and love ever after. Miss F at seventeen looked about fourteen, if not less, and acted about twelve. At fifteen she had probably looked about ten and acted like an eight-year-old. The thought would never have even occurred to Edgar The Ears. For him Miss F wouldn't even have existed. She would need to get to voting age before he would even think of smiling at her, and even then he probably wouldn't bother. People of that age weren't likely to vote for him.

Actually the statistics show they aren't likely to vote. That would definitely put her beyond his radar.

'Well, that's a serious accusation,' I said, taking out my notebook and pen to put things on a formal footing. And to start putting the pressure on. 'I think we'd better start off with some dates for this seduction.'

She looked back, still sucking her spoon. I think she had realised that she'd overstepped the mark.

'He didn't, really,' she said slowly, the spoon still in her mouth. 'I – I made that up. It sounded more interesting.'

I looked back at her, the thin smile turning into one of bitter resignation as I realised the truth.

'You've never met him before, have you?' I asked. 'You don't even know who he is, do you?'

She shrugged and burped. The Lime and Mint Treble can do that to a person.

'I'm bored,' she said, dropping the spoon into the remains of the Treble. 'And anyway, he's probably done something wrong. Otherwise why would he be on trial?'

Don't you just love it when people come up with that sort of nonsense? He must be guilty, he's on trial isn't he? Especially when it wasn't Edgar The Ears on trial in the first place.

Which was a distinct pity.

And what I really, really hate is having to defend the rights of a swine like Edgar The Ears, a – thing – I would quite happily see nailed to the desert floor so that he can die slowly, frying in the sun.

Okay, well perhaps "nailed" isn't quite the right word not with all that desert sand and stuff and -

Anyway, back at the Milk Bar.

'If you're bored,' I said, standing up and putting my notepad and pen back in my pocket, 'maybe someone should play some practical jokes on you.'

Locking you up in your room for a few years would be a start, I thought.

'That would be fun,' she replied, eyes now wide like a child's. 'Do you know any practical jokes?'

'Perhaps pour some salt into your Treble?' I suggested, the first thing that came to mind, probably because of the salt shaker on the table.

'Wow! That would be wicked!' she exclaimed. 'But they'd have to do it without me seeing, coz otherwise it wouldn't be a surprise.'

I pinched the skin between my eyebrows, the way you do when you suspect a huge headache has just landed and is now taxi-ing into the front left lobe of your brain prior to setting off the afterburner.

'I tell you what, let's play hide and seek,' I said. 'Close your eyes and count to twenty.'

'Okay,' she replied, closing her eyes and putting her hands over them, her mouth moving silently as she counted.

I took the lid off the salt shaker and poured the contents into her Treble. Then I dropped down and hid beneath the table in the next cubicle.

'Twenty!' I heard her say, followed by: 'Oh, he's gone. What a funny little man.'

Funny?

Little?

Then the exaggerated sound of noisy consumption of a Treble.

'Oh! Someone's put salt into my Treble! Oh! That's so wicked!'

I closed my eyes for a few moments. I couldn't believe what was happening. She was actually enjoying the remains of the Treble. With a full shaker of salt in. I crawled away. Enough was enough. At the counter they charged me five pound forty for the Treble and ten quid for the salt. They'd seen that sort of thing before. As I left I almost bumped into the knees of Miss F's mother. She probably wasn't used to men crawling out of Milk Bars on their hands and knees. I noticed, as you do in such situations, that she actually had very nice legs.

'Ah, Miss F's Mother,' I said, standing up and straightening my tie, as if a grown man crawling around was a perfectly normal thing to do. 'I don't suppose you've ever met Edgar The Ears, have you?'

'No,' she replied, eyes blinking. 'I hear he'll be appearing in court tomorrow afternoon though. I'm looking forward to seeing him.'

'Will he? Excellent. Can't wait. Oh, I think Miss F is inside waiting for you.'

'Yes, I promised her I'd order a Lime and Mint Treble for her if she was good. You have to bribe them at that age, you know.'

I smiled.

'Don't tell her until it's in front of her,' I said. Two Lime and Mint Trebles? Miss F would be throwing up for about a week.

Okay, it was probably pretty nasty of me. But she had teenaged herself at me. And she didn't have any of the facts I was looking for. Halfway through the week and all I had were shreds of stories. At that rate I was going to end up having to invent the facts, and the courts do not like that sort of thing.

'It's a gorgeous little town, isn't it?' Miss F's Mother said, apparently in no hurry to go inside.

'Very much so,' I replied. 'You've definitely never met Edgar The Ears before?'

'No, I don't get involved in politics. Have you been to the East Gardens? It's a lovely park apparently, I was thinking how nice it would be to relax on the lawn, enjoying the sun. Miss F will want to run around, I know, so it would be nice to have some company.'

'I've heard of the gardens. What about your husband? Perhaps he's met Edgar The Ears.'

'Oh, I don't think so. Or there's the History Museum, I hear they have an excellent section on sexual mores through the ages.'

'They do? Well, that sounds unmissable. So, no relationship between yourself and Edgar The Ears, then? Never been on the same committee or anything like that? Parent-Teachers Association?'

'Not that I can remember.' She laid a hand on my arm and looked over my shoulder. 'I'd better go in, Miss F is waving at me.' Then she looked into my eyes. 'I'll see you later.'

I couldn't help but wonder, as I watched her walk into the Milk Bar, whether she had been deliberately ignoring my questions. On the one hand she appeared to have little interest in him, yet on the other she had said that she was looking forward to seeing him.

Now that's strange.

I've just realised. I know I spoke to Miss F in the Milk Bar on the Wednesday, in the afternoon. I've got it written down in my notes. And I also have this very distinct memory of Miss F's mother telling me that Edgar The Ears was appearing in court the next day. But he appeared on the Wednesday afternoon, so she must have told me on the Tuesday afternoon. Except I clearly remember her doing so after I bumped into her rather attractive knees while leaving the Milk Bar.

Which was definitely, one hundred percent certain, on the Wednesday afternoon.

Weird.

I shall have to have a ponder on that one. I could shift that scene back to the Tuesday afternoon. But it just wouldn't seem right

Very weird.

I'll see if Beazeley spots it when he comes back to planet Earth. If he doesn't I won't worry too much about it.

Definitely very, very strange, though.

Marshmallows.

Chapter XXII. The One Good Deed

Beazeley's had a lie down and seems a little better. He seems to have recovered from the (whisper: cheerleading) incident. He's gone through the previous chapter and hasn't mentioned anything, so I'll just leave it as it is for the moment. It's probably not that important in the overall scheme of things. Just one of those anomalies best left alone. A bit like knowing that you left your mug of tea in the lounge but finding it on the top of the tall bookshelf in the passage, the one that hasn't been dusted for a couple of months. There's just no way that you'd forget the act of climbing high enough to put the mug there, let alone the question of why. The best thing is just to ignore it. And make a fresh mug of tea.

So, here we are, fresh mug of tea and Wednesday evening. That Wednesday evening.

Jenny made me think of that tall bookshelf in the passage. She dusted it this afternoon. Then she came in here to remonstrate with me over my lackadaisical cleaning habits. They aren't lackadaisical. I just don't dust. Certainly not the tops of bookshelves that you need to stand on a chair or something to see.

And then, having given me a lecture on house cleaning, she looks out the window and sees the young woman opposite washing her windows again. She asked me if I'd noticed.

"The woman across the road washing her windows? No, Jen, I hadn't really noticed her. I've been far too busy with this, you know that," I replied.

"Bloody liar," she said, and walked out to the kitchen.

Me a bloody liar? I'm not the one hanging around here while not mentioning some person Beazeley thinks is downright evil.

Anyway. I've put Jennifer out of my thoughts totally.

Wednesday evening. The tension.

During the day almost everyone had been on edge. Two members of the jury had been murdered. Or, to be more accurate, and I like to think that accuracy is the sine qua none of everything I do, one jury member and a bag lady who could have been mistaken for a member of the jury. I was pretty nervous myself. About the trial. After all, we only had twelve jury members left – and two of those were locked up overnight, and another was actually a jury member's mother. If any more of them got done in we'd have too few to constitute a proper jury and the trial would have to be restarted, maybe months later, perhaps never. I couldn't face the thought. I even have to admit feeling a bit of a heel in feeling just a twinge of gratefulness that The Clowns hadn't got away.

Add to that Mr Ball's less than encouraging performance and I was getting close to the chewing of fingernails stage. I'd tried to find out which rooms the two lawyers were in, just in case they might have left their copies of the book lying around, but without any success. Mildred One was always on duty in reception, and I couldn't get near the register. I did ask a few people if they knew, but received different answers, so that was no good. I considered tailing them, but there wasn't time. In fact, as the afternoon passed I began to become more aware of just how little time there was.

Admittedly, if I had got at the register the first name I would have been looking for would have been the Nun With Guitar. And cleared up that number 13 nonsense straight away.

With evening and twilight came a greater tension. In the gloom people were literally jumping at shadows. Switching on the low-wattage lights in the corridors did not help an enormous deal. There were just too many alcoves, corners, niches and sundry hiding places a murderer could be lying in wait. I noticed quite a few people checking the ceilings out in case someone was hiding there. Thinking about it, quite a few of those ceilings were pretty high. With the lights casting shadows all over the place there probably would have been one or two spots where someone could hide, say from a rope attached to a hook. Pity I didn't think about that at the time.

I can't say that I personally was too concerned about waking up with a knitting needle sticking out of any part of my anatomy. There was no reason for anyone to want me dead, unless whoever it was was some random psychopath, in which case the probability was that someone else would get it before me. The thing about psychopathic killers is that they tend to go for relatively easy targets. Not often you find them taking on a fully armed Marine in preference to some little old lady fast asleep. And I'd been careful to casually drop hints into various conversations to suggest to people that I was an ex-Marine, and that I went to bed every night with a forty-four magnum in my hand under the pillow, a Samurai sword next to me, and a hunting knife strapped to my leg.

One on each leg.

The truth was that the closest I'd ever been to being a Marine was having gone to the beach once. And the only weapon I had was the defunct Teasmade. But if anyone tried entering my room while I was asleep they would get that Teasmade over their head. If there was more than one, they'd just have to queue like any decent Englishman or woman would do.

Why have I suddenly thought of icecream?

Unfortunately the rest of the residents had rather more fertile imaginations than mine. Bunny Blue told me that the rabbits were convinced the killer was targeting them. Why, I don't know. Apparently the discussion went something like this:

- Mrs Baggs was wearing blue. The killer probably mistook her for a blue bunny.
- But Hugo was wearing faded black.
- Was he?

- Yes, definitely.

- Pause.

- They probably thought he was a bunny in mourning, then. Stands to reason.

You can't fight that sort of thinking. Might as well bury your head in a bowl of molasses and breathe in. Or maybe bury their heads in a bowl of molasses and shove a carrot up their costume.

But the problem with situations like this is that people don't know who they can't trust, so they end up trusting almost no-one. That's in addition to the tensions you'll find arising in a group of strangers cooped up together in artificial surroundings. People quickly form cliques and begin playing underhand political games.

That evening the usual suspects were in the lounge watching news on the television. Apparently there had been a multiple car pile-up which didn't involve an Audi, so Vicar Preachy was happy to watch. Mrs Plum sat contentedly knitting. Her new knitting needles were marvels of the inventive mind. Vicar Preachy had nicked Judge Beak's golfing umbrella for one, sharpening the ferrule to a point. A stake from some innocent gardener's patch made up the other. From the faint aroma I guessed that it had been holding up runner beans.

'Evening, all,' I said, taking a chair next to the table near them, giving them the you-can-trust-me-like-I'm-your-friendly-Uncle-Joe smooze.

'Hic my hic Uncle hic Joe hic turned hic out hic to hic be hic a hic serial hic womaniser hic,' said The Prim Maiden Aunt primly, in a French accent, her tic racing from eye to eye with the effort this extended speech had cost her, looking as if it might play pinball with her mouth.

'Woman have always been oppressed,' Miss F contributed automatically, mindlessly, her attention on the television, looking far too healthy for someone who had gorged themselves on two Lime and Mint Trebles, one with added salt. 'Pity the guy in the Mercedes wasn't going faster.'

'My Uncle Joe was a drinker,' Miss F's Mother said. 'A secret drinker. It was common knowledge amongst the family.'

'Do I have an Uncle Joe?' asked Miss F hopefully.

'Every woman has an Uncle Joe,' replied her mother. 'Not necessarily her uncle, nor named Joe.'

'You could say that all men are Uncle Joe,' Strawberry Mousse stated.

'It's a sad world,' sighed Vicar Preachy. 'Do you think it's time to surf the channels again, Miss F?'

'Okay,' Miss F replied cheerfully. 'Maybe we can find that porn channel again.'

'I don't want you watching too much porn, Miss F,' admonished her mother. 'You don't want to turn into a sofa potato.'

'Isn't that "couch potato"?' enquired Vicar Preachy.

'Quite possibly, Vicar Preachy. I have to confess I prefer the Saint James version.'

'Now you come to mention it,' said Vicar Preachy, 'I did tell you about *ficus-indica* didn't I?'

'Saint Ficus Indica? Yes, Vicar, I seem to recall you mentioning her. She was burnt at the stake, wasn't she?'

'I fancy a steak,' said Miss F.

'Oh, not Saint Ficus Indica. I meant *Opuntia ficus-indica*. That's the variety of prickly pear I'm cultivating. It's from South America originally, not easy to grow in these climes.'

'Oh? That is interesting, Vicar. So it climbs. My goodness.'

Throughout this inane chatter I had managed to retain the quiet smile which showed how much I empathised and agreed. In reality it was incredibly difficult to restrain the urge to take Mrs Plum's new umbrella and drive it through each and every one of them.

Opening it afterwards for full satisfaction.

'So, reached any conclusions?' I asked mildly, as if making polite conversation rather than digging for information.

Shovels.

'My mother thinks it's one of the staff,' said Miss F without taking her eyes from the television. 'The Prim Maiden Aunt thinks it's God's justice being meted out. I think it's a plot by the ruling manocracy to keep women enslaved.'

'It could have been an accident,' suggested Vicar Preachy. 'Two accidents, that is. They could accidentally have fallen on the needles while cleaning them before returning them.'

I guessed that they were talking about the murders. I wasn't.

'You could be right,' I said. 'What about the trial? Getting any feeling for the facts?'

'We can't discuss the trial,' sniffed the Major. 'The judge has made that quite clear. Quite clear. About not discussing the trial.'

'A fine man,' I said through gritted teeth, laying stress on the word "man" for Miss F's benefit.

'One hic of hic the hic old hic school,' agreed the Maiden Aunt. In a French accent. Miss F pursed her lips at the television screen.

'I bet those aren't natural,' she said.

'I suppose,' I said with a sad sigh, 'he must be somebody's Uncle Joe.'

'Stuff and nonsense,' said the Major. 'He's a judge. He can't be anyone's Uncle Joe. He's a judge. Can't be anyone's Uncle Joe'

I noticed that the Major had kept extremely quiet during the interchange. I was pretty certain that he was definitely somebody's Uncle Joe, and had no wish to be found out. Something else I was pretty certain about. The only things that that lot were interested in were television porn and who the murderer was. I decided to retire to the Baby's Arms for a relaxing drink. Hanging around with that lot was likely to drive me to drink, I might as well get a head start.

There was a strange sort of mood in the air. As I walked into the Baby's Arms a group of little chip monks came rushing out, cowls down and habits flying, jabbering in that strange, high-pitched voice they use when excited. One of them noticed me coming in and aimed a kick at my shin, but I managed to jump out of the way in time. They can be vicious little creatures when in the mood.

Most of the bunnies were inside. Bunny Blue was obviously making great strides. Bunny Pale Pink sat next to him, holding his paw while looking up at his face with eyes of adoration. Nearby the barmaid was trying to separate two bunnies fighting each other, rabbit punches flying like snow. Matilda was next to Bunny Pink, sitting with the look of someone who wishes she could find a bunny like Bunny Blue. Behind her Sad Sid nursed a drink. And behind him, again in the shadows, stood the outline of Bunny Evil. I got myself a whiskey and a double Bloody Mary for the Nun With Guitar and went and sat down next to her.

'Not often you see that sort of thing,' I commented, watching the battling bunnies.

'It iz ze tenzion,' the Nun With Guitar replied in that wonderful accent, taking a sip of the Bloody Mary without looking up from her book.

'I suppose it must be. What's the latest from the jury?'

She turned her head slowly and looked at me over her glass before putting it down. I recognised that look. It was the look of a mother about to say "You haven't really done your homework, have you?" – or a girlfriend about to say "You don't really love me, do you?"

Jeez I hate it when they do that.

'Vor a momend I zought you had kome do be vit me,' she said. 'But I zink you prever me az a member ov ze jury, rather zan me az me. Ziz iz true, iz nod it?'

'Can you separate parts of a person out?' I asked. 'You are a member of the jury. You are a nun. You are wearing a guitar. All these are parts of the you that is the totality. When I speak to the juror do I not speak to all of you?'

The look on her face told me that she didn't quite buy my sweet talk.

'You left a pieze oud. I am alzo a voman. I have a voman'z eyez. A voman'z needz. A voman's dezirez. A voman'z viewz. A voman'z bunionz on ze veet vrom vearing voman'z zhoez.'

'I hear you, sister,' I said, wondering what she was on about, but knowing she wasn't talking about the trial. I finished my drink and stood up to go. It was a pity. In another time, another place – maybe on a glorious golden beach on an idyllic island – we could really have hooked up. If I had let myself be less hard-headed and practical about circumstances I might even have imagined that there could be a time and place for us right there and then.

I paused before going, the way you do when you don't really want to leave.

'What are you really doing here?' I asked. She gave me a thin, bitter-sweet smile.

'I am on ze pathway do paradize,' she replied.

'Earthly paradise?' I said suggestively. Or in a tone that came as close to being suggestive as you can when trying not to chat a nun up.

'I am in no hurry vor heaven,' she replied.

We looked into each other's eyes for a few moments. I had that same strange stomach-turning feeling, that this was a woman I might never understand but I'd be happy to spend the rest of my life not understanding. Some things don't make sense, some things don't need to, they just feel right.

'Number 13,' she said, returning to her book. 'Do nod be lade. I do nod like ztaying up avter eleven ov ze pm.'

I nodded and left. I knew there was no 13. Believe me, there never is. Part of me wanted to believe that the looks she was giving me meant that she felt the same way I did. The logical part pointed out that, if that were the case, she'd have told me her real room number.

But would she then, if that happened, retain that incredible allure of mystery? Perhaps part of the attraction was her holding out the illusion of room 13, something that was both there but not there?

Or maybe it was a test I had to go through. I had to believe in her. There was a 13 in there somewhere. It wasn't 113. It wasn't 131.

Maybe it was 31 but she read upside-down?

No, I'd checked that already.

Perhaps it was 213 and the 2 had fallen off.

Or perhaps someone had slipped something into my whisky, and it hadn't been an aspirin.

I returned to the hotel. I decided to wander around the corridors for a while. I wandered lonely as a crowd for a few hours. That's what the poets get wrong, I reflected. Being on your own isn't to be lonely. Being lonely is being alone in a crowd. As I turned a corner I almost bumped into Matilda returning from the Baby's Arms, presumably having given up on finding a soul mate that evening. She squeaked and shrank back. Behind her I could see Sad Sid skulking in an alcove. Poor sod.

'What are you doing on your own?' I asked her. I shook my head and tut-tutted. 'Hasn't anyone told you that the police have ordered everyone to travel in pairs for the duration?'

I did some more tut-tutting at the foolishness and innocence of such a good-looking young bunny. Then I looked behind her as if suddenly spotting Sad Sid.

'Now that's fortunate,' I said. 'Sid, come here a minute.'

Sid shuffled forward slowly and eagerly. That might sound like a contradiction, but it was the shuffle of a shy bunny who thinks his chance might just have finally come, but doesn't want to rush things and make a total prat of himself, he just wants to rush things in case he loses this chance.

'Sid, this is Matilda,' I told him. 'Matilda, this is Sid.'

Obviously I didn't know what their real names were, but they didn't object.

'Now, Sid, until things get sorted out I want you to stick with Matilda. Look after her. I want the two of you to stay together wherever you go. Within reason, of course. Even without reason, if the fancy takes you. Understand?'

Sad Sid nodded his head so emphatically I thought it would come off. Matilda gave a slow, shy bat of the eyelids to say yes, and looked demurely at Sad Sid out of the corner of her eye, a little smile on her gentle face.

'Good, now hold paws and be off with you.'

Sad Sid took Matilda's unresisting paw and they hopped away. For the first time Sid had a spring in his hop. One of his ears was even standing upright. I could have sworn his costume had gained a sleek new shine.

After I had watched them hop off I turned and casually walked on. As I drew abreast of the nearest alcove I whipped in, surprising Bunny Evil. Before he could react I kneed him in the goolies and, as he went over, brought my elbow down in the general area of his kidneys. He collapsed with a strangulated burst of breath, falling into the foetal position.

'You leave those two alone,' I said, holding up one of his flop ears and whispering into it, 'or you'll think what you've just received is pleasure compared to what else I can do to you.'

Then I left quickly before he could recover.

You know, considering how things turned out in the end, uniting Matilda and Sad Sid was the one thing I could look back on with a sense of satisfaction.

One good deed.

Chapter XXIII. Vicar Preachy Has a Moral Crisis

The Nun With Guitar sat on a rocking horse at the top of a mountain. She was looking down at me. She wore nothing but her wimple and make-up. Her long black hair streamed over her the front of her shoulders. Streaks had been dyed white. They looked quite natural.

'I'm Lady Godiva,' she called down to me. 'Vant a rite?'

'It's not safe!' I tried to shout. The wind was blowing against me. Too strong. 'The mountain's not safe,' I screamed against it.

'Look, I kan vly,' she called, raising her naked arms. As I watched, battling against the wind to get to her, her arms sprouted feathers. They turned into wings. She turned into a pigeon. She flew down and dropped something onto my head. It bounced off and fell into the green-blue grass. I picked it up. It was written in hieroglyphics. Moving hieroglyphics. Men and women and eyes and cats and dogs and squiggles dancing sideways across the page. I looked up. Down below the Nun With Guitar was wading into the surf.

The Jello started up.

'Come back!' I shouted. 'Come back! Come back! It isn't safe!'

The Jello grew louder.

I mounted the rocking horse and bounced after her.

The Jello grew louder.

The rocking horse reared and I tumbled off. Down, down, down, down, down, down ...

The Jello grew louder.

A fin appeared in the distance.

It was followed by another fin.

Then another.

The Nun With Guitar reached her hand out to me over the sand dunes.

The Jello crescended.

The Nun With Guitar opened her mouth, about to scream.

And then I woke up.

God, don't you hate weird dreams like that?

You wake up thinking, "What was all that about, then?"

Did it have any meaning? Was it revealing something deep about my subconscious desires implanted during my potty training? Or did I just have too much cheese before going to bed?

What fascinates me about dreams like those – I'd prefer it if someone else could have them rather than me, mind – is that they're capable of any interpretation you fancy. Psychologists make their living by dreaming up ever more fanciful notions. The Nun With Guitar's breasts were hidden by her hair – obviously a mental fear of bare breasts, often called the Daily Mail Disease. The rocking horse rearing – obviously an unresolved accident with a rocking horse while young. The mountain and the surf: maternal images suggesting that – I don't know, make your own theory up, it'll be just as good as any.

In tribal cultures I could have made a religion out of dreams like that. Call them visions, tell the people that there is one true god and he wants us all to smite our neighbouring tribes, after which we all have to go around naked apart from wearing wimples. Talk about missed opportunities. Only a couple of thousand years or so between now and my inventing a really interesting religion. Oh, well.

Beazeley's recovered sufficiently from whatever latest nervous disorder ailed him to come pester me again. I've left him in the kitchen with a copy of Lady Chatterley's Lover. I told him that it was the Reader's Digest condensed version of what I've written so far. When I last saw him he was looking very pale.

And Jenny's promised to pop in at lunchtime! Much, much looking forward to that. I've considered the matter of this other summer beach she fancies and come to the conclusion that there's no way it could be Edgar The Ears. So whoever it is is merely some unfortunate competition which I'll have to deal with. If Beazeley doesn't like him he can't be much trouble. In fact, thinking about it, Jen was probably just winding Beazeley up, she enjoys doing that. Which is something else we have in common.

We can go for a walk after lunch. How to get rid of Beazeley, though, that's the question. Maybe give him War And Peace and tell him that it's what I managed to finish off this morning.

Speaking of which, let me get on. Thursday.

You know, now that I come to think about it, it's funny. Monday was sunshine from dawn to dusk. Tuesday dawned bright and summery, and started with the discovery of Mrs Baggs. Wednesday was also a glorious day, except for Hugo the Accountant who was in no position to appreciate it. Thursday – Thursday began with the sound of a Jello. And we all know what that means. Something ugly, nasty, dangerous and shark-shaped is heading your way. I slipped silently from my bed and padded over to the door, putting an ear against it to listen.

Thought so.

I whipped the door open and grabbed Alberto by the neck. He had been on his knees, playing his Jello into the keyhole. I dragged him up until his face was just below mine.

'Do you take requests, Alberto?' I asked slowly, in a tone that suggested "No" wasn't the right answer.

'Si, senhor. Of course, senhor,' he gasped.

'What about, could you shut the hell up?'

That's when I discovered that there is a piece for Jello titled "Could you shut the hell up".

It's in B flat, apparently.

He put the bow's strings to the Jello and scraped it softly. It came out as an Adagio.

He played it slowly with my hand around his neck. As he got towards the end I let him go.

'You no lika my playing?' he asked plaintively. 'I thoughta you lika my playing. You saya how good it is just a-tuning up. I play just specially for you.'

I patted him on his shoulder.

'Sorry, Alberto, I do lika – I mean I do like your playing. It's just there's this tension in the air, and I wasn't expecting a morning serenade. I wasn't sure whether the person playing the Jello outside my room didn't also have a knitting needle with my name on it.'

'Ah, I understanda, senhor. Is great tenseness. And funny weather. And people not like idea of being murdered. I understanda perfect. I no lika myself.'

'Great, great. Why don't you take a coffee break or something?'

'Hokay. Oh, by the way, Charlie sends his apologies. His missus is extra-nervous and he can't leave her. But he send his regards.'

'Thanks, Aberto. Pass mine on to him, won't you.'

'Will do. Toodle pip.'

It was only after I had closed the door on his receding figure that I realised that Alberto's fake Czechoslovakian accent had disappeared from his last couple of sentences. He was as English as I was. Well, there you go, I thought as I turned my attention to showering and shaving. And he was really only following me because he thought I liked his Jello playing. It was a nice thought. Probably a total lie, but a nice thought. A nice lie. Unlike the nasty ones.

Having showered I began dawn patrol of the corridors, awaiting the morning scream. There wasn't one, but, as Alberto had mentioned, the weather was – well, I can't tell you exactly what the weather was like, or Beazeley would have another conniption, so let me describe it this way.

Storm clouds. Vast, looming, black, really black, black, storm clouds. A howling wind coming in waves, whipping off the ocean. Whipping so hard it brought the taste of salt sea to Wellbury. Driving sudden flurries of litter and sand. Lightning. Jagged lightning splitting the horison. Beams of sunlight suddenly appearing from nowhere, highlighting a house or street sign briefly before immediately disappearing. Almost like curtains suddenly rent in two to reveal the riders of the apocalypse before the curtains fell back to cover the scene and leave you looking nervously around, wondering where the riders were now, feeling that they weren't very far away and were watching you before having their version of a little fun with you.

Even worse. **Ryders**, not riders.

There, that should do nicely. If that doesn't get the hair on your neck standing up, think of something that does. A spider just above your head. The rattle of a snake just behind your chair. A twig breaking in the empty forest at midnight where no honest person apart from yourself should be. The sudden sound of silence in the plane at 30,000 feet where previously the engines had been playing. Whatever works for you.

That sudden breath of nothing just behind your neck.

Finally, having patrolled the corridors fruitlessly, I went down to breakfast, wincing at the crashing of thunder, thunder which – I think "pealed" is the word normally used. This thunder didn't peal. It crackled and boomed every thirty seconds or so, like an artillery bombardment. Very un-English, I must say.

I'm pretty much a straight kind of a guy. I don't let my imagination run away with me just because there's a bit of bad weather out there. But I could understand the feelings I saw on the faces of those gathered for breakfast that morning. And most of them weren't there to have breakfast. They were there to have company. The bunnies were in their corner with their tray of carrots, but none were nibbling.

They all looked up as I entered the lounge. Bunny Pale Pink was in Bunny Blue's arms, either terrified or pretending to be so to get the most out of things. Matilda, I noted, was in Sad Sid's arms. Good on you, Sid, hope it works out, I thought. I knew it wouldn't, but you can always hope the hope, whatever the probable reality.

I waved a hand at them, along with an assuring smile, an assurance that stopped somewhere about two millimetres behind my lipstick. They reminded me of what I had done to Bunny Evil the previous evening. I was sure he wasn't the type to forget a grudge, and I didn't like not knowing where he was. He'd be waiting for me somewhere, and not to shake hands and discuss the good old days over a pint.

'You sure get on with them rabbits,' The Quiet American noted as I sat down. Everyone was there, apart from The Clowns. They were kept overnight at the police station. The Quiet American had continued his quest to prove that the number of loud Hawaiian shirts on this earth is unlimited, this morning's one being a combination on the theme of purple and puce.

Strawberry Mousse was painting her nails pink. Miss F and Miss F's Mother were reading another Mills and Boon, Miss F's Mother's arm around her daughter's shoulders, both having decided that Thursday was peaked cap, pony tail, white t-shirt and baggy olive combat trousers day. Bottomed off with standard flip flops. The Maiden Aunt was practising being prim while the Major refined his glare on a tea cup. Mr Sleepy snored away behind the couch. Mrs Plum sat endangering anyone within three yards with her knitting.

The Nun With Guitar was consuming a tub of yoghurt in the suggestive manner only she could achieve. That day's habit was shimmering red, with more shimmer than red, millions of sequinned dots, and the usual ventilation strips just where you don't want your eyes to pay attention to on a nun. Vicar Preachy sat with a pad on his knee, the stub of a pencil in his fingers and a faraway look in his eyes.

'I try to get on with everyone, far as I can,' I replied to the Quiet American. I had the urge to say "Tolerance is my middle name", but I'd realised that he had a tendency to take things too literally.

'Heel, if Ah was at home Ah'd be shooting the critters,' he replied. 'It's been a right real revelation, being over here.'

"Over here again" I felt like correcting him.

'Revelations mean different things to different people,' I noted.

'Yoh sure can say that again.'

No, I didn't. It was tempting, mind.

'I am so glad we haven't had another accident this morning,' said Vicar Preachy. 'I've being trying to write my sermon for Sunday, but it is so difficult under these trying conditions.'

'What's the sermon on?' I asked, to be polite.

'It's a sermon about the Sermon on the Mount.'

'My goodness,' I said.

'Colonche,' he replied.

There was a pause as I searched for an appropriate answer to that.

'The Indians made it from prickly pears,' he added.

'My goodness,' I said.

The Nun With Guitar looked at me and smiled, dragging a spoon slowly, very slowly, out of her black-lipsticked and open mouth. Then she licked her lips with her pink tongue.

'I have alwayz zought ze mound very impordand,' she said. 'And kvite probably colonchez, doo.'

'I'm glad to hear you say that,' responded Vicar Preachy. 'Although we come from different sides of the true faith, at least we can agree that the sermon is the crux of our ideas.'

'Yez, crux,' said The Nun With Guitar, again slowly, still looking directly at me. 'It iz juzt perhapz vun or doo ledderz oud of zat zat ve mighd uze differendly.'

'Yoh know, that's something that really had me perplexed when Ah first got to these shores,' noted The Quiet American thoughtfully. 'The way you Brits spell strangely. Now take the letter Zee –'

'I zink I mighd dake a vew zees,' The Nun With Guitar said, standing up. 'Kould zomeone vake me up ven it'z dime do go-go? Room 13,' she added, looking directly at me. 'Zhall we zay half an hour before go-go dime? It mighd give uz a chanze to discuzz ze crux.'

The Quiet American looked at me thoughtfully as The Nun With Guitar removed herself and her guitar. Languidly.

'Whal, pardner, I can't say that as how I understand you Brits properly, but dang me if she wasn't trying to tell you something.'

'She was,' I said, sipping my coffee. 'There is no 13. Believe me, there never is. And if there was, she would never take it. The Irish never do.'

'She's Irish? Ah wondered where the accent came from. A great people, the Irish.'

'Absolutely marvellous,' I replied. No doubt The Quiet American has since told bemused Russians how much he admires Dublin, and which part of the Emerald Isle do they come from?

'What does this mean?' Miss F asked. '"He granted her ablution."' She looked at Vicar Preachy. 'Vicar Preachy, according to this a priest witnessed a girl's ablution. What does that mean?'

Vicar Preachy coloured. He licked his lips nervously.

'It's a misprint,' Miss F's Mother said. 'It should be "He granted her absolution." Not so, Vicar Preachy?'

'Er, quite possibly,' replied Vicar Preachy.

'What does that mean?' asked Miss F. 'Absolution? Is that one of those ceremonies where they carry statues of Madonna around?'

'It's the forgiveness of sins,' Miss F's Mother said. For some reason Vicar Preachy was becoming even more nervous. I could understand the embarrassment of having to explain to a fifteen-year-old-seventeen-year-old teenage girl what ablution meant, but with absolution he should have been on much firmer ground. If anything it looked as if he were wishing for that rare phenomenon of the ground opening up and swallowing him.

'I, er, I think I'll go for a walk,' he said, standing up suddenly, pad and pencil dropping onto the carpet.

'They'll be serving breakfast soon,' Miss F's Mother said.

'I want double eggs and bacon for breakfast,' Miss F said. 'With steak.'

'I, er, don't feel that particularly hungry,' Vicar Preachy muttered, half-way to the door.

Up until then I had mentally dismissed Vicar Preachy as what he appeared to be, a mild, innocent vicar with an enormous bald dome, which, thinking about it, was a silly thing to do. On the face of things there was no reason to think that he might ever have had anything to do with Edgar The Ears, but he was a member of that jury, and that should have made me wonder why. His behaviour that breakfast made me realise that he was concealing a secret. It might not have anything to do with Edgar The Ears, but if it did I needed to know about it.

And if it didn't I still needed to know about it.

Apart from that he was one of the last possible sources of information I had. If I didn't get anything out of Vicar Preachy it would be time to start concentrating on Mr Sleepy, which sounded a futile task, or, worse, Mrs Plum, who would definitely be a fount of information, all of it absolutely useless.

Devon cream.

Now when a man like Vicar Preachy misses breakfast it's obvious he has a serious problem. And with a man of the cloth that can only mean one thing: a moral crisis. Or quite possibly an immoral crisis. It was easy to work out where he would have gone. The cathedral. I gave him five minutes before following him, pretending to the others that I had forgotten something in my room.

'He's going to follow Vicar Preachy,' I heard Miss F say as I left the room.

'Double egg and bacon on its way,' I called back. 'With steak.'

'Oh, yummy,' trilled Miss F. 'But I know you're going to follow Vicar Preachy anyway. So nah-nah-nah.'

I was tempted to go up to my room, collect something and return, just to prove her wrong. It didn't last long. That cathedral and Vicar Preachy were calling. And I was going to answer the call.

Now there are some experts who can identify a cathedral just from the description of a sliver of stained glass or a streak of marble – call then cathedrologists. (Think of really, really boring train-spotter type people.) (Yes, perhaps that is a little bit of tautology.) So I can't tell you exactly what it looks like, or you'll have one of the clever-cloggs geeks on the Internet saying "I know where Wellbury really is, it's down in Dingly Dell" before you can say "fishnet stockings". So let me describe the cathedral in such a way that the story works without giving too much away.

(It's not in Dingly Dell, by the way. Honest Injun.)

First let's give it some arches, turquoise arches. All cathedrals have arches. All the older ones, anyway. And some gables. Orange ones. A few flying buttresses whizzing all over the place. And let's say that the original cathedral had some additions in, oh, say the eighteenth century. The roof was raised by a mock-Tudor second wall built on the original arches and gables. And instead of stained glass windows it has a stained glass roof. The sun comes streaming down onto the sinners below. Old Archangel Gabriel looks down with his beady eye, as if he were floating in the clouds. There's only one entrance door, and that's three foot high, to force the congregation to enter on their knees.

Right, that should about do it.

Not forgetting the crackling thunder and barrages of lightning, of course. Coarse salt spray everywhere. Even though we were nowhere near the coast.

Whoops.

Anyway ...

Crash-bang-whallop-what-a-picture.

I crawled stealthily in through the three-foot high doorway, keeping as low to the ground as I could. Not to show that I was holier than anyone else, just to make sure Vicar Preachy didn't see me before I saw him. I spotted him as soon as my eyes adjusted to the multi-coloured dim light shining down from on high. I peeped over a pew and there he was, kneeling, head down, hands grasped together, his bald head and remaining tufted hair lost in prayer. Next to the confessional booths. They had a sign over them: "Confessions: 8am to 10am, 4pm til late. £5 per half hour. Bulk discount available.'

Ah! I thought. Excellent! A Roman Catholic cathedral. I like Roman Catholic cathedrals. People in them will believe anything. After all, they believe in the Holy Sea. Where the Holy Seals live, I suppose. And if Vicar Preachy was desperate enough to go into a Roman Catholic cathedral it was obvious that he was in a mood to believe anything and everything. I just knew that I could sell him fifteen copies of "Debbie Does Dallas" and convince him that it was a documentary about the virgin birth. Or Mary Magdalene's early life, anyway. I crawled around on my hands and knees, careful to keep out of Preachy's sight. I was looking for a door. A specific door. One with "Private" on it. Or "Staff Only". Or "No entry". Or "Verboten". Or whatever the latin is for 'You cumma in here you die painfully. Bless you." Rooms are only really interesting when somebody wants you to stay out of them. And the one I was looking for would contain vestments. In other words, Fancy Dress.

Something to dress up in to fool Preachy into thinking that I was an important servant. of Rome. I soon found it. I fiddled the lock, slipped in and began going through the cupboards.

What joy! I should have expected it. A cathedral would mean a bishop. And a bishop's garments. Or arch-bishop. Or Vice-bishop, I'm not sure how you tell the difference. Mitre. Flowing purple cassock. Shepherd's crook. The works. It was like Hollywood. I quickly donned the purple cassock and mitre. The cassock was a little big for me – the bish was obviously a portly sort of chap – and I had to hoick it up quite a bit, tying the belt, or whatever it's called, around my midriff to keep it up. I tilted the mitre over my eyes slightly, just in case Preachy should look too close and recognise me. Then I walked out as serenely as any real archbishop might, at home in his own cathedral.

Any real archbishop trying not to trip over his cassock in the half light.

I sidled up to Preachy, keeping my face to one side as far as possible. A sudden ray of sun came through stained glass roof: Archangel Gabriel face reflected on Preachy's bald head, almost like a tattoo in the middle of those devil's tufts of hair; in the strange light I could have sworn that old Gabriel winked at me from Preachy's bald bonce. The heavens had parted to let that single sunbeam through. Anyone less cynical than me might have considered it an omen.

Or a threat.

'You may enter the confessional, my son,' I said in as deep a voice as I could muster, as an extra-special boom of artillery thunder echoed around the gables, 'I'm starting early this morning.'

He started, which gave me time to glide into the priest's side of the confessional. It turned out to be the sinner's side. The priest's side always has a chair. The sinner gets to kneel. But I thought it best to stay there and pretend that I knew what I was doing. I stood in the corner next to the grill, keeping myself in the shadow. Preachy hurried into the other side.

'Do I pay now or after?' he asked breathlessly, obviously unused to the form.

'Now would be better,' I said. 'We take all major credit cards.' If he paid up front he'd be more willing to spill the beans.

'I'm afraid I only have cash.'

'Cash is fine. Just slip it under the grill.' And you can't cancel it like you can with a credit card.

'I'm afraid I only have a ten pound note.'

'I have change, my son.'

He slipped ten pound note underneath the grill. I hoicked up the cassock, found my wallet, and returned a five pound note.

'Deus sui generis,' I said. It sounded Latin. I'd heard something like it not long before. Couldn't remember where, but it sounded close to authentic.

Though I was tempted to add, "Hocus Pocus Slowly Malone".

It was a game we played as kids.

'I'm sorry?' asked Preachy.

'God is so generous, my son. How long is it since your last confession?'

'Ah. Um. Er. Well, to be honest, this is my first. I'm not actually a Catholic, you see.'

'That's okay, my son, in this cathedral we're multicultural. You wish to confess your sins. Go ahead. The clock is ticking. Be as quick as you can, my son, I try not to over-charge.'

'Ah. Um. Er. Well, um, you see, I've done a very terrible thing. Something I can't forgive myself for.'

'Have no fear, son, I'll do the forgiving bit. That's part of the job. I am sure that what you did is not as bad as it might seem. Tell me.'

He paused. And then said:

'I gave Edgar The Ears absolution for all his sins.'

I couldn't believe what I was hearing. I mean, yes, I know Christianity is supposed to be a forgiving religion, ignoring what some might think of as historical evidence which might go against the validity of that understanding, but even so, absolving Edgar The Ears? That illegitimate low-down total and utter piece of shark's droppings' shadow on the lowest shelf of the sea floor? The man must be mad. Totally and utterly mad. Not bonkers. Not crazy. Simply and plainly mentally and legally and completely insane. From a great height. In triplicate.

Mashed Swede with extra fruit in.

'What in hell's name made you do that?' I asked.

'Well, it wasn't in hell's name, it was actually in heaven's name, that's the point –'

'Yes, yes, let's not discuss the finer points of theology. The question is – why?'

He hesitated before replying.

'He put a gun against my head.'

'Figuratively, I presume.' It was obviously some religious analogy, Edgar the Ears wouldn't go near a gun.

'Literally. Put a gun against my head. Said he'd pull the trigger, I'd be dead.'

'Did you play the fandango?'

Pause.

'Is that a Catholic thing?'

'A minor sect. They're all thunderbolt and lightning. Banned in seventeen countries and Guatemala.'

Just then a particularly close bolt of lightning hit earth. Counting away until the rumble of thunder came I worked out that it must have struck about one block away. I wondered whether someone had just given me a hint of what was waiting for a person who pretended to be a bishop as soon as said person stepped out of the cathedral.

'They sound very, very frightening,' Vicar Preachy said.

Beazeley's just said that he thinks I'm getting carried away now. (He really does talk like that. Or whine like that, maybe I should say.) Well, Beaze, old boy, you want to write it your way, you write it your way. This one is my show.

You ...

No. Not going to say it.

Now, where was I? Ah, yes, back in the confessional. With the thunder and lightning outside.

For a moment I wondered if Vicar Preachy knew what I was talking about. I wasn't sure if I knew myself. I think I was just making it up to keep him talking. I was still shocked by his confession. He looked so innocent behind the grill with his bald head, devil's tufts of hair, studded dog collar and lead hanging down his back I felt it difficult not to take him at face appearance, a mild and simple vicar of the parish.

'Let's get back to this absolution business,' I said. 'I thought your lot didn't go in for that sort of thing.'

'We don't, as a rule. It seemed a special occasion.'

'You can say that again. Look, if you absolved him of his sins because he was threatening to kill you, then that's not absolution. It says so on page 293 of the Dummies' Bishops' Guide to Absolution. Paragraph five, subsection eight point one.'

'Ah, but subsection eight-point-one, clarification section four-b specifically states that absolution given while having a gun pointed at your head remains absolution.'

Bugger. I hadn't realise there was actually a manual on that sort of thing.

'That only relates to calibres less than .22. Can you remember what type of gun it was?'

'It doesn't matter what the calibre was. You're only trying to make me feel better. I should have had the strength of faith to refuse.'

By now he was actually weeping. Not a pretty sight. An idea struck me. Vicar Preachy appeared determined to play the role of the martyr. The sort of person who would list in detail all of his transgressions, a bit like the drunk sobbing on your shoulder that he wished he had never left the missus giving you a detailed break-down of his missus's better qualities. Which normally amount to "She's a wonderful wife. And she's a wonderful wife. I tell you, she's a wonderful wife. There's not a woman in the land –" Zonk. Sound of bottle over head.

'What you have done is obviously a serious matter,' I said. 'You can only atone for it by telling me all the sins for which you absolved him. Start with the first.'

'Um – but what about the secrecy of the confessional?'

Ruddy pedant.

'This is the confessional,' I pointed out. 'What you say will go no further than this booth.'

Well, maybe just a little further. Okay, quite a lot further. Most of the serious dailies. All of the tabloids. Possibly a slot on ITV, though they don't pay as well as they used to. Blue Peter, as an outside possibility. Hell, even Heaven and Earth on BBC1 if I could find the right angle. Radio Four's Thought For The Day would get an interesting make-over.

I'm not proud. I'd even sell to Reynard.

It'll cost them though.

'I see,' he said slowly. 'Well, the problem is that he said that he didn't have time to go through everything – that there was too much, and could I give him a, well a sort of blanket absolution. So I did.'

For the second time in five minutes I found myself not believing what I was hearing.

'Not even one?' I asked desperately. 'Not even something about bribes? Mistresses? Strange sexual habits? Anything? Ginger-bread men? Profiteroles. _____s? Exploding bully beef?'

'Exploding bully beef?'

'It doesn't matter what! Anything!'

'Nothing, I'm afraid.'

I slumped against the wall and slid down it until I was on the floor. So near and yet so far!

'Bugger!' I said softly to myself. Just not softly enough.

'Pardon?' asked Preachy.

'Ah, er, I was thinking of Bunter,' I said. 'The seminal work on absolution. Thrilling read.'

'I haven't managed to finish that, I'm afraid. I get to page three and tend to fall asleep.'

'Ah, well, you see, there you go,' I said, thinking I might just have spotted a gap. 'Now if you read Bunter in full you'd find that blanket absolutions aren't binding.'

'They aren't?'

'Oh, no. No, no, no. Definitely not. For absolution the penitent must confess each of his sins individually. And for some sects, if it's a woman, she has to provide a drawing too.'

'They do?'

'Oh, yes. Not that we go for that here, of course. Not any more. But definitely, yes, blanket absolution isn't supported by any denomination. Goes totally against theological thought. Against the later thinking. Bunter's quite clear on his position regarding paragraph five. He's devoted section thirteen to it.'

'He is? He has?'

'Oh, yes, most decidedly. So, you see, you haven't given Edgar The Ears absolution at all.'

'I haven't?'

'Not at all. But what you do have to do is go to him, explain the circumstance, and get him to tell you everything in minute detail. Then come back here and pass it on – I mean tell me.'

There was the tiniest of pauses.

'I am not going anywhere near that offspring between Mephistophelies and a rattlesnake again,' Preachy said, standing up. A little heated, I thought. 'If he comes anywhere near me I shall shove an *Opuntia* up his rectum. A big one. Thank you for your help. You've relieved me of a great burden.'

'Not at all. Just say five Hail Marys, bow to the east and nod your head three times at midnight.'

'I'll do that,' he promised. 'And thanks again.'

'And make sure that you vote the right way in the trial.'

'Oh, you needn't worry about that,' he said as he stepped out of the confessional. 'I know exactly how I'm going to vote. I've been looking forward to that. Oh, yes, I've been looking forward to that a lot.'

I peeked through a crack in the door, watching him stride out of the cathedral, dog lead flapping behind him. The thought crossed my mind that I seemed to be solving everyone else's problems without getting any closer to the information I wanted. I gave him five minutes and then left myself, quickly. I didn't want to be found there by the real bishop. It was almost time for confessions to begin. I dropped Preachy's five quid into the charity box as I left. After all, render unto the church what is theirs.

And just in case little Baby Jesus was waiting outside with a rocket launcher or bolt of lightning for a specific someone who had masqueraded as a servant of Rome ...

... 13 ...

I was half way back to the hotel when I realised that I was being followed by a gaggle of old Belgian nuns singing the Te Deum. You know the type. Dull blue habits. Flying, starched white wimples. It took me a while to realise why they were following me. I'd forgotten to take the bishop's clothes off. They obviously thought that I was some great and reverend personage. I turned, bowed to them and smiled. Then I raised my hand as if I were about to bless them. They knelt down, bent their heads and closed their eyes. I legged it round the corner before they could realise that I was gone, cassock flying. I stripped the robes off as I ran, folding them up in a bundle. I put the bundle on top of my head and pretended to be a porter delivering clothes. When I re-appeared in the street a block away the nuns were still in situ, waiting for their blessing. I'm told they're still there. They started a new order, The Sacred Nuns Of The Awaiting Blessing. They're allowed ten minutes off every four hours to have a pee or drink a glass of water from the local stream. Apparently they get really, really excited when a thunderstorm looms. All sensible people get indoors. They start singing and praying as if there's no tomorrow. Which, if you're going to kneel outside in the middle of thunder, lightning, hail, etc, could well turn out to be true.

I got back to the hotel, wrapped the bundle of vestments in some – well, I was going to say brown paper, but that might give the game away. So, let's say I rolled everything up in one of the hotel rugs and posted them back to the bishop, along with a note saying that they had been found in the spare room of the local knocking shop. I hoped that that would put the bishop off asking too many questions about where they had gone to.

Then I picked up one of those gadgets builders use to detect pipes and electrical cable buried in walls and hurried off to the courthouse.

I've never been able to get one of those things to work. They either beep continually, suggesting that the wall is chock full of plumbing and wires, or make absolutely no sound, even when pushed against a live light switch.

To be honest my DIY skills are pretty minimal at the best of times. The last time I tried anything the hammer head came flying off and broke a window.

That didn't matter, because I wasn't on my way to check any walls. I wanted a rummage around Judge Beak's rooms, just in case he had inadvertently left any notes lying around in a carelessly locked cupboard somewhere. It was a thousand to one chance. If only Judge Beak had been the forgetful kind.

But it was a chance.

The gadget was my excuse if anyone turned up unexpectedly. I'd tell them that it was a health and safety check, to make sure there wasn't any loose electricity flowing around the walls, something like that. That might sound like a silly excuse, but, don't forget, there were several thunderstorms overhead that morning. Leaky electricity was the order of the day

Beazeley's face has just gone pale. Well, paler than usual. For some reason he appears to think that breaking into a judge's rooms or locked cupboards is somehow worse than breaking into anywhere else.

I would have thought breaking into a police officer's place would be worse. Especially if they were armed.

Jenny has just popped her head around the door, looked me up and down a few times, and announced that she thinks I would look quite sexy dressed as a bishop.

I'd better get back to that Thursday before I have a chance to think about that concept.

This time was definitely last-chance saloon.

Chapter XXIV. The Case is Closed – Oh, No It Isn't

The first thing I noticed after I had picked the lock to Beak's rooms was the desk. A big, clunky thing, probably oak, with a solid front, the sort that hides the sitter's legs, and always makes me wonder if the person I'm talking to is wearing any trousers. (I'm told that that's an interview trick: if you're nervous, imagine the interviewer isn't wearing anything from the waist down. I tried it once, but it just gave me the giggles.)

(But I'll never forget the interview I went to where the interviewer stood up at the end and showed that they weren't wearing anything below the waist.)

(I didn't get that job. I didn't want that job.)

First port of call was the wastepaper basket underneath the desk. At least you don't have to break into them. I had just bent down and leaned into the desk footwell to get it when I heard someone unlock and open the door. I decided that pretence was the best defence, took out my gadget and crept underneath the desk. Ninety-nine times out of a hundred that trick works. People don't look for anyone hiding – working – underneath a desk. They just pick up whatever it is they've come for and leave. This turned out to be the hundredth time, I realised, as Judge Beak's bony knees suddenly appeared in front of my face as he sat down.

Well, I say bony, but he was wearing his robe. The outline of those knees just looked very bony from two millimetres away. I decided to keep up the pretence and run the gadget over his knees. It beeped.

'H'your onour h'thed h'thomething?' asked a voice.

Fortunately there was a mirror behind the judge – a robing mirror, I presume. One of those antique things on a frame on wheels. Hinged at the middle of the frame so that it can be tilted. I've never quite understood why they're made like that. This one was obviously slightly loose. It kept tilting back and forth as if someone behind it was playing with it. I was crouched down with my head between my knees, just below the desktop, but by squashing my face sideways and squinting to the right I could see Mr Crane's angular form reflected in the mirror. And next to him, the reason for the mirror slowly pirouetting, Mr Ball hopping ponderously and nervously – and slowly – from fat flat foot to fat flat foot. I could feel the reverberations coming through the floorboards.

'Just my knees beeping,' said Judge Beak. 'They do that when you get to my age.'

They do? I thought to myself. Oh, well, in that case ... I waved the gadget in front of his knees again.

Beep.

He was right, you know.

The gadget didn't show whether it was reading electricity, gas or water.

'Now, Mr Ball, Mr Crane, Mr Crane, Mr Ball,' said the judge, a hand coming down underneath the desk to scratch his beeping knees, almost picking my nose at the same time, 'we know each other well. I know you would not request such a meeting without cause. Please, go ahead.'

Beep. Scratch, scratch.

'MOST UNCONVENTIONAL,' Mr Ball said, carrying on with the jumping from foot to foot trick. 'MOST, MOST, UNCONVENTIONAL.'

'H'your onour, h'most h'dithtrething,' Mr Crane put in, wringing his hands.

'I see,' said the judge. Thoughtfully.

Beep. Scratch, scratch. Wring, wring, jump, jump.

'What is?' asked the judge after a legal pause.

'BOTH OUR CLIENTS,' bawled Mr Ball.

'H'both, h'your onour,' said Mr Crane. I could see him in the mirror, shaking his head sadly. It clipped a hanging light fitting which began circling just above him. His budgie scuttled around his head trying to avoid it. The light began throwing strange, swinging shadows and light around the room.

'Both?' asked the judge.

Beep. Scratch, scratch.

'BOTH,' confirmed Mr Ball.

Legal pause.

'They've both done what?' asked the judge.

'DROPPED THE CASE' – Mr Ball.

'H'dropped h'the h'cathe.' – Mr Crane.

Stunned legal pause – the judge.

Extra-stunned silence – me. In fact my stunned silence was so much more stunneder than anyone else's I'm surprised no-one heard it.

'They can't have,' Beak said finally, the incredulous note in his voice the type of tone someone might adopt when told that there really were fairies in the back garden.

'INCREDIBLE.'

'H'unheard h'of.'

'Both of your clients?' asked the judge.

'H'yeth, h'your onour. H'my h'client h'advithed h'me h'that e h'wath h'dropping is h'cathe.'

'AND THEN MY CLIENT SAID SHE WAS GOING HOME.'

'H'and h'my h'client h'thaid e h'wath h'going ome.'

'AND THEY'RE BOTH GOING HOME.'

The judge considered this for some while.

'We cannot abandon the trial just because the plaintiff and defendant have gone home,' he said finally. 'It might set a dangerous precedent.'

'OBVIOUSLY NOT, YOUR HONOUR.'

'H'of h'courth h'not, h'your onour.'

'It would go against natural justice,' the judge said.

'NATURAL JUSTICE, NATURALLY.'

'H'againtht h'all h'prethedent.'

'In a case of public interest we must reach a conclusion.'

'PUBLIC INTEREST.'

'H'concluthon.'

The judge nodded slowly. Scratch. Beep.

'We have started,' he said. 'We will finish. There is no law which requires the defendant and plaintiff to be present. We have a judge, lawyers and jury. That will be sufficient.'

'WE HAVE BEEN PAID UNTIL FRIDAY. WE ARE HONOURABLE MEN.'

'Onourable h'men.'

'Technically it is quite feasible to continue a trial without plaintiff or defendant,' noted the judge. 'In a way you could regard them as nice-to-have extras, but not essential.'

'QUITE SO. NICE TO HAVE.'

'H'exactly, h'your onour. H'opthonal ekthras.'

The judge stood up suddenly.

'To court!' he exclaimed. 'The show must go on.'

I closed my eyes as his red robe swished out of sight, trying not to exhale very loudly. When I opened them I saw a jet black eye looking at me through a gap between the mirror and its frame. A jet black eye redolent of knives, poisons, spells, and calm murder.

An emotionless jet black eye redolent of knives, poisons, spells, and calm murder.

And then the court recorder was gone.

I clambered out from underneath the desk, fourteen dozen different muscles I never knew I had all complaining very loudly. It took me a good few minutes of stretching just to get the larger ones to quieten down. And then I hobbled off to the court. With Norah The Nose and Edgar The Ears out of the way there was a good chance someone was going to let something slip, and I was determined to be there when it happened.

Which, as it so happened, I was.

....

Chapter XXV. Hector and Horace Have Their Great Moment

I arrived just as everyone was sitting down after standing for the judge's entrance. Immediately I could sense that the atmosphere had changed. The jury obviously knew that neither Norah The Nose or Edgar The Ears was going to be there. They lacked that tension that had seeped out of them previously, the tension of people trying too hard to pretend they weren't interested. The Quiet American had a portable DVD player on his lap. He was watching Dr Strangelove. I don't think he realised that it was a comedy. In fact I don't think he even realised that it was fiction. These Yanks can believe in some strange things.

The Nun With Guitar was strumming it softly, appearing to look into the distance, apart from the occasional glance she shot in my direction. She was obviously trying to tell me something. That's the trouble with Nuns With Guitars. They seem to think you're psychic or something.

Miss F was reading a magazine while tapping her foot to the beat of the guitar, a woman's magazine, the type that contains the latest recipes, heart-wrenching tales of women struggling in a modern world, of women betrayed by dastardly deceiving men, and fifteen ways to have better sex. Vicar Preachy calmly perused an A3 size, hardback edition of *Prickly Pears Of The World*, presumably now feeling secure that he wasn't headed for eternal damnation for granting Edgar The Ears absolution. Mrs Plum knitted away happily.

The Quiet American was polishing his pistols as he watched his DVD. Mr Sleepy snored quietly away – in tune, this time, to the guitar – Strawberry Mousse's scarf once again hovering an inch above his face. Strawberry Mousse was painting her toenails, a bare foot stuck up on the balustrade of the wobbly jury box. The Major was playing patta-cake with the Prim Maiden Aunt. Miss F's mother had a hand on her daughter's shoulder, and was looking at the ceiling in the way mothers do when they trying to work out what they're going to make for dinner. All very cosy.

The judge's nose had even managed to fall asleep straight away. A record. And the most interesting thing was that Mr Crane and Mr Ball were now in the sentinels of the witness stand and the prisoner's dock. And Mr Crane had been given a table to stand on. A good solid table. A "this table was not made for breaking no matter how fat the bloke on top is" table. It was almost as tall as the dock wall. And it made him a foot higher than Mr Crane.

At last, equality.

More than equality.

Mr Ball was finally a foot ahead.

Mr Crane appeared to realise this as he stood looking up at the rotund little figure. For once he eased his vulture's head from between his shoulders and stood on tip-toe to attempt to reach vertical parity.

'H'now, h'Mithter Ball,' he began slowly trying to hypnotise the owl-head opposite and above, 'h'we h'fathe h'the h'real h'truth.'

'YES, MR CRANE, AND YOU ARE LOOKING THE REAL TRUTH IN THE FACE. I AM THE TRUTH.'

'H'I thay, Orathe, h'that'th h'a h'bit h'throng.'

'Sorry, Hector, I was developing my voice as Mrs Nose.'

Judge Beak snorted, started, said "A good school" before falling asleep again. Nobody seemed to notice.

'H'ah,' said Mr Crane, 'h'I h'thee. H'good h'point.'

He paused for a few seconds before smoothing his ears back in a poor imitation of Edgar The Ears.

'Mr Crane, you are of course doing your job as a lawyer, I understand that. And doing it very well. I would dispute that with no-one. As a lawyer, of course, your duty is to fight for your client, no matter how repugnant you might feel that duty. Would you not agree?'

Well, blow me down. He might not have had the ears for it, but he was doing a good job of imitating Edgar The Ears' oily approach. He'd got rid of the lisp and eccentric approach to his h's.

'NATURALLY I WOULD AGREE, MR CRANE. BUT IN THIS CASE MY DUTY IS NOT IN THE LEAST REPUGNANT. IN FACT I FEEL MORE THAN EVER THAT I AM IN THE FOREFRONT OF THE FIGHT FOR THE PUBLIC INTEREST, WHEREAS YOU BELONG TO THE FORCES OF EVIL, ATTEMPTING TO SUPPRESS FREE SPEECH AND HONEST FICTION.'

Mr Crane blinked.

'Orath, h'that h'didn't h'thound h'like h'Mitherth h'Nothe,' he pointed out.

Mr Ball's owl-head cocked itself sideways as he pondered this.

'I was replying as myself, Hector. It's a little confusing, doing things this way. I'm not sure whether I'm Horace or Norah.'

'H'very h'true, Orathe.'

Mr Crane scratched his bald head in thought, causing his budgie to retreat to his neck. Mr Ball sucked the end of his wig as he too pondered the problem.

'H'what h'we h'could h'do, Orath,' suggested Mr Crane, 'h'ith, h'I'll h'athk h'a h'quethton h'ath h'me, h'and h'you h'anther h'it h'ath Mitherth Nothe. H'then h'you h'come h'over ere h'and h'I h'go h'over h'to h'your h'dock h'and h'you h'athk h'me h'a h'quethton h'ath h'you, h'and h'I h'anther h'it h'as Mithter Nothe.'

'I think that would work very well, Hector,' Mr Ball said. Then he looked down. 'But what about my table?'

'H'ah,' said Mr Crane.

He pulled at an earlobe. The budgie scuttled to the other side of his neck.

'H'we h'could h'get h'the h'usher h'to h'move h'it h'for h'you h'eath time,' he suggested.

Oh, boy, this I had to see. First they'd have to find Happy Harry, and then convince him to lug a heavy table from the top of one dock, down into the well, and then back up another dock about every five minutes. And then the spectacle of Mr Crane and Mr Ball hurrying up and down appealed, especially when they tried to remember who exactly they were supposed to be each time. It promised to be good entertainment, if nothing else. I leaned forward and rubbed my hands.

But there's always someone around to spoil the party.

'Thank you, Mr Ball,' said Judge Beak, waking up. 'Well, members of the jury, you have heard the concluding cases of both the prosecution and defence. We will now adjourn for lunch. I'm told there are hot tarts for dessert. And after lunch you will retire to the jury room to consider your verdict.'

And then he was on his feet, the recorder's hand shot out, the metallic request to stand sounded, everyone was half standing and half sitting, and the judge was gone.

'But we haven't done our final speeches,' pointed out Mr Ball plaintively. 'And I had a really good one this time. I was going to use the word tranquillity.'

'H'I'd h'managed h'to h'get "peekaboo" h'in,' replied an equally miserable Mr Crane. 'H'and h'that h'wathn't h'eathy. H'ethpethially h'in h'iambic h'pentameter.'

'I was going to use free verse. It seemed appropriate.'

Both mused with crumpled faces on the sheer unfairness of life.

'But, you know, Hector,' Mr Ball said, perking up suddenly, 'we don't need Judge Beak here to do our concluding speeches. After all, surely defence, prosecution and the jury are sufficient.'

'H'an h'exthellent h'point, Orathe,' Mr Crane enthused. Both turned to the jury box, broad beams on their faces.

Which disappeared as they realised the jury had done a runner as soon as they realised what was likely to come. There was just the slow rocking of an empty jury box which has been deserted at high speed. Even The Clowns in the well of the court and Sergeant Johns were no longer there. Though in his case he was probably more interested in lunch than avoiding the final speeches.

'And when you think about it, Hector, do we really need the jury?' suggested Mr Ball.

'H'not h'thethe h'daythe, Orathe. H'quite h'legitimate h'to h'give h'our h'concluding h'theethes h'without h'a h'thury.'

'Go on, then, you begin,' said Mr Crane, sitting down on his table to enjoy his fellow lawyer's speech.

The one with "peekaboo" in it.

I crept away as quietly as I could. I couldn't see their final speeches being of any benefit to me. Especially when I heard Mr Crane say:

'H'ladieth h'and h'thentlemen h'of h'the h'abthent h'thury ... '

If that was iambic pentameter then I'm Joan of Arc.

You know, I'm beginning to wonder if using all the religious imagery is a good idea. It's starting to sound like the Seven Deadly Sins. Sloth, greed and sex five times nightly.

Oh, bugger, now what have I done. God, I hate it when that happens. Someone mentions something – the three ships that Columbus had when he brought civilisation to the Indians, and you think, yes, they were the Rita, the Pita and – what the hell was the third? And you spend the next two weeks trying to remember, refusing to look it up because you know you know the answer. Only now it's not three pesky little ships, it's Seven Deadly Sins. Let me see, gluttony, that would have to be one. Sex. Sex has to be in there somewhere, it always is.

Sex and ...

Whipping cream?

No, it's no good. They just won't come. Maybe I should ask Jen. But if I ask Jen will she think that I'm suggesting something? And if she does, will she like the suggestion? If she doesn't, will she belt me before storming out, returning five seconds later to collect her handbag and belt me a second time?

Nope, it ain't worth it. I'll just have to try remember them on my own. Let's see: sloth, that's one. Gluttony, two. Lust, three. Envy, four ... four ... four ...

Pride.

Chapter XXVI. Interview with Norah Nose and Edgar Ears

I bet Beazeley ten quid I could get a Unicorn into this. He accused me of "tampering with the facts". Eejit.

Jenny said she'd agree to go on a date with me if I did get a baby Unicorn in.

Jen, I don't think we should take a baby Unicorn away from its mummy. That wouldn't be fair. And bringing in the mummy Unicorn would crowd things a bit, don't you think?

Okay, Jen's happy to settle for a little Unicorn.

I'm going to do it. Oh yes I am! Watch this space! Watch out for that little Unicorn!

.........!

Back to reality for the moment. Back to Wellbury High Court and Added Assizes.

As I was creeping out of the court I met The Clowns coming up from the well of the court, escorted by Sergeant Eric Johns – if you can call a man struggling for breath after having climbed a few steps an escort. They could have outrun him just by falling over and rolling away. I didn't understand why they didn't do a runner. The judge hadn't made the "perverse" ruling he had promised to, so all they had to do was disappear for less than twenty four hours and they could claim their inheritance. So long as the ruling came after the Friday they were in with a chance.

'How are you two getting along?' I asked. 'Managing to keep cheerful amidst the slings and arrows of outrageous fortune?

They looked at me, confused.

They looked at each other, confused.

They looked back at me.

Still confused.

'I haven't noticed any slings or arrows,' Bonnie said, trying to be helpful. 'What do they look like?'

'Just a manner of speaking, kid, just a manner of speaking. Police cells not too depressing, are they?'

'Oh, no, we aren't staying in the cells,' Bonnie replied, smiling happily, 'they're redecorating the cells, so we're staying at Inspectors Summers' house. We've given our word we won't run away.'

It was my turn to look at him in confusion. His face had the innocent and open expression of a naive young man who sees nothing strange in being detained at an inspector's house while the cells at the local nick are being redecorated.

Sergeant Johns was listening to us while catching his breath – or, more accurately, using the impression of listening to us as an excuse to catch his breath.

'Come along, you two,' he said, 'it's way past my usual lunchtime, and if we don't get a move on the rhubarb crumble will be gone.'

'The food at the police station is just the best I've ever had,' enthused Clyde, 'much better than the hotel.'

'And afterwards Inspector Summers is going to take us for a drive around Wellbury,' added Bonnie.

'They took us to the cinema last night. It was great fun.'

'But we must be off, Sergeant Johns here gets hungry very easily.'

'And Squish will be waiting for us.'

They waved and left. They waved and left before I had a chance to ask for the name of the medication they were on. A police inspector taking two clowns for a drive to see the sights? Or along to the cinema? They'd have everyone staring at them. And the food at the local nick was better than the hotel? The hotel might not be five star quality in the cuisine department, but it was generally pretty good. Far better than anything a plod shop would come up with for anyone detained on suspicion of being naughty. Still, each to their own taste.

Maybe they liked burnt bangers and mash three times a day, or whatever the cook at the nick canteen could manage.

I returned to the hotel. There was something I had to do. One last desperate attempt to salvage something from the wreck. Catch Nora the Nose or Edgar The Ears before they left and find out why they'd dropped the case. If they hadn't already left, and Mr Ball had certainly seemed to think so. Fortunately I found Norah in her room, packing her suitcases. She'd finished five, and was on the third last one. She was wearing the lime-green outfit with matching shoes. It shouted "pillar of the community" and "I do good works". Which I happened to know she didn't.

'I'm Judge Beak's private secretary,' I introduced myself, 'Henry Herbert Higgins. He's asked me to pop over and sort out a few loose ends.'

She gave me a look I'm not unused to. The kind of look that says, "I know you're lying".

'I didn't know Judge Beak had a private secretary,' she said, turning her attention back to the suitcases.

'Not many people do,' I replied. 'That's why it's called being private. I won't take up too much of your time, Mrs Nose. The judge just wants to know – why did you drop the case?'

This time she gave me a full-on look which stated categorically, with extra footnotes and enlarged contents page, that she knew that I was lying. Then she gave a half smile, one of those Mona Lisa type "why don't you come up to my room" smiles. And snorted.

'Let me tell you a story,' she said, continuing with her packing. 'You can decide whether or not to believe it. I'm not really bothered either way.'

'Go ahead.'

'Let's say there were two little children named Lough and Trewth. Now "Lough" can be pronounced two ways, "Luff" – a version of

"Love" – or "Low", take your pick. But I will say that Lough was a little girl of about five or six, with the most winsome face, shiny blonde hair, trusting blue eyes that looked deeply and earnestly at the world around her and the people in it. Her mother doted on her.'

I nodded. She was obviously talking about her own children. In a coded fashion, of course.

'It could also be "Loo",' I pointed out helpfully.

'What?'

'"Lough",' I said. 'It could be pronounced "Loo", like "through".'

She gave me a rather filthy look.

'Who's telling this story, Porridge-for-brains, you or me?'

'Erm, you?'

'Right, so shove a sock where the sunshine don't go, okay?'

'Hokay.'

She turned back to her packing.

'"Trewth",' she continued, 'well, is that another way of saying "Truth" (with a capital T, of course), or is it an abbreviation of "Strewth!", an old fashioned ejaculation of surprise or bewilderment, commonly held to be itself a corruption of "God's truth!"? Whichever you prefer, Trewth was but a baby, a gurgling bundle of six or eight months who only stopped chuckling to sigh with pleasure at the brave new, wonderful new world in which he found himself. The sort of baby a mother would give her life to protect. Such as when his father threatened to take his ex-wife to court to get custody of the children.'

'I saw you with them the other day,' I said.

'They've been with me in court every day,' she replied.

'Yes, but I'm not allowed to mention that.'

'Yes, I see. You're right, you can't. Isn't that terrible.'

I could sense a certain sarcasm in that remark. It certainly wasn't a question. Not even a rhetorical one. It didn't have a question mark at the end.

'But no judge in his right mind would separate you from your children,' I said. 'You aren't a secret drinker, or addicted to drugs, or anything like that, are you?'

'Edgar knows some nasty people. When I was married to him it felt as if I were living in the reptiles' enclosure at London zoo. Though that's probably being unkind to the reptiles. The point is, a bent judge – well, he probably has a list of them in his address book. And all of them in his pocket, of course.'

I was about to suggest that it would have to be a big pocket, but she didn't look the type to appreciate such a sense of humour. Not just then.

'Which is why you wrote the book,' I suggested.

'Now you're getting the hang of it, Pfb.'

I ignored the Pfb.

'You never intended to publish it. It was a bargaining counter.'

'Well done. You're a fast learner, sweetie-pie.'

'But – does it really contain – well, all the details, the real story behind Edgar The Ears?'

'Everything anyone could possibly ever need to know.'

I could feel myself beginning to sweat at the thought. People speak of throwing the book at someone. If that book got thrown at Edgar The Ears it would be like dropping a ton of bricks on him. Well, a bit of a mixed metaphor there, I suppose, but my mind was in a bit of a whirl.

'But surely – surely it's your public duty to publish. People can't go on thinking he's squeaky clean when he's –'

Words failed me.

'Public duty can go swing with a coconut,' she replied, putting on a hat and checking her appearance in the mirror. 'My duty is to my children. That's all I care about. Edgar's agreed to a one-off lump sum payment, and to keep away from the children. The children and I fly out to Australia tomorrow. You won't ever see us again. And now, I must go. You can help the porter with my luggage if you've got nothing better to do.'

She stroked my cheek with her nose as she walked out.

Beazeley has just protested that Lough was an objectionable little whining brat, and that Trewth did nothing but cough and choke and crap the whole day long. Is that how you saw them, Beazeley? And, if so, I thought you didn't want them recognised? I shall add a special note awarding you personal recognition for that description. Maybe I'll also add a personal description of you so that your brothers at the bar will recognise you.

Beazeley has suddenly felt the need to lie down. On the carpet. Next to the desk where I'm currently working.

Ah, that's better, I never realised a foot rest could be so comfortable. Don't worry about the stains, Beazeley, I'm sure you'll be able to get them out.

Now, where was I? Ah, yes ...

After Norah The Nose left I wandered down to the private bar. Rumour had it that Edgar The Ears was fond of a snifter of expensive brandy when under pressure. I didn't hold out much hope for finding him there, but to my surprise there he was, smoothing back an ear.

The rest of the bar was deserted. It was just the two of us. I couldn't help but wish that it had just been the one of us. Either one.

'Herbert Henry Higgins,' I introduced myself.

'I know,' he replied before I could continue, 'Judge Beak's private secretary.'

'Well, yes, actually –'

'And you just want to tie up a couple of loose ends.'

'Funny you should –'

'Such as why I've decided not to continue the case.'

'I, er, yes, the judge would like that little point cleared up, yes.'

He smiled. He lit a cigar and took a slow sip at his brandy snifter. He radiated honesty and confidence. And oil.

Then his left ear pinged open. He swiftly smoothed it back into position.

'My wife – ex-wife – has finally seen sense,' he said. 'She has realised that there is nothing to gain in publishing totally untrue lies and slander about my private and public lives.'

'What about totally true lies and slander?' I asked. I couldn't help it. It just slipped out. It was either that or punch him one in his face.

You have to hand it to him. His smile didn't even twitch. He'd have been telling the passengers on the Titanic how much they were enjoying themselves right up until the last bubble disappeared from the surface of the sea. Using a loudhailer and speaking from the first lifeboat launched, of course, but he'd still be calm and confident. If only for their sake.

'Those would be even worse,' he smiled.

'Strange that she's off to Australia with a lump sum payment and the children,' I noted.

'Is that what she told you? Dear, dear, she is a fantasist. She lets her imagination run away sometimes, I'm afraid. It's one of the reasons I had to divorce her, I'm afraid. She's getting treatment, but never finishes the course.'

I recognised the approach. Politicians call it rubbishing your opponent. The academics call it ad hominem. We plebs call it playing the man instead of the ball.

'But you have agreed to pay her a lump sum?'

'A small amount.' Right ear pinged open. 'A little something to ensure she doesn't become destitute.' Left ear pinged open. 'I'm afraid, under the agreement, I can't give you the exact amount, though it would confirm the facts that I'm giving you.'

Both ears flapped around like sails in a wind that can't make up its mind whether it's coming or going.

He finished his brandy and stood up.

'Any time you need further information just give a call. I'm always available.'

And that was a whopper. He was incredibly good at being suddenly unavailable.

Still, who can say they haven't been stuck on a phone listening to a recorded voice saying, "Your call is important to us"?

He walked out, the picture of a sincere, honest politician with both lying ears flapping at full blast. I knew I would never get an honest, open fact from him. But the trial wasn't over. There was still the afternoon and the Friday. Something would have to come up. I'd decided that I was definitely going to purloin – borrow – one of the copies of the books, either Ball's or Crane's. How, I didn't know. I never do until it happens. Some people plan ahead, only to find themselves scuttled when the plan goes wrong. Me, I just make it up as things go along. It normally works.

Normally.

Ninety-nine times out of a hundred.

It was the last round in the last last-chance saloon in the last town on the last road to nowhere.

And funnily enough, for what it's worth, this time turned out to be one of the ninety-nine ones.

....

It just wasn't what I was expecting.

....

Indigestion tablets.

Chapter Twenty-VII. Fiddling the Jury's Verdict

I noticed a magazine Beazeley's bought. "Post-modernist Art for Today's Artist". You won't believe this, but the cover shows a nun naked, apart from wimple, sitting on a rocking horse, hair streaming forward over her shoulders to maintain her upper modesty, the head of the rocking horse obscuring other naughty bits. So that accounts for that silly dream. I must have glanced at it in a newsagent and then forgotten about it. It probably whirled around my subconscious looking for an exit before finding one in my dream.

The interesting thing is that it's not the real Nun With Guitar. Close, but it doesn't have the Goth makeup. And she's a blonde – the one on the cover. And she looks a bit vacant, like between the ears she's on holiday. My Nun With Guitar had eyes that seemed to see into your soul. And behind those eyes there was more frenzied activity than a January sale. An extremely intelligent January sale.

Does that sound a bit of a contradiction in terms?

An imitation. The nun on the magazine cover. The photographer probably heard about the real Nun With Guitar and came up with a weak imitation. After all, she doesn't even have a guitar. How can you have a Nun With Guitar without guitar? Honestly.

Back to that Thursday.

Time was running out. Norah The Nose had left. Edgar The Ears had left. I didn't have any tricks left up my sleeve. I don't think I ever had any tricks up my sleeve, come to think of it. I never thought I'd need any. Overconfidence. I was going to turn up at the trial, get some substantial evidence, encourage the jury to do the right thing, possibly nick a copy of the book from one of the jurors, and Bob's your uncle. Only in this case Uncle Bob hadn't turned up. Now all I had left was the jury. Get their verdict to come out the right way and I could make things up for ages knowing that I was protected by a reliable verdict from a trustworthy jury in an open court. In my business that's almost the equivalent of being given a licence to print money. Edgar The Ears would be in the position of a pirate firing off his last salvoes as his cannon sank beneath the sea. And he'd know it. Oh, he'd still fire them. Give him that credit at least. He'd go down pretending to fight. But he would be beaten.

So long as the jury came to the right verdict.

Once I knew the jury had returned from lunch to consider their verdict I slipped into their room disguised as an Italian ice-cream salesman. That is, I was disguised as an Italian, not the ice-cream. And of course, it wasn't ice-cream, that would just be silly. It was the highest grade Jamaican hash available in London. I had bought it the week before, remembering the old adage my uncle had passed on to me: "Remember, boy, as long as you've a joint you've a friend".

It was only later that I found out he was talking about his hip replacement.

'Whal, what say we take a secret ballot?' suggested the Quiet American. 'We do it quickly enough Ah reckon as how we'll have time for a hand of poker or two. I haven't had a game so long I declare I'm suffering withdrawal symptoms.'

'Gold Vlaky,' the Nun With Guitar said to me, the slight smile on her black lips suggesting that she had rumbled my disguise but wasn't going to say anything. I passed her the thin cigarette and she lit up with relish.

Well, yes, a lighter, but it had "Relish" printed on it.

'Oh, this bit is especially tricky,' said Mrs Plum, concentrating on her knitting. 'Could someone vote for me, I need to concentrate. These curly bits are always tremendously tricky.'

'Well, I don't mind,' Vicar Preachy replied. 'I could vote yes on one and no on another. That would balance things out, as it were.' He paused. 'No, sod it, guilty on both. That son of a bacteria's backside's got it coming.'

See what happens when people don't concentrate? The book was on trial. Norah The Nose was the defendant, not the plaintiff. A guilty verdict would mean publication would be banned. Just as well I was there to put things right.

'Ah'll have a Corona Confusion,' said the Quiet American. 'Now, who's in for a quick game?'

As the Quiet American began dealing the cards, illegal cigar sticking out of the corner of his mouth, the Nun With Guitar sat on the edge of the table, one leg on a chair, and began strumming her guitar.

'Jezuz vantz me vor a zunbeam, oh yez he doez,' she began singing.

The others began tapping their feet in time to the tune. I was the only one who noticed the small pistol strapped to her thigh.

Okay, there wasn't a pistol, but there was a garter, and boy were those nice legs! She definitely should have had a little Derringer strapped to one.

'Oh yez he doez!' she sang with fervour, the guitar beginning to swing.

'Oh yes he does!' echoed the others.

'Are two jacks a good hand?' asked Vicar Preachy.

'Real good,' assured the Quiet American. I'll see your shoes and raise you a sock, padre.'

'Zatan iz my zalvation! Oh, yez he iz!'

'Oh, yes he is!'

'I've always wondered,' said the Prim Maiden Aunt, 'in strip poker, does size count when betting?'

Amazing. Give her a roll-up and a hand of cards and the hiccough has gone. And the accent.

'A good question, ma'am,' replied the Quiet American. 'In Texas Rules it does, but you need a tape measure. So Ah reckon we just stick with good old Queensbury. Unless anyone's got a tape measure on their person. And is willing to bet it.'

'Ze devil'z in my botty, oh yez he iz!'

'Oh, yes he is! He's in my body!'

'I've never played strip poker before,' said Strawberry Mousse. 'I hope it isn't too difficult.'

'Easy as falling off a log, hun,' replied the Quiet American.

'Zatan iz my frient, oh yez he iz!'

'Oh yes he is! He is my friend!'

'What would you go on this hand?' Strawberry Mousse asked the Quiet American, shading her cards to him so the others couldn't see.

'Hell, hun, that's a good hand you've got there. I'd bet my pants on that one.'

'I'm zinning in ze zunzhine! Oh, yez I am!'

'Oh, yes I am! Sinning in the sunshine!'

While they weren't looking I slipped their votes into my pocket and replaced them with ones I'd prepared earlier. Like my uncle used to say, you can never be over-prepared.

Though he had been talking about hip joints.

I left them before the smoke got to me. The Nun With Guitar was letting it rip. Even the poker players were singing and moving to the tune. Strawberry Mousse had lost her top. Miss F and her mother had acquired tambourines from somewhere, and were shaking and shimmying it together, swinging their hips so that they bounced off each other, laughing and singing. The Quiet American's paunch rolled like a jelly fish without his shirt to hide it. The Vicar had managed to retain his clothing, but he was jerking like a puppet on a string, dog collar flying around like an electrified whip. Mrs Plum's hair had flopped over her forehead, and there was a demoniacal glint in her eyes as she knitted, faster and faster.

Mr Sleepy slumbered on.

I went to have a stiff drink. I needed one before returning to the court for the jury's verdict. In fact I had two. And a third just to prepare myself. Then I went back to the public gallery.

The moment of truth was at hand.

Or so I thought. I didn't realise that truth likes to have a few moments rather than just the one.

Chapter XXVIII. Crisis in Court

It's one of those strange experiences. An hour before I had seen the entire jury getting high as hell, stripping off their clothes and dancing to an evangelical music gathering celebrating Satan. Then there they were, sitting in the creaking jury box, fully dressed, looking as if they were a perfectly respectable, normal jury. Apart from Miss F, who had a dreamy look on her face, head resting on her mother's shoulder. And the Major, who was smirking, and was sitting a little closer to the Prim Maiden Aunt than previously. With his hand on her leg.

The court usher pressed the button, the request to rise came forth, the jury rose. Judge Beak entered and sat down. With a strange clunking sound. The sort of clunking sound you only remember afterwards. That's when you realise the significance of the strange clunking sound. And the way he had appeared to stagger just before sitting down.

The jury sat.

In fact, Judge Beak's nose had looked really pale when he first appeared, come to think of it.

His wig looked a bit peaky too.

The lawyers composed themselves and waited.

Silence.

'H'your onour?' enquired Mr Crane, standing up and flapping his wings.

Silence.

'H'your onour?'

Silence.

'H'he h'could't 'ave h'fallen h'athleep h'that h'quickly, thurely?'

Now there was dead silence in the court as everyone arrived at the logical conclusion that this time there was something seriously wrong

315

with Judge Beak. This time it wasn't going to be forty winks and a shower to wake up. The jury leaned slowly forward for a better look. The jury box creaked and moved. The jury leaned slowly back.

'I think he's collapsed,' said The Quiet American. 'Doesn't look like he's gonna wake up anytime soon.'

'Tweak his nose! Tweak his nose!' screamed Mr Ball, in his excitement forgetting to boom.

Mr Crane's wig gave a "cheep" and flew off to investigate Judge Beak's nose.

'Ahididie! Ahididie!' screamed the recorder, followed by something in a strange and fearful language as she leapt from her chair, desperately trying to jump up onto the judge's bench but failing to get a handhold.

At this moment Mr Sleepy woke up. He threw Strawberry Mousse's scarf from his face, took one look, bounded from the jury box into the well, and lifted the little recorder up onto the judge's bench. Once she was sitting with the judge's head in her lap he sat down, stretched out, and fell asleep.

It was the only time I ever saw Mr Sleepy awake. The only time I ever saw him do anything. And that was an act of mercy.

You will never see any plaques to people like Mr Sleepy. No monuments will be graced with his name. No streets or roads named after him. You won't find a "Mr Sleepy Lane", no "Mr Sleepy Avenue". At most he might achieve a hollow. Even his gravestone will probably read "Not dead, just snoring. We think." Yet there are countless other Mr Sleepies out there, performing the occasional act of kindness. Quiet, anonymous people, men and women, living out quiet, anonymous lives, unsung, yet the backbone to a truly great nation.

Beazeley is on his knees, praying.

Jen is killing herself laughing.

Laughing far too much to read this, so while I have the opportunity, may I say that she has the most gorgeous laugh I have ever heard.

Accepting that I never actually heard the Nun With Guitar laugh. Not a full, belly-blown belter.

Of course, her smiles were to die for, and her lips ...

...

Back to the Thursday afternoon. Concentrate, man, concentrate, you're almost there.

Cullen skink.

'H'quick, h'we h'mutht h'get im h'to othpital,' cried Mr Crane, wide eyes battling with his eyebrows for occupation of his face.

'There's a stretcher in the First Aid kit outside,' squeaked Mr Ball.

They each opened the door to their little dock and scampered outside. Minutes later they re-entered wearing bright-green paramedics' overalls over their lawyers' clothes, Mr Crane carrying the front of a stretcher, Mr Ball the rear. They stopped in front of the judge's bench. The recorder hopped down while Mr Crane reached over and pulled the judge across the bench, lowering him to Mr Ball. Once Judge Beak was on the stretcher Mr Crane again took the front, Mr Ball the rear, while the recorder hopped astride the judge's stomach, pumping at his chest, struggling to hold on at the forty-five degree angle created by the difference in height between the two lawyers.

As they passed the recorder's desk she leaned quickly over and pressed a button before returning to her chest exercises.

'This court is duly adjourned,' said a metallic voice.

They trotted out.

Then, silence, apart from the receding wail of an ambulance siren taking Judge Beak and his nose to the intensive care unit.

Beazeley has just reminded me that in real life the judge was discovered to be stone dead on the bench.

Plonker.

I am not going to say it.

No.

Not the X-word.

Plonker times two.

The trial.

That was it, I realised. That was definitely the end of that trial. I watched the jury file wordlessly out. They wouldn't be giving their verdict. Not even the verdict I had carefully prepared for them.

Only one looked up at the public gallery. The Nun With Guitar, of course. She raised an arched eyebrow, waved gently. And she was gone. And her Guitar was gone. And then the court was empty.

A small, dainty hand. With long fingers. Soft, long fingers.

I took the original votes out and looked at them. For the record written on the voting slips were:

Not guilty.

Guilty.

Yes.

No.

X.

Baked Beans. Bread. Milk. Kitty litter.

Clowns: one vote each way.

Darling I will always love you.

One was a parking ticket.

And the final one said: "Number 13, Victor, Or-E. Iv you're interezted. Bevore eleven."

Ha!

. . . 13 . . .

Ha.

Ha.

Chapter XXIX. To Have and to Hold and to Lose (Bugger.)

How's this for a conversation:

"Strawberry Mousse's boobs are too big" – Jen.

A puzzled silence – me.

"Jen, my sweetness and my light, darling, you are the only woman who can make my heart sing, and Strawberry Mousse never existed. Not in that way, anyway" – me.

"Her boobs are still too big" – Jen.

Sigh – me.

"Okay, Jen, okay, I'll make them smaller" – me.

"I think you fancied her" – Jen.

"Jen, in real life she was eighty-seven years old, had false teeth which kept falling out, and was actually a he" – me.

A suspicious pause – Jen.

"You're lying" – Jen again.

"Jennifer, if you don't believe me, ask your brother" – me.

"He won't tell me anything about it. He's too scared" – Jen.

"Well, I'm telling you. The question is, will you believe me?" – me.

Another suspicious pause – Jen.

"Jen, what on earth makes you think I fancied her? If I had fancied anyone there, don't you think it might have been the Nun With Guitar?" – me.

A short laugh – Jen.

"I knew you were making all that up about the Nun With Guitar. No man would fancy a nun. They just don't" – Jen.

Weary rubbing of face – me.

"You did fancy her, didn't you? That pink woman with the big boobs" – Jen.

Hitting of head against brick wall – me.

"Jen, word of honour, I'll swear any oath you want me to that I never fancied Strawberry Mousse. What else can I say that will make you believe me?" – me, desperately. Desperately, desperately, desperately. God.

"I'll go make some coffee" – Jen.

Cheeses. What is it with women? You let them do your shopping, next thing you know they're treating you like you've been married for forty years and they're afraid you might be enjoying yourself. And how, precisely, am I supposed to concentrate with her giving me the evil eye the whole time? It's bad enough trying to keep my mind on bum when she wanders around the room bending over to pick things up. She has a very attractive – figure. I think she does it on purpose. Some women do, you know.

Better get on with it, I suppose. Before she gets back, sees this, and dumps a mug of coffee all over me.

I don't think I'm going to bother with the little Unicorn. It doesn't seem worth the hassle.

But then again, maybe it's, I don't know, that time of the month or something.

Maybe I will have a shot at the little Unicorn.

I'll have to think about that one. Let's get back to the Thursday.

Right. Thursday. Thursday evening.

That Thursday evening, if it could really be said, again a la Wordsworth, that I wandered lonely as a cloud, it would have been one of those miserable, heavy, dark clouds that bumps along a moor. The ones that look as if they are about to burst into tears at any moment. The ones that you have an urge to feed a sweetie to and tell them to buck up, worse things happen at sea, and look, Mr Sun has got his hat on.

Well, maybe not the best analogy, but I wasn't the happiest bunny around.

I passed the happiest bunny in the corridor as I was moping along. He was blotto, standard empty vodka bottle in his paw. (How is it that bunnies like that always manage to finish the last drop before passing out?) I was tempted to follow his example, but fate intervened. Just as I was about to turn and head for the bar a door opened and Mr Ball looked out. He was dressed in civvies. I had presumed that, off-duty, he would wear one of those mustard-coloured check suits with waistcoat that look incongruous to modern eyes, but in fact he was wearing blue jeans, white t-shirt and leather jacket, black hair brylcreemed. Or jelled, these days, I suppose. Hell, vajazzled, even, I hear that's the current fashion. James Dean, apart from fifteen stone and two feet or so. And the glasses.

What is vajazzling, anyway?

'The telephone's not working,' he informed me.

Ever notice that? You're down in the seventh hell of the Pits Of Despair, you couldn't give an enema for anyone else's problems, but they have to tell you them all the same. I mean, for crying in a bucket. Was I arsked about whether or not his telephone wasn't working?

Problem is, you kind of pick up on this British thing about being polite. Especially if you are British. Which I was at that moment.

So I nodded sociably. And, since that appeared to have exhausted his conversation, I also tut-tutted sociably. Then I tsk-tsked sociably. I think the only reason that I didn't head on somewhere else was that I felt so low and miserable I might as well pass the time exchanging inanities with an overweight James Dean.

'I'm leaving on a fast train,' he added. 'I was trying to telephone reception to get a porter to take my bags down.'

I nodded. There was a silence.

'Going away?' I finally asked.

'Don't know when I'll be back again,' he replied.

He turned to look at his suitcases before I could make a comment about it being so sad to say goodbye.

'It's my back,' he said, frowning at the suitcases as if they were the cause of his bad back. I was about to commiserate when I noticed something on top of one of the suitcases.

The book.

That book.

THE book.

THAT book.

The BOOK.

That BOOK.

One of only two copies.

!

Stop that.

Somewhere a Jello played one short beat.

I hesitated. There it was, less than six feet away. It contained everything they didn't want the world to know. It was a goldmine. A literal goldmine.

Two beats.

....

Well, okay, not actually, literally, a goldmine, it didn't have people running around digging holes in the earth or blowing rocks up with dynamite or gelignite or blowwy-upper-powder, but you get my drift. Six. Six feet away. Six miserable feet away. All I had to do was hit Mr Ball over the head, nick the book and run like hell.

Three beats.

Maybe hit him over the head twice.

Just to be sure.

Perhaps not. I had to get hold of it without anyone realising that I had borrowed it.

Another idea struck me.

'I was just on my way downstairs,' I said. 'I'll mention it to a maid, shall I?'

Three beats, pause, fourth beat. Beethoven's Fifth, played quickly.

James Dean turned and blinked at me.

'Really? Very kind. Very kind.'

'No problem,' I replied and raced downstairs. By now the Jello was following me in full flow. Playing a theme I thought I recognised. The 1812, with real cannon.

If Mr Ball wanted a member of staff to carry his suitcases downstairs for him, he would get one. And that one would be me.

Racing downstairs, of course, in that hotel, meant I went up a floor, turned right, right, right, tripped down three steps, and landed up outside the staff room. I listened at the door for a few seconds. No-one inside. I opened the door and shot in. Three cupboards. No time for sophisticated dibbing of the locks. Rip open a door. First one contained green frogs for some reason. Fluffy, toy green frogs. Piled to the top of the cupboard. Or they were until I opened it. I fought against a cascade of green, fluffy, toy frogs until I came to the second cupboard. Rip open another door. Just what I was looking for. Staff uniforms. Not a moment to lose. Take off shoes. Roll up trousers. On with black leggings. Maroon top over my shirt. Zip up canary yellow skirt around waist. Polka-dotted white scarf around neck and into maroon top. On with dark green apron. Force feet into high-heeled pale blue toe-pinchers. Oooh, they hurt. Own shoes into apron pockets. Couple of lemons into blouse for verisimilitude. They slip down to navel. Take them out, tie a piece of string to them and hand them round my neck, popped into blouse. Check in mirror that bum doesn't look to big in skirt.

It did, but I didn't have time to go on a diet.

I needed a wig. Open third cupboard. Brooms, brushes, buckets. And a mop. That will do. Try to pull mop-head off its handle. Won't come off. Twist it until it's at a ninety-degree angle. Push handle down back of maroon top until mop-head over my head, instant wig. Chuck in some glitter and attach little furry green frog as modernistic scrunchy. Scramble through drawers. An old compact. Just enough rouge to cover stubble. A new lipstick. Helium green. No time for fashion. Apply thick layer to lips. Check in mirror. Dust a hanging strand from cheek. Not perfect, but it will do as long as I keep my face turned to the side. Mildred X. The ugliest looking waitress the Railway Tavern had ever seen. But at least my hair colour was natural. Sort of grey-off-white-drain-dirty-looking. Open door and quickly look for any passers-by. No-one. Race along corridor, from alcove to alcove, up stairs, Jello screeching like nobody's business.

Okay, for "race", read "hobble". That blasted mop handle was killing me. And the shoes weren't doing me any favours either. I began to wish I'd worn flats.

Get to Sleeping Bunny Bacchus. He's now stretched across the corridor, blocking my way. No choice, can't jump over him in those shoes, will have to walk over him. He's probably used to waking up with strange footprints all over him.

Just then he wakes up, opens one bloodshot eye. Opens both bloodshot eyes, wide. Jumps up and runs away, screaming "Pink elephants! Pink elephants! Mummy! Mummy!" Falls up stairs. Falls back down stairs. Hits head. Sinks gratefully back into a dreamless sleep. I carry on. Hobble on. Get to Mr Ball's room. Knock softly on door. Undertall James Dean opens door. Jello suddenly goes silent. Very silent.

'Heyick,' I say, face sideways, nodding at suitcases.

James Dean looks at suitcases.

Looks back at me.

Nods.

'That was quick. Yes, if you could take my suitcases down.'

326

Sidle into room. My back to James Dean. Slip – squeeze – book into apron pocket next to shoe. Must look strangely pregnant on one side, with a square baby onboard. Pick up suitcases. Turn around, head down. Follow James Dean downstairs, carrying suitcases. Jello picks up again, slowly his time.

Well, "carry" would be perhaps the wrong description. I don't know what he had in them, but lead bars would be my guess. It wasn't long before I was heaving them along the floor, humping them up stairs, banging them down stairs, sweat pouring, mingling with whatever residue was in that mop. It smelt like all the lavatories in London which hadn't been cleaned since the battle of Trafalgar.

Finally, finally, we reached reception, and I managed to drag those freaking suitcases out to where his taxi was waiting. Heaved them into the boot. Waited for tip. Just for show. I wasn't worried about a tip, I was impatient to get back to my room. Where I could read The Book.

He hands over a sick squid.

Cheapskate.

'You can keep the book,' he said, squeezing himself into the back seat. 'Every word in it is true.'

Door slams closed and he's gone.

I watched the taxi leave, surprise and other stuff dripping from my eyes. So he knew I'd half-inched it. And wasn't bothered. I almost broke into a cheer. He wanted the contents made public. He couldn't do it himself. But he couldn't be blamed if a super-criminal stole it. And he'd given me something worth much more than any measly tip. I hurried back into reception, as fast as anyone could wearing high heels and a mop handle shoved down their back.

'Heyick,' I said as I passed Mildred One.

'Heyick,' she replied, absorbed in the evening paper.

"Your slip is showing," I think that Heyick meant. I wasn't particularly bothered.

Quick, back to room with precious cargo. Slink from alcove to alcove.

I almost made it. Just as I was in spitting range a door opened, the Jello gave a few quick beats and Mr Crane appeared. Mr Ball had been James Dean. Mr Crane was Noel Coward. Smoking jacket, far too small, the sleeves about six inches short of his wrists. Shiny black trousers. Pinched patent-leather black shoes. Monocle. Cigarette holder. (White.) Smoke wafting slowly but surely from coloured Soubrani cigarette. Toupee hanging on to side of head, artificial brown.

'Ah, just the person,' he said. 'I'm leaving on a fast train.'

'Heyick,' I said, trying to move on.

'Yes, exactly, the phone doesn't work. I need someone to carry my bags down.'

I was about to give him a no "Heyick" when I noticed.

The Book.

That book.

Etc.

THAT BOOK ...

On top of one of his suitcases.

I had Mr Ball's book, with Mr Ball's annotations. Mr Crane's book was now in my reach. With his annotations.

Two goldmines. Explosive. Bang bang time.

Two Jellos began playing.

I don't know who was playing the second.

Lady Luck was smiling on me. Not smiling, giving me a humungous great broad beam, thirty-two white teeth sparkling, and the biggest wink in history, both thumbs up, saying "Go for it, kiddo". All I had to do was take a little chance. One little chance.

So I took it.

'Heyick,' I said, hobbling quickly in. Back turned to Mr Crane as I made to pick up the suitcases. Cram book into other apron pocket alongside other shoe. Pregnancy now shows square baby wearing boots. Or maybe it's twins. Follow Mr Crane out, head down.

Cheeses, those suitcases! Okay, Beazeley, I'll change that later, don't want any blasphemy in this. I'll invoke Buddha instead, okay?

Heavy? Weighed tons? There ain't a cliché in the world as would describe the sheer agony I went through. Drag suitcases along corridor. Hump upstairs. Bounce downstairs. Following Mr Crane. Sweat has now incorporated all ablution conveniences not cleaned since man first tried walking upright. Fifty years later, reach reception, dripping wet with something that started off as sweat but is now grey slime. Heave suitcases into back of taxi. Wait for tip, trying to disguise gasping for breath. Just manage to pull wrist away before driver slams car boot down on it.

He hands over seven quid.

Well, he was taller than James Dean. He could afford more.

'You can keep the book,' said Noel Coward as he folded himself into the rear seat of the taxi. 'Every word is true.'

I swayed on the pavement, leaning against a lamppost, watching the taxi leave. Both books! With implicit permission to use the contents as I saw fit. Obviously each thought I could only interpret things their way. Well, we'd see about that.

And despite appearing for Edgar The Ears he knew where his true moral duty lay.

I tottered back into reception.

'Heyick.'

"Your slip is still showing."

'Heyick.'

"I still don't flying care."

Back to room, a long, painful journey. In room, sank onto bed. Ignored mop handle in back. Jello building up. Did eenie-meenie-minor-mo. Decided on Mr Crane's version. Took out book. Sighed happily. Very happily. Very, very happily. Opened it. Jello comes to a crashing crescendo.

Nothing.

Blank.

Completely, utterly, totally ... blank.

Not a word. Pages pristine. Not a note, jottle, doodle. Dandy. Just frigging dandy.

Blanketty blank blank.

I was so, so, so close to saying the X-word.

But there was still one throw of the dice.

The other book.

Took out Mr Ball's book, knowing what was coming, hoping it wasn't.

It couldn't be.

Not after all the tears and pain and sweat and blood and custard.

No.

Yes.

As feared and expected, pages innocent of prose, a book of empty white space. Not even that last, contradictory page some technical manuals have, stating that it was left deliberately blank.

I could have cried. In fact I did. I could have thrown those books against the wall. I didn't. I was too tired.

Too, too tired.

I lay there for ages, staring at the ceiling. That was it, then. All for nothing. All for absolutely, blinding, effing, blasted, blooming, blinking, nothing.

I felt as drained as the mop, except without the odour.

Eventually I decided that I needed a drink. I leaned over to the phone to call room service.

The phone wasn't working.

Well, at least the lawyers hadn't been lying about that.

I staggered to my feet and stumbled out of the room. Right at that moment I absolutely needed a stiff drink. Nothing else. About a whiskey-bottle full to kick off with. After that I'd get serious about the whole business.

I'd just pulled the door to behind me when I heard it again. The sweet, soft, dulcet tones of a Nun With Guitar singing. Singing my life out. I listened for a few moments, the siren call teasing me away from the nectar of the gods.

I just didn't have the energy.

I'd done thirty-one. It was time to see about one-one-three.

The first "1" could have dropped off.

I really didn't have the energy.

Alternatively there was room 130.

The "0" might have come loose.

Or 131, 132, 133 ...

It was a complete wild goose chase.

A waste of time.

While my whiskey was waiting.

My double whiskey.

Tullamore Dew, nectar of the gods.

I turned to the wall and solemnly hit my head against, slowly, three times.

Then I set off for the first floor.

Coming up the stairs I caught a glimpse of the first room number.

101.

And then, as I entered the corridor, 102 ... 103 ... 104 ... 105 ... 106 ... And still the lady sang ...

... 107 ... 108 ... 109 ... 110 ... 111 ... 112 ...

"Floor equipment store: Staff Only: By Order: No unauthorised admittance" ...

... 114 ... 115 ... 116

I stopped and went back.

What should have been room 113 was a staff equipment store.

They weren't taking chances, these people.

So. It had to be between 130 and 139.

I continued along the corridor slowly. Mostly because I was dead tired. Partly because I felt the end was near. I was going to find the clue behind this 13 business. One of them was going to be missing the third digit. I would knock. The Nun With Guitar would open the door ...

And then ... ?

I got to a turn in the corridor.

Facing me was room 120.

I hesitated for a second.

Her voice was clear. Clearer than ever.

What, exactly was I going to say? What was I hoping for? A family of Happy Families?

I decided that I'd play it by ear.

I took a breath, smoothed down my lapels.

And continued walking.

121 ... 122 ... 123 ...

Six to go ...

124 ... 125 ... 126 ...

Three to go ...

127 ... 128 ... 129 ...

And turn into a new corridor.

I fell back on my backside.

There was no new corridor.

Just a brick wall.

Which I had just walked into.

I sat and looked at it for a few moments. In other circumstances it might have looked like a perfectly normal wall.

There was no 130 ... 131 ...

Still the song came ...

Came through the wall.

A wall I wasn't going to get through any time soon.

I stood up and approached it.

I felt it.

I patted it.

I ritually banged my head against it.

Three times.

You win.

Then I went looking for someone I knew I could find.

It took a while, but eventually I found him.

Sleeping Bunny Bacchus.

Forcing the mop handle up the back of the blouse I managed to sit down on the step next to him. I patted his pockets until I found what I knew would be there. A full bottle of vodka.

'Cheers,' I said, cracking it open and taking a deep pull. His nose wrinkled a cheers back at me. 'Here's to Shit Happens.'

It was not the best of times to find Bunny Evil standing in front of me.

With a butcher's knife in his paw.

Looking really, really evil, and really, really unhappy with somebody.

Like me, for a start.

Sometimes you don't really want to be at the front of a very long queue.

He had a cynically sad smile playing around his lips.

As if he was really, really glad to see me.

But I wasn't about to be really, really glad to see him.

Now, of course, the fact that I'm sitting here right now writing this shows that he didn't end up eviscerating me, so I won't pretend that that happened. Although, thinking about it, I could claim to be a ghost writer, that would do the trick, after all we already have three ghosts.

But then I wouldn't get to go out with Jen, which I'm determined to do.

Okay, maybe I could still go out with Jen if I were a ghost, but I can't see it lasting. For a start, if I were dead, we wouldn't have many shared interests, especially the ones most young couples have uppermost in their minds.

Or downermost.

And, anyway, being a ghost would mean having to talk to Hugo.

Fortunately, in real life, Bunny Evil really didn't actually kill me. But that still leaves me with the problem of the little Unicorn. What you could call the elephant not in the room as it were.

I shall have to think about that one.

Anyway, there we were, me sitting on the step next to Bunny Bacchus with Bunny Evil standing over me ...

With a vicious knife in his paw, claws extended ...

'I should owe you one,' he said in the tone of a bunny thinking of the slow and enjoyable pain of someone else. I shrugged. I think I was too tired and too depressed to care. He put a paw in a pocket somewhere, the knife and claws disappeared and a wallet appeared. He flipped it open. "Arthur Penbottom, Private Detective. No job too Snorge." read a badge.

I still don't know what that means.

Snorge?

Who cares.

'You lost me my job,' he continued. 'I was supposed to look after Matilda and see that she didn't get involved with anyone. Her father's extremely wealthy and extremely jealous of his little princess. And extremely unimpressed that I lost sight of her and allowed that Sad Sack to get into her life. Fired me straight off, her father did.'

'Sad Sid, I called him,' I replied, not really giving a damn. I reached into my pocket, underneath the waitress's clothing and passed him my card.

'Irene the Happiness Fairy?' he asked.

'Sorry, give that back a moment.'

I took out a pen, put a line through Irene, wrote something above and handed it back.

'Victor, Or E, the Happiness Fairy?'

'My new name,' I said. 'I had a makeover.'

'Sometimes you have to, I suppose.'

I shrugged.

'I was here to do a job,' I said. 'First time I ever failed.'

He sat down next to me.

'Me too,' he said.

I passed him the vodka bottle and he took a pull.

'Actually, I really owe you some thanks,' he said. 'I should never have taken the job in the first place. Her father's an evil, manipulative summer beach. The sort of control freak who wants to keep his daughter in a glass cage as if she were a butterfly, instead of letting her grow up and become her own person.' He took another pull of vodka and passed the bottle back. 'And then the way you caught me in that alcove – well, that showed me I'd become a bit too cocky. I'm one of the best, but there's always that danger of thinking no-one can beat you. I was lucky it was you. There are other people who wouldn't have stopped with an elbow in the kidneys. And there's always someone who thinks they're younger, faster, better looking, and wants to prove it.'

'Glad to have been a help.'

'Yeah, well, just don't try it again sunshine, I'll be ready for you next time.'

'I doubt there will be a next time,' I sighed. 'I'm screwed. You're fired. He's pissed.'

'Reckon he got the best deal.'

Somewhere in the distance we heard the theme tune of all large cities – a siren. It rapidly came closer until it was in the street below. Bunny Evil stood up, wandered into the alcove and looked out the window. 'Black Landrover,' he noted, 'police car. It's hit a fire hydrant.'

I stood up and joined him. Down below a black Landrover was parked half on the pavement, blue light flashing on the side of the roof as the fire department unwittingly paid for its wash. The siren had been switched off and all was silent again. Normally I would have been off to investigate like a shot. That evening I was just too, too tired.

I went back and sat down next to Sleeping Beauty with the bottle of vodka. Bunny Evil joined me. I waved the bottle under Sleeping Beauty's nose. His whiskers twitched. He opened his mouth. I poured a slug down his throat. Then I took a deep pull myself as he sat there, eyes closed, licking his lips happily. I passed the bottle over to Bunny Evil.

'I wish you hadn't called me Bunny Evil,' he said. ' I think I'm more of a Bunny Suave. Or Bunny Sleek. I made this costume myself, you know.'

'Yes, well, sorry about that. Bit late to change it now, though.'

'I suppose so.' He sighed. 'Oh, well, if the word gets out I'll just say it was my cover for this case. I can be anyone I want, really. I was an old woman with a shawl and a walking stick once.'

'Big teeth?'

'Sorry?'

'Oh, sorry, I was thinking of a different story.'

'One with a happy ending?'

'Happy endings are out these days, I'm afraid. It's this austerity thing going around.'

'Pity.' He scratched his nose. 'You couldn't let me end up leaving with – I don't know, say the Nun With Guitar? Hand in hand?'

'Not a chance.'

'Bunny Pink? I like her. She's just my type.'

'Trust me, she isn't.'

'Well, that's it then, I suppose. On my own again, as usual, all alone.'

'Me too.'

'Could be worse.'

'I suppose so.'

'Nice costume, though.'

'Thanks.'

There was a pause.

'Why didn't you make her Nun With A Gun?' he asked.

I made a face.

'Wish I had, really. Would have fitted. But what kind of gun? Hand-held machine gun like that Stocky Rallone, I reckon.'

He thought for a moment.

'Good point,' he conceded. 'Not a machine gun, no. And that Derringer idea of yours, well, it wouldn't really fit, would it? It would have to be something like a forty-five, but slim-line black velvet, and you don't get those nowadays. I had one, but it wore out just as it became comfortable.'

'Nope. That's always been the problem, the whole way through. They just don't make them the way they used to.'

Of course, had it been anyone else, or had I been a bit more smart or a bit more lucky or a bit more good looking, just then the Nun With Guitar would have appeared between us, sat down, put an arm around each of us and said:

'Boyz, I tink I'm more ov an RPG type Lady, you know vat I meaning?'

And that would have been another whole other kick-ass type story.

And boy, would he three of us had fun, and I know what I meaning.

But it was not to be.

Sadly, it was not to be.

And so we sat in happy companionship. Sleeping Beauty Bacchus, Bunny Evil and Mildred X. Listening to the sounds of Ave Maria being sung in a haunting low voice to the accompaniment of a guitar.

'There never is a room 13,' I commented more to myself than anything.

'No,' Bunny Evil agreed. 'They get your hopes up. But you're right, there is no 13. Believe me, there never is. The numbers go 11 … 12 … 14 … 15 … There never is a … 13 …'

'I once stayed in a hotel where the numbers went 11 … 12 … 00 … 14 … 15 … The 00 was for special people only.'

'Hey, I stayed there once.'

…

'God, I'll never forget that weekend,' we more or less said in unison. And with a heavy heart at remembrance of chances lost.

'Why is it you always remember the one who got away?' asked Bunny Evil rheumatically.

I didn't know the answer.

So, more or less, ended that Thursday, or as much of it as I remember.

Yes, Beazeley, thank you. Upright fire hydrants are American. They wouldn't have them in Wellbury. I know. The thing is, at the time I was just too knackered to invent a decorative fountain. But, just for you, we'll make it a decorative fountain. Made of marble. Fifteen foot high and thirty wide. Very pretty. Italianate.

It gleams in the moonlight.

People throw coins into it, you know.

Then they make a wish.

Some of them come true.

I know I did.

Throw a coin at it, that is.

But no, I'm sorry, you can't have a happy ending in this one.

Chapter XXX. Going home

Writing that last chapter last night really took it out of me. I felt every bit as knackered as I had been at the time. Now, with a good night's sleep behind me and a long hot shower – plus past the first cup of coffee stage – I feel refreshed and ready to begin the final chapter. Cruck knackles, stretch fingers, and here we go.

Actually, being tired last night had its compensations, in a strange way. I was a bit abrupt with Jen when she was about to leave. She asked me what my problem was. (I like that, my problem! She's the one who's been tetchy as all hell.) So I made some sarcastic comment suggesting she ask her boyfriend, the totally evil wazzer Beazeley was talking about. She looks at me in total silence for a few seconds before bursting out laughing, and the tells me that I'm the totally evil wazzer that Beazeley mentioned.

Then she stalks out and slams the door.

I was too tired and surprised to go after her. Besides which I had a suspicion that door slamming is her way of telling me that it, if there ever was an it, is definitely all over. So imagine my surprise when she turns up again with Beazeley this morning. She said she was only interested in the final chapter, nothing else. I apologised profusely (I'm not sure what for, but that isn't unusual) and asked her to give me another chance. She turned her nose up, said "you'll have to show you mean it" and flounced out to the kitchen.

I know she's the right one for me. Anyone who can make my heart stutter by flouncing out of a room has to be the right one.

Then she came straight back in, told me that Beazeley has a date, which shows that he at least is one step ahead of me, and flounced out again.

Beazeley has a date? Must be with the young woman across the road. I noticed him trying to chat her up yesterday. Poor girl.

Oh, well, best of luck to him. I know who I want to go out with. It's just a question of how to make it happen.

Having flounced out twice Jen came back in with some coffee and asked, in that tone she has of pretending not to be interested, why I haven't mentioned Beazeley in the trial. I pointed out that I had. I just had to disguise him. Now she's going through everything again, determined to work out which one he was without me telling. Beazeley's doing the same thing. Why, I don't know. Some people are like that. Tell someone you wrote them into a book and they just have to know, "Which one am I?" Well, truth is the whole world is in this one.

So, Pat, Sam and all the others from you-know-where, if you want to know which one was you ...

Guess.

And don't worry, your secrets are safe with me. I've made a note of them in the Appendix to remind me not to tell them to anyone.

But while Jen and Beazeley are otherwise occupied, I have a chance to ponder something. Initially I thought Jen was that perfect one, and mostly I still do.

Okay, I definitely still do.

It's just I would like the occasional day when my brain doesn't get turned to mush.

I suspect that's why they invented golf.

But I should have known that, as an actor, she's a natural critic. She says that I have too many women in. (That's feminism for you. First of all there are too few women. Then there's too many.) And Beazeley's decided that there are too many middle-class, middle-age white characters, and that I must make space for ethnic minorities. I told him, Beazeley, you just show me where it states that any of the characters are white, green, pink or purple. If you want to read them as white, that's your problem. You can read them as Red Indians for all I care. Sorry, Native Americans, the ones who didn't know they were American until the Founding Fathers popped over to explain the situation to them.

And then I asked him whether he would like me to be more descriptive of the real people there. No, strangely enough, he didn't. He's remarkably good at changing his mind, is our Alfred. And he missed the obvious point that I've described the court recorder as Asian, which kind of opens a slight hole in my "white, green, pink or purple" argument, but the counter-argument would be that all the characters have been disguised, so the court recorder probably wasn't Asian in the first place.

But down that road lies lunacy.

Actually, I rather wish I'd included a nineteen-year-old Swedish au pair and a Sioux chief in full battledress, headgear and all. I'm sure I could have made space for them.

One of those sarky native Australians from Crocodile Dundee.

Anyway, Friday. It's Friday today, just as it was Friday then. And, coming to the final chapter, it feels pretty much the same. It felt like end of term time. The end of summer school. Or end of summer camp time, if you're a Yank, I suppose. Total strangers brought together for a short while, intensive emotions, totally unexpected situations, and then suddenly you come to the last day and it's goodbye, love and kisses all round, exchange of addresses, promises to write, knowing you never will.

Course these days it would be e-mail, or tweeting, or that other thing, Swipe or whatever it is. Just isn't the same.

So all this took place before the WWW.

Friday ...

And the lucky ones will have had a bonk the night before. Possibly the start of a new relationship which will endure for eternity.

Or maybe just a bonk.

I hadn't even managed that.

(When I mentioned "summer school" I was talking about one for grown-ups, I'd just like to make that clear. If anyone had the image of a children's summer school, turn that into a sweet and innocent kiss.)

I hadn't had one of those either.

First thing in the morning I took the mop back down and up to the kitchen. Inside Mildred Two was sitting on the floor looking as if her boyfriend had dumped her, her pet puppy had run away and the doctor had told her she had two hundred years to live, but they'd be boring as hell and she'd take up watching tins of paint dry as an interesting hobby.

'Hello, Mildred Two,' I said, as cheerfully as I could manage, 'what's up? Oh, I found this mop in the corridor.'

Her eyes suddenly lit up, as if her boyfriend had come back on his knees, her pet puppy had returned from foreign parts with fabulous adventures to relate, and her doctor had said there had been a mistake, and she had only two days to live and they wouldn't involve paint.

'Moppy!' she exclaimed. 'Oh, Moppy! Moppy! Moppy!'

She grabbed the mop from my hands and clutched it to her bosom. Then she dipped it into a bucket of suds and began to mop the floor, dancing and singing.

I felt good that I had, however unintentionally, brought some cheer into her life.

But there are some strange people out there.

Around eight o'clock I wandered into the reception. Bunny Blue was standing there, paying his bill. The smart bunny costume was wrapped up in a clear plastic bag. Obviously the time for his disguise was over.

In real life he looked a bit like a young Robert Redford.

Stewed prunes.

'So everything sorted?' I asked. 'Love's rocky road smoothed, clear sailing ahead, moonlight and roses, that sort of thing?'

He grinned ruefully and pulled an earlobe.

'Unfortunately not,' he said. 'I thought that this was it. The real thing. I knew I had to make a move last night, it was my last chance. So I did.'

He sighed.

'You know, sometimes people aren't everything they appear to be.'

I nodded. I knew that well. I'd looked into mirrors before. Real ones. Ones that reflect reality. Not those antique ones in the dim lit corridors of the Railway Tavern.

Though, in my morbid and depressed state, I did wonder whether those mirrors in the Railway Tavern reflected real life more truly than others. Not as distinct, but more honestly.

You look into a mirror and see your soul reflected back at you. And you start freaking out because you realise your soul's just an amorphous blob of grey.

All that work you did on your abs, wasted.

'So what happened?' I asked, trying to push away my reflections in favour of his. He completed paying his bill, picked up his suitcases and bunny costume.

'She turned out to be a he,' he said, holding out a hand, which I shook. 'A transvestite bunny, would you believe? Just my luck. Anyway, good luck. See you.'

He paused and turned as he was walking out.

'By the way. I hear they've arrested Mrs Plum for the murder of Mrs Baggs. And Hugo the Accountant.'

And then he walked out, slumped shoulders suggesting that he was losing the fight to look on the bright side of things.

'That true?' I asked the receptionist. 'They've arrested Mrs Plum for the murder of Mrs Baggs?'

'Heyick,' she replied, agreeing, tossing her head in the direction of the hotel bar, straight hair falling on bouffant side.

'And Hugo the Accountant?'

'Heyick.' Yes. And Hugo the Accountant. Straight hair back in place.

'How could they arrest him? I thought he was dead.'

She didn't reply. She just looked a Heyick at me. Removing all the swearwords it translated as "Now you are being very, very, very silly. Baboon-brain."

She and Norah must have been talking.

Well, well, I thought, turning towards the bar. As I walked I spotted Bunny Pale Pink hiding almost out of sight at the top of the stairs, a tear falling gently from each eye.

No, Jen, Beazeley wasn't one of the Mildreds. Try again.

A tear falling gently from each eye ... right, that's it. Onwards and upwards ...

I'll never forget that sight, that scene. That moment. Say what you want about Bunny Pale Pink being a ... transvestite bunny. Those tears ... Well, I guess it doesn't matter how you hurt when you hurt.

Slap me with a kipper ...

Anyway, life always goes on. It's only in our personal spaces where we find time to stop and cry. Outside the sea keeps rising and falling, whether we want to Canute it or not. And, of course, Canute didn't. One of those strange contradictions where you learn that the fable the would-be historians have passed down is totally different from what Canute was actually trying to show. Poor sod.

Ahab and Moby Dick had a whale of a time. They just didn't enjoy it that much.

One day I'd like to write the story of Bunny Pale Pink. Hopefully it will have a happy ending. I can't see how, but ... Well, it shall just have to wait, I suppose.

Inside the bar I stopped short. I'd expected to find Detective Inspector Summers, I'd a gut feeling that he'd be there. Or she. What I didn't expect to find was both Mr and Mrs Inspector Summers. Nor that they would be exchanging a very intimate kiss.

Get a hotel room for God's sake.

'Ah,' said Mr Inspector Summers, noticing me and standing up while Mrs Inspector Summers quickly re-arranged her hair and blouse. 'Take a seat, we've been expecting you.'

I took a seat as ordered and looked from one to the other. There was a tug at my leg. I found Squishy looking up at me. I picked the kitten up and put her in my lap. She made herself cosy. While giving me that "You are a very strange person" look. "But you have a nice lap so I'll forgive you."

'I hear you've arrested Mrs Plum for the murder of Mrs Baggs,' I said, stroking Squishy, who began to purr. 'I was rather surprised, to be honest. I kind of presumed it was the recorder. Those eyes ... '

Inspector Summers' eyes widened in mock surprise.

'Minti?' he asked. 'She's only eight. How could a little eight-year-old girl do such a thing?'

'Eight years' old? You mean she's not some Indian assassin?'

Summers chuckled. Even Mrs Inspector Summers had a slight smile on her face which suggested that she was trying to retain a neutral, ice-cold professional police officer's approach, but found it difficult in the face of some doofus who couldn't recognise an eight-year old child when he saw one.

'She's the judge's granddaughter,' Summers explained. 'A love child of his son's. And she's Scottish, not Indian. Grew up in Glasgow.' Another smirk. 'You mean you didn't know that? I thought you knew everything.'

Sarcastic git. I'll bet he didn't know that until that morning either.

'She looks Indian,' I said, at a loss for anything better to say. And going against my usual philosophy of, if you haven't got anything to say, don't say it. And when you have got something to say, don't say that either.

'I think her grandmother came from India,' Summers said, taking a sip of coffee, apparently having decided to give up on the smarmy know-all role. 'Judge Beak only found out about her last week when her mother died. She – Minti, the little girl – was left alone in the world, apart from her mother's will which requested that Judge Beak should be told about her. The judge has been protecting her since then. I think he was at a total loss as to what to do with her.'

'Apart from the fact that he fell totally in love with her,' Mrs Inspector Summers said. 'And she with him. Instead of being a lost little soul alone in the world she found out that she had a lovely granddaddy who wore funny clothes, but was also looked up to. A man respected in the community. A judge. And he was delighted to find out that he had a granddaughter.'

'But the Clowns – aren't they're his grandchildren?'

'Yes. But adopted. Minti is directly related. His son was the black sheep of the family. Which was a pity, because he was an only child.'

I nodded slowly.

'And he was faced with the problem of the tabloids finding out that a respected judge now found himself with his son's eight-year-old love child who looked foreign,' I said. 'Should be a heart-tugging little story, but people would still sneer.'

'Precisely. Which is why you aren't going to mention it.'

'Of course not,' I promised faithfully, if somewhat absentmindedly. I tickled Squishy under her chin and she purred again, giving one of my fingers a gentle and playful bite.

'But at least you could tell me about Mrs Plum,' I said. Or pleaded. 'How did you know it was her?'

They looked at each other.

'Would you like to begin, darling?' asked he.

'Go ahead, my sweet,' said she.

My sweet? You must be joking.

Vomit.

'It was obvious from the start that she was the guilty one,' Frank Summers began, getting a frown from his wife which stated quite plainly that he was the only one who had thought it obvious, if indeed he ever had. 'Ninety-nine percent of the time the owner of an implement used to commit a crime is the one what done it, so to speak. It was Mrs Plum's knitting needle, wiped clean of fingerprints, a bad mistake to make. Had anyone else planned the whole thing they would almost certainly have worn gloves when stealing the needle, and when killing Mrs Baggs. They wouldn't have bothered themselves with wiping it clean.'

He sipped at his coffee, and Mrs Inspector Summers continued.

'The second give-away was the trick with her bag when she pretended to find the needle missing,' she said. 'It was the old trick of holding the bottom of the bag with the needle inside, making sure she had a firm grip on the needle, and turning the bag over to make it appear as if there was nothing left in it. People like Mrs Plum do not turn their bags over in public like that.'

'The problem was proving it,' Frank Summers said. 'And the second problem was preventing her next victim from getting the final call.'

'Now wait a minute,' I interrupted, 'why did she kill Mrs Baggs, and how did you know there would be a next victim?'

'Oh, that was obvious,' Frank Summers said breezily, earning himself another dirty look from his partner. 'She was just your typical motherly-looking psychopathic grandmother wreaking vengeance on the world. She couldn't stand Mrs Baggs' wittering, so she decided to get rid of her. Once we knew that, we knew that there would be a next victim. Unfortunately we were too late to save Hugo the Accountant. But that made it even more important to prevent a third killing.'

'And if that was true, if she were your typical motherly-looking psychopathic grandmother wreaking vengeance on the world,' Mrs Inspector Summers said, the stress on "if" telling me that she hadn't been convinced at the time, 'then she had almost definitely done this sort of thing before. Which would mean that she would almost definitely have a record. Which she did. She had escaped from a secure mental prison. Or perhaps insecure is the word. They tried to hush it up. The prison governor was afraid of losing her pension. It was only late last night that we managed to make a match.'

I nodded again.

'The black Landrover that crashed into the fire hydrant, sorry, decorative marble fountain – that was you?'

This time Frank Summers received a glare from his wifer. I guessed it was her personal Landrover.

'Ah, yes,' he said, standing up, 'well, we must be getting along.'

'Before you go – who was the next victim going to be?'

'The Clowns,' he replied. 'Remember her saying how sorry she felt about them? She'd said the same thing about Mrs Baggs before sending her to another world. And Hugo the Accountant.'

'But they were locked up overnight, the Clowns,' I said. 'She couldn't get at them during the day, and they were locked up overnight. Or, perhaps not locked up, but staying with you.'

'Exactly.'

The penny dropped.

'You arranged it. You had them arrested. Deliberately. That's why they were staying with you rather than being held in the cells?'

'It was the judge's idea,' replied Frank Summers. 'He knew who they were. He pretended not to recognise them. He knew he only had to keep them safe until today so that they could come into their inheritance, and then, of course, when we told him that they were in danger he came up with the plan to keep them safely locked away. Come on, Squish, tuna time.'

I lifted the kitten, who had fallen asleep and then woken up instantly at the mention of tuna, and handed her to him. The kitten yawned, gave me a friendly parting scratch with her tiny claws and a look that said "Yes, a very strange person. But I like you. The skirt doesn't do anything for you, though."

'Well, it will make an interesting story,' I said as they prepared to leave. He turned and gave me the sort of smile which said that I was about to be told something funny which I wouldn't find very amusing.

'It's still *sub-judice*,' he said. 'You can't write a word until it's over and ruled otherwise.'

'But – but of course it's over,' I protested. Fairly weakly.

'I doubt that it will ever be over. Unless Judge Beak returns from another place. I mean the hospital. And then re-opens the trial. Pretty unlikely, I would say.'

Stymied. Flipping, frigging, stymied. Kippered in a basket. The last light at the end of the well-known tunnel had flickered out.

'Well, at least you can tell me – what was in the book – what wasn't in the book – what was supposed to be in the book – is it true?'

He winked at me and they walked out.

'Darling,' I heard her say, 'you haven't forgotten that my mother's coming for the weekend?'

'Damn, I had forgotten,' he replied in the manner of someone regretting that they'd been reminded of a dental appointment. I couldn't help but hope for a moment that his mother-in-law was the mother-in-law of all mothers-in-law. Just then he popped his head around the door and looked back into the room. His leather jacket swung slightly, and Squishy's head also appeared, about a foot below his.

It isn't often you see that sort of thing.

'By the way, you haven't seen a little Unicorn running around anywhere nearby?' he asked. 'A little Unicorn, not a baby Unicorn.'

'A little non-baby Unicorn? No. Have you lost one?'

'No,' he said, winking again. 'I just thought I'd help you win your bet.'

And then he and Squishy were gone.

On second thoughts that Summers isn't such a bad bloke. In fact I think I could get to quite like him.

Beazeley, you owe me ten quid.

Beazeley's just claimed that he never agreed to the bet. God, I hate welchers like that.

No, Jen, Beazeley wasn't Mr Sleepy.

So where do you want to go for our first date?

Okay, okay, we'll decide later then.

But we are going on a date, aren't we?

Jen says that, even though Beazeley thinks I'm a cruel and heartless summer beach, and she's inclined to agree, she's decided that she will let me take her out. Not only that, she will generously permit me to pay.

Good deal, I reckon.

Beazeley really is just an awful judge of character, you know.

Anyway, back to that Friday morning.

I stood in the bar for a few minutes, hands stuffed down trouser pockets, with what I presume was a grim look on my face. Then I decided that I might as well hang around reception in case there was the slightest possibility of retrieving anything from the whole miserable debacle.

To my surprise The Ghost was lugging his suitcases towards the front doors.

'You aren't leaving, are you?' I asked him.

'Too ruddy right I'm leaving,' he replied. 'That flipping accountant is driving me nuts. Keeps going on about how his life was ruined because he had a small thingy. Do I look like the type of ghost who could give a flying duck?'

'No,' I had to agree. 'Not the type of topic that you could debate for any length of time. Not the kind of conversation that gets a dinner party lively.'

'Dinner party?' he asked aggressively. I took the hint.

'Idle conversation taking place without any suggestion of dinner or any other foodstuffs especially including those enjoyed by the carnivorous human,' I added quickly. He nodded.

'If he wasn't dead already I swear I'd kill him. That's one of the drawbacks to being dead.'

'I suppose it would be.'

'Anyway,' he said as I followed him out into the street, 'there's an opening for a ghost in a fringe play in London. The pay isn't that good, but the company should be interesting.'

'I might be in London in a few weeks,' I said as he hailed a ghostly hansom cab. 'I'll look out for it. What's it called?'

'Hamlet,' he replied as the cab's horse dropped a grey-white steaming deposit onto grey-white cobblestones.

'Hamlet? That's hardly a fringe play, is it?'

'It's all in Norwegian. Or Swedish or something. Nobody understands a word. Not even the actors. It's had great reviews.'

I scratched my jaw as he entered the hansom cab and closed the door.

'Well, break an arm and a leg, as they say.'

'Do they? Ruddy stupid thing to say to a ghost. Come on driver, make it smartish, I'm in a hurry.'

I watched the horse and cab clip-clop away silently, about two inches above grey-white cobblestones. And then it was suddenly tarmac again.

You know, I was in London two weeks after that. I checked out the tourist guides to fringe art, and there it was. "Hamlet in Norwegian or Finnish or Swedish or something". "A work of art!" screamed the Daily Echo. "Marvellous concept!" shouted the Rattling Bones. "Triumph for British genius" bawled the Sulking Guide Weekly.

So I bought a ticket over the Internet and went. Only to discover that the theatre where the performance was supposedly taking place had burned down in the Great Fire of London and was now a Tesco food emporium. I asked one of the shelf packers when the performance was to begin. He gave me a strange look and called security. They escorted me out – very politely, I must point out – but I could have sworn that the security boys – a man and a young woman – thought I wasn't the full box of hazel nuts, if I could put it that way.

Do you ever wish to travel back in time to find out whether they would have been given a standing ovation?

No?

I'm down here again.

Must be just me, then.

354

However, I digress. And whenever I do that Beazeley gets nervous. And Jen starts to read things into what I've written that were never there to begin with. So let me hastily repair to that Friday morning.

No, Jen, nor the Jellist.

Friday morning ...

I meandered my way back to reception thinking how strange it was. Everyone had different interests, expectations, hopes. For me it was the trial and the book, and that had now, apparently, gone west. Or south, or north, or wherever it is that these things go. For The Clowns, it was staying anonymous until the Friday morning. For Bunny Blue, the chance of true love. Poor guy. I also felt sad for Bunny Pale Pink, in a way. I hoped some of the other bunnies had had better luck. They deserved it, poor things. I just hoped that Sad Sid and Matilda had hit it off. Bunnies like that get so few breaks in life, you feel like crying when they mess one up.

When I reached reception Miss F, Miss F's Mother, Strawberry Mousse and Vicar Preachy were all checking out. They had enough bags to fill a bus. A big bus. An ocean-going-state-of-the-art-cargo-carrying bus. I guessed that somewhere along the line they had found time for a shopping spree. Miss F and her mother were wearing identical red and white floral halter-neck dresses, which made Miss F look almost her age, and gave the impression that they were carrying a sign which said "Don't mess with the mum and daughter cause we're having fun and we ain't done".

Strawberry Mousse hadn't been able to relinquish the pink and white, but she had dispensed with the bright pink jacket and opted for a soft white blouse and only slightly pink skirt which softened her normally aggressive exterior.

'Now have we got everything?' Vicar Preachy was asking.

'Don't fuss, Desmond, dear,' Strawberry Mousse said. 'If we've forgotten anything they can send it after us.'

Desmond? Dear? Blimey, someone had been getting friendly overnight.

'Hello!' exclaimed Miss F, seeing me and for once showing unalloyed delight. 'We're going to Cornwall!'

'Cornwall? That should be nice,' I replied in that manner you use when trying to share the eagerness of a child, and failing miserably. Fortunately the others were too happy to notice.

'We've never been to Cornwall,' Miss F's Mother explained. 'We were talking about it last night in the Baby's Arms, and decided we'd all take the weekend off and walk along the beaches. You could come too, if you want.'

'I am going to buy a bucket and spade,' announced Vicar Preachy, 'and I won't care what anyone says. And we're going to have cream teas, fresh clotted cream and jam and scones. And fudge. Hot fudge.'

'I'd love to come,' I said, quite honestly. 'Unfortunately there are a couple of loose ends I need to tie up.'

'Thanks for everything,' Strawberry Mousse said. She came up to me, put her arms around me, and assaulted me with her bosom, giving me a kiss on the lips. It was a case of being literally gobsmacked. Instead of the feeling of being attacked that I expected it was rather pleasant.

I could have done with another of those.

'Yes, it has been an interesting week,' Miss F's mother said, taking Strawberry Mousse's place and giving me another full on the lips smooch.

'Pity about the gardens,' she said. 'Perhaps some other time?'

'Mmmmm,?' I replied.

'I'll never forget you,' declared Miss F, deciding to emulate the adults, throwing her arms around me and crushing my face with hers. As Vicar Preachy stepped forward I hurriedly put out my hand just in case he decided to contribute with a Christian kiss.

'Best of luck,' I said, shaking his hand. It curled around mine and squeezed. Not the limp, wet-fish handshake I rather expected. He leaned forward and whispered in my ear.

'I've told my wife that I'm going to be staying with a Catholic bishop discussing theology,' he chuckled in a low voice. 'If there's one thing I've learnt from this week it's that life is too short. I've come to the conclusion that God wants us to be sinners so that He can enjoy us repenting. And I intend to follow His will. Sin and repent. Sin and repent.'

He stood back and winked at me. For a moment I wondered whether he had worked out who exactly that "Catholic bishop" had been.

'And you know something else you can use prickly pears to make?' he asked.

'No?'

He leaned forward again.

'Mescaline,' he whispered and stood back again, smiling broadly.

I leaned forward. I felt I owed it to him.

'Vicar Preachy,' I whispered, 'do me a favour.'

'Of course, my son. What is it?'

'Avoid the profiteroles at all costs.'

He blinked.

'If that's your professional opinion.'

'It is indeed. Have a good trip. Enjoy yourselves.'

'Look after yourself,' Strawberry Mousse said. I stood watching them walk out, shaking my head, wondering whether I had missed something in the accepted norms of saying goodbye to someone who was a relative stranger. When I turned around again the recorder was checking out. I said something bland about hoping Judge Beak was recovering well.

'Hae hoo hot h'noo,' she replied, stemming her tears with a massive man's red handkerchief, picking up her suitcases and walking away.

'Poor thing,' said Mildred One behind me, 'she really loves him.'

I turned around to look at her.

'Heyick,' she said, tossing her head ambiguously while wiping a tear away from her eye.

And then The Clowns turned up. Clyde and Bonnie, looking like your average sweet young couple in love, very eager and very much in a rush. She was wearing one of those blue puffy skirts with loads of under-skirts beneath, white top, white shoes and white bobby-socks last seen in a Rockwell painting circa 1953. He, for some reason best left unexplained, was wearing black leather lederhosen, white shirt and espadrilles.

'Isn't it wonderful!' exclaimed Clyde. 'Isn't it marvellous! Isn't it wonderful!'

'Fantastic,' I agreed, wondering which particular part of this best of all possible stinking worlds she was particularly in love with at that moment.

'Bonnie, run and catch Minti before she leaves,' she told her husband-to-be. 'I'll sort out the bill and things.'

'Yes, my darling,' replied the obedient Bonnie, 'kiss me goodbye before I go! Kiss me goodbye before I go! Kiss me quick!'

You need a kiss before disappearing for all of about two minutes?

Young love. Really.

And then I whistled silently, pretending to be studying the ceiling's architecture as they indulged in the type of kiss foreigners are reputed to enjoy. Since two such clean-cut young people would never have read about such a thing, nor seen it on any screen, I could only presume they had experimented and hit on it as being their preference.

'Heyick,' whispered Mildred One, wiping a little tear from each eye.

After about ten minutes they had to come up for air.

'Go, now, Bonnie, before Minti leaves,' said a breathless Clyde. He blew her a kiss and ran out the door. She watched him go with bright eyes, her hands clasped together in front of her chest.

By that stage I was knee deep in vomit and sinking fast.

But very nice vomit.

'Isn't it just really, really wonderful?' she asked, turning back to me.

'Which part?' I asked, smiling back in spite of myself.

'We've got a sister!' she exclaimed. 'Minti is our sister. Now we can start our married life already with our own little family. I've always wanted a little sister to love and to look after.'

Well, that was true, I suppose. I hoped that Minti had a lot of patience. Being looked after by those two would have been like being smothered in cotton wool all day.

Still, some people like it that way.

Looking at her cheerful face I was tempted to give her a friendly chuck underneath the chin. Trouble is, last time I tried that was with a fourteen-year-old convent girl. She had responded by laying me flat with a single uppercut to the chin, and then stomped all over me goolies. That sort of thing tends to make you careful about trying these things. Instead I merely said, 'That's great. I'm sure you'll have a great life. Oh, by the way, happy birthday.'

'Oh, thank you!' she exclaimed, giving me a kiss on the cheek, flinging her arms around me and hugging me with a body-rubbing tingle which made me envious of Bonnie. The way she used her body, well, he was in for an interesting honeymoon. Enthusiastic amateurs normally beat the professionals every time.

'You've got lipstick on your lips, and it isn't mine,' she giggled. Then she sparkled back, danced over to the reception counter, settled her bill, and then waltzed out carrying five fully-packed suitcases. For a moment I thought Mildred One was about to burst into tears. She was saved by the sight of Bunny Bacchus staggering into reception to check out. As it was still early he was only half-cut. Mildred One looked at him disapprovingly, which was a bit of a waste – Bunny Bacchus had probably last noticed a disapproving look about fifteen years and a million vodkas ago.

'S'rr bill,' he said, carefully placing a half-full bottle of vodka and his wallet on the reception counter and then staggering back and forth slowly as he searched his pockets for the wallet he had just placed on the counter, using the exaggerated care such bunnies do in that type of situation.

'H'swallet,' he finally decided, 'h'stollen.'

Mildred One picked up the wallet and waved it in front of his eyes.

'Heyick.'

I presume a translation isn't necessary.

'Ah, swallet. Swallet. M'swallet.' He stopped in his slow gyrations, waiting for the next thought to arrive in his brain.

'S'rr bill,' he repeated, remembering why he was there.

'Heyick,' said Mildred One, mouth turned down, handing him a printout listing his charges. He took it, peered closely at it while leaning forward, forward, until his top half was lying sideways on the counter, reading the printout. Or looking at it. He fumbled his wallet open and began counting out fifty-pound notes.

'Hsone! Hstwo! Hshree! Hs ... Hs?'

Mildred One impatiently took the wallet from him, counted out the notes, took change from the till, put it in his wallet, and put his wallet and receipt into his pocket. Then she came around the counter, pulled him vaguely upright and turned him around, pointing him in the direction of the doors.

'Hsright!' he decided, and began staggering towards them. He veered slightly and walked into the aspidistra. Alberto looked back at him. They gazed at each other for a few seconds.

'Hsberto!' Bunny Bacchus exclaimed.

'Si, senhor.'

'Hsmy friend, hsberto!'

'Si, senhor.'

'Hsmy favour't Shellist!'

'Si, senhor.'

'Hsone more time, hsberto!'

'Si, senhor.'

'Play it again, hsberto!'

'Si, senhor.'

Alberto took up his Jello and began to play a slow march. Bunny Bacchus pulled himself as upright as he could, picked up his suitcase, turned around towards the exit, found himself facing reception, carried on turning until he was pointing in the right direction, and began marching out, kicking his legs out, singing "He ish trampling the vineyard where the grapesh of wrath are shtored ..."

And then he was gone.

'Heyick!' Translation: men!

'Zere iz vun zing you kan rely on about a man,' said a Russian accent from the stairs, 'and zat iz zat you kan never rely on a man.'

It was The Nun With Guitar. She'd chosen an all-white habit with shimmering silver for this last day. Sequined silver dots rippling like thousands of little blinking lights, all winking at me as she moved. Rippling dots. They should make a song of that.

A lament.

She wafted slowly down the stairs and across to the reception desk and asked for her bill.

'Viktor, or E, vy did you nod kome do me?' she asked, coming towards me and gently laying a hand on my arm. 'I azk only zis of you: vy ypu did nod kome do me? Ve kould have played good muzic dogether, you and I. Vy you did nod kome?'

'I vanted to. I mean, wanted to. But you know the life of a Happiness Fairy,' I replied as cheerfully as I could. 'Busy, busy, busy. Waving that wand, trying to make the world a better place, there's just not enough time.' I decided not to mention kneeing Bunny Evil in his nuts and then sitting on a staircase sharing a bottle of vodka with him. It would have sounded just too macho. And not something the Happiness Fairy would be likely to indulge in.

She stroked my smooth cheek with her black-painted nails.

'You zhould zhave lezz ovden, Viktor, or E,' she said. 'It vould make you more addracdive.' Then she turned to pay her bill, her face hidden by her wimple.

'Where to now, sister?' I asked, trying to smile. Trying not to show my heart breaking. Trying to think, it was just a brief encounter, you'll get over it, lad.

'Anozer hodel, anozer hope zat I'll meet ze man ov my dreamz. Zuch a piddy you never made id. Maybe ve'll all ged happy in Heaven.'

'Good luck.' I fished around for something to say. Anything to prolong the moment. Anything to keep her there. The sort of thing you do as a silly teenager, not believing that the girl you're talking to could have any interest whatsoever in you, while she's doing and thinking exactly the same thing. It's one of the reasons I'm never quite sure about theory of evolution. If we are that evolved why does every generation go through the same miserable, horrible period?

'Say,' I said, an idea popping into my mind, 'that song you were singing yesterday – the one about Satan. It just seemed a strange one for a nun to sing.'

'Timez have zhanged. Ve no longer have do endure zackcloth and azhes. And I like zatin. I prever id do zilk.'

'Satin? Ah, I thought you were saying Satan.'

'Yez, many pipple do. Perhapz id iz ze agzent. Or perhapz id iz vat pipple vant do hear. People kan zee and hear zingz which are nod zere. Or nod zee zingz zey do nod wizh do believe in. Zuch az ze number 13, vor exzample.'

She gave me one final meaninkful look, picked up her guitar and bag and valked out.

'Room number 13,' I chuckled as best as I could, turning back to the receptionist. 'That corny old chestnut. There is no 13. There never is. Believe me.'

'Heyick?' she asked. She picked up the key the Nun With Guitar had left on the desk and offered it to me. The tag read:

... 13 ...

Nuts.

Nutty nutty nuts nuts nuts.

With fried squirrels on.

I raced to the door. Some Japanese tourists were just entering. They bowed to me. I corkscrewed a bow back as I ran past, almost giving myself a hernia. I ran out onto the steps. The Nun With Guitar was sitting on the top of a number thirty-one bus as it drove away, legs folded in the lotus position, sheer white silk stockings shining in the sunlight.

She had her legs folded in the lotus position, not the bus, just in case that isn't clear.

She was looking back at me, playing the guitar, softly singing ...

'Zomevhere my lov, zere vill be zongs do zing, zomevhere ...'

As the bus turned a corner, just before it was lost to sight, she raised a hand and waved goodbye. Slowly. And sadly.

The guitar kept playing.

I lifted a hand in response.

A warm wind came softly through, blowing soft as the kiss of silk.

And on the wind a whispered adieu.

'Da zvidahnia, Victor, or E.'

And then the bus and The Nun With Guitar were gone.

...

And there were no more buses.

...

And there were no more buses.

...

And there were no more buses.

...

No trams, planes, automobiles, cycles or passing ricshaws. Just a single, solitary bicycle wheel padlocked to a lamp-post.

And it had a puncture.

I said the X word.

Silently.

I traipsed back into the hotel. The Nun With Guitar was the one thing I could have salvaged from the wreckage of the week, and now she too was gone. Gone, without even a kiss from those death-black lips.

Sometimes you just feel like crying.

Sometimes you just feel like sobbing.

Sometimes all you have left are the ....

Such miserable thoughts were partly pushed to one side for later masochistic entertainment as I re-entered the hotel. The Japanese party were all bowing respectfully and deeply to Matilda and Sad Sid. Matilda and Sad Sid bowed back. The Japanese, obviously confused, but holding to their manners and tradition as it they were lifelines, bowed back to the bunnies. Matilda and Sad Sid bowed back.

'You two leaving?' I asked, coming up to relieve all of them before they did their backs in.

'Yes,' squeaked a breathless Matilda, looking up at Sad Sid with devotion. Sad Sid gave me his paw.

'If you ever need any stationery,' he promised. I nodded.

Stationery? What the flip was he on about?

'Good luck,' I said. It seemed to be my mantra for the day.

'I hope,' squeaked Matilda, 'I hope you find what it is you're looking for, one day.'

She kissed me on the cheek and they hopped away to happiness. I wiped a tear from my cheek.

Those whiskers had got in my eye.

I turned back to the reception counter. The Japanese party were going up the stairs, saying "Heyick?" to each other while using their hands to indicate large ears and pom-pom tails along with question marks.

'Has the MI5 agent left?' I asked Mildred One.

'Heyick,' she replied, meaning no, not yet.

So, maybe I should take her up on her offer.

But, of course, that was not meant to be. She and the Quiet American came down the stairs, holding hands.

Kumquats.

'Time to check in mah guns,' the Quiet American said, laying the holster on the desk.

'Why's that?' I asked.

'Whal, because they belong to the hotel, son,' he replied, as if that should be obvious.

I turned to the MI5 agent as the Quiet American signed his slip.

'So, did you get your story?' I asked.

'No, sadly not. Back to the lathe on Monday, I'm afraid. Still, K Wyatt and I are going to London for the weekend. Who knows, maybe something will come of it.'

K Wyatt? The Yank's name was K Wyatt? Who knew it? Did you know that?

'Best of luck,' I said to change the mantra slightly.

'You too, pardner. Come on, MI5, the hot lights of London are just a-screaming at us to get there.'

And that, as they say, is a true and faithful account of what happened at the trial, as far as I can relate. Jennifer thinks it's too unbelievable, Beazeley thinks it's too obviously true, so what can you do?

Beazeley wants to know when the unhappy ending is coming.

Beazeley, the Nun With Guitar and I missed out on the perfect relationship because of flaws in our characters, our total inability to relate on the temporal plane while being soul-mates on the spiritual. She was an unholy infatuation and I fell for her hook, line and sinker. We could have danced Nirvana in Paradiseo's moonlight if we had taken our chances when we met them. But we baulked. We failed. We had heaven in our grasp and we watched it slip and float away. And on a flipping number 31 bus. How much more tragedy do you want? Tell me, Beazeley, which particularly unhappy ending are you looking for?

Ah.

Apparently Beazeley thought that Clyde and Bonnie would turn out to be Strawberry Mousse's long lost children, which would mean that they would end up as a happy family, but unable to marry each other. Cheeses, Beazeley, who the hell is going to believe in a coincidence like that? Get a grip, man.

Jen has finally given up and wants to know which character was Beazeley.

Simple. He was the Prim Maiden Aunt. The "buns" were the earmuffs his mummy insisted he wear in case he caught cold. And the hiccoughs were him stuttering as he does. Poor thing.

Beazeley's just pointed out that he doesn't have thin lips.

I think he's still having trouble with the underlying concept here.

Okay, Beaze, I'll give you a trout pout. How's that? Anything else you want? Film star looks? A Mohican?

Oh, god, he wants a Mohican.

And a Guardian Angels' leather biker's outfit.

And reflective sun glasses.

And a new dress. Apparently he doesn't like grey. It doesn't suit his pallor.

Who does he think I am, Flipping Father Christmas?

Some people, really.

We can't really finish without giving Edgar The Ears the type of fate he deserves. Maybe it didn't happen in real life, but, what the hell, we can give him a truly gruesome end here, the sort he deserves.

Let's see ... Poisoned by his ex-wife Norah The Nose? Hmm, fitting, but that would get her into trouble.

Run over by a bus? Too quick.

Run over by a bus several times? Far too quick.

Trampled to death by a herd of hamsters on speed? Wearing little rugby boots with the studs filed into points? A nice thought. Unfortunately we'd have to twist things just a little too far to get there. They don't make rugby boots that small.

I know.

Let's say that there was this incredible gust of wind. Just as it arrived Edgar The Ears had told two very naughty porkies, and both his ears were unclipped. The wind caught his ears, lifted him fifty feet, and purely by chance dropped him into an open manhole. One which led to the sewers. The effluent was in full tide and swept him deep into the depths of London's Victorian drains. The walls are too slimy to climb. So, since then, he's being keeping his nose just above the scum line, looking for a way out.

Which he will never find.

Right, that's Edgar sorted. All done. Time to wrap up.

Jen wants to know why I was at the trial in the first place.

Let's just say Edgar The Ears' house was on the paper round of my first girlfriend when I was a kid. He messed her around from start to finish. She was the only kid I knew who ended up owing the news agents money – and there was nothing I could do. It might have been a long time ago, but you never quite forget the first love, do you?

Wendy, her name was. Her family left the neighbourhood about a year later. I was devastated for over a week.

Jen thinks that's ever so sweet. She's gone to make a cup of tea for me, which gives me the opportunity to mention that it's actually true. Work gave me two weeks off when I told them I was seeing voices, I noticed a mention of the trial in a local newspaper, and I thought, right, Edgar you snoek's rectum, come-uppance time. It's one of those things I suppose all young children think of when someone older and bigger and more powerful screws up their life for them, that dream that one day they'll meet the baboon's bottom on equal terms and pay off old debts. So Wendy, if you read this, I hope you'll be happy to know that Edgar The Ears won't be reading any free newspapers for a long time. For ever, in fact.

And I hope the braces came off eventually.

Jen's back. She wants to know if we can end with a wedding. She likes happy endings.

Of course we can, Jen, why not?

Okay, I know I said we wouldn't, but like Maynard Keynes said, when the facts change we should change our minds. And Jen is a new fact. A very, very nice new fact.

Breaking news, everyone: Clyde and Bonnie are getting married soon, everyone is invited.

And, Beazeley, you aren't going to stop me making that happen, whatever you do.

He thinks it's a good idea.

I've been a bit hard on Beazeley, I suppose. So I've decided to give him the honour of thinking up a title for this book. He said, "Just leave it blank". So that's what I'll do.

Thanks Beazeley.

I can type those final words:

The End

Now your sister and I are going to a movie.

See Ya.

Appendix

Now they've both gone back to the kitchen ...

Remind me to complete this some time. What Strawberry Mousse said to Miss F.

And quite possibly a few pictures of Pom-pom girls.

A lot of pictures of a lot of Pom-pom girls.

Just for Beazeley.

Leave it blank?

He's off his perch.

What else was I going to put into this Appendix? I'm sure there was something... Hmm ...

Ah, well, it'll come back to me.

One other thing: that jury box. Just a second while I give one of the struts a slight kick ... that's it ...

... Pop ...

... Crinkle ...

... And ...

... Splat ...

I always keep my promises.

Now, let me see, I didn't use the X-word, did I?

Don't think so.

Time for a brandy, I think. The good stuff, for a change.

Right, shut down and switch off.

There.

Oh, and

...

That does feel so good.

Right, brandy time. In the special balloon glass.

Chapter Thirty One

He thinks I don't know how to use his laptop. I do. And I'm not at all the way he describes me. I'm a caring, sensitive person. And the Major never stroked my knee. He wasn't the type. He made all that up.

And I am going out in a date tonight.

I'm going out with The Nun With Guitar.

Really, I am.

And afterwards we're leaving town.

Her convent won't let us get married.

So we're eloping to a new world.

So ner-ner-ner to him.

He's a right *Halichoeres bivittatus*.

So ner-ner-ner again.

But when I am gone

think not of me as Beazeley,

nor even the Prim Maiden Aunt,

but rather as a flying fish,

because that's where the answer lies,

my friend:

a Piscine in the wind.

See, I can do those too.

Signed

Alfred J. (Julius) Beazeley.

(Not my real name, of course.)

You know, he was right. I can see my reflection in this screen.

Disclaimer: All characters in this message are entirely fictional. Any resemblance to any person alive dead or in any other condition is entirely fictional. Furthermore ...

Oh dear. The system just crashed. I hope it saved what I was writing.

Still, who cares. After a couple of Bloody Marys with celery the Nun
With Guitar becomes quite

...

Now it really has crashed.

But while I remember, Pfb ...

So long ....

And thanks

This page has not been left unintentionally unblank.

This one has.

Oh yes it has!

Postscript: Wedding Day

And on with the show, take a bow, folks, here comes the happy ending after all ...

Fade in joyous music with booming noise of song accompanied by The Nun With Guitar's guitar supported by a Czechoslovak Italian Alberto on the Jello.

And a sixty piece orchestra in the background. We can afford it.

Oh yes we can!

Satin is my salvation. Oh yes it is!

Oh yes he is! Oh yes he is!

There they go, dancing down Main Street, Wellbury, UK, Britain. Past the Baby's Arms, the Railway Tavern, cathedral and court house with added Assizes, local crowds and the cast of the Harvest Festival applauding like there's no tomorrow. The Clowns dressed in wedding white, holding hands and skipping along, unconsciously knocking over Italianate fountains left, right and centre. A colourful bouquet of orange, red and yellow in Clyde's free hand. Judge Beak's nose just behind his granddaughter in her blue sari, who is doing the eight-year-old version of just having fun. Strawberry Mousse, kicking that pink skirt out wide. Vicar Preachy on cymbals, his dog collar whipping dangerously around his neck as he does the fandango. The Quiet American line dancing with Miss MI5 With Moustache aka Julia the Journalist. The Major doing a mix of fox-trot and Congo, his uniform fully restored, peaked cap at a jaunty angle, Sam Browne belt polished to a mirror, buttons shining, shoes gleaming and moustache beaming. Miss F jiggling her small chest enthusiastically and shaking that tambourine as loud as she can. Miss F's Mother alongside her, keeping one eye on her daughter while jiving to some personal memory which is bringing a little smile to her lips. Mr Sleepy being pushed in a wheelbarrow by a Morris dancer trying to hold his nose, Bunny Bacchus in another wheelbarrow alongside, vodka bottle firmly in paw. Bunny Evil sitting on the front edge with a bottle of vodka in his paw, dark glasses on his nose, a sadly cynical smile on his face. Mrs Plum knitting for the world, turning full circle with each purl. Just behind her Mr Crane, whose attempt at Boogie Woogie is best not described as a vulture doing the waltz. Mr Ball, whose enthusiasm is breaking the paving tiles. All the other bunnies, led by Sid and Matilda. Three ranks of Mildreds, fronted by Mildreds One, Two and Three in their staff uniforms. With Igor in the middle, dragging his knuckles, but looking very happy. Followed by a puzzled little Unicorn who just a few seconds before was contentedly nibbling helium in the Forest of the Silver Beams and is wondering how he got here and who these strange people are.

And the ghosts of The Ghost, Mrs Baggs and Hugo making a special return visit, having a wail of a time, walking through the old lampposts.

The Inspectors Summers keeping an eye on things, parked just out of range of the Italianate fountains, Mrs Inspector firmly behind the wheel.

And the girl next door with her bucket and Daisy Dukes ...

And the Postman ...

A choir of chip monks singing in sweet harmony ...

Beazeley next to the Nun With Guitar, playing a saxophone ...

A nineteen-year-old Swedish au pair and a Sioux chief in full battledress, headgear and all ...

And one of those sarky native Australians from Crocodile Dundee.

Oh yes he does! Oh yes he does!

Yeah, man ...

Wait a shoe socking second.

Beazeley?

Beazeley?

Beazeley!

How in the name of all that's tarnation did he get in there?

X

Let's keep going. The show must go on. There may be trouble ahead
...
I'll rub him out later ...

....
....
....
....
....
The Jello is playing ...
There's a large number of little fins around here ...
Circling ...
Hundreds and thousands ....
Circling ...
Jello ...
Yes, I'm afraid we're going to have to face it ...

This time it really is ...

Finns to the left of me, Finns to the right of me, it really is indeed ...

Finis

web: www . dughaille . info

www.ingramcontent.com/pod-product-compliance
Lightning Source LLC
Chambersburg PA
CBHW071155250626
47159CB00001B/97